WINDSWEPT

"Like all the best speculative fiction set in the future, *Windswept* is also about the way we live now, and Adam Rakunas tackles what matters most with a metric ton of humor and heart. A promising, thrilling debut."

Robert Levy, author of The Glittering World

"Lush and exotic, Rakunas's *Windswept* is like the booze that powers his world: a delightful cask aged añejo rum that keeps revealing greater complexity and depth the more time you spend with it. I didn't realize I had been lacking rum-running space opera in my life, but after *Windswept*, I definitely have a thirst for more."

Mark Teppo, author of Earth Thirst *and co-author of* The Mongoliad

"Adam Rakunas is one funny SOB, and now everyone's going to know it. *Windswept* is a zippy, zany ride, with more fast turns than a Wild Mouse rollercoaster. There's more witty banter and laughs per page than anything I've read in years, making this, my friends, the rarest kind of science-fiction-comedy novel: one that's actually funny. Buckle the hell up."

Daryl Gregory, award-winning author of Afterparty *and* We Are All Completely Fine

ADAM RAKUNAS

Windswept

ANGRY
ROBOT

ANGRY ROBOT
An imprint of Watkins Media Ltd

Lace Market House,
54-56 High Pavement,
Nottingham,
NG1 1HW
UK

www.angryrobotbooks.com
twitter.com/angryrobotbooks
And a bottle of rum

An Angry Robot paperback original 2015

Copyright © Adam Rakunas 2015

Cover by Jessica Smith
Set in Meridien by Epub Services

Distributed in the United States by Random House, Inc., New York.

ISBN 978 0 85766 478 5
Ebook ISBN 978 0 85766 479 2

Printed in the United States of America

9 8 7 6 5 4 3 2 1

For Anne, my parents, my grandparents,
and everyone who has to punch a clock

All the world that's owned by idle drones is ours and ours alone.
We have laid the wide foundations; built it skyward stone by stone.
It is ours, not to slave in, but to master and to own.
While the union makes us strong.

Ralph Chaplin, "Solidarity Forever"

ONE

I was sitting at my usual stool at Big Lily's, talking with Odd Dupree about his troubles down at the plant, when something big and stupid came crashing through the front door. Vytai Bloombeck's head swiveled like a pumpkin mounted on a sack of compost as he scanned the faces of the regulars. I tried to duck beneath the ironpalm bar, but it was too late – he had zeroed in on me.

"Padma!" he shouted, moving toward me like a runaway cargo can, "I got something, make us both righteously wealthy, like Jesus would want." He shoved Odd to the side as he plopped into two chairs. Odd's eyes rolled back into his head from the smell. Bloombeck's job was to fish blockages out of the city's sewer mains, a Contract slot he'd kept since Time Immemorial because no one was stupid or desperate enough to take it from him.

"Not even Jesus wants you, Bloomie," I said, wincing at the stabbing pain in my right eye. My pai was supposed to float text warning me that Bloombeck was within one hundred meters, but, thanks to the vagaries of my brain chemistry and the implant's firmware, the damn thing always gave me an electric jab in the retina *after* he'd shown up. I'd complained to every tech I know, and they all shrugged their shoulders and gave me the Santee Anchorage Song-and-Dance about how We Don't Have the Proper Tech, We Don't Make Enough to Care about Your Problem, Just Wait for the Next Bloody Update. The Oh-God-It's-Bloomie warning squatted between a migraine and my period on the pain scale, and the only treatment that worked was avoiding him. "You want to talk to me, you make an appointment."

Bloombeck gave me his weird smile, all upper lip and blue gums. "You're looking mighty fine today, Padma," he said.

"Oh, stow it," I said, holding my mug against my right temple, hoping the warmth would soothe my headache. If my pai hadn't continued to be so useful, I would have paid a doc to jab a needle in my eye and burn the damn thing off my optic nerve. Maybe I could do that when I retired. If I retired.

"Whatever you have can wait until I'm done with Odd." I pointed to the other end of the bar, the part closest to the open lanai. The fresh air off the ocean would help mitigate his scent. He grumbled away, leaving a wake of distressed people.

Odd ran a finger through his thick, gray beard, pushing aside the bristles that covered his faded Indenture tattoo, a caduceus. He hadn't been a doctor or a nurse, but a pharmaceutical test subject for LiaoCon. The long years of his Indenture had left him a nervous, twitching wreck. Odd had been lucky to walk into his Slot, where the heaviest thing he had to operate was the crayon he used to mark pipes slated for replacement. He shivered as he looked at me. "So, you think you can get me moved to a different shift, maybe?"

"Getting you off graveyard's gonna be tough," I said. "You just don't have the seniority."

"I'm the oldest guy there," he said.

"Yeah, but you've only been on Santee six years," I said, blinking up his Profile on the Public. "It's a long line ahead of you, Odd."

"Glenn wants us home at the same time." Odd's eyes flickering like hyperactive birds. "Is that too much to ask? I do good work, I don't grumble. Doesn't that count for something?"

"Of course it does," I said, looking at him and giving him a calm smile in the hopes he'd relax. I'd already plied him with two fingers of Uncle Mbeki's Finest Kind Blend, but it just made his eyelids droop while the rest of him twitched. "But there are people who've been here twenty who're waiting for someone to take their Slot. And you know how much the traffic's dried up."

He held up his hands. "I don't want to be a bother, I know things're tight for everyone. It's just…" A quiver ran down his back, down his arms, into his fidgeting fingertips. "I wonder sometimes, was this worth it? Breaching and coming here?"

I put my hands on his, holding them until they stopped shaking. "You really think you would've been happy if you'd stayed on that lab ship? Getting stuck with every weird anti-viral and arousal pill they cranked out? You think you'd still be alive? You'd think you'd have found Glenn?"

He shook his head, his movements calm and steady.

"I know working graveyard sucks," I said. "I did it too. I pulled a lot of crap shifts all over: at the brush factory, at the lifter base, even in Steelcase. I ever tell you I drove a crane for two years?"

He gave me a loose nod.

"And all that time, no matter how tired or dirty or sober I got, I never once thought I'd made a mistake coming here." I took a sip of tea, hoping Odd would buy all this. "You have a good hard think about it, you'd agree. Breaching is never a mistake."

He kept nodding, his head bobbing more and more. I thought that would have been enough for him, but then a thought must have come loose in his brain, because he stopped and said, "Yeah, but I still want to see my husband at breakfast. In the morning. I'll take whatever you got. I'd even go to a refinery."

"Odd, you know I wouldn't do that to you. I know the treatment plant isn't the greatest, but, Jesus, you really want to go to a place like Sou's Reach? You think your gig's bad now?"

Odd shrugged, his bony shoulders stacking up around his ears. "I hear Saarien's a fair guy. He tries to work with everyone."

"Just wait until the harvest rush when they're working past capacity and you haven't slept in a week and you're slipping and sliding all over the place and trip right into the holding tanks. You slip in the water at our plant, you'll smell horrible, but you'll come out alive. You won't if it's molasses. You move out of Brushhead into that shithole, he will own you. And I couldn't let that happen to you."

"Then what can you do?"

I sighed and blinked up every job listing I could think of. No one at the treatment plant would want to trade away a decent Slot, not even if I paid them off. I could probably talk to another Ward Chair, see if they'd be willing to swap bodies, but I knew everyone held on to whatever they had. Ever since the Big Three decided our blessed little mudball wasn't on an economically viable route, refueling traffic had gotten lighter and lighter, and that meant Contract Slots had gotten scarcer and scarcer. I heard whisperings that the only thing keeping Santee Anchorage from getting cut out completely was the fact that we sent more industrial molasses into Occupied Space than anyone within a six-jump radius. I suppose if I stuck with the Union long enough, I'd be promoted to those circles, but I had other plans, and all of them involved me no longer giving a shit.

Wait. Shit. There. A job flitted past my eyes, and I rewound it back. "Niccola Witt is going on maternity leave. She'll be out for a year."

Odd wrinkled his nose. "She does pollution control at the bottom of the plant. Her job stinks more than Bloombeck's."

"Odd, it's not like you'll be wading into the ponds without protection. You'll get a full environment suit and a rebreather. Well, you'll get *her* suit, 'cause we can't afford a new one, but–"

"I don't know, Padma. What happens when she comes back?"

"By the time she does, there'll be people to fill her Slot *and* yours."

He leaned closer, the always-scared look fading from his eyes. "You got a line on something?"

Bloombeck materialized out of nowhere. The smell hit me just before the needles in my optic nerve. "Padma, I really need to tell you this–"

I turned toward him, slow and steady. "Is it about your back dues?" I rubbed my eye to ease the pain. "Last I checked, you're coming up on five years' worth. And we haven't even talked about penalties."

Bloombeck scratched his face. His ink, a pair of crossed hedge clippers under a Union fist, redshifted under his grubby fingernails. I could never remember which of the Big Three he'd worked for before he'd Breached his Indenture, but you could tell they hadn't valued him even then. The inkwork was uneven, like someone had just stamped his face with a spiked rubber pad before sending him away. At least when WalWa had tattooed me, they'd taken their sweet time, the bastards.

Bloombeck pointed at his temple. "I just texted you for an appointment. You're free right now."

"Since when?"

"Since your four o'clock cancelled."

I blinked up my calendar and saw that, sure enough, Estella Tonggow had stood me up again. Bloombeck had snaked her spot. I took a deep breath, wondering for the umpteenth time why our Union forebears hadn't allowed me the power to beat the ever-loving crap out of people like Bloombeck. I knew that all kinds of people from all kinds of backgrounds Breached from the Big Three, and that we had to embrace everyone, but, Sweet and Merciful Buddha, even Vytai Bloombeck would have made them change their minds. "I will be with you in one moment."

"But—"

"Bloombeck, if you don't shove off, I will call up Soni Baghram and have her arrest your ass."

"For what?"

"Loitering with intent to annoy. Wait your turn."

"Baghram wouldn't do that," said Bloombeck, giving me a little sneer.

"You want to bet?" I said. "You want me to call up the nice police captain and ask her who she's more likely to listen to?"

I turned back to Odd. "You want the gig or not?"

He nodded, his face lighting up. "You're the best, Padma. When do I start?"

I blinked over a few forms to fill out. "Get that back to me by tomorrow, and you can get rolling next week."

Odd hugged me, then danced out of the bar. I looked back at Bloombeck and said, "Now, what can I do for you? And it had better involve you turning into a giant stack of money, 'cause I'm not interested in whatever scam you're cooking up."

"What makes you think I got a scam?"

"Because you're talking."

"What if I told you I knew about a bunch of people who wanted to Breach?"

"How could you come by info like that?"

"I got ears everywhere, and these ears tell me there's a WalWa colony seeder six days out," he said.

"Anyone can see the shipping queue, Bloomie."

"But can they see there's been grumbling ever since they came in from the Red Line?" said Bloombeck. "I heard it coming through the wireless."

"How can you get reception all the way down there?"

He shrugged. "The piping, it does weird stuff to signals. But, look, these people know the Union runs this place, and forty people want to jump ship. That's a good digit, yeah? Help you make your number?"

"It would, but only if I knew how much this would all cost me."

"Only three hundred fifty yuan," said Bloombeck. "That's

how much it'll take to bribe the radar control officer at Sand Point–"

"Stop," I said, looking out the window toward the lifter. Even though the giant black ribbon of coral carbon was twenty klicks offshore, its massive width filled the south window as it reached into space. The crawler platforms glinted in the late afternoon sky as they brought empty fuel tanks down to the water and full tanks and cargo cans to the sky. It was a sight that would have filled me with calm and contentment, but for the sweaty presence of Bloombeck. "I think you've said enough."

Bloombeck brightened. "So, you're in?"

"No, I said 'stop' because I've now hit my monthly limit for hearing your stupid shit," I said, pointing to the door. "Get lost."

"But you haven't even heard the deal!"

"Bloomie, if it involves the words 'bribe' and 'radar control officer,' then I don't need to hear any more." I waved my hand at him and closed my eyes. "Now get the hell out of here. You're blocking my breeze."

This was the time of day when the land began to cool, sending the wind back out to sea. Big Lily had all the windows open, so I got a noseful of Brushhead's afternoon scents: the laundry house up on Taupo Road where the proprietor kept plumeria, hints of naan and baguettes from Giesel du Marque's bakery. There was the sweetness of citrus from the Shareholder terrace farms, the tang of arcing steel from the shops of Repair Street, the swirl of boiling molasses from six hundred distilleries, all of them heady and full and rich, and none of them able to cut through the rancid stink of Bloombeck's odor.

I opened an eye. "You're still here."

"Forty Breaches, Padma," said Bloombeck. "This is all completely on the level."

"Your level isn't even level," I said, waving for Big Lily to bring me another tea. "You're so crooked it defies physics."

"But I know how to work an angle, and I got a winner," he said. "You just hear me out, and you'll see."

I took a sip. "If you know about the Breaches, why do we need to bribe anyone?"

Bloombeck blinked. "Uh, what do you mean?"

"I mean, forty people wanting to jump ship. Even on one of those big colony seeders, someone would hear the grumblings and do something to shut it down. Call in some Ghosts."

"Yeah, but this far out? With the little traffic we get now?" said Bloombeck, hunching closer to me. "You really think the Big Three care about us anymore?"

"I don't see WalWa closing up Thronehill or slowing their demand for our cane," I said. "But, still, even if this magical forty avoid attention, how would they get down here? They wouldn't steal a shuttle or do anything flashy. They'd hide in an empty fuel tank or a cargo can or something that would let them avoid attention. They might even follow your lead and slip down through the bilge on Garbage Day."

"Hey, that *worked*, didn't it?"

"By accident, if I remember your story correctly," I said. "Still, it's got me thinking about bribing the radar control officer."

"Well, *someone's* got to cover for those people–"

"That's a Union job," I said. "And can you think of anyone in the Union who'd pass on information about forty Breaches when they could keep it for themselves? You walk into a Union Hall with all those fresh bodies, people are going to fall over each other to get you whatever you wanted. Wouldn't you?"

Bloombeck opened his mouth to protest, then sagged back on his barstool.

"That was a nice try, Bloomie," I said.

Bloombeck's flabby arms plumped against his sunken chest as he sputtered, "Don't you want to make your number?"

"Of course I do," I said, "but I still want to respect myself in the morning."

Bloombeck hissed, then leaned back in at me. "You think you're so hot, with your payout and your brown-nosing with Tonggow. Like you've ever done anything for us here. You're just ready to live it up on Chino Cove with all the other Co-Op fatasses."

I slammed my fist on the bartop hard enough to shake everyone's mugs. Despite the stench, I put my face right in Bloombeck's. He flinched.

"Up until now," I said, "I have been practicing some restraint, out of respect for Big Lily. She doesn't like fights in her place, and I don't want to get on her bad side."

I grabbed an empty mug and held it up to Bloombeck. His eyes crossed as I tapped the mug on the bridge of his nose.

"That's why I am going to use my words," I said. "I let you slide on dues, Bloomie, because it's not worth the effort to chase you down. You don't register on the Union's bottom line, the same way you didn't register with your employer when you Breached. If you did, you think they would've let you roam around in your ship's bilge?" I gave him a gentle tap on the forehead with the mug. "But when you annoy me like this, you make me wonder if maybe it *would* be worth squeezing that cash out of you, just because I'd have an excuse to kick your ass from one side of the island to the other. It's like when the Big Three decides they need to make a show and send out Ghost Squads to sabotage each other. Or when they get their goons to crack down on Indentures so they don't get ideas about Breaching. You ever see a goon work somebody over with a riot club, Bloomie?"

Bloombeck shook his head, his jowls shivering.

"I have," I said. "I had to take a lot of classes in hostile negotiation in business school, and I did really, really well. You want to see what I learned?"

He shook his head again.

"Then get lost."

Bloombeck's eyes opened wide, and he tumbled over himself and a couple of seats on his way out.

I took a deep breath and sat back, blinking up a link to the Public and loading up the traffic queue from the top of the lifter. All the ships coming and going from Santee Anchorage lay there, listed in neat little rows, a spreadsheet that could tell all kinds of stories if you knew how to read it. Ten years ago, that story would have been one of scrapes with goons and derring-do on the high seas, of fishing Breaches out of the ocean like pickles from a barrel. Now there were only half a dozen supercarriers swinging by to grab a few billion barrels of industrial molasses, and those beasts barely needed to refuel from our ocean.

There were four colony seeders en route for refueling, but there was no way to tell if any of them were the ship Bloombeck had talked about. I scrolled them away until I saw the ships I knew were the real deal. I'd dug their names out of news reports, stolen Big Three financials, and all the gossipy whispering that traveled around Occupied Space faster than light. I smiled as I saw them: fifteen LiaoCon Xinzang-Class ore processors coming in from Nanqu. Fifteen claustrophobic nightmares filled with choking gases and horrible rations and enough people who would want to jump ship even if there weren't a sprawling city at the bottom of the anchor. I had been making payments to people who ran orbital traffic control, enough for them to run broadcasts on my behalf and keep quiet. There was always a chance they could screw me over at the last minute, but that was a risk worth taking. Besides, the messages they'd broadblasted into space made a point of telling people to ask for me by name, all but ensuring I'd get the credit for them joining the Union.

I watched the queue for a few more minutes. The LiaoCon ships were still four hours away – a little tight for my timing, but I'd be able to take care of business before the miners started their descent.

Business. Gah. I blinked up the time: quarter past four. Damn Tonggow for ditching me at the last minute. How a woman that scatterbrained could make a rum as good as Old Windswept was a mystery. How she managed to keep her distillery running was an even bigger mystery. She'd been doing something right, though, for her to keep producing as well as she did, and, as long as she kept it together long enough for me to buy the place off her, I could make sure there was always a steady supply of Old Windswept...

My scalp tingled at the thought of the still running dry. I sipped my tea, but it was too late. My fingers grew cold, and my eyeballs watered, and that voice scraped across the back of my brain, dry as bagasse and sharp as nails: *You really think they're going to make it? You pushed away a good thing with Bloombeck, like you push away everything good, and now Tonggow's not here, and you'll never make it to six o'clock...*

The breeze blew through the seaward windows again, carrying the cool green from the ricewheat paddies and the cane fields way out in the kampong, the bite from cane diesel engine exhaust, the heavy tones of coral carbon being spun into lifter cable. The first Breaches had called it getting windswept, back when they came down the cable and decided that their lives were worth more than their Indentures to the Big Three. It sure as hell beat holing up in Thronehill on the corporate side of the fence with the office drones, all of them breathing triple-scrubbed air and never getting a noseful of this. I breathed deep, forcing myself to relax, tamping back The Fear. I would not let it get out. Not today.

Big Lily walked up with my tea. "One of these days, I really *will* call Soni to bust that twerp," I said.

"I would think Captain Baghram would be busy fighting real crime," said Big Lily, setting down the mug. "Besides, you'd have to catch him doing something illegal, and I don't think even Bloombeck is stupid enough to try that in here."

"Soni and I are good enough friends that she'd do that for me," I said. "Especially if I paid her off."

She made a face. "I'm sure she'd charge you a pretty penny to lock him up. Save your money. It's not worth dipping into your budget for the likes of Bloombeck." She got a fresh bottle of Nelson's Column from underneath the bar. "You want a little extra?"

"You know I don't drink until after six o'clock."

"Yeah, though I've never understood why."

"Girl's got to keep some mystery."

"What's the fun in that?" she said, opening the bottle. She gagged, and some of the rum splashed on the bartop.

"What?" I said, and then the smell hit me, like mustard and raw sewage. My eyes watered as my throat tightened. "Christ, Lily!"

People ran for the windows, and someone hit the massive fans that kept the place cool during the peak of summer. The air freshened, though the stink lingered, the puddle staining the bartop's finish with yellow streaks. "You ought to tell your friends in the Co-Op about that," said Big Lily as she capped the bottle and tucked it into a trashcan.

"What, you, too?" I said, eyeing the stain. What looked like steam rose from its lightening surface.

"Me, what?" said Big Lily.

"Everyone thinks I have some magic pull with the Co-Op, just 'cause I'm talking with Tonggow," I said.

She grabbed a rag to clean the bar, eyeing the now-fizzing discoloration. Then tossed the skunked bottle in the bin and pulled up Beaulieu's Blend instead. "Well, I hope you work things out with her. You've been talking about buying her place as long as she's been talking about retiring. And better you than someone else. She makes a hell of a rum, and I'd like it to stay that way."

She didn't know the half of it. I eyed the Beaulieu's and blinked up the clock. Four twenty-seven. Jesus.

I blinked up the two numbers that ruled my life: the number of people I'd recruited into the Union, and my cash reserve. I knew both numbers by heart, since they hadn't changed in the past six months: 467 and 120,300. I'd fought like hell to get those people included in my headcount, and I'd scrimped to keep that bank account as filled as possible. It was enough money to buy out Tonggow now, but I needed the pension and completion bonus to get through the first few years of production. And I wouldn't get there until I'd recruited five hundred people. It was so close I could taste my first batch of Old Windswept. Those mining ships would come in, those people would emerge from the can with my name on their lips, and I'd never have to deal with this crap ever again.

"You looked at your numbers again," said Big Lily.

"You bet I did," I said.

"Just don't go crazy with it," she said, pouring a splash of Beaulieu's into a rocks glass and giving it a swirl. "Take it from a Shareholder who's been in your shoes: what you do for the Union is important, but being your own boss? That's more important." She took a sip, then nodded. "At least Bill Beaulieu is still up to standard."

"I'm sure he'd be thrilled," I said.

"Hey, he was a Breach once, just like you, just like me," said Big Lily. "He came here with nothing, did the same shit-work we all did, and he earned his way up and out. If a nice guy like him can make it, you're a shoo-in." She laughed, and I blinked away my numbers.

"It hasn't happened yet," I said. "Besides, those people might not Breach after all. Some other recruiter might nab them for their headcount. Carmody or Leslie Paik. Even Neil Scoon might rouse himself from his tomato patch to get 'em ."

"Or Saarien," said Big Lily.

"Es*pecially* Saarien," I said. "You know how many Breaches he's pinched from me?"

"I think we all do, Padma."

I sagged onto the bartop, careful to avoid the stain. "Every time I've gotten close to adding someone to my headcount, he snatches them away. Like those economists! You have any idea what we could do with that kind of expertise in Brushhead?"

Big Lily shook her head.

"Me neither, but I'd have done *something* with them. Instead, he keeps 'em all working in that deathtrap he calls a refinery, sucking away funding from the rest of us. Hell, now he's talking about turning Sou's Reach into an artisan community!"

"That'd be something," said Big Lily.

"He stood up at the last Union Board meeting and said, 'We need to acknowledge and nurture our innate creativity.' Walked away with a hundred thousand yuan to make glassware or some crap like that. Just because he has the highest headcount on the planet."

"I know he's pissed you off by poaching bodies from you, but that's how it was even during the peak times. Everyone wants out of their Slots, and recruiters want to make their numbers."

"Yeah, but does he have to be such a dick about it?"

Big Lily shrugged. "Evanrute Saarien may an asshole, but he's a *loyal* asshole."

I almost spat on the bar, then thought better of it. "To himself, sure."

"And to the Union," said Big Lily, wiping the highball glasses clean. "He's gone to the mat for his people, got his head cracked in the same picket lines as the rest of us. He may get wrapped up in all his speeches about the Struggle, but we're on the same side, Padma."

"His ego crowds out anyone else on his side."

Big Lily shook her head. "You sure you're not pissed because of what he used to do? A little transference, maybe?"

"Saarien isn't the only former Corporate recruiter here," I said. "What about Chenisse Lau? I used to hang out with her a lot."

"You used to get in fights with her a lot," said Big Lily. "Remember that year I banned you both from here?"

"She started it," I said, looking into my tea. "Saying I didn't pay attention to my Ward. What the hell did she know?"

"My point, Padma," said Big Lily, "is that, while I can appreciate your desire to get your payout, there's still plenty here to focus on. Chenisse was right: your Ward has to come first."

"If you're trying to tell me to go along with Bloombeck for the good of the Ward–"

"Oh, hell, no!" Big Lily laughed. "But what you did for Odd? That's what you should be doing more of. Especially since it gets you stuff like this." She put a plate of kumara cakes before me.

I smelled the sweet steamy cakes. "Oh, you are a doll." I broke open a cake and took a bite, the hot filling burning my tongue.

Big Lily shook her head, then took out a fluted tasting glass off the rack behind her. She set it down in front of me, next to the bottle of Beaulieu's.

"I told you, it's not after six," I said, reaching for another cake.

"It's not for you," she said, nodding to the other end of the room. I followed her chin and saw a guy sitting by the window. He wasn't really my type, but he had a chest like a rum barrel and eyes that didn't look too hard. "He's been watching you all afternoon."

"You have the best way of looking out for your customers."

"It's my job to know what my customers need," said Big Lily, throwing me a wink and walking to the other end of the bar.

I grabbed my tea and the bottle and the glass and walked over to the window. The man with the not-hard eyes looked up at me.

"I like your taste," he said, flicking his eyes at the rum.

"It's not my favorite," I said, sitting down across from him. He had a circle of stars around his Union ink, the sign of someone who'd put in time on the anchor. "But I still like to share it."

He nodded as I poured him a shot of Beaulieu's. "Sharing's good."

"So am I." We clinked glasses.

TWO

The only good thing about my former employer damaging my brain was that I didn't need an alarm clock.

My eyes popped open just before the muezzin cleared her throat and started the evening Maghrib. The Emerald Masjid stood two blocks away from my building, and its speakers were just in line with my second-story flat. It was like she was in my ear, calling me to prayer along with the rest of the faithful. I blinked up a clock: five forty-two. Almost time.

I slipped out of my bed and into my bra and pants. As I pulled on a shirt, Anchor Boy stirred, one muscled arm flopping over where my waist would have been. He had been good – really good – and I really didn't want to wake him and send him packing. Still, six o'clock was six o'clock, and I wasn't in the mood to explain what was about to happen. I grabbed his shoulder and shook him.

"Uh?" he said, his eyes flickering open. "Hi, uh…" He blinked, trying not to be too obvious about pulling up my profile and name. "Padma?"

"Very polite," I said. "It's time to go."

He nodded as he levered himself up. "Hey, you're right. Happy Hour is about to start over at–"

"No," I said. "Not time for *us* to go. Just you."

He sank to his elbows. "I do something wrong?"

"Nope," I said. "You were great. But I need to be alone now."

Anchor Boy gave me a smile, which evaporated when I didn't return it. He shrugged and got up.

For a brief moment, when he pulled on his shorts and reached for his coveralls, I thought about saying, *No, please, stay*. I never had company at six o'clock, and he'd been so attentive in the sack, maybe it would be the same when we had our clothes on...

No. I had to do this alone, or it wouldn't work. That's what Dr Ropata had said, and he'd been right about everything else everything so far. I leaned against the door frame, my hands behind my back, watching Anchor Boy get dressed.

"Be careful up there," I said. "Wouldn't want you to lose focus and press the big stop button."

"It's actually a series of switches," he said, grabbing his deck jacket and walking to the door. "I don't suppose there's any point in asking if I can call you?"

"You can try," I said, tapping my temple. "My pai's a little messed up, though."

He nodded. "Look me up if you ever get it fixed," he said, then clicked the door behind him.

I counted to five before leaping up and locking the door. I pulled every window shade closed but for the one in my tiny sitting room, the one that looked out over all of Santee City clear to the ocean and the massive lifter complex offshore. It was a view that would have cost a fortune but for the fact that Marjorie Ling, the landlady, was one of the first Breaches I fished out of the water after I became a recruiter. She still threatened to raise my rent to match the market every year, but a bottle of Still Standing Silver and the reminder that she owed my ass kept the price under control. Marjorie gouged the bejeezus out of her other tenants to make up for it.

The row houses of Brushhead rolled away on the gentle hills until they ran into the cane plants in Budvar and Faoshue. In the mornings, when the breeze came off the ocean, the smell of molasses and cooking sugar would drift up from the exhaust vents, overpowering every other scent my neighbors made. On some days, like the middle of summer when the refinery at Sou's Reach had busted and no one had taken a shower in weeks, the smell from the cane plants was the best thing in the world. It was also a better alarm clock than the chimes my pai made despite my turning off that option years ago.

I watched the sun begin its dip toward the horizon, and the water in the Ivory Canal sparkled like a billion fifty-jiao coins. In the middle of the canal were the rusting boxes of Partridge Hutong, my first home when I came to Santee, and I had to admit even they looked good in this light. There was no way in hell I'd ever go back there, of course, same as I'd never go back to night shifts at the water-treatment plant that had given Brushhead its name. I couldn't see the plant from my window, and that was a bonus. The pile of rusting pipes and misshapen holding tanks made Partridge look like a palace. The plant may have kept everyone employed, but that didn't mean I had to love it, not like I loved the rest of the Ward.

The gentle golden glow sparkled off the rooftops as the neon signs of the bars, strip clubs and churches winked on.

Somewhere out there, shifts were changing, people were going to or from work, opening bottles of rum or throwing away the dead soldiers. I took in one more breath, watched the light glint off the lifter ribbon, then closed the last shade, turning the room completely dark. The blackout shades had cost a month's wages, but they worked better than my old method of tacking heavy blankets over the windows. Looked nicer, too.

I sat at the kitchen table and reached under, found the candle and bottle I kept there and set them both in front of me. The candle was from an old hurricane kit, one that had been used and refilled a dozen times so far. It wasn't important. The bottle was.

It had a triangular base and was made from bumpy green-blue glass. The bottle's label was a cartoon of a woman's foot propped up on a lanai railing, overlooking the coast at Saticoy, a few klicks north of here. It was quite a pretty foot, manicured and smooth, and there was a string tied to the big toe. At the other end of the string was a box kite, high up in the cartoon sky, pushed about by some men in clouds, blowing on the thing. I had been using this bottle of Old Windswept for the past year, and it would last me another six months, if I was careful. And I was *always* careful.

The bottle was cool and comforting in my hand, like a heat sink drawing away all the tension from the work day. Hour after hour of dealing with angry people unhappy with their shifts, their supervisors, their Contract slots, and, just for extra texture, having to fend off Vytai Bloombeck–

I winced at the stabbing pain in my right eye and groaned. God, just thinking about him made my pai twitch. Terrific.

The pain receded, and I blinked back the video buffer to earlier this afternoon. I watched Bloombeck's offer again, just to remind myself that turning him down had been the right thing to do. *"Forty Breaches!"* he said, and I blinked it off. Enough.

I caught a lick of afternoon breeze and smiled. The same wind had caught me the first time I'd stepped out of the WalWa office in Thronehill, and I hadn't looked back. I could do the same with Bloombeck's deal. I could do the same with The Fear, scraping around up in there, especially now that it was six o'clock.

I lit the candle, and it sent out a warm yellow glow, like my flat was inside a stick of butter. I watched the flame dance to my breath, then closed my eyes and did what Dr Ropata prescribed all those years ago: I imagined me, sitting at my table, the candle and bottle in front of me. Then I let the camera in my mind pull back until I was outside my building, looking down over Brushhead. Then, farther back, until I could see the entire city below me, a smudge of buildings and streets in the middle of hectares and hectares of swaying green industrial sugarcane stalks. Then, even farther back, until I was above Santee Anchorage, where I could see the thin black line of the lifter reaching up to the orbital anchor, now surrounded by ships coming and going.

Then out into open space, watching my solar system's four other planets and yellow sun shrink to tiny points as my mind traveled beyond the Red Line, where it was safe enough to jump between systems. And farther still, until I could see all of Occupied Space, the stars and planets where people had made their way, where the Big Three tried to buy and sell everything and everyone, where other Union people fought and worked and lived and died, and then all the way out and out and out to the vast, limitless reaches of the Universe in all its wonder, its glory, its beauty.

I opened my eyes, then unscrewed the bottle. The cinnamon and pear scents from the Old Windswept washed over me, and I lifted the bottle to my lips, remembering Dr Ropata: just enough to taste, not enough to call a drink. It was a fine line, but I'd had enough practice. The rum sloshed as I tilted it back–

The minaret speaker crackled to life with a spike of feedback so loud I jumped out of my chair. I also banged my teeth against the bottle as Louise Ellison, the muezzin, sang out in Old Arabic, *Woe unto those eternal travelers; may they reach their destination with God!* Even with everyone pai'd up and Public terminals on every corner, sometimes the fastest way to spread important news was from the rooftops. I'd have to check in, see what the deal was, what ship went down, but that could wait. I lifted the bottle again...

And now the carillon at Our Lady of the Big Shoulders began to chime. What the hell? Vespers wasn't for another hour, and, even then, this was a Wednesday. Louie Kwan, the organist, had the day off, and he only sat down to play if something big was going on. Something like–

Then I recognized the music: "Eternal Father, Strong To Save." Louie usually let the Emerald Masjid take care of the salvation business unless it was more than one ship. As he rolled around to the end of the first verse, and I knew there'd be people in the city taking off their hats and singing along: "Oh grant Thy mercy and Thy grace, to those who venture into space."

And then a shofar sounded off. Then a conch shell. Then a whole chorus of horns, bells, voices, all of them calling out to the sky, which meant that it had been one hell of a mess up in orbit. Still, there was nothing I could do on the ground, so I lifted the bottle–

And then silence, except for one lone trumpet, sounding over the rooftops. For a brief moment, I hoped it was someone just adding a grace note to the proceedings, but then I recognized the tune – one that Big Lily and the rest of the old miners would play whenever one of their number died. I went to the window, pulled open the blinds, and looked a few blocks west to where Big Lily's bar was.

She stood on the roof, her skirts snapping in the evening breeze. She had a trumpet to her lips, and she was blowing a song from Dead Earth: "Gresford," the Miners' Hymn. We may have all been one big Union, but every trade mourned their own in their own way. The ships that had gone down must have been miners. I'd have to go back to Big Lily's to pay my respects, but only after I'd taken this sip, and...

Mining ships. Oh, shit.

I blinked up a link to the Public and loaded the traffic queue. I scrolled until I saw them, the fifteen LiaoCon ore processors, now at the top of the lifter, waiting to offload, and–

One by one, the names blinked, then turned blood red. Within a minute, all fifteen ships were listed as lost in transit with all hands. Four hundred sixty-two souls. Oh, those poor fucking people.

...and those twenty-seven you'd counted on... hissed The Fear before it laughed and laughed and laughed.

I looked at the bottle of Old Windswept, then blew out the candle and got up. It wouldn't do me a bit of good now, not with the sinking feeling in my gut over all those deaths combined with my rising anger at how they probably died. LiaoCon padded their bottom line by skimping on maintenance, by using cheap materials, by running ships twenty years past their hulls' expiration dates. Four hundred and sixty-two people, all worked to death, just to make some fucking LiaoCon Shareholders a few extra yuan. Hell, even the ships' potential destruction was probably part of some actuarial equation, a loss against future profits. My heart pounded as I got up.

I pulled on my cargo trousers and boots, well worn and almost ready for a resole, then my deck jacket, the one I'd borrowed from Wash eleven years ago and had forgotten to return. Through the window, I could hear the traffic sounds and background noise of the neighborhood had picked back up: the sizzle of tritip roasting on outdoor grills, the two-tone beep of tuk-tuk horns, the sounds of bar bands tuning up. Union people would always pause for a remembrance, but they sure as hell wouldn't stop. The city was in the middle of a shift change, and that meant everyone was moving. It would be the perfect time to get in touch with someone inside Thronehill, one of those now-thawed fishsticks who'd realized how screwed they were and wanted to poke back at their corporate masters. Problem was, it would take days to get in touch with someone friendly, and that was just to put out feelers about possible Breaches. Getting hard data, that could take weeks. Hell, it had taken six months just to learn about the LiaoCon ships.

Could I wait another six months? Seven? A year?

My head buzzed with a text from Estella Tonggow, apologizing profusely about missing our meeting because of a mishap at the distillery and, if it wasn't a problem, could we reschedule for tomorrow or until after she'd stopped the imploding piping?

Why bother? hissed the voice from the back of my head. *You'll never be able to buy her place now with those ships lost. And what'll you do if you can't get your daily snort?* My vision blurred for a brief moment, and it took a few breaths to bring the world back into focus.

There was another text: and did I get her gift?

I hopped downstairs. Mrs Karpinski, one of my neighbors, sat on the front stoop. In one hand, she held a smoldering pipe; in the other, a small package wrapped in orange paper. "Evening," she said, the smoke circling around her head. She had a compass tattooed on her cheek, evidence of her long days as a ship's navigator for LiaoCon. "Courier dropped this off for you. I was going to bring it up after I finished my evening constitutional."

"That stuff's going to kill you, Mrs K," I said.

She snorted and handed me the package. "If all those cosmic rays haven't done me in, a little tobacco sure as shit won't do the job."

The paper was tucked into tight folds, and it looked too expensive to tear open. I undid the folds, and there was a coral steel flask. There was no inscription on it, but it didn't need one. I unscrewed the cap and took a whiff, and the smell of Old Windswept washed over me.

Mrs Karpinski sighed, and I offered her the flask. She took a tiny sip and shuddered, her body melting against the building. "Oh, that is *lovely*. That from Tonggow?"

"It is," I said, pocketing the flask. "Her way of apologizing for canceling on me. It's been happening more than I'd like."

She waved away the smoke from her pipe. "You worried she's going to sell to someone else?"

Yes, cackled The Fear. "Nah," I said.

Mrs Karpinski patted my arm. "I wouldn't, either. We used to work together at the refinery at Beukes Point, you know?"

"I didn't."

She grinned. "Oh, yeah. Estella pissed off one supervisor after another because she insisted that *her* way of doing things was the best. Once she made up her mind, she wasn't going to change it. I don't think buying that distillery has altered her thinking. If she's going to sell to you, she's going to sell to you." She took a puff from her pipe. "But I'd still make sure I sent her a thank you note pretty damn pronto."

I gave Mrs K a kiss on the head and walked down the steps. I started blinking in a text to Tonggow, making sure to use proper spelling and grammar. Ever since I first met her, Tonggow insisted on propriety, and I liked that about her. When I had first heard rumors about her retiring last year, I had barged my way into her distillery to demand she sell to me at bulk rates. She just smiled and offered me tea and cakes and made me feel welcome, despite the fact that I had behaved like a complete ass. I had made up some story about how I appreciated her rum and wanted to make sure it didn't change. OK, that wasn't a complete fabrication. I just didn't tell her *why*.

Of course I could reschedule, I texted, *maybe tomorrow at ten-thirty?* I willed The Fear away, sending it deep into whatever pit it hid in. This was no time to listen to The Fear. This was the time to make sure I could buy the distillery, even if that meant my only lead was (and it hurt like hell to admit this) Vytai Bloombeck. Even though I *knew* he was full of shit, it was better than nothing.

I blinked up the time: quarter past six. The bars and cafes and strip joints would be full, which meant Bloombeck would be trolling, probably down at the shabbier end of Murdoch Street. I wasn't in the mood to walk there, so I ducked through alleys until I was on Sway Street. I raised my hand to hail a tuk-tuk, and a bright green job ripped out of traffic and bumped over the curb in front of me.

"Murdoch and Kadalie," I said, climbing in. "And floor it."

"Meter's busted," said the tuk-tuk driver, a skinny girl with streaks of grease and a pair of wheels inked on her cheeks. "Trip'll cost you two fifty."

"That's a little cheap, but what the hell." I got out three yuan and held them up to her.

The driver looked at the bills like they were dead fish. "Two *hundred* fifty."

"Really?" Anger overwhelmed any last protests from The Fear as I blinked up her face on the Public. No hits, which was a neat trick for a Union hack. I didn't get a handshake from her pai, either. I peered closer at her ink and saw it had been made with a pen, not with a needle. If she wasn't a runaway from the kampong, I'd buy a hat just to eat it. "How do you figure?"

She scratched her chin, leaving a little smudge. "Shifts have changed, so all the other drivers are doing the commuter thing. You're on business, 'cause no one who looks like you would go to that neighborhood for fun."

"Sounds like you've got me twigged for a rube," I said, glancing at the empty caneplas envelope on the dash where her hack license should have been.

"Nah," she said, grinning. "Just desperate. I know my customers."

"Then you should know this." I reached into my pocket and pulled out my Union card, the one with WARD CHAIR written on it in large, don't-fuck-with-me letters.

The driver's eyes flickered from me to the card and back again. "No charge," she said, kicking the tuk-tuk into gear. "Would you like me to wait while you conduct your business?"

"That would be lovely," I said, licking my thumb. "One more thing." I reached over the seat and swiped her cheek clean. "You really ought to use permanent marker. Union hacks aren't crazy about fakes."

"Right," she said, her voice tiny. She stomped on the gas and shot us into traffic.

Brushhead had been awake all day, but the place really came alive at night. As we zipped down the sloped streets, barkeeps opened their windows as merchants hosed off their sidewalks. The neon glow from the theaters blinked on with the sodium lamps, and the crushed coral pavement smelled wet and tangy. We drove along the Ivory Canal onto Clipner Road, past the swing-shift gangs heading for their gigs on the cable or at the cargo depot or any of the hundreds of places that Union people still had jobs. I leaned over the driver's seat and said, "How long you been off the farm, kid?"

"Six weeks," she said, her voice barely carrying over the tuk-tuk's motor.

"Your family know you're in the big, bad city?"

She shrugged. "They're too busy with crops. We got some kind of fungus, and I got sick of dealing with it."

"Intriguing," I said. "But that doesn't answer my question."

She shook her head. "I'll be home for harvest."

"You want to stay in Brushhead?"

She nodded.

"What's your name?" I said, blinking a picture of her.

"Jilly."

"Jilly what?"

"Just Jilly."

I've never been a fan of the Freeborn way of single names.

I attached a note to her photo: GET HER JOB, SURNAME.

"OK, Just Jilly," I said, as we slowed behind a convoy of lorries stacked high with cane. "If you can get me to where I want to go in the next five minutes, I might forget to log this whole conversation."

Jilly nodded. "You mind if I put on some music?"

"As long as it's got a good beat, fine."

She knocked on the dashboard, and the sounds of a banghorchestra thrummed from beneath the seats. Jilly stomped on the gas, and the tuk-tuk hopped onto the sidewalk. A few choice beeps of the horn cleared the way as we screeched around a corner and down into the dirtier part of Brushhead.

THREE

Murdoch Street was half a block long and always felt like a cave. There was something about the way the buildings smashed together, the way the rooflines leaned out into the street, the way the sun never hit the sidewalk that made the whole place feel like it should have been a mushroom farm instead of a collection of run-down bars. It wasn't scary so much as it was depressing as hell. Despite decades of the Union, the Co-Op, and even WalWa trying to fix the place up, it never changed. This was where the people who fell through the cracks got stuck. It was also one of the few places in the entire city where Vytai Bloombeck was allowed to loiter.

"You sure about this, boss?" said Jilly as she pulled up the parking brake. The warm glow of early evening bathed Kadalie Boulevard in deep golden light, none of which crossed into Murdoch. Even the bare fluorescent bulbs in front of the bars couldn't hold back the murk.

"Relax, kid," I said, climbing out of the tuk-tuk. "You had plenty of dark nights out in the kampong."

"At least there I could see the stars," she said, pulling her arms inside her shirt.

Normally when I wanted to find someone, I just grabbed the first person I knew and said as much. My request would fan out over the Public, and, in a matter of minutes, I'd be sitting down to tea and cakes with the object of my search. There was no way in hell I could do that with Bloombeck because a) I didn't want anyone to know that I had anything to do with him on purpose and b) everyone would laugh and say, "This is a joke, right?" and nothing would happen. I was left with doing things the old-fashioned way: walking along Murdoch Street until my pai gave me a headache.

It took six bars until I got a poke in the back of my eye. The place had two windows, one covered with a plywood sheet and the other in grime. It didn't even have a name, just a hand-scrawled paper sign above the door that said DRINK. Figures Bloombeck would be in here. He wasn't an alcoholic, but the people he bothered usually were. I nudged the door open with the toe of my boot then stepped into the dark.

Three people looked up, their faces ghostly from the little bit of light that seeped in behind me. None of them had any ink; they were probably Freeborn people who'd left the kampong to look for work and wound up getting trampled. They all eyed me for a moment before huddling back over their drinks. The bartender, a man with an eclectic collection of facial scars, gave me a look, then nodded toward the back, where the darkness got even darker. I took a few breaths so my eyes could adjust, then plunged into the middle of a sea of tiny tables, half of them covered with empties, and the other with unconscious people. Crouched over one of the drunks was Vytai Bloombeck.

I put a hand on his shoulder, and he snapped upright.

"I swear, he said it was his turn to pay!" he screeched, holding his hands over his head. A few ruined five-yuan bills quivered in his grip.

"Sit," I said, pointing to an empty table.

He took a breath after hearing my voice, and all the tension seemed to leak out of him as he plopped into a chair. "So glad to see you, Padma, I–"

"Stop," I said, sitting across from him. "You are going to tell me everything you know about these Breaches, and you are going to do it with a minimum of bullshit or I call Captain Baghram to come down here and arrest you for rolling drunks. Start."

"OK, OK," said Bloombeck. "So, my guy–"

"Who is he?"

"Come on, Padma, you gotta give me something–"

I tapped my temple, the universal sign for I'm Making a Call on My Pai.

"Jimney Potts!" he blurted. "Jimney knows all about the ships with the Breaches, I swear!"

I took my finger away from my head and laughed. "Bloody hell, Bloomie. Jimney owes me more than *you* do."

"You think he don't know that?" said Bloombeck. "I seen his profile on the Public! He's holed up tight in Thronehill, thinks you won't go in there to get him."

"But he saw *you*," I said, poking him in the chest and wishing I hadn't; it felt like prodding a bag of gelatin. "If he's so busy hiding, why'd he take the risk to talk with you?"

Bloomie licked his lips and shrugged, which made him look even more pathetic. "We're old pals, you know? We shared that flat in Partridge Hutong after you moved out–"

"*Don't* remind me," I said, wiping my finger on the table. "The way you were always banging around at all hours.

Whatever shift I worked, you were always awake."

"I had things to do," he said.

"So did I, and they usually involved getting a good night's sleep," I said. "What did Jimney tell you?"

"He was between shifts in the burn room, and he overheard some security guys talking about beefing things up on the anchor 'cause they wouldn't be able to catch the ship in transit. Even caught the name."

"Which is?"

"Oh ho," said Bloombeck, shaking his head. "Not until you help me out."

"I told you, that radar control thing won't work."

"No, I got something *better*," he said, licking his lips. "I got this neighbor, Brittona Snow, owns plot of land out in the kampong, a quarter hectare out at Sag Pond, right?"

"For what?"

He shrugged. "A little heirloom cane on the side. Nothing that'll get her into the Co-Op, but, you know, she's got a home still, makes an OK batch. I help her to sometimes. Anyway, a couple of years ago, this debris rains down on it from the corporate side of the fence, right? WalWa burning their weekly paperwork, and it just turns her crops to mush. Wipes it all out. Brittona goes to her Union rep–"

"–who is?"

Bloombeck made a face. "Evanrute Saarien. Brittona works at Sou's Reach."

My heart sank, then bobbed back up with a burn that hurt. "Figures that asshat would be involved."

Bloombeck grinned. "You still sore at him?"

I made a fist, then made myself relax. "It's not worth getting into. Continue."

"Anyway, Saarien says he'll bring it up with WalWa, and

the whole thing would have gone away, *except*" –he leaned across the table, his rummy breath making my eyes flutter– "just this evening, Brittona says WalWa wants to buy her out. For five K."

"Then that's that," I said. "WalWa rains garbage on Union grower, Union beats up WalWa, grower gets compensation. The great circle of labor continues."

"But isn't that a big deal?"

"No. They pay off farmers for bits of messed-up land all the time, and five thousand's pocket change for WalWa."

"No, wait," said Bloombeck. "I always get that wrong. Isn't a K supposed to be a million?"

I looked at him. "Bloomie," I said, "did WalWa pay off your neighbor with five *million* yuan?"

He nodded, giving me a blue-gummed smile.

"Even the biggest cane plantations aren't worth a quarter mil," I said. "Five million for a lousy quarter hectare?"

"Ain't it all crazy?" said Bloombeck.

"Insane," I said.

"Brittona, she takes the money, of course," said Bloombeck, "and that's what got me thinking: we ought to get in on the same deal."

"And what deal is that?" I said.

"Getting bought out!" said Bloombeck, his piggy eyes wide. "That's why I want to give you this information about the Breaches: it's collateral."

"Bloomie, where do you keep getting all these big words?" I said. "You're starting to scare me."

"Like I said, I know how to work an angle," said Bloombeck. "If I tell you about the Breaches, then you owe me. And then *you* can pay me back by helping me buy a little cane farm that'll get stuff dropped on it so *I* can file a complaint and get bought out. Hell, we can even get some of that Union infrastructure money to make improvements, and that'll mean we can get even *more* cash out of WalWa."

I looked at the rum behind the bar. It was past six o'clock, but getting drunk was beginning to look like a good idea. "I'm still not clear where I come in."

"I got an eye on one of these parcels off Saticoy."

"What parcels?"

"The ones that are next to the Old Windswept Distillery."

"And what do you propose I do about that?" I said.

Bloombeck shrugged. "Well, I hear you're trying to buy the place..."

"'Trying' is not the same thing as 'owning,'" I said. "And I'm sure as hell not going to jinx the deal by bringing you into the mix."

"I ain't gonna ask for much," he said. "Like, half a hectare."

"That's more than I'd be willing to part with, *if* it were my call," I said. "Which it's not."

"But it *will* be!" said Bloombeck. "And once WalWa dumps stuff on it, I'll give you a cut of the settlement!"

"Even if this information were accurate," I said, "which I very much doubt, considering how much weed Jimney Potts smokes, it's not worth making a deal with you."

"It could be."

"Saticoy is upwind from Thronehill," I said. "Did you think about that?"

He shrugged. "The wind could always change."

"Oh, God," I muttered, then nodded. "Fine. I'll do what I can, if I can."

Bloombeck straightened up, a neat trick for a pile of crap like him. "Plus three hundred thousand yuan."

One of the things I learned in business school was how to deal with a ludicrous offer: you nodded like you were considering it, then you came back with an equally ludicrous counteroffer. I gave Bloomie the nod, then said, "Make it one fifty."

"Hey, I'll go for tha–"

"One *hundred* fifty," I said. "Then a decimal point, then two zeroes."

A weak cry fluttered from Bloombeck's belly. "Who do you think I am, Padma? You think I'll stand for that kind of insult?"

"Yep," I said, rising from my chair.

"OK, OK, OK!" he said, reaching toward me. "I'll take it!"

I smacked his hand away. "What do I get in return?"

"What do you mean?"

"You think I'm going to haul my ass all the way to Thronehill and track down Jimney just on your say-so? You're gonna have to do better than that."

Bloombeck nodded, then flashed his ruined teeth. "Only if you make the deal. One of us's gotta blink it in."

I sighed. One hundred fifty yuan wasn't pocket change for me, but I could spend it without feeling too guilty. "Fine," I said, blinking up the forms and filling in my data. I shot it over to Bloombeck, who took his sweet time filling in his part. He blinked the finished contract to me, and then I double-checked the thing, its ISO-20K-compliant font hovering in air: I would give him one hundred fifty yuan and help him secure a plot of land near Saticoy, and he would give me the name of the ship.

"Of course, I still have no way of trusting this information," I said. "I'm surprised Jimney even remembered who you were."

"I got the proof," said Bloombeck, "but it goes into escrow."

"How you learned that word, I'll never understand," I said. "OK."

I blinked on my pai's video capture, sending the feed straight to the Public. "I'm looking at Vytai Bloombeck, Partridge Hutong, Brushhead, Santee City," I said. "He and I have just struck a contract, transaction number whatever–"

"Hey, do it right," said Bloombeck.

I blinked up the contract number and read it aloud. "I'm putting one hundred fifty yuan in escrow for the information he's selling me, and I'll release the funds upon delivery blah blah blah boilerplate boilerplate blah blah blah."

"And I'm looking at Padma Mehta, 42 Samarkand Road, Brushhead, Santee City," he said, "and I approve this contract."

"God help me, so do I."

We closed our feeds, and the escrow officer on duty checked out the deal. The approval blipped through, and Bloombeck stared at me. "Well?" I said.

"Well, what?"

He shifted in his chair. "Aren't you going to offer me a drink? You're always supposed to share a shot once you've closed a deal."

I raised a fist. "Only shot I'll give you is one to the nose."

"I'm just saying, it's tradition."

"Yeah, but not a good one," I said.

"All the same," said Bloombeck, looking toward the bar and raising a finger.

"Jesus," I sighed. "Fine." I turned around and did the same. The bartender started to pour two shots from the bottle in front of him, then caught my glare and reached under the bar. The light glinted off the foil Co-Op seal on the new bottle's cap, and I nodded. I knew I couldn't afford to be choosy in a place like this, but I'd be damned if I was going to drink export rotgut.

The bartender brought the bottle and two glasses to our table, then left when I handed him a tenner and a few fifty-jiao pieces. "Make with the proof, and it had better be solid."

"The drink first?"

I grabbed the bottle, a seven-fifty of Nelson's Column, a silver. Deirdre Fantone, the distiller, used coral steel tanks for aging, so the rum had a sharp flavor, like getting punched in the face with a grapefruit. I imagined the cap was Bloombeck's neck as I twisted it and cracked the seal. My warm, fuzzy feeling vanished as the room filled with the smell of mustard gas and raw sewage. The unconscious drunks around us all bolted upright, and I grabbed Bloombeck by the scruff of his neck and hauled him out as the bartender yelled to clear the room.

Outside, the air wasn't much better, but at least it didn't make my eyes burn. I still had the bottle in my hand; most of the rotgut had swished out as I'd ran. I held the bottle up to the light and saw black flakes and oil slicks swirling inside. I blinked a picture and sent it to Tonggow along with a note (*Co-Op product going bad?*) before tossing the bottle into a nearby storage crate that was acting as a public trash can.

"Ugh, what was that?" choked Bloombeck.

"Nothing that's relevant," I said. "Ship name. Now."

"OK," he said, then looked away.

I leaned forward. "You *do* have proof, right? 'Cause if you don't, you know the law says I can have that contract voided *and* be allowed to kick your ass all over the island."

"It's with Jimney," he said, beads of sweat forming along his hairline. "He insisted."

"Jimney Potts doesn't know *how* to insist," I said.

"Still, it's with him. In Thronehill." He gave me a sheepish grin. "Guess we're going on a field trip, huh?"

"No, I am," I said, getting up. "You wait here. I'm going to show Jimney a new meaning of the word 'insist.'"

"I really think I should go with," said Bloombeck, eyeing the exit of the alley. "Me and Jimney, we're pals. I worry."

"That's what I like about you, Bloomie," I said, following him toward Kadalie. "You care."

Jilly huddled up in the front seat of the tuk-tuk. She took one look at Bloombeck and said, "*That* isn't riding in my rig."

"Watch your mouth, scab," said Bloombeck.

"Is that any way to talk to a future member of our Union?" I said, climbing in next to Jilly.

Bloombeck looked at Jilly and sneered. "Some muck-scratcher from the kampong's gonna come into *our* Union?"

"Bloomie, if we can let you in, we can sure as hell let her in." I patted Jilly on the shoulder. "Fastest way to WalWa HQ, kid. And just ignore him. I usually do."

"Why aren't you now?"

"Business trumps hygiene. Drive."

Jilly shook her head, but pulled a U-ie onto Kadalie and headed toward the setting sun. We bumped over the Sway Street Bridge, across the green waters of the Ivory Canal, and sped up the road to Thronehill.

FOUR

If Brushhead's crammed architecture and riot of smells were one end of the Santee Anchorage experience spectrum, then Thronehill was the polar opposite. Every corner was planned down to the millimeter, its buildings were all square, squat and made of the same gray pourform. It was built entirely by WalWa people, and it felt it. The air was cold and clammy and made me want huddle inside my deck jacket, even though it was summertime. Whether it was a trick of microclimate or some urban heat sink effect, I was never sure. I hated coming here. The Fear loved it.

After a brief drive through the edges of the kampong, we came to the district gate. A lone WalWa security goon stood in front of this, mirrored helmet shield flipped up, riot hose trained on us. "This district is closed to nonessential personnel," he said. (At least, I think it was a he. I knew there were women who became goons, but the armor and steroids made it tough to tell them apart.)

I put my Union card in his face. "I'm as essential as they get, stud. Shift it."

The goon took a step back, blinking like crazy as he tried

to make sense of my card and the messages it triggered in his pai. I waved it around, his beady eyes following. "Still need to see a work order," he said.

"OK," I said, tucking the card back into my pocket. "Say... what kind of armor you wearing?"

"What?"

"Armor, stud, what kind?"

The goon snorted. "Mark Six."

I nodded, then put my hands on his waistband. "Good to know," I said. "The emergency release is still exposed on the Mark Sixes." I grabbed two red tabs on his armor and yanked as hard as I could. There was a hiss, and the caneplas plates clattered to the ground, leaving him naked to the breeze.

I jumped in the tuk-tuk. "Make sure to ask for an upgrade. Might save your life." I patted Jilly's shoulder, and we scooted into the frigid streets of Thronehill. I didn't have to tell her where the main office was; it was a good ten stories taller than every other gray box of a building, and the street signs all pointed the way in giant orange letters. Even with the reduced trans-stellar traffic, there were hundreds of other WalWa departments in this district, all the good little Indentures beavering away to fulfill policies that had probably changed when they were still in transit. Fewer and fewer of them got promotions that allowed them to flee up the cable, so it was just a matter of time before they all Breached or sealed themselves inside the giant Colonial Directorate building so they could hide from the big bad world they pretended to manage.

"I already regret listening to you, Bloomie," I said, shivering under the buildings' shadows, "and we've only just gotten here."

"It'll be worth it," said Bloombeck. "Pull up to the main office ahead, kid."

"I know where it is," said Jilly, the fear in her voice replaced by annoyance. She would go far.

"You stay here," I said to Bloombeck as we squeaked to a stop.

"But—"

"Bloomie, you really think they're going to let your spivey ass in there? This is official Union business, and you are not a Union official."

"But how're you going to find Jimney?"

"I'll follow the smell."

The main office loomed overhead, like someone had dropped a block of granite from orbit. It was one of the first structures to be built after the lifter, and it was a prime example of Big Three architecture: take the worst of native materials and turn it into the least functional of buildings. The only things that worked were the elevators and the atmosphere purifiers. The black caneplas doors squeaked open, and a blast of triple-scrubbed air from inside made my nose twitch. A pair of goons, their riot hoses at the ready, stood on either side of a battleaxe of a receptionist.

"Hi," I said, flashing my card. "Here on business."

The receptionist held a scanner to the barcode, and her desk chimed. "Mehta, Padma," said the desk with a pleasant female voice. "Santee Anchorage Freelancer's Union. Level Three access."

Every piece of Big Three hardware that talked used what we called the Univoice. It bubbled out of all sorts of salvaged, obsolete, or stolen gear. It was one of the few Big Three bits of tech that didn't annoy me, though that didn't stop me from figuring out ways to make the Univoice cuss.

"You get all that?" I said, giving the receptionist a broad smile.

"I know who *you* are," said the battleaxe. "I knew before you brought your... air in with you."

"Then you know to call off the steroid munchers," I said. The goons tightened their grips, and I blew one a kiss. "Jimney Potts. Owes me dues. I'll find my own way."

The receptionist twitched, making the WalWa logo inked on her cheek crinkle. "Follow the lighted path," she said. "Or we cannot be held responsible for what happens."

"I appreciate the thought," I said, scratching my cheek with my middle finger, right on my Union fist. The receptionist sneered and stabbed a button on her desk; a line of golden tiles lit up, snaking past the desk and into the bowels of the main office. I waved at the goons as I followed the Yellow Brick Road.

The interior halls were painted stomach-churning shades of brown and red, like someone had thrown a dozen hedgehogs in a blender and smeared the results on the walls. Some genius in WalWa's Work Environment Conditioning division had probably done a study to figure out what colors made people feel small and insignificant and had come up with this result. I whistled the WalWa corporate anthem, making sure to hit the high notes with extra gusto every time I passed some doomed office drone, his eyes staring dead ahead into oblivion. The lit tiles ended outside a janitor's closet; the scents of chiba and body odor leaked out from underneath. I didn't bother to knock.

Jimney Potts sat on an overturned pail, his eyes unfocused and bloodshot and locked on the wall opposite him. He wore bagasse-pulp paper coveralls filthy with black soot. A tarnished metal nameplate that said *POTTS* hung from his chest pocket. "Jimney," I said.

He kept staring.

"Jimney!"

He jumped, his paper clothes crackling with caked grime, then looked around the room until his eyes focused on me. "Oh, hey, Padma," he said, absently scratching his ass with a hand broom. "Aren't you out of your Ward?"

"Delinquent dues hurt us all, Jimney," I said, blocking the doorway of his closet.

"Oh, yeah," he said, blinking a little too slowly. The air scrubbers in the hall whined, trying to clean up the THC odors that hovered around his body like a heat haze. "And I'll get it, I'll get it. It's just I got a wife, four kids, there's only so much cash to go around..."

"And you wouldn't have any cash at all without your Union gig," I said, wondering who in hell would marry Jimney, let alone reproduce with him.

"Oh, yeah," said Jimney, now fiddling with bottles of cleanser on a nearby shelf. "Hey, the Union's done all right by me, Padma."

"And you can do right by the Union by telling me what you told Bloombeck about that seeder."

"Oh, I don't know about that," he said, shaking his kumara-shaped head. "But, you know, maybe if there's a finder's fee..."

"Jimney, who do you think pays that fee?"

He screwed up his face, like I'd just asked him to calculate the trajectories of every can coming down to sea. It was one thing to deal with someone who's windswept, but people who made their own magic breeze required extra patience.

Finally, he said, "Oh, yeah. That's really deep, Padma. It's all a big cycle."

"Right," I said, doing my best to steer his stoned logic back to the topic at hand, "and the big cycle needs new members, and new members might be arriving on that colony seeder. What can you tell me about them?"

"The ship's got a real pretty name," said Jimney. He smiled, and his eyes glazed over.

I thumped the door, and his whole body shook. "I know," I said. "Tell me about the Breaches."

"What?"

"The Breaches. On the colony seeder."

"What colony seeder?"

"The one making the water drop in six days," I said, forcing my hands into my pants pockets so they wouldn't go around his scrawny neck.

"What do you want to know about that?"

"Everything."

"OK," he said, digging through his filthy coveralls. "Um, last week, I was cleaning the executive lounge, working the stalls, you know?"

"Not really."

"I had the stall door closed so I could scrub off the graffiti–"

I put a hand over my mouth to hide my smirk. The only graffiti in this building was written by me. I made a point of freshening it up every few months, just to remind the WalWa people the Union was there, ready for them if they ever wanted to join.

"So, I got the door closed, and these guys come in, and they're talking about this ship having crew trouble, and I caught the name..."

"Which is?" I blinked up the shipping queue. I'd spent the past six months focusing on the mining ships and hadn't bothered to pay attention to everything else in transit. I cursed as I saw there were a lot of blank data fields. No way to tell which was the seeder.

"Yeah," he said, nodding a little too much. "And then, a few days later, I'm in the burn room, sweeping the shreds back to the fire before I leave my clothes behind–"

"Hold it," I said. "You leave your clothes behind?"

"Yeah," Jimney said, fingering the black streaks on his coveralls. "Always burn it at the end of the week. WalWa policy. Plus, I don't have to do laundry."

"Of course."

"So, I'm sweeping the shreds, finishing up, and these two goons are walking outside the burn room, and I hear them talking. They're all worked up, because they got this security alert, saying there are, like, forty people causing trouble on this ship. I hear them say it's on the way–"

"What is its name?" I said. "And when is it making its fuel drop?"

"Oh, wow," said Jimney. "Hold on. Lemme think. Numbers make my head hurt."

I wondered if this happened to anyone in a citywide office. Is this why my boss had wanted to spend all his time in the local titty bars instead of being out in the field?

"I got it!" Jimney said with a broad smile. "The *Rose of Tralee*. They were making landfall today."

"Today? Bloombeck told me it was in six days."

"Hey, how is he?" said Jimney. "I haven't seen him in, like, almost a week. Said he was buying next time we got together. Is he here? Should we go say hi?"

Before Jimney could move, I stepped back into the hall and slammed the closet door shut. He made a few feeble protests as I barricaded him in with a trash barrel. He'd get out eventually, but right now I had to lose as much deadweight as possible.

I blinked up the queue again, and there it was, an hour from hitting orbit: the *Rose of Tralee*, a WalWa colony seeder fresh in from Goodluck, bound for someplace in the Beyond. Now Bloombeck's story made sense; Santee wasn't popular for local traffic, but it was one of the last fuel stops before jumping past the boundaries of Occupied Space. Leaving Santee was, essentially, a one-way trip. That, plus all that travel time (two years out of Goodluck to jump, then two years to here, then two more years to the Red Line and Beyond) gave the crew plenty of time to contemplate how long and shitty the voyage ahead could be.

Plus, forty Breaches. That would easily put me over the top, give me a few Breaches to pass on to other recruiters to put them in my debt. I'd always have a need for labor, Union or otherwise, and it would go a long way toward helping the distillery succeed.

Still, Jesus! Just like Bloombeck to get his timing messed up. This would have been great news a week ago. Now, it was just a potential pain in my ass.

I slipped outside the main building, smiling and waving to the stone-faced receptionist as I ran to the tuk-tuk.

"Padma, I been thinking," said Bloombeck, climbing out of the tuk-tuk. "It's not fair, the price we agreed on. I want to up it to *three* fifty–"

I grabbed him by the shoulder and flipped him out to the ground. "Drive," I said. Bloombeck howled in protest as Jilly stomped on the gas. "Head for the coast."

"Anywhere in particular, boss?" asked Jilly as she dodged a caravan of WalWa Indentures biking toward the main office. I heard the cry of *Union parasite!* before we skidded around a corner.

"Sou's Reach," I said, "and go faster than you did before."

Jilly nodded and steered us onto the sidewalk. We passed the line of vehicles at the exit cordon, and I waved to the still-naked goon as we bounced onto Brapati Causeway. The tuk-tuk's engine protested, but she didn't let up until the first whiffs of rotting sugar hit us thirty-six minutes later.

FIVE

The Recovery launches weren't so much boats as they were planks with delusions of seaworthiness, and the sailors lounging around were in danger of being overrun by empty rum jugs. None of them looked competent or sober enough to do anything, which made things that much easier when a black and yellow police bumblecar screeched to a halt in front of the Recovery office and disgorged six cops who proceeded to arrest their way in. As soon as the cops cleared the dock, I tore a blue boy in half and gave one piece to Jilly. "Find me something big enough to haul forty people and you get the other half."

She protested until I held up two more C-notes. As she scurried away to steal something appropriate, I bounced to the launches. They were even more terrifying up close, less ships than collections of scabby paint and rusted parts. I hopped onto the least cancerous of the boats, fired up the cane diesel engines, and hoped for the best as I cast off. The launch gurgled and creaked as it hit wake, and the noises only got worse once I turned into open water.

No one else in the harbor made a move toward the

smoke columns, now turning white from steam. That was encouraging: no one from another Ward had managed to get the jump on me, and the lack of WalWa traffic meant I just might pull this off. I cranked the throttle up to maximum, despite the engine's whining protests. The smell of heated saltwater filled my nose, along with boiled fish. Hot drops were hell on sea life.

Soon, the cans were in sight: four gray cylinders, each thirty meters long, bobbing along the swell, their heat shields acting as ballast. Scorch marks from the re-entry scored their sides, and I wondered if they were dropped on purpose or by accident. Drop cans could withstand the fall, but the G-forces were brutal to anyone stowing away inside. Most Breaches preferred to hitch a ride just before the empty cans were strung on the lifter's downward cable, hoping the cans' shielding would protect them from Santee's Van Allen belts. Either was a tough way to jump ship.

I pulled alongside the closest can and tossed cane rubber fenders over the side to keep the boat from smashing on the can's hull. Proper protocol for Recovery involved a lot of decontamination and quarantine, but I was in a hurry. I grabbed the biggest wrench I could find on the launch and banged three times on the can. The thick steel rang, hollow like a cave.

Then there was an answer: a furious pounding from inside, and the unmistakable cry of "Get us the hell out of here!" *Us.* Oh, that was a sweet sound. I scooted the launch up to an access hatch, and, despite the poor condition of the tools on board, managed to crack the seal and open. "Anyone in there injured?"

"Yes!" came a chorus of voices. Excellent. I knew those *How to Breach* pamphlets had been a good investment.

"Good," I said, tugging on the hatch as hard I could. "Then, on behalf of the Santee Anchorage Local of the Universal Freelancer's Union and the Ward of Brushhead, I'd like to offer you assist–"

The hatch gave, and I tumbled back on my ass. When I stood up, five pasty people in damp WalWa coveralls looked up at me.

"OK," I said, wiping the rust off my hands. "Get on board, and tell everyone else to step lively."

"There's just us," said one of them, a woman with a ruined smoker's voice. She was all muscle and had a patch over her right eye. Her face was bright red and wealed by burn scars, crinkling what looked like a tattoo of crossed wrenches. For the briefest of moments, I thought I knew her. No, I *knew* I knew her, even though I had never met a one-eyed ship's engineer in my life. Was she someone from my days in the Life Corporate? No, that was impossible. No one from my previous life had ever Breached.

I held out a hand, and she took it with a grunt. I shuddered as she squeezed so hard I felt my fingers pop. I may not have known her, but I was sure I wouldn't like her.

The others followed her: a pair of old ladies whose ink had faded, a gaunt white guy whose coveralls were three sizes too big, and a middle-aged woman dragging a body by the shoulders. They all huddled on the deck like sheep, glancing up at the sky, as if they expected a WalWa security boat to smash down on them.

"Good," I said. "Now, let's get the others."

"What others?" said the gaunt man. BANKS was stitched over his left breast pocket, and he had scales tattooed on his cheek. A lawyer. Great.

"There are supposed to be forty of you," I said.

Banks shook his head. "Just six. Well, I guess that's if you want to include Thanh." He nodded at the body.

I looked at him, then climbed over the lot of them to the hatch of the fuel can. There was nothing but the smell of rank seawater. The only pings I got were from these six, and one had no lifesigns. I looked back at him. "My source told me that me that forty of you were going to Breach."

Banks shrugged. "There were just the six of us awake. I mean, unless some of those fishsticks were thinking about it, but it's not like they could tell us–"

I grabbed him by the front of his coveralls. "THERE WERE SUPPOSED TO BE FORTY OF YOU."

"I'm sorry, I'm sorry!" he said, and the way his eyes went wide and watery told me enough. There were only five Breaches, six with the corpse. I was short of meeting my obligation. Vytai Bloombeck had lied to me, and, worst of all, I'd fallen for it.

I thumped the side of the can, and it rang back, hollow. I could hear The Fear laughing, its chainsaw voice bouncing around my skull. I rubbed my temples, pushed back the tingling paralysis creeping up my spine. No, no, I would not give in, I could make it until tomorrow night–

And then the breeze picked up, strong enough to blow away the smell of re-entry boiled fish and carbon. It came from far out to sea, heavy with salt spray, just a little chill in the warm morning. Out of habit, I inhaled, brought the smell through my nose and right into my brain. It had been so long since I'd been on the open water that I'd forgotten just how *clean* the air was out here. Brushhead didn't have real air pollution, but it was all such a riot of smells that it masked the tang of the deep, deep sea.

My new passengers didn't pick up on this, of course.

How could they? They'd spent years stuffed inside a floating tin can, breathing recycled farts in the musty seeder's air; their noses were shot to hell. I wanted to tell these people to breathe deep, enjoy their new freedom, but all of the recruitment talk could wait.

"Well," I said, "this isn't what any of us were expecting, so let's just get to shore and we'll worry about the rest later. Is anyone injur–"

I got a tickle behind my eye. It wasn't as bad as the Bloomie Is Nigh alert, but it was enough to make me nervous. Something was coming. I steered us so the shoreline was in view and saw sunlight glint on the water. I blinked in a zoom and saw four WalWa skiffs zipping toward us. "Oh, shit," I said, cranking the throttle to maximum and bringing us around.

"What are you doing?" said Banks.

"Getting a move on," I said, nodding at the skiffs.

"But we're heading out to sea!"

"Look," I said, dodging the can, "in twenty minutes, those boats will be within firing range. They'll hose us down with riot foam, which will freeze us in place, and then you are beyond fucked. Me, they'll just rough up, but you? You'll never see daylight again."

"And I appreciate that," said Banks, "but wouldn't we be safer on land?"

"Yes, which is why you're going to do what I tell you to." I grabbed his skinny shoulders, pulled him in front of me, then put his hands on the wheel and throttle. Then I started to get undressed.

He blinked and looked away. "OK, I might have hit my head during re-entry, so I may just be imagining this–"

I grabbed his face, and he jammed his eyes shut. "I need

you to keep your shit together," I said. "I also need you to open your eyes so I can send you instructions."

"My pai isn't working well," he said.

"Is it working well enough for me to send you a picture?"

He nodded.

"Then open your fucking eyes, please."

Banks did, and our pais did a handshake. I sent him a photo of the coastline, making sure to highlight the Emerald Masjid, then sent a shot of Jilly. "When I let go, start a count to twenty. Then point the boat toward that green tower in the first picture there. When you get to shore, that girl in the second picture will be waiting for you. Do *not* go with anyone but her, got it?"

He nodded.

"Good." I patted his cheek. "See you around, counselor," I said, then jumped overboard.

SIX

My balance was a little off, thanks to not making my Six O'Clock. It wasn't my most graceful dive, but it got me clear of the launch. I worked my way to the surface, thankful it wasn't mating season for the squid. I would have enough problems with the WalWa skiffs and didn't need a batch of horny, tentacled beasties thrown into the mix.

Once I got topside, I was glad to see the launch zipping away. I swam toward the WalWa boats, blinking up a distress signal from my pai. I made sure to put it on all channels; some signal buoy would put it out on the Public, which might attract someone who was looking for action. It might also attract anyone allied with Sou's Reach, but that was a chance I could take. This late in the day Saarien's minions were probably unconscious or on their way to it.

The skiffs were half a klick away and gaining. I blinked up a zoom to see if their foam cannons were armed, but could only see the boats hopping over the spray and now heading toward the cans. Better to assume they were ready to fire, which meant getting their attention pronto.

I blinked up a picture of the skiffs and fired it out to the

Public with a landstamp and a note: *NOW DROWNING.
WALWA NOT COMING TO MY AID. AVENGE ME WITH
LAWSUITS AND STRIKES.* I waited a few moments, and the
skiffs veered hard to port, right toward me, though they had
slowed down a bit. Did that mean WalWa had a watch agent
on the Public that scanned for anything I said? It had been a
while since I'd gotten that kind of rise out of them. I'd have
to see what kinds of hoops I could get the boat crews to
jump through once they'd hauled me on board.

Then my head buzzed with a message: *we're coming to get
you. stand by.* That was quick, seeing how the skiffs were still
a ways off. Then I looked at the message signature: *banks.*

I kicked and pushed myself up to get a better view and saw
the recovery launch was heading my way. I also saw that it
was now loaded with people. *HEAD TO SHORE, DUMBASS,*
I texted back, but the launch kept chugging toward me.
Great. Not only did Banks not follow instructions, he was
also one of those lazy twits who shorthanded all his texts.
What else should I have expected from a Big Three lawyer?

I kicked up again to look at the WalWa skiffs; they had
cranked up the speed, and a quick zoom showed their round,
warty riot foam cannons were aiming in our direction. I
swam at the launch until they were close enough to throw
me a line. My shoulders burned as I hauled myself on
board. The Breaches, all pale and pooped, gave me goggle-
eyed stares as I climbed over them to the pilot house.

"Do you not know how to follow instructions?" I said,
shoving Banks away from the wheel. "I told you to head for
shore, not to come back and get me."

"But it's choppy out here, and–"

"This? This is a calm day," I said, spinning us about and
putting the throttle to All Ahead Flee. "I could have swam

all the way home if I'd wanted. You think I don't know how to handle myself?"

"No," said Banks, "I just thought–"

"Until you've had a solid meal, two beers and your pai's firmware reburned, you don't *get* to think," I said, looking over my shoulder. The skiffs bounced over the waves, and would be within firing range in minutes. "You know why? 'Cause you don't know shit about what goes on here. Everything you've learned about life went right out the window the minute you entered that can. You got me?"

Banks blinked a few times, then said, "I do. Turn us around."

"Oh, so you've had a change of heart?" I said. "Can't deal with someone who's Union calling the shots?"

"No," said Banks, "it's just that the only way out of here is to turn us around. We're not as fast, but we're more maneuverable, and by the time they come about–"

"Look," I said, "I don't know what they taught you about naval warfare in law school, but I can assure you that it's wrong. Those skiffs are all loaded down with enough riot foam to freeze us for a month, and they'll be good and ready to fire as soon as we're in range."

Banks nodded. "Good. You see my point, then."

"Did you hit your head during re-entry?" I said. "They're gonna be in range in thirty seconds, and once they start shooting and that foam starts setting–"

And then I realized what the mad bastard was getting at. I cranked the launch around hard. "Everyone, hold on to each other!" I yelled. "Duck down low and don't let go. You," I said to Banks, "start throwing as much useless weight overboard as you can. Except yourself."

"So, I'm not useless?" said Banks.

"The day's still young."

He gave me a smile, then moved about the launch, chucking everything over the side. I braced myself against the wheel as we barreled toward the skiffs, the clock ticking down to zero. I blinked the numbers out of my field of vision as all of the WalWa boats opened fire, their cannons bursting like kids spitting cupcakes out of their mouths. The foam loads sailed overhead, splashing in our wake and expanding into giant, marshmallow islands. The cannons kept going, every barrage sailing over the screaming Breaches, but all falling just behind us. The gunnery crews must have been going nuts trying to level their guns as we blasted straight through their flotilla. By the time we passed the skiffs, the deckhands were shooting their riot hoses at us, but they just didn't have enough oomph. When the skiffs finally came about, they were stuck in the middle of their own now-setting foam. They fired a few more rounds, but the shots went wild and had that air of desperation I so love to get from WalWa. As I turned the overcrowded launch to shore, I allowed myself a smile.

"Are you one of the whores?"

I turned around. The middle-aged lady with the dagger stare was at my elbow, her eyes hollow in the dusk shadows. "What?"

"The whores who lure men down from the corporate side," she said, her voice a broken pennywhistle. "I know all about you. I've seen the shows, read the manga. You people sell each other out, turning innocents into sex slaves, make others fight for sport. I know all about this place, all the flesh and sin."

That was when I realized I was still in my underwear. No one had ever accused me of prudery, but damned if it wasn't difficult to stay cool when I was undressed. I pulled on my clothes with as much speed and dignity as I could muster. "Ma'am, how long have you been working for WalWa?"

"All my life," she said, indignant. "I was born in a company hospital, went to company schools–"

"–and consumed too much company media," I said, stifling the urge to mention her coming out of the company gene pool, too. WalWa loved its Indentures to interbreed, since servility is a recessive trait. "There aren't any slaves on Santee, except for the Big Three Indentures."

She stiffened. "I was never a slave!" she cried. "I was free to work and buy what I wanted! I was taken care of!" She pointed a bony finger at the corpse on the foredeck. "I was perfectly happy taking care of those people, but Thanh had to keep dreaming! He couldn't see what a good thing we had!" She turned toward the body and spat. "Where's your freedom now, you asshole?" And then she turned on me: "Take me back! I want to go home! I don't want to be a slave! I don't want–"

I slapped her. Not hard enough to send her to the deck – as much as I wanted to – but with enough pop to shake her. She put a hand to her cheek, but she shut her mouth long enough for me to kill the throttle and climb to the top of the pilot house. The other four Breaches looked up at me.

"This launch is going to shore," I said. "When we arrive, you'll have a choice: you can go to the WalWa Colonial Directorate, where you'll likely be tried on the spot for Breach of Contract and sentenced to spending the rest of your life working in the bowels of the building, *or* you can take a risk and find out just what life has to offer when you're free. It's not an easy choice to make, but it'll be the first real one a lot of you have ever had. Until then, unless you've got a medical emergency, sit the fuck down and shut the fuck up." I climbed back inside the pilot house and slammed the throttle. The launch lurched against the surf as the engines buzzed back to life.

Banks made his way back to my shoulder. "Not the best motivational speech I've ever heard."

"Not the best one I've given," I said, giving him a closer look. His pale face was as lean as the rest of the Breaches, but his was the only one that didn't look miserable. In fact, he looked downright happy, his eyes surrounded by laugh lines. "You a critic?"

Banks's smile broadened. "I've heard enough to know when they're sincere."

"What, were you in marketing, too?" I asked.

"What makes you say that?" he asked.

"The glaze in your eyes," I said. "It comes with WalWa's Sales and Leadership Program. They still using the needles?"

"Not in Legal," he said, tapping the scales on his cheeks. "Well, not the little ones, anyway."

He said it so deadpan that it took me a moment to realize he'd made a joke. Now I had reason not to trust him: lawyers only joked when they were about to screw you.

"You'll have to forgive Mimi," he said, nodding to the old lady. She now sat next to the body, gently stroking his wispy hair. "Thanh was the only thing keeping her going, and with him gone..." He shrugged, his smile lagging a bit.

"You known them long?" I asked.

"Two jumps," he said. "They're company lifers, doing botanical caretaking. I spent a lot of time helping in the gardens."

"What, giving legal advice to begonias?"

"No, as a passenger. I can't do hibernation."

"No one should, not the way WalWa does it," I said, and then The Fear tickled the back of my brain, sending icy slivers down my spine. *You missed six o'clock*, it said. *Let's remember your* own *hibernation…* I gripped the steering wheel and focused on sailing.

"What's going to happen to her?"

I cleared my throat. "Well, hell, Counselor, you should know."

"Not really," said Banks. "I covered real estate, not Service Relations."

"If she decides to stay, her life's over."

"What, they won't ship her back?"

"Maybe in the alternate universe you came from," I said. "In *this* reality, WalWa pinches every penny, which means they're not about to pay the gravity tax for some Breach who has a change of heart. She'll be lucky if she ever sees natural sunlight again."

This time, his smile actually went away. "Sorry, I didn't know."

"You do now," I said, hanging onto the wheel as the launch bounced over the breakers. "If she decides to stay, she can get a job at a plantation as a staff botanist. She can open a flower shop. She can start a street kindergarten teaching kids about water lily filtration. Whatever she wants to do, she'll be free to do it. That's more than the Big Three could ever promise her."

We puttered along, and Banks said, "And what about me? If I stay, what could I do?"

"Are you kidding me?" I said. "Santee property law makes a hurricane look orderly. You just have to pass the bar exam."

"How tough is it?" he asked.

"Depends on how much you can drink."

He looked at me, and I gave him a wink. What the hell. His smile returned, still overly broad and annoying, but it never hurt to groom legal talent. A future rum magnate would need all the lawyers she could get.

"Still, how do I know you're not going to sell us into slavery?" he said.

"You're just going to have to trust me, aren't you?" I said.

"That's what my recruiter said before they shipped me out."

"Yeah, but did they ship you to a place like this?"

As the launch bobbled on the swell, a splash of water bounced off the hull and sprayed us. Everyone started, except Banks, who blinked, inhaled through his nose and said, "My God... does it always smell this good?"

"Every day," I said. "Every single day."

SEVEN

The sky was electric purple by the time we approached shore. Everything glowed, like it had been spray-painted with gold. "Wow," Banks said at my shoulder.

"Not bad, huh?" I said.

"It's almost enough to distract me from that horrible factory you're steering us toward."

"We're only steering *near* that horrible factory," I said. "And it's an industrial cane refinery."

"Oh," said Banks. "That changes everything."

"It should," I said. "No refineries, no molasses."

"And no city?"

"Worse," I said. "No booze."

"A tragedy."

"Look, this isn't Planet Paradise where diamonds and hookers bubble up out of the ground," I said, zooming in on the beach to look for Jilly. "The only natural resources this place has are a lot of ocean and soil that grows sugarcane. The prices for sea water and industrial molasses are set, and with the way traffic's been shrinking, the only thing that brings in extra cash is rum with a Co-Op seal."

"You know I was joking, right?"

"Yeah," I said, "and I wanted to make sure you knew I wasn't. If it weren't for rum, we wouldn't have the cash to help people like you stay free."

Banks cleared his throat. "In that case, I'm excited to see the lovely refinery that protects and supports us all."

"Hey, there's no need to go overboard," I said. "The place *is* a dump."

I'd told Jilly to wait for us at the north end of Sou's Reach on a strip of beach that no one claimed as their turf because of its proximity to the refinery's waste pipes. Sou's Reach didn't want to be responsible for the sticky, stinky mess, and none of the bordering Wards wanted to deal with the potential for cleanup. It was the perfect spot for a pickup, and I couldn't help but grin when I saw Jilly standing there, a green and brown WalWa corporate bus behind her. The launch bumped up onto shore, and we climbed out into the black, foamy surf. The one-eyed Breach carried the body.

"You are getting such a raise," I said as we approached Jilly. "But I'm afraid this ride's a bit bigger than we need."

"No worries," she said, then looked at the ground.

"What?"

Jilly looked back at the bus, then shook her head. There was a squeak of metal, and she leaped back as the bus's rusty suspension gave way. Three dozen burly, dirty men with no necks and grimy coveralls climbed out. It took me a moment to recognize the insignia on their left pockets: they all worked at the cane refinery. There was one more squeak from the bus, and a man in a shiny white suit hopped to the ground and walked toward me. "Sister Padma," said Evanrute Saarien, "what are we to do with you?"

"Nothing, Rutey, if you know what's good for you and

your testicles," I said, as Jilly ran to my side. "You OK?" I asked her.

"They were blocking the road as I pulled up," she said. "Made me stop and let them on."

"Were they armed?"

"No."

"Then next time, step on the gas," I said. "When you have ten tons of steel and they only have one ton of flesh, you win."

"Sister Padma, don't take it out on the girl," said Saarien, his voice slick as a molasses spill. "How was she to know how we do things in the city?"

"True," I said, "how could she know you hire former goons for your brute squad?"

I heard one of the Breaches gasp.

Saarien shook his head. "You would say something like that. Something that mocks our brothers and sisters in the Struggle against the harshest strains of corporate bondage."

"Once a goon, always a goon," I said. "What do you want?"

"Me?" he said, putting his manicured hands on his lapels. "I want nothing but to help these people and give them the opportunities and joys that Indentured life could never bring."

"If that's your way of saying you want to pinch them for your headcount, get stuffed," I said. "You may have stolen everyone else from me, but you're not getting this lot."

Saarien's smile didn't lose an erg of energy. "Sister Padma, you really think they'd be better off in Brushhead? Cleaning out sewage? Where's the fulfillment? Where's the advancement? I can offer them positions that they'll be able to move out of quickly and easily. How many people do you have toiling away in the same Slots?"

"That's beside the point! I made the recovery, and that means I get to add these people to my headcount."

"But you recovered them under false pretenses," said Saarien. "I mean, really, Sister Padma... calling the police on my crew? What kind of Solidarity is that?"

"The same kind you used whenever you snagged Breaches for yourself?" I said. "You really think throwing more people into your refinery is going to make it work better?"

"Our output is the highest on Santee," said Saarien.

"Because everyone else's places are starving for the parts and labor you keep taking for yourself," I said. "Maybe if you actually listened to everyone else during Union meetings instead of whining about what *you* need, you'd remember that."

"Looks to me like you're the one putting herself ahead of what's good for the Union," said Saarien. "I hear you spend more time trying to get in good with Tonggow than you do with your own people."

I bit back a shout. "Rutey, what does it matter to you if I add five more people to my headcount? They'll still be in the Union. Isn't that what matters?"

"What matters is that you play by the rules," said Saarien.

"I do," I said. "And the rules say whoever makes the recovery gets the bodies."

"Bodies?" said one of the old ladies.

"You *are* going to kill us!" screeched the other.

"It's just an expression," I said over my shoulder, but Mimi was already bawling, and the two semi-comatose old ladies joined in. I turned to put a hand on Mimi's shoulder to calm her, but got a punch in the face instead. Not a slap.

A close-fisted, arm-swung-way-back haymaker that had me seeing stars. I staggered, lost my footing and collapsed in a heap.

When my head cleared, I looked up at the Breach with the scarred face. Her one good eye narrowed. "Don't you ever lay hands on her again." And then she kicked sand in my face.

By the time I got to my feet and wiped the sticky muck from my mouth, the Breaches had filed behind Saarien's thugs and onto the bus. One of the goons had draped the dead Breach over his shoulder like a stack of cane. "Hey!" I yelled, staggering to my feet, "they're with me, you assholes!" The goons turned, and one of them put a hand the size of a baby in my face. I slapped it away, which felt just like slapping a brick wall coated in meat.

As the bus rumbled away, Saarien leaned out a window and waved. "Thank you for supporting Sou's Reach again, Sister Padma!" he called, holding up a closed fist. "Solidarity!"

"You bastard!" I yelled. "If I get my hands on you, I'm going to pound you until your brains are jelly!" I tried to give him the finger, but my now-throbbing hand couldn't move.

"That wasn't the picture of Solidarity that I'd expected," Banks called out from behind me. I spun around; he was peeking out from the launch's pilot house.

"What are you still doing there?" I said.

"I'm not a fan of conflict," he said, hopping off the boat. "Those guys looked like they were full of it."

"They're full of something," I said.

"He wasn't with WalWa, right?" said Banks. "Some kind of undercover thing? I mean, that guy's white suit looked like something out of Corporate Recruitment."

"That's because he was, before he Breached," I said. "I guess he liked the cut of the clothes."

"And he runs a refinery? Shouldn't he be doing, y'know, recruitment?"

"He does," I said. "But he also has to eat, and that means he has to hustle, just like the rest of us. It's not like the old days when you had ships lining up ten deep at the anchor, all of 'em full of crews waiting to jump ship. If we want to stay free, everyone works at everything, including the dirty stuff." I wiped my good hand on my jacket. "Though how that son of a bitch keeps that suit clean is a mystery."

"You don't get along?"

"No, no, we're the best of friends. That's why I let him shanghai your buddies to his little molasses pit." I patted his shoulder. "Come on. If you ever want to see them again, we need to move."

"Where?" said Jilly.

"There," I said, pointing to a sand dune just ahead.

"What for?"

"Better signal."

From the top of the dune, we had a clear view of Santee City, all its lights now blazing in the purple twilight. I took Banks by the shoulders and turned him toward the Emerald Masjid, the warning lights on its spires fading on and off. "Your pai working?" I said.

Banks blinked, then nodded.

"Good," I said. "Dial nine-nine-nine, then tell whoever picks up that you're a Breach, and your friends have left you behind. They're on a WalWa bus heading up the beach, toward the big green tower."

"Why me?"

"Authenticity," I said. "Dial."

Banks shrugged, then relaxed. His eyes glazed over, then he repeated what I'd told him, giving me a puzzled look the whole time. "They just thanked me and said to wait here," he said. "Who was that? The police?"

"Nope," I said. "Nine-nine-nine dials straight to the local WalWa HQ."

The blood rushed from Banks's face. "I called WalWa?"

"Yep," I said. "They've probably got you tracked and pinpointed as we speak."

Banks opened his mouth, then grabbed me by the lapels of my deck jacket. "How could you do this to me?" he shrieked. "How could you turn me back in?"

"Relax, counselor," I said, flipping his hands off me. "Just because they know where you are doesn't mean they can get you. Besides, you're with me."

Banks tensed again. "That hasn't been working so well today."

"Hey, I got you this far, right?"

Banks nodded.

"Then I'm going to get you the rest of the way," I said. "We just have to catch up with the bus and get your shipmates back."

"You planning on calling some secret reinforcements?" said Banks, trailing behind.

"In a manner of speaking," I said.

"I'm starting to learn not to trust your manners," he said.

It was a short hike to where Jilly had stashed her tuk-tuk behind a pile of rusted, rotting piping, right on the stinky side of the refinery. "Keep the lights and stereo off," I said to Jilly as she cranked the engine. "And hang back a bit."

The only good thing about being on this beach was that

the roads sucked for bigger, heavier vehicles. That meant we could make up plenty of ground that the bus couldn't. Within a few minutes, the taillights came into view. "Stop here," I said, and Jilly eased into the brakes.

"Is this when the backup arrives?" asked Banks.

"Soon," I said, leaning out of the tuk-tuk and looking up at the evening sky. "OK," I said to Jilly as I climbed out, "you're going to go back to Brushhead straight for the Union Hall. Ask for Lanny, tell him I sent you, and that you need a provisional hack license."

"I'm not getting a license," said Jilly.

"Then you're also not getting this," I said, holding up the second half of the fifty-yuan note along with the two C-notes. "Nor this beautiful signing bonus."

Jilly's eyes grew wide at the bills. "I have to take a test?"

"You know how to stop, start, and steer," I said, "that should be enough. Wait at the Hall. I'll get word to you tomorrow. Go."

She nodded and turned the tuk-tuk around. Banks hopped out. "Oh, no," I said.

"If you're going to rescue my friends, you're going to need me," he said.

"What, so you can convince them to stay, like you did back at the beach?" I said.

"I was outnumbered," he said. "And scared."

"It's about to get even more crowded and scary," I said. A few bundles of lights appeared over the horizon, slowed, then started to get bigger. As Jilly zipped away, Banks stared at the sky, his mouth opening wider as the lights got stronger.

"Right on time," I said. "You may want to cover your ears."

Banks gave me a funny look, but he put his hands to his ears as a gentle whine from overhead grew bigger and louder. A dozen searchlights flicked on at once, making the road so bright you'd think it was noon. The whine became a hurricane shriek as four WalWa fast-attack airships descended on the bus, their rotor fans kicking up a blinding dust storm. The airships hung around the bus like angry, armored birds, an effect made worse when the loudspeakers screeched to life.

"YOU ARE IN STOLEN PROPERTY. STOP THE VEHICLE AND PREPARE TO BE SEARCHED."

i would like to leave now, Banks texted me.

EIGHT

Follow me, I replied, then hit the dirt and crawled toward the bus.

this doesn't look like leaving, texted Banks.

You're going to have to trust me.

moving toward the dangerous people.

Repeat: You're going to have to trust me.

do i have a choice?

Of course. You can come with me or stay.

what kind of a choice is that?

More than you had before.

The airships descended, their rotors spinning dirt in our faces. The intakes created Force-Ten dust devils that could flay a person in seconds. I hoped the pilots hadn't gotten sloppy and stopped following their procedures, otherwise my obituary would start with "Sucked through a fan like a bug" – not the way I wanted to be remembered.

still trusting you though i have now wet myself

When I say so, we get up and run.

All four ships were just a few meters off the ground, their screaming turbines rattling my teeth. I counted down as the ships got closer and closer, the dust devils getting bigger and bigger, swirling around each other like dervishes until they almost touched–

GO.

I ran for the bus as hard as I could, not taking my eyes off its taillights, even as the rotor wash threatened to knock me off my feet. I ran as the dust battered my face like so much buckshot and got into my lungs, ran until the airships were right on top of me–

The rotors screamed as the pilots goosed their throttles, the dust devils blowing into each other and canceling each other out. The path was clear, and I charged past the airships and dove underneath the bus as the ships clanked to the ground.

As I lay there, the bus's driveshaft a few inches above my nose, I felt something grab my leg. I looked back; Banks was on his stomach, spitting and coughing. *i think i shat myself*, he texted.

I promise not to tell.

how did you do that?

Standard WalWa blockade formation, I texted. *They put out a final blast of air to clear the landing space so the goons aren't in the middle of a dust storm.*

how did you know

Business school. Hostile Acquisitions workshop. Lost a lot of classmates during finals.

i am so glad i'm a lawyer.

Above our heads was a maintenance hatch, its latches scarred by years of broken socket wrenches and beat-up pliers. The Colonial Directorate gave all the funding towards their air and ocean fleets, which meant their bus mechanics never got the new tools or parts they kept begging for.

And just for a little extra kick in the teeth, WalWa policy wouldn't allow the mechanics to buy from us, so the poor bastards had to work with broken, worn-down equipment. Fine with me; it meant I could unbolt the hatch with my multi-tool without any problems.

I lifted the hatch a few centis and peeked in. It was easy to spot which feet belonged to the goons, with their beat-up WalWa combat boots. The Breaches clustered in the middle of the bus. Two pairs of pipe-cleaner-thin legs bunched together in one seat: the old ladies, I figured. One pair of feet flopped at weird angles – that had to have been the Breach who'd died. Mimi and One-Eye sat opposite, Mimi's legs crossed and One-Eye's feet planted square on the ground. Even from here, I felt nothing but menace from One-Eye, like she stewed in a cloud of anger. There had to be more to her than an engineering background; everything about her screamed "security training." *What's the deal with the one-eyed woman?*

ellie? ship's engineer.

Why's she so protective of Mimi?

just protective of all of us. kept ship going. kept us going.

Can you talk with her?

Banks's eyes went wide. *walwa could trace call, know i'm here.*

They already do, I replied. *They care more about the bus. Ask her where Saarien is.*

Banks sighed, then nodded. His eyes glazed over for a moment, then he snapped back to attention. *not on bus. got out when airships arrived.*

He ran?

Banks's eyes glazed again, then he shook his head. *no, got off, walked toward airships. still there.*

I crawled toward the nose of the bus, getting close enough that I could see, sure enough, a pair of white trouser legs standing opposite WalWa standard-issue combat boots. I couldn't hear who Saarien was talking to or what he was saying, but I could see Saarien hopping up and down, probably out of fury. I grinned at the thought of him pulling his best How Dare You Do This dance in front of a bored goon commander. The longer Saarien kept it up, the better my chances of stealing back my Breaches.

I crawled back to the hatch. *You took Command Presence, right?* I texted.

sure, replied Banks.

Good, then follow my lead. I cleared my throat, took a deep breath, then slammed the hatch open. "Nobody move!" I roared from the back of my throat as I climbed into the bus. "Heads down, hands in laps! You! Don't you look at me! Eyes down! DOWN!" I yelled to a goon who had started to turn his meaty head. I elbowed him on the neck, and he stared down at his boots. Poor bastard: out of armor for a few years, but his programming from WalWa Security Services ran too deep. He had no choice but to obey the boom in my voice.

I walked to the middle of the bus where the four remaining Breaches huddled. Even One-Eye (no way I was going to start calling her *Ellie*) looked small and scared, one arm thrown over Mimi's back. They were surrounded by Saarien's ex-goons, who were just as hunched over and shuddering. For a moment, I thought about bluffing the goons off the bus, maybe getting them to think they were doing Saarien's work if they listened to me, but the whine of the turbines and the sudden clomp of four dozen pairs of hobnailed boots said that was a bad idea. The real goons, the ones who were armed, completely surrounded the bus.

How do we get this bus through the cordon? I texted Banks.

thought you had a plan

Winging it can only get you so far. Ideas?

we really need the bus?

How else do we get away?

Banks looked around, then stared at the access hatch in the floor. *we stay. bus goes.*

I looked at him, then at the hatch, then at the hostages, and all the dots connected. *You devious monkey.* I stomped up to the two old ladies, and put my hand on one of their shoulders. She rolled up in a ball, taking the other with her until they were on the floor. I looked at Banks, who shrugged. *this will make it easier to move them*, he texted, then scooped one up by her armpits and guided the clump of old lady to the access hatch. They shivered the whole way, until Banks put a hand on one of their necks and whispered something. They both straightened up, nodded to him, then slid through the hatch.

happens all the time, texted Banks. *you just have to tell them this is a drill, and they calm down.*

Will that work on the other two?

let me get them up, he texted. *you get thanh.* He nodded at the body, sitting upright on its own.

Why me?

Banks winced as he grabbed his lower back.

Are you kidding me? I texted.

threw it out on re-entry.

Jesus. I reached down to Thanh's shoulder; it was cold, probably from the trip to shore. I had no problem handling the dead; I'd worked enough labor riots to get an honorary membership into the Undertaker's Local. Still, there was something about the way Thanh's eyes had rolled back, the way his mouth lay wide open, that made my skin crawl. I pulled on his shoulder, and he rattled.

It wasn't the sound of air leaving his lungs. As I picked up Thanh's corpse – which was a lot heavier than a man his size should have been – it sounded like he'd eaten a handful of machine parts. At first I thought he'd broken some bones, but when I hefted him over my shoulder, I heard the distinct *clink* of metal on metal from somewhere in his midsection. Christ, what was WalWa doing to their people during hibernation?

There was a peep, and I looked up at Mimi's big, saucer eyes as she pointed a trembling finger at me. She had one arm wrapped around Banks, and the other around One-Eye, whose angry face looked even more terrifying in the airships' floodlights. *Calm her down*, I shot to Banks, but Mimi's peep turned into a cry, then into a wail loud enough to cut over the idling turbines outside. A few of the goons stirred, and one turned up at me, the light dawning in his beady eyes that, wait, we weren't a threat...

I dropped the body in the goon's lap; his programming went right out the window when Thanh's arms flopped around his neck. "MOVE!" I shouted to Banks as I ran up the aisle.

One-Eye snarled, but I ducked low and put my shoulder in her stomach. The air whooshed out of her lungs as I kept moving, bumping One-Eye into Banks and Mimi and sending all four of us tumbling through the access hatch. We hit the ground with a *whump*, and there was a brief moment of stillness.

Then Mimi started crying again, this time building up so loud she drowned out the airships' engines. I crawled off the pile of bodies, pushing them aside until I could see Banks. *Get her quiet.*

Banks put his head close to Mimi's, but she wouldn't shut up. Her shrieking built up in volume and pitch, and then she gulped for air and cried, "THANH! WHERE'S MY THANH?"

"Jesus Christ, lady, he's dead!" I yelled. "And you will be if you don't shut up and get moving!"

"WHERE'S MY THANH?" Mimi wailed, and I thought about slapping her again until I caught One-Eye's glare. Even in the dim, I could see the scars wrinkle in a way that said, *Go ahead. Just* try *to touch her.*

"Fine," I said. "Fine, *I* will get your Thanh. And you," I said, pointing at One-Eye, "will get her the hell out of here. Wait here until I signal Banks, then run."

"Where?" said One-Eye.

"You'll know." I climbed back into the bus, right in the middle of a scrum of Saarien's goons. They all stared at me, the way a dozen starving wolves stare at the one little chicken that accidentally wandered into their pack. One goon actually licked his lips. This required something brilliant.

I pointed at the front of the bus. "Oh my God!" I screamed, "they're coming!" They all followed my finger, which gave me enough time to jump on the goon nearest me and climb over his shoulder. Before he could react, I hopped to the floor and ran to the driver's seat. One goon grabbed at my collar, jerking me off my feet. My tailbone flared as my ass hit the ground, paralyzing me long enough for the goon to reel me in. I got it together long enough to crab-walk towards him, moving faster than he expected, then rammed my head right into his crotch. The goon howled and let go, giving me time to get up, run to the front, and fire up the bus. The engine wheezed and protested, but I stomped on the gas. The bus lurched, knocking the goons backward. The gears rattled as I tried to get it into second, and I managed to text Banks (*GO!*) before we rammed one of the airships, sending us all flying forward. There was a shriek of shearing metal and the crunch of broken glass as the windshield smashed apart, sending a rush of hot air into the already stuffy bus.

I looked up from the steering wheel into the mirrored facebowls of a dozen goons – real, live, armed WalWa goons, pointing their riot hoses at me. I froze, then cursed myself for freezing, when there was a shout from the back of the bus, "OH GOD, IT'S ON ME!" I looked back: Saarien's meatheads were in a pile on the floor, with Thanh's body on top of them. They squirmed to get away from the corpse, but all of their pushing and pulling made Thanh's hands flop around, slapping each of them in the face. It was like a demented game of "Why Are You Hitting Yourself," played by sick, sick children. It was also my cue to flee.

I threw the bus into reverse and bolted from the driver's seat as the first volley of riot foam splatted its way in. The scent of stale vanilla filled the bus as the foam expanded, like a pudding from hell, and I shoved Thanh's body off the pile of goons. It hit the floor with a rattling thud, and I leaped into the open hatch, pulling the body behind me as the foam seeped over the goons. I could only look up as the bus rolled overhead, the thud of heavy boots following as the whole mess slipped downhill past me and toward a gap in between two airships. The WalWa goons gave chase, firing their riot hoses at the bus, only to gum up one of their own airships. Three of the airships took off to chase the bus, while the other strained against the now-hardened foam. I looked around to make sure everyone was eyeballing the unfolding disaster, then fireman-carried the body as fast as I could in the opposite direction.

After what seemed like forever, I was back in the darkness, my lungs burning and legs wobbling. I put the body down, again with the rattling, then sat next to it. "I hope you're worth it," I panted to Thanh, the starlight reflecting in his dead eyes.

Thanh, thank God, said nothing.

Got your man, I texted Banks. *Where are you?*

There was a rustle, and the Breaches crept up to me. The two old ladies shivered, and Mimi stroked Thanh's hair. *we saw you running here*, Banks texted.

Anyone see you?

He shook his head. *they were too busy watching the bus and foam show. but aren't they still tracking me?*

No, I was lying about that.

why?

To get you to panic and do what I said.

Banks shook his head. *tell me you learned that in B-school.*

Crisis Management was one of my favorite classes, I replied, getting to my feet. *We have a bit of a walk, so keep quiet until I say it's OK.*

can we still text?

Keep it person-to-person, and you're fine.

no, meant you and me.

I looked at Banks, whose face was twisted up in a strained smile.

Sure, I replied. *Just don't expect a great conversation.*

fair enough.

One-Eye already had the body over her shoulder and

one arm around Mimi. I pointed at the lights of the city, put a finger to my lips and started walking. The Breaches followed, and I made mental notes of how best to beat the hell out of myself for taking this stupid deal with Bloombeck. All this headache, and for five (no, six, even the dead could join the Union) Breaches.

everyone's sorry, by the way, texted Banks.

For what? Not trusting me? Going with that white-suited scumbag instead of me?

in our defense, none of the fliers and graffiti said this is what breaching would be like.

Sure they do, I replied. *We cover it under the section headed "BEST CASE SCENARIO." No one bothers to read the worst cases.*

could it have gone worse?

You could have been crippled during re-entry. Someone could have gone overboard. We could have been attacked by squid.

squid? what, are they giant mutants?

No, they're average size.

so what's bad about that?

Getting pecked to death by ten thousand razor-sharp beaks isn't a pretty way to go.

We walked in silence, then Banks texted, *this is a hell of a paradise you have here.*

Not even corporate life is round-the-clock glamor, I replied.

it was a little glamorous.

I was about to reply when headlights flashed over us. Everyone hit the ground without my prompting, and then the wind shifted and the smell of lime and rotting cane washed over us. *It's OK,* I texted, then got up and ran toward the lights, waving my hands.

what are you doing? texted Banks.

Getting us a ride.

if it's like the last ride, i'd rather walk.

The lights belonged to a giant canvas-covered truck that shuddered to a stop. The smell of its cargo punched me in the face: a few months' worth of rotting palm fronds, decomposing fruit peelings and the remnants of every rum barrel on this side of the city. "Yo, Papa Wemba!" I yelled. "Give a girl a lift?"

Papa Wemba stuck his head out the window, his massive gray dreadlocks curling down the side of the cab. "Padma, are you the reason why my cargo got searched and I got probed by a pack of goons about ten minutes ago?"

"Did you enjoy the probing?"

"Hell, no!"

"Then it wasn't my fault."

Papa Wemba shook his head. "What did you do this time?"

"If you give me and my friends a lift, I can tell you all about it," I said, motioning for the Breaches to come forward.

"Is that a dead body?" asked Papa Wemba.

"Does it change things if I said it is?"

Papa Wemba sighed. "You know there'll be more goons on the way back to town, right?"

"Yes, Papa Wemba."

"And you know that time is money, right?"

"You know I do, Papa Wemba."

"So how much money are you willing to part with to make good time?"

I blinked up my bankroll, just out of habit. One hundred eight thousand, five hundred fifty-two yuan. I could make up the difference by the end of the week. "How much time does five hundred yuan buy us?"

Papa Wemba chuckled. "You *must* be in trouble to pay that much." He jerked a thumb toward the back of the truck. "Get in. Mind the eggshells."

I blew him a kiss and hustled the Breaches into the back of the truck. "We are *not* sitting on garbage," said Mimi, freezing up as the smell hit her.

"This isn't garbage," I said. "It's pre-compost."

"It smells like garbage."

"But it pays better," I said. "Get in, or get left behind."

Mimi looked at One-Eye, who nodded. Mimi climbed in, followed by One-Eye, still shouldering Thanh's body. Banks and I helped the old ladies get over the tailgate, then hopped in ourselves. "Find a pile that's crunchy and dry," I said, pulling the canvas flap behind me. "Then hunker down."

"How much longer?" asked Banks.

The truck rolled, then picked up speed. "Half hour, tops," I said. "Papa Wemba won't bother to take any main roads, now, not for that kind of cash."

Banks grunted as he sat on a pile of palm fronds. "You trust him?"

"I trust how much he values five hundred yuan."

"Is it always about money with you?"

"What, you never thought about your pay grade when you were still with WalWa?" I said. "You never thought about billable hours, or what you could *buy* with those billable hours? You never thought about good food, good booze, all the stuff money made possible?"

"Sure, but that was all for after," said Banks. "You know, when I did my thirty years."

"Then it's time to start thinking about it *now*," I said, shifting the pre-compost until it felt comfortable. "Nobody starves here, but if you want anything above subsistence living, you'll have to pay for it, and that means working for cash. Everyone here hustles because everyone has plans." I smiled. "Give it some time, and you might make some for yourself."

Banks leaned against the side of the bed. "So, what's yours?"

The Fear laughed. *Tell him. See how fast they all go running back to WalWa once they know what kind of person you are.*

I shrugged. "Still working on that part." The Fear hissed. *Nice try,* I thought, then closed my eyes and thought about how to get another seventeen people to fall out of the sky.

NINE

The compost truck bumped over the Sway Street Bridge, sending a load of half-rotted cane leavings over my legs. "Sorry about that!" called Papa Wemba from the cab. "Shocks are still a little off!"

I wiped the slime from my pants, leaving streaks of black. "Where did you get this stuff?" I called. "It looks like it's already broken down."

"It's the last of the salvageable bagasse from Jerzy Yutang's fields," said Papa Wemba. "He got hit with some nasty fungus, wiped out most of his crop."

I tried wiping my hands, only to have the black streaks get bigger. "You sure this is safe? Shouldn't he have torched the whole yield?"

"The piles will be hot enough to kill off any pathogens," said Papa Wemba. "Though you're probably going to want to use a little bleach on your clothes."

"Terrific," I muttered.

"Tell me wherever we're going has laundry," said Banks.

"Where we're going has a new wardrobe for all of you," I said. "Unless you're married to those coveralls."

"God, no," said Banks, plucking at his filthy lapels, now streaked black. "These things itch like hell. We only rated paper clothes, you know."

"Then they'll burn that much easier," I said, peeking through the canvas. We were on Wedge Boulevard, a mostly residential street right on the edge of Brushhead. It was the usual Wednesday night traffic: people sitting at sidewalk tables outside The Mead House and the few bulgogi joints, the sounds of people having dinner coming from the upper-story windows, and the last of the shift-change traffic petering out.

"Looks nice," said Banks behind me.

"It is," I said. "Brushhead's a good neighborhood to start out in; plenty of housing, plenty of jobs, plenty to eat."

"Oh, tell me more about that part," said Banks. "If I never see another bowl of WalWa NutriFood, it'll be too soon."

"They still have the same three flavors?"

"There's a fourth now," said Banks. "They combined the first three. Tasted like imitation crab and old chewing gum."

"Lovely," I said. "I always did like how they had to put the word 'food' in there, like a reminder that it was supposed to be edible."

"Nothing's too good for us Indentures," said Banks.

"That'll change, once we get you settled," I said. "A couple quiet nights, and–"

My pai flashed a call from Soni. I got the groans out of the way before I took it. "What's up, Soni? The payment not get through?"

"What the hell are you doing to me? First it's rescue on the high seas, now you've turned my precinct into a mess."

"What are you talking about?"

The truck turned a corner into what sounded like a

cricket riot. Papa Wemba called from the front, "You better get up here, Padma."

I climbed over the piles of coffee grounds and mulched bagasse to the front of the truck bed. I threw aside the canvas to get a view through the windshield, and my jaw dropped. We were now on Koothrapalli Avenue, Brushhead's main drag, and the street was a sea of bodies. I saw a lot of smiles and laughing in the neon glow, which was always better than an angry mob, but still distressing.

Then I saw the people waving signs: *WELCOME, FRIENDS! SLAVES NO MORE! FREE AS IN BEER!*

"I'll have to call you back," I told Soni and hung up before she could protest.

The signs were sloppy, obviously hand made this evening. Who could have told the crowd? Soni wouldn't, because she hated crowd control. Jimney couldn't, because he was probably still stuck in the broom closet. That only left...

Vytai Bloombeck pushed his way through the crowd and thumped the truck's hood. He waved at the crowd like a game-show prize girl and gave me a blue-gummed grin.

"This delay is gonna cost me," said Papa Wemba.

"Me, too," I said, blinking him fifty yuan. "Get us off Koothrapalli as fast as you can and go to the Union office on Reigert."

"Not the Hall?"

"Hell, no," I said, blinking him another twenty. "I'll meet you there. Don't let anyone know who's in the back." I turned to the Breaches. "Everything's OK, just a typical Wednesday night. I'll be right back."

"What about this?" said Mimi, pointing at the garbage.

"Can't be any worse than your old ship, right?" I said, then dove into the cab and out the door and into the street.

People slapped me on the back and tried to put beers and pierogis into my hands as I made my way to the front of the truck.

"Padma!" cried Bloombeck, holding his arms aloft, like he expected a hug.

I grabbed his wrist and spun him away to an empty stoop. "Hey, everyone, let's not stop a working man here!" I yelled, pointing to the truck. "Time is compost and compost is money and" – I got in Bloombeck's face – "I am going to feed you to the squid. What are you doing?"

Bloombeck's face fell. "You don't like it? I thought you'd like it."

"Like what?" I said. "A mob? How'd you even get this many people to talk to you?"

"You're upset?" he said. "I figured this was good news, the kind of thing that'd make your rep even better."

"I need you helping my reputation like I need a nail in my skull," I said. "It's not your place to go sticking your nose in my business."

"Yeah, but this is everyone's business," said Bloombeck. "You'd got forty Breaches, and a whole bunch of people could move up and–"

I looked back at the signs, then saw who was holding them. There was Gene Snout, a sonic landscaper who'd Breached eight months ago and now worked as a cargo checker on the lifter depot. There was Vimi Van, who'd managed the road crew in Thronehill for the past year; she wanted to open a butcher shop. And every other bright, hopeful face was someone I'd recruited, slotted into some shitty Contract job, and left until I could find their replacements.

I turned back to Bloombeck. "You son of a bitch, you

blabbed. You blabbed to everyone, after I told you *not* to, after we made a *deal*–"

"–which I kept up–"

"–except you *didn't*, because you *blabbed*!" I yelled, blinking up the contract I'd just signed a few hours ago. I scanned the whole thing, then grinned as I hit the magic clause. "Section seventeen, paragraph eight, clause six, sub-clause two: 'All parties shall keep this agreement in confidence. Any breach of this confidence renders the contract null and void.'" I slapped Bloombeck on the head. "Deal's off, Bloomie. Find someone else to buy your scam farm."

I turned back to the sidewalk and got two steps before he grabbed my jacket sleeve. "But–"

"But what?" I said, spinning around and flipping his hand away. "But I should help you, even though you broke our agreement? But I owe you, because we go back a long way? But, no, Padma, you're completely right and I'll leave you alone because I know anything I say won't hold up in court?"

"But... you already paid for this," he said.

I felt a bubble in my stomach. "Paid for *what*?"

He waved his hands toward the crowd. "This! I mean, yeah, *you* didn't pay for it, but I told everyone you would, because, you know, you're going to make your number and all. And I figured, since we're in business–"

I grabbed him by his greasy lapels. "We are *nothing* but null and goddamn void."

"Well, *now*, yeah, I see that," he said. "But I made the arrangements, people to fill the crowd, the sign makers, the band–"

"Band?"

There was a burst of horns, and the crowd cheered and parted as the Brushhead Memorial Band fired up "For She's a Bloody Great Union." Within two bars, everyone swayed and danced as the band strutted down the middle of the street, all dressed in their red and gray jackets and white pants. The woodwinds circled, the brass and drums following, and then they set up right in front of Papa Wemba's truck, which still hadn't been able to move.

I looked down at Bloomie, who tried to give me a smile. "You got them to put on their *uniforms*?" I said.

"Well, it's a special occasion, so—"

"Do you have any idea how much this will all *cost*?"

"Eight hundred sixty-five yuan," said Bloombeck. "It would've been an even grand, but I talked the band down when I told 'em it was for you."

In the back of my head, I could hear the crowd singing along with the band ("And so say all of us, and so say all of us, for she's a bloody great Union..."); everything in the front of my brain said I could strangle Bloombeck and get away with it. *Your Honor, this piece of shit completely overstepped his bounds, making business decisions like this, especially when this was only supposed to cost me a lousy one hundred fifty yuan...*

Papa Wemba caught my eye, then pointed to the masses and tapped his wrist. Time was money. Of course it was.

I left a still-blubbering Bloombeck on the sidewalk, waded through the crowd, then climbed on the hood of the truck. The band was drowned out by the roar of the crowd, a sound I would have welcomed and loved at any other time. All those people, they'd looked to me to help them out, and here I was, about to deliver.

Except I couldn't.

I held up my hands, and everyone stilled. "Thank you—"

I started, before someone yelled, "We love you, Padma!" and the cheering started again. One of the trumpets tooted away, and the band started up, and I yelled, at the tops of my lungs, "THERE AREN'T FORTY BREACHES!"

It took me a few more tries before everyone got quiet, and I could feel the waves of love turning into something hot and ugly. "There are not forty Breaches," I said, loud and clear.

"Then how many are there?" said Jordan Blanton. As a LiaoCon architect, she had designed suborbital hanging gardens; now she'd been helping muck out the city's sewage pipes for sixteen months. The stars on her cheeks had started to look as hard as her eyes.

I opened my mouth, about to say *six*, but then looked at everyone's faces. Their good mood was gone, their faces growing hard as people remembered the shitty jobs they had and would continue to have while a few of their neighbors would luck out. Anything less than the forty Bloombeck had crowed about would give this mob an excuse to become a riot. Union people could put up with a lot of bullshit, but this would be too much.

So, I took a deep breath. "Evanrute Saarien pinched them, so there are none," I said, bracing myself for the first of many flung bottles.

There was a moment of silence. Then the signs sagged, along with the faces. People shuffled away, heading into the bars and cafes. I jumped off the truck, and Jordan just shook her head. "Jordan, I tried," I said.

"I should've known this was all crap when I heard it from Bloombeck," she said, her eyes getting a little damp. "But then you show up in this truck, and I thought, maybe it's my turn. I can get someone to take my Slot, start designing again–"

"You will," I said.

"Heard that one before," said Jordan. "About sixteen months ago." She gave me a little wave, then melted into the crowd.

I opened the truck's shotgun door. "Let's go," I said, climbing in.

"You're gonna mess up my seats," said Papa Wemba.

"Bill me," I said, slamming the door behind me and waving up the road. "Drive."

It was a short hop to Reigert and Handel, and we slipped behind the Union satellite office, which took up all of an old shophouse. "I need to make a pickup here anyway," said Papa Wemba as he stomped on the parking brake. "Wednesday night is AA at Our Lady, and that means a lot of coffee grounds."

"Glad we could provide," I said, opening the door.

"Hey," said Papa Wemba, reaching over and touching my arm. "You got nothing to feel bad for, Padma. You're gonna bring in new blood to the neighborhood, and people will remember that."

"Yeah," I said, slipping out. "The problem is that only six people will remember. Thirty-four others will still be pissed at me."

I lifted the back flap, and the Breaches stared at me. "Can we get up from the pre-compost now?" asked Banks.

"It's garbage," I said, opening the tailgate. "Only call it pre-compost when you need a favor."

I blinked my keycode to the back door and ushered everyone in. "Welcome to my backup office," I said, flicking on the lights. A few moths skittered into the air, kicking up tiny dust puffs. The air was stale, probably because I hadn't opened the windows in eight months.

"Backup office?" said Banks with a grin. "You mean, you actually do work?"

"Everyone here works," I said, my tone sharper than it should have been. "Sometimes, the work's a little weird. I usually spend my time making sure everyone in the neighborhood gets what they need to do their jobs. And right now, you all need clothes and showers and food."

"And jobs?" said Mimi.

"We'll worry about that later," I said, opening a cabinet and pulling out towels and toiletries. "Sixty years ago, before the Hall got built, the Union used this place to organize strikes. People took turns scrubbing up and sleeping so the picket lines would always be manned. Not that we've had anything to picket since WalWa closed the support factories and the Big Three slowed their refueling traffic, but what the hell. Water's hot, towels are clean." I handed soap and a towel to each of the Breaches, then walked over to a stack of boxes, all filled with clothes. "Leftovers from last year's charity drive. Boxes are arranged by size, so grab one before you head upstairs. Should be enough in there to last the week."

"What happens after a week?" asked One-Eye. "You kick us out?"

"If I don't find you lot jobs in a week, I'll kick myself out," I said. "If there's one thing this planet isn't lacking, it's Union jobs."

"What about Thanh?" asked One-Eye, pointing to the corpse.

"The kitchen has a walk-in freezer," I said. "We can put Thanh in there for the night, then we'll bring him to the Olmos Brothers tomorrow. They run the neighborhood funeral parlor."

One-Eye grunted, then heaved the body into the kitchen.

"Now, is there anything you can't or don't eat?"

"Nope," said Banks.

"No," called One-Eye from the freezer.

"I'm a enzymatic legumiglutiphobic vegan with a mastication preference," said Mimi.

"What the hell is that?" I said.

"She only eats pre-chewed nuts and vegetables," said Banks.

I blinked at him, then looked at the old ladies. "How about you two?"

One of them shook her head. The other said, "No eggplant, please."

"Right," I said. "I'll be back in twenty minutes. I am locking the door behind me. Do not, under any circumstances, leave this building with anyone, not even if they say they're with me."

"Are we prisoners?" said Mimi, her voice quivering.

"No," I said. "You're perfectly free to go, but I'm pretty sure you won't get very far without someone trying to rip you off or snitch you out to WalWa. Right now, you guys are in legal limbo: you're not quite free from Indenture, and you're not under the Union's full protection. It's a crappy situation, and I apologize for it, but I promise to explain it all after you're clean and fed."

"I wouldn't mind you telling us now," said Banks.

"I would," I said, "because you all stink to high heaven, and I'm not going to sit inside with you until you've showered and burned those coveralls." I pointed to the stairs. "Find a room, make yourselves comfortable. I'll be back."

I waited until they filed upstairs, then hurried out, pulling the door behind me and blinking the deadbolt shut. I also caught a glimpse of myself in the mirrored office windows: I looked like hell, my hair frizzed out, my face smudged, my deck jacket covered in garbage that would never come out. I peeled the jacket off and tossed it into a nearby garbage bin; it had been years since Wash gave me that thing, and I think he'd have understood.

At the konbini six doors down, Mooj Markson, the owner, had brought in the produce stands and replaced them with grills, and my stomach grumbled at the smell of pork satay and yakitori. "Hungry there, Padma?" he said as I grabbed a dozen finished skewers and looked for something Mimi would eat.

"Got some backlogged paperwork to do," I said, scooping pickled daikon, roasted burdock, and a few other kinds of banchan into tiffins. "And I can't really get much done at Big Lily's tonight, you know?"

"Yeah," said Mooj, rubbing his ink, a pair of crossed wrenches. "That was a hell of a thing, the way the whole fleet went down."

"Tell me about it," I said, spooning up a container full of roasted palm nuts. I had no idea how to make them pre-chewed for Mimi.

Mooj nodded. "All fifteen of them had hull breaches. Heard from some friends who do orbital recovery, and they said it's like the ships just decided to stop holding themselves together." He flipped a row of skewers. "Stands to reason, in a ugly sort of way. The Big Three run their gear ragged, do the bare minimum of maintenance, then just write everything off when it falls apart. Just like with us."

"Yeah," I said, wiping peanut dust off my hand and looking inside the shop. Rows of rum bottles lined the shelves behind the counter. "Give me a seven-fifty of Stillson, too, please."

"Fine choice," said Mooj, nodding inside the store. One of his clerks pulled down a seven-fifty and handed it to me. Stillson was a good starter rum, and, while I had no intention of getting the Breaches loaded, I would be remiss if I didn't give them all a taste with their dinner.

Mooj handed me the food, all done up in a bundle. "How much?" I asked.

He shook his head. "On the house tonight. Figured you could use a break, what with this crap Bloombeck tried to pin on you."

"Thanks, Mooj." I blew him a kiss and turned to the sidewalk.

"And say hi to the guys at the office, yeah?" Mooj called after me.

I stopped. "What guys?"

"Your buddies, the ones who got here before you?" he said, pulling the skewers off the grill. "About a dozen of 'em , big guys. Maybe you want to bring 'em some extra yakitori?"

I ran. The front door to the Union office wouldn't respond to my keycode, and the deadbolt held no matter how hard I yanked at the handle. I dropped the food, grabbed the garbage can and rammed it at the caneplas window, once, twice, three times and it smashed open. My deck jacket had spilled to the ground, and I threw it over the jagged edges as I climbed in. "Banks!" I yelled as I raced up the stairs. There was a light on the fourth floor, and I took the steps two at a time.

"Mimi! Everyone, get out of here! They're back! They're–"

I collapsed on the fourth floor landing, out of air and energy, just in time to see the Breaches all sitting on couches, surrounded by twelve angry people. They carried pipes, cricket bats, and looks of fury on their inked faces. Jordan Blanton stood in the center of them. "Saarien got there first, huh?" she said.

Banks looked from behind one of the men and said, "You still got us dinner, right?"

TEN

"Don't," said Jordan, holding up a hand. The other held a heavy pipe wrench. She tapped it on her thigh as she paced back and forth. I nodded and clamped my mouth shut.

"You *lied* to us," said Jordan, pointing the wrench my way. "You think someone wouldn't see you unloading five strangers into this office? You think we're that stupid?"

I stayed still. Even if Jordan wanted to me answer, it was probably best to let her run out of gas.

"Sixteen *months*, Padma!" said Jordan, poking the wrench at my chest. "You know how much extra methane I've breathed? How the stink doesn't leave my body unless I have a two-hour steam bath every night? How many times I've had to apologize to my family for leaving in the middle of dinner during the Tasting Festival because the toilets in Chatham have backed up?"

I crossed my arms, and Jordan said, "What, you don't have an answer?"

"Am I allowed to give you one?" I said.

"No," said Jordan. "No, you are not, because whatever answer it is will be complete and utter bullshit. And we are tired of that." She pointed at her chest. "My doctor says I'm going to develop eight kinds of horrible diseases within a year if I stay underground. How do you think that's going to affect my design work? Who's going to want to hire a landscape architect who's crippled and smells like sewage?"

"We want jobs," said one of the men.

"Shut it, Remy," said Jordan, pointing the wrench at his head. She looked at me. "We want *better* jobs."

I nodded, then held out my hands. "If I may?"

Jordan shouldered the wrench, then gave me a weary nod.

"How much better do you want your jobs to be?" I asked.

Jordan snorted. "I want them to be what you promised them to be."

"You have that," I said, trying to blink up the folder on the Public where I kept all of my recruitment contracts. I got a network error. "Just pull up your paperwork. It's all there in black and white."

"It's just more bullshit."

"No, it's what we talked about," I said, trying to pull up the contracts again and getting an even angrier network error. "You and I sat down for an hour and went over the kind of experience you had, then we matched you up with your job at the plant. You turned down four other Slots."

"That's because they were all about processing bagasse or working as a cable tender or cleaning squid nests off of the docks," said Jordan.

"And none of them involved crawling up to your neck in filth," I said. "Yet you took that job, anyway."

"Because you said it wouldn't last long!" said Jordan. "You told me there were always new Breaches, and that someone would come down the cable to take my Slot!"

"And you're going to hold it against me that they haven't?" I said. "You think I *wanted* you to stay in that Slot for that long?"

"I think you've been spending more time working for Estella Tonggow than you have for us," said Jordan, popping me in the stomach with the wrench.

I shoved it aside. "And I think you're on some seriously dangerous ground."

"I'm sorry to interrupt," said Banks, holding up a hand, "but is it OK if we start eating?"

"No!" Jordan and I said, and she pointed the wrench at my head. "We want a better deal."

"Then you're going to have to take it up with someone who has authority," I said. "I'm just a recruiter and an organizer. I can't change contracts that have already been signed."

"Signed under false pretenses," said Jordan.

"Really?" I said. "You want me to pull up the video I shot when you signed up? I made it clear that there were no guarantees that you'd be able to get out of your Slot right away."

"I don't need to see it," said Jordan, "because I remember you telling me that there were *always* new jobs."

"With no guarantees," I said, trying to blink up my archives on the Public. Sixteen months ago might as well have been a lifetime. Had I really said that to Jordan?

"I don't care anymore," said Jordan. "None of us do. We're up to our armpits in piss and shit and that fucking black mold that clogs the intakes, and we can't handle it! And we never get the support we need from the City Works Committee or the Union or *you*."

"I've been busy."

"It's your *job* to take our calls," said Jordan. She nodded, and everyone in their crew aimed their assorted power tools at the Breaches, who froze. My heart stopped. I watched as Thor Becker, a nice guy who did bonsai in his spare time, put the muzzle of a portable bolt thrower to Mimi's head. She didn't breathe, just closed her eyes and her mouth and tried to make herself as small as possible.

"You really don't want to do that, Thor," I said.

"You're going to get these people to take our jobs," said Jordan.

"There are others in line ahead of you," I said.

"That's not my problem," she said. "It's yours."

"Jordan, you know that isn't the way it works," I said, blinking in a call for someone, anyone to get their asses in here and stop this. Why now, of all times, did my pai refuse to connect?

"That isn't going to work," said Jordan, pointing at her temple. "Luce dropped a few jammers when we arrived."

"You realize that's a crime, right?" I said.

"So's spending every day parading in this city's filth," said Jordan. "Besides, it's going to be our word against yours, and yours isn't going to have a lot of weight after we prove you lied to everyone."

"I didn't lie," I said. "Saarien really did get these people first. I had to call in WalWa to scare him off."

"Uh-huh," said Jordan. "Tell me another one."

"No, she really did," said Banks. Luce Hagenbuch tapped Banks on the ear with the muzzle of a blowtorch and shook his head.

"Can't we talk about this?" I said, backing toward the door. "Without the weaponry?"

"Nope," said Jordan. "And you can stay where you are."

"It's just really crowded in here," I said, not stopping. "Maybe on the stairwell?"

Jordan raised the wrench and took a step toward me. "Come back here!"

"Plus, the food's still outside," I said.

"It is?" said Banks, rising from his seat. Luce pushed Banks back down so hard he slipped off the chair. Banks grabbed for a handhold, but only knocked the chair back into Luce's shins. Luce howled as he went down, and the blowtorch flashed once. A lick of flame skittered across a desk, and, as everyone turned to the fire, I jumped through the door.

I wasn't running away, I told myself. I was going to get help. I was going to stop this injustice. I was going straight to the precinct house where I would tell my good friend Captain Baghram about the hostage situation brewing under her nose. I was going–

My vision blurred until the whole world looked like it was inside a blender. My legs locked up, but my momentum carried me down the stairs. I heard The Fear chortle as Jordan tackled me from behind – *Told you you wouldn't make it*. I didn't have time to argue.

We both tumbled into the office's reception area, money bouncing out of Jordan's pockets as we hit the ground. Stars danced in front of my eyes as my head bumped a desk. We both staggered to our feet, and I could hear Jordan yelling, though I couldn't understand any of it. My head was fuzzy, and my ass still hurt from my fall on the bus. Jordan raised the wrench over her head. The only thing that kept me from getting brained was the fact that I puked on her boots and collapsed. That was enough to throw off her swing; the wrench crashed down into the floorboards, and I rolled away from her feet.

"This isn't the way to do things," I gasped, wiping flecks of vomit from my chin as I crawled toward the shattered window. Pieces of broken caneplas crunched under my palms.

"Shut! Up!" Jordan tugged at the wrench, trying to extricate it from the recycled bamboo.

"Going right to physical threats? You've been around too long to know that won't work." I grabbed the open window frame to steady myself and breathed in the night air. God, it tasted good.

Jordan roared as she tore the wrench from the floor.

"I mean, shit, you didn't even try to *bribe* me," I said. Jordan charged, and I sidestepped in time to trip her up. Jordan sailed onto the sidewalk, landing with a heavy *wuff*. The wrench clattered away, lost in a tangle of feet. A small crowd had gathered, and I waved as I stepped through the open window.

"Contract dispute," I said. Everyone nodded, then dispersed to the nearest bars.

The tiffins from Mooj's were still outside, as was the bottle of Stillson. I scooped them up, then grabbed Jordan by the belt loops and hauled her to her feet. Blood streamed from her broken nose and various scrapes on her cheeks. I helped her through the window, making sure to give her head an extra bump on the closest desk as we navigated through the office.

At the bottom of the stairs was the loose change that had fallen out of Jordan's pockets. I let go of her long enough to scoop it up, and noticed one of the fifty-jiao coins had a weird finish. It felt way too light, and its surface felt more like caneplas than metal. I bent it between my fingers, and the thing snapped in half, a few bits of wiring and circuitry frazzling out the edges. I held it down to Jordan's face. "Where'd you get the jammer, Jordan?"

"Fug you," she said.

"And now I've got that on video," I said, blinking my way back into the Public. I set my pai on live streaming as we made our way up the stairs.

"See, Jordan, this isn't the way intra-Union discussions are supposed to go," I said, steering her up the stairs and looking the other way when I walked her into the bannister. "If you have a problem with your recruitment contract, you're supposed to contact your rep during office hours. If you aren't happy with the answer you get, you can always go to the Union Arbitration Board, where you'll be given a hearing in a timely fashion. Your satisfaction is what makes the Union go 'round. If you're not happy, we're not happy, and we're not happy until–"

We entered the fourth-floor dorm, and I turned my head away so fast my neck popped. I blinked and blinked until I was sure my pai was off, then looked back in the room.

Jordan's gang sprawled on the ground, all of them bound with old clothes and covered with bruises. Their weapons lay in pieces in a neat pile in the middle of the room. The Breaches sat all on the couches, looking exhausted. "What the *hell* happened here?" I said.

One-Eye shrugged. "We defended ourselves."

My hands went limp. The tiffins rattled to the floor, and Jordan fell to her hands and knees. "You *what*?"

One-Eye pointed at Thor, who was unconscious and had a number of purple lumps growing on his cheek and forehead. "This asshole had a gun pointed at Mimi, and I didn't like that."

"First of all, it was a bolt thrower," I said, "and, second, do you have any idea what you've done?"

"Of course I do," said One-Eye, crossing her arms and smirking. "We stood up for ourselves."

"No, you didn't," I said, clenching my hands so they didn't go around her throat. "You assaulted Union people."

One-Eye shrugged.

"Are *you* a Union person?" I said.

One-Eye shrugged again, but her smirk flagged a bit.

"*No*," I said, pointing at her as I stepped over the unconscious crew. "*You* are still an employee of Walton Warumbo Universal Unlimited, and that means—"

Jordan coughed. "It means you have fucked up in a great, big way."

One-Eye's smirk was gone. She shifted in her seat. "How bad is it?"

"Bad," I said. "Keep-you-out-of-the-Union bad. Send-you-back-to-WalWa bad. Put-your-ass-on-the-lifter-without-a-spacesuit bad. About as bad as it gets."

Jordan got up on her elbows and laughed. "You want to make that deal now, Padma?"

I thought about the broken jammer in my pocket. There was still the possibility of calling the cops and getting Jordan and her crew nailed for assault and interfering with Public transmissions, but that would be undone by any video of One-Eye disarming the hell out of her captors. It was built into every Contract between the Union and the Big Three: Any physical assaults on Union people that were not dealt with swiftly and harshly would turn into a shitstorm that would spread across all Occupied Space. I blinked my pai back on and looked at Jordan. "What are your demands?"

She wobbled to her feet and wiped the blood from her

face. "Slot transfers, effective immediately. You put us in some place where we get fresh air, real sunlight, and no goddamn sewage."

I put up my hands. "OK."

"Also, you pay us for pain and suffering."

"Fine," I said, pointing at the bottle of Stillson. "Drinks are on me."

"Oh, no," said Jordan. "It'll take at least five hundred each."

Three grand? Used to be a measly hundred yuan would be enough to pay for a good coverup. I blinked the money to an escrow account, then sent the link to Jordan. "You'll get it when I get what I want, and you know what I want," I said. "Now get the hell out of here."

"What," said Jordan, grinning through the streaked blood and snot, "you're sending Union people out of our own office?"

"Out."

Jordan nodded as she untied her crew. They scooped up the pile of parts and shuffled out of the room. "Man," Thor muttered as he passed, "that old lady can *hit*."

"She's not *that* old," I said, looking at One-Eye, who gave me the bird.

"Is that dinner?" said Banks, pointing at the tiffins.

"Seriously?" I said. "That's all you can think of?"

"All I've had to eat is NutriFood," said Banks. "Can you blame me?"

"Not really," I said, realizing I hadn't had anything since that kumara cake at Big Lily's. The smells of spilled daikon and burdock were killing me. I handed containers and chopsticks all around, hoping the palm nuts would pass Mimi's muster. The bottle of Stillson was intact, though a little scraped.

"Is that stuff any good?" asked Banks as he chewed, a yakitori skewer in each hand.

"It's not bad," I said. "Nice bite, a sweet aftertaste. A little simple, really, but it'll go well with dinner."

"Plying us with food and booze, just like our bosses said you would," said Banks, tearing the chicken off one skewer with his teeth. He ate like someone who hadn't seen food in a year. Then I remembered he hadn't. Jesus, eighteen months with nothing but NutriFood. Hibernation seemed like a pleasant alternative.

–and the Fear reared its ugly head, grinning with icy teeth at the thought of hibernation. *Oh, it was so pleasant in there, wasn't it? Just close your eyes and remember-*

I excused myself and did my best not to run into the bathroom. I splashed cold water on my face, then gripped the sink, trying to remember what Dr Ropata told me to do: focus on the drain plug, not look in the mirror, and say to myself *I am* here, *I am* here. I blinked up the time: ten fifty-two. A little under seventeen hours until six o'clock tomorrow evening. I could do this.

I toweled my face dry, found some glasses, then set them on a table, the picture definition of a perfect Union recruiter. "Twelve years ago, I was in the same position as you guys," I said, picking up the Stillson. "I was tired, and hungry, and scared out of my mind because I'd just left behind everything I'd ever known. It's like you've just challenged a giant to a fight, and then the giant actually looks down at you." I swirled the rum in the bottle. "Hieu Vanavutu, the guy who recruited me, did something for me on my first night as a Breach that made all the difference. He poured me a drink. Not a lot, just a sip from a distillery that's since gone out of business. He wasn't trying to get me loaded" – I said this to Banks, who smiled and held up his hands in mock surrender – "he was telling me I was like everyone else on this planet. We're all scared, we all aren't sure what's going to happen, but we all look out for each other. So. Let's have a drink, and get some rest, and–"

I cracked the bottle cap, and the stench of mustard and dead dogs filled the room. I gagged and dropped the bottle, rum spilling everywhere and turning the room into a gas chamber. "Out!" I choked, "out!" We hustled down the stairs, the smell following us. One of the old ladies, the one who couldn't eat eggplant, stumbled, and I picked her up and carried her out into the street. The air was fresh, but that didn't stop me from feeling like puking again.

I set the old lady down and asked if she was OK. She gave me an unsteady nod and said, "I think I would like to go home now."

"Me too," I said, putting an arm around her shoulder. "Everyone here? Good. We are now going to my place."

"Why?" said One-Eye.

"Because I know there's nothing there that can kill us. Come on."

We took back streets and alleys, and arrived at my flat a few minutes later. Along the way, I'd texted a konbini run by Freeborn and ordered more food, making sure not to get any rum when they tried to upsell me a fifth of Stillson. Three skunked bottles in a day? Either the Co-Op was getting lax, or someone had started poisoning the cane. Whatever it was, I didn't have the energy to cope with it now.

The kid from the konbini met us at the front door to the flat, and I tipped him extra to forget the size of the order and how many people were with me. Banks, Mimi and One-Eye had managed to clean up while I'd been at Mooj's, so the old ladies took turns showering while we ate in silence. They changed into some old coveralls I saved for muck work in the garden, and then I grabbed fresh pajamas and staggered into the bathroom, not even bothering to look at myself in the mirror. I knew I was a wreck.

The hot water was better than sex. All the salt and mud and sweat washed away, along with the last bits of me that wanted to stay awake. The only thing that kept me from falling asleep in the shower was the blast of cold water as the hot ran out. I was too tired to blame my guests, so I just toweled off and got dressed. Everyone was asleep when I returned: the old ladies had curled up on my bed like a pair of cats, Mimi sacked out on the couch, One-Eye on the floor with her back to the wall.

Banks was in the sitting room, staring at the snuffed candle and the bottle of Old Windswept. He turned to me and said, "Buy you a drink?"

"That's not for company," I said, grabbing the bottle and holding it up. He hadn't drunk any, as far I could tell. That meant I wouldn't have to knock it over his head.

"The good stuff, huh?"

"I said, it's not for company." There weren't many hiding places in my flat, so I just opened a kitchen cabinet and rattled the bottle behind some plates.

"OK," said Banks. "Sorry."

"Look," I said, resting my hands on the counter. "It's been a really, really long day. I'm exhausted, I have two old ladies–"

"–Gricelda and Madolyn–"

"Sleeping in my bed, and this one" – I pointed a toe at One-Eye – "looking like she's on guard duty. You are not regular Breaches."

"There's no such thing," said Banks. "Breaches come from every career category, every walk of corporate life–"

"–and stop quoting my own goddamn pamphlets at me," I said. "There is something seriously weird about all of you, and... you know what? You could all be the heads of the Big Three for all I care. In the morning, I'm finding you all jobs and flats and counseling and pre-chewed acorns or whatever you need, and then I am going back to work, because there are only six of you, not forty. Thanks for not convincing more people to jump ship with you."

"We were it," said Banks. "You know how WalWa likes to keep its crews light."

"I know they don't let lawyers participate."

"I was a special case."

"Special as in 'exemplary' or as in 'polite antique euphemism for mentally retarded'?"

"Well, I *am* a lawyer," he said, trying to keep his grin from exploding all over his face.

I exhaled, and the last of my strength went. "Don't sleep in that chair," I said. "You'll tweak your back. Sleep on that one." I motioned to an overstuffed highback I'd gotten from a moving sale. It was the comfiest spot in the flat, other than my bed.

"Thanks." He peeled himself from the chair, still looking like a scarecrow, even in new clothes. "Hey, is there a way to read up on the law here? I'd like to know what we're getting into."

"You're not going to sleep?"

He shook his head. "Almost getting killed three times in one day has me a little wired."

"Here," I said, tossing him a pad. "You can access the Public on that, or at least the guest stuff. When we get you all signed up tomorrow, you can just use your pai."

"Assuming we all sign up."

"Shut up, Banks."

"Good night."

I sat at the dining room table, looking at the candle. The Fear tried to come back, but I told it to fuck off until tomorrow. I put my head down and was out.

ELEVEN

There was something about the way riot armor rustled that woke me faster than cold water. I could hear it in the hall: plates of caneplas scraping against each other, the fizz of priming riot hoses. I opened my eyes and immediately regretted it: the light leaking around the edges of the curtain was bright and sharp, slicing right into my brain. I didn't need to blink up the time to know that it was early; the city outside was still quiet, which was why I could hear whoever was ready to kick in my door as clear as if they were a herd of elephants at a ballet recital. My back seized as I slipped out of the chair, but I kept it together long enough to grab the cricket bat I kept by the umbrella stand. I glanced around the flat: everyone was still here and asleep, except for Banks. He was gone, and the pad sat on the table next to a fresh candle.

I tiptoed to the side of the door and squared off, cocking the cricket bat so I could score a six off whoever was about to break in. Cops? Goons? Goons *and* cops? That would be new.

There was a knock. "Du Marque Bakery, with a delivery

for Mr Banks?" came a cracking boy's voice from the other side of the door.

I brought the bat down a centimeter, then stopped myself. "What?" I said, then cursed myself for speaking.

The rustling sound again, and then the boy said, "Yeah, I have a dozen assorted pastries and some coffees and–"

I threw open the door, bat still cocked, and there was a kid in delivery whites with two canvas bags that smelled like baked goods and caffeine and love. Foamed milk spattered his shirt. It hadn't been riot armor I heard; it was the kid's cargo. He started and took a step back, then said, "Uh, don't worry, I wasn't planning on asking for a tip."

"Who ordered all this?" I said, putting the bat down and looking into one of the bags; the gorgeous scents of cinnamon and yeast rose up and made my nose very, very happy.

"Mr Banks," said the kid.

"Who?"

"White guy, really skinny? Said he had to run some more errands, and said you'd pay for delivery."

I thunked the bat on the floor. "He said what?"

Banks appeared at the end of the hall. "Oh, good! Giesel sent over the food."

The delivery kid gave me a shrug and held out his hand. I blinked up DuMarque's Bakery and found a ridiculously marked-up bill in my name, but blinked in payment anyway. "Where the hell have you been?" I said to Banks as the kid set down the bags and slunk away. "And what part of 'Don't go outside' did you not understand?"

"It seemed safe enough," he said, picking up the bags and giving them a smell. "Bread. God, I missed bread. You can't have yeast inside a seeder, did you know that? Gets into the vents, mutates, does weird things with the engines–"

I put the bat against the wall, blocking his path inside. "Did anything that happened to you yesterday not sink in?"

"Padma, I was out for twenty minutes," said Banks. "I got up, I was hungry, I saw you had nothing in your fridge except for a few almost-empty bottles of rooster sauce, and I smelled the bakery. How can you not eat there every day? It's incredible."

"Don't change the subject," I said, giving the wall an extra tap with the bat. "I don't care what you and the rest of your friends did when you were Indentures. You do not know how this city, how this planet, how anything here works until you've worked with me."

"What's there to learn?" said Banks. "I've already gone through the Union Charter and the Co-Op structure and everything I could read–"

"What if you'd gotten lost and couldn't find your way back? What would have happened if you'd gotten in an accident? What if one of Jordan's people had gone out last night and blabbed all about you?"

"What, you don't trust your own people?"

"I don't trust *any* people," I said, "especially when there are big things like money, jobs, and baked goods on the line. Anyone who didn't like your face could have pinged your pai, found you weren't on the Public, figured out that you're still a Breach, and dimed you to WalWa. You could have been disappeared, and there wouldn't be a damn thing any of us could have done except light a candle in your memory. Idiot."

Banks looked at the ground as he trudged inside.

"Oh, knock it off," I said, following him into the flat.

Banks shrugged as he set the bags on the table, then

handed me an almond bialy. He took a croissant out of the bag, breathed in its smell, and took a bite. "You gonna eat that?" he said between chews, pointing at my bialy.

"I'm too angry to think right now."

"Then can I have it?"

"Hell, no," I said, taking a bite of bialy and opening a cup of coffee. The other Breaches stirred and shuffled into the kitchen, then brightened up when they saw the food. Mimi and One-Eye bowled over each other to get to the table, and the old ladies moved faster than hungry teenagers at an all-you-can-eat. They tore into rolls and slurped coffee, pausing only to gulp in air before attacking their next helpings.

"Ladies, I know it's been a while since you've had real food," I said, finishing my first bialy and starting a second, "but you need to eat slower so you don't get sick. Giesel DuMarque never skimps on the butter."

"Thank God," said One-Eye. "I haven't had butter in four years."

"Or cream," said one of the old ladies.

"Or meat," said the other.

"Just NutriFood," said Mimi. "That was rough."

They all grunted and kept eating.

I left them to their carb binge and walked out onto my lanai. The morning haze had burned off already, leaving a few traces of cloud in an otherwise flawless sky. The sidewalks steamed as the sun hit the last of the morning dew. It was going to be a beautiful day, which only pissed me off that much more. I should have been able to take the morning off, maybe enjoy a second bialy, chase down leads on more Breaches. Instead, I was going to have to spend the day begging.

I blinked up a link to the Union Hall's transport line, and

smiled to see Jilly had, indeed, gotten herself a provisional license. The smile disappeared when I saw that Lanny had stuck me with a processing fee, an expediting fee, and a Don't-Make-Me-Do-Work-Past-Sundown fee. He'd also charged me for Jilly's new hack medallion, which meant a total of one thousand yuan out of my account. I'd probably get it back in a few months, considering how much hustle Jilly had, but I still wasn't in the mood to drop that much cash for a kid from the kampong. I texted Jilly through the transport office and told her to get here right away.

I also blinked up the news feed for the past twenty-four hours. There was one mention about the shattered window at the office on Reigert, but since neither my name nor Jordan's appeared in the article, I shrugged it off. The local busybodies could gossip all they wanted; as long as there was nothing on the Public, it wouldn't affect me in court.

There was also no mention of the *Rose of Tralee*'s crew jumping ship. In fact, the colony seeder only appeared in the daily docking manifests, which was odd. A seeder usually got a few mentions on the Public, if only because it stimulated a lot of debate about making sure the Union would have a presence at their destination, or whether sending ships Beyond was worth it, or all the blather that starts in bars and ends up in essays and bad songs. There wasn't a peep of that.

There was also nothing from Evanrute Saarien. Four years ago, Dolly Jo Bialowsky, a recruiter from Underhill, rescued a group of Breaching air-processing techs before Saarien did. He responded by screaming bloody murder all over the Public, railing about how Dolly was creating schisms within the Union and that competition was the bane of a strong Union and how tradition was the backbone of a Union society, all polite ways of saying "Fuck you, those bodies were mine." He wound up taking her to court, and the suit went on for so long that Dolly Jo went broke and had to go back to a Slot herself. I expected the same treatment for me, but Saarien, as far as I could tell, was silent. There wasn't even a mention of his daily schedule of appearances in Sou's Reach. Either he was laying low to plot some horrible revenge on me, or I'd thrown him for a loop by calling in WalWa. That meant I had some time.

But not much. I had to get this crew signed on the dotted line, and that meant finding them Slots. Or, rather, finding Slots for Jordan and her buddies so I could fit this lot into the soon-to-be-vacant Slots at the plant. As Jilly pulled up in front of my flat and honked, I waved and went back inside. Everyone had fallen back asleep, except Banks, who was absently chewing on a bagel while looking at the pad. "You know," he said, "we still haven't gotten to try any of that rum you talked about."

"It can wait another eight hours," I said, sitting down to lace up my boots. "I'm off to get you jobs, and then we can talk about booze."

"Can I come?" said Banks. "They're all going to be knocked out for the rest of the day, and–"

"Hell, no," I said. "You can keep reading and eating."

"We're out of food," said Banks. He pointed at the now-empty canvas sacks.

"Too many carbs," I said. "See, if you'd stayed put, I'd have made sure you got a balanced breakfast, not an overload of sugar and butter."

"Then you can show me where to get lunch," said Banks, smiling. "Please, Padma, I'm going to go nuts in here. I need air. I need space. I need sun."

The way Banks perched on his seat, coiled and ready to leap up, reminded me of a baby cane viper. They're cute as hell until they learn that they have poisonous fangs. Still, if he was going to be a lawyer here, he might as well start learning now. Besides, with Jordan and Saarien keeping quiet, it would likely be a safe and boring trip.

"Fine," I sighed. "Just don't get in the way."

"Yes, ma'am," he said, hopping to his feet.

Down in the street, Jilly sat in the driver's seat of her tuk-tuk, tapping at the wheel with her thumbs. "They wanted to take out my sound system, boss," she said. "I told 'em you liked the volume big."

"The bigger, the better, kid," I said, hopping into the back. "You get squared away with Lanny?"

She tapped the laminated card stuck above the mirror. "Good thing my folks aren't wired, or they'd have heard and hauled me back to the kampong."

"Just keep your head on straight, and that won't happen," I said. "Now, we got a busy day, so hop to. Get us to the steam plant in Faoshue, and floor it."

As Jilly pulled into traffic, Banks said, "So, what's on the agenda?"

"We meet with someone who owes me a favor, and I cash it in," I said.

"And if that doesn't work?"

"It will."

We edged through the morning traffic, Jilly's head bobbing with the music. Banks kept sniffing the air, like a dog who'd been let out for the first time in months. As we crossed the Ivory Canal, he turned to me and said, "Why did you go into Service?"

"It beat being a consumer," I said.

"No, really."

"Yes, really," I said. "I grew up in a free settlement on Vishnu's Palm, and we'd see all the news and shows on our pirated feeds, all the *stuff* that corporate citizens got access to, and I looked around our crappy little house and said, 'To hell with this.' When I was thirteen I took the exams, got good marks, and signed an Indenture contract for forty years. Never looked back."

"But you Breached," said Banks.

"Because I found out how shitty corporate life was," I said. "If you're not backstabbing your way to get ahead, you're flinching to make sure no one gets a knife in you. I got out of B-school and took a job with WalWa's entertainment division right in my own backyard. I ran a stadium, the whole operation. Thought it would be safer, because no one was going to use it as a stepping stone. Almost got killed in a beer riot because my assistant was out to get me."

"Really?" said Banks. "That must be a hell of a story."

"It's really not," I said. "Remember the Tsokusa Blight?"

He nodded. "Ugly business."

"Incredibly ugly," I said. "Only time the Big Three quit fighting each other and worked together. There was supposed to be a benefit concert at the stadium, and me and my assistant – this woman named Nariel – we worked our asses off. I let her take credit for a lot of ideas, got her name out there, helped her get promoted in pay grade. But it turned out she was undercutting me at every turn. She'd call up vendors and cancel orders in my name, get contracts mis-signed. She thought she'd get ahead by clawing over me. I had to undo all this crap, order more straws and napkins, only to have her storm into my office and complain about the workload. 'I didn't sign my life away to do this kind of grunt work,' she said, then left only to sabotage me more. About two weeks before the concert, I heard there was an opening in Colonial Management, so I figured if I'm going to go through this much trouble, the stakes had better be worth it. I put in my transfer and dumped the whole thing on her lap."

Banks shrugged. "So?"

"So, there were riots."

"Riots, as in multiple?"

I nodded. "I had all the distribution chains lined up, and Nariel was supposed to make the calls, do the followup, execute the plan. When she started canceling orders, she forgot which ones to re-up, so things got jammed, and she had to arrange for last-minute deliveries, all of which interfered with the beer trucks, not just at our stadium, but at every one on the planet. By the time they opened the taps, the crowds had been standing in the sun for eight hours, and they binged and things got ugly. Did you really not hear about this?"

"I knew about the blight, but the rest of it? Fourteen years ago I was still farming potatoes and concrete. All this might as well have been happening on the moon, for all I cared."

"That's where the worst riots were," I said as we zipped around a loaded cane truck. "Vishnu's Palm had two satellites, and both were a mess. Projectile vomiting in low-G. Nasty business."

Banks shook his head. "And all this got laid on Nariel's lap?"

I nodded. "Like I said, I had it all planned, but she didn't do the groundwork. She got busted back to a Grade Six, and then I don't know what happened to her."

"So you just left her holding the bag."

"Hey, if she wanted the responsibility, then she could take the blame. By the time this was all underway, I was already a fishstick. Does that make me the bad guy?"

"Maybe a little," said Banks.

"It was not a very professional, compassionate move," I said. "In fact, I admit it was downright petty, but, Christ, people got promoted and demoted all the time. The smart ones used it to their advantage, made new connections, found another way to get a leg up. The rest..." I shrugged.

"Is that going to happen here?" said Banks. "Someone crosses you, and you leave?"

"Hell, no," I said. "Now I get even. Take a right here, kid."

TWELVE

The day did not go as I had planned.

In Faoshue, Manny Kreese, who did steamfitting at the coconut oil plant down there, gave a sad shake of his pumpkin head. No, he didn't have any open Slots. Not anymore. Too much hassle.

In Whaui, Su-Yin Tags was polite when she said the recycling plant had just gone through a turnover and couldn't afford to let their newly trained Contract people go, not with garbage season approaching.

In Cheapside, Mama Gertrude took a break from stirring her compost pits to tell us, in no uncertain terms, to fuck off.

And on and on at every Ward we visited. We putted from one meeting to another, from Beukes Point to Jotzi, down and down my list of people who owed me favors, all of them unable to repay me just now. (So sorry, Padma, it's just not the right time/quarter/phase of the moon.) "This makes no sense," I said as we crawled along Landry Underpass. We'd just gotten the bum's rush in Budvar, a Ward with a long history of cooperation and football hooliganism with

132

Brushhead. (Hard workers in Budvar, but they're a pack of bastards on the pitch.) "Even the people who'd told me to my face they could help are backing out."

"Maybe they got better offers," said Banks.

"I doubt it," I said as we approached the border of Steelcase, the low shops giving away to giant warehouses. "This is one of those deals you only pass up if you've taken a blow to the head. And even then, there are clauses in the Union Charter to override this shit."

Steelcase had the second-biggest holding depot in Santee. The Ward was a collection of warehouses, molasses storage tanks streaked with rust and grime, and blind alleys. Loading cranes zipped overhead on the coral steel trellis that enveloped the entire Ward, carrying massive cargo cans in their rusty jaws. The grid of two-hundred-meter-high uprights and four levels of maglev rails left a spiderweb shadow on the streets. The trellis was the only thing straight and square in Steelcase. Back when this place was under construction, Hurricane Minh had blown so hard that the buildings, their new pourform foundations still wet, moved from their original layout into this claustrophobic's nightmare. I didn't mind coming down here, but Jilly was white-knuckling her way around.

"This is out of my turf," she said, slamming on the brakes as a panel truck screeched around a blind alley. "I don't like it, boss."

"You didn't have any problems bootlegging fares in Brushhead," I said.

"That's different," she said, wringing the wheel. "I could see when the cars were coming there."

"Relax, this is a friendly neighborhood," I said, looking at the black streaks lining the buildings. It hadn't been that long since I'd visited, but it seemed more run down than I remembered. Wash must have been having as bad a time as the rest of us.

"You know someone here?" asked Banks.

"The Ward Chair," I said. "We go way back."

"You trust him?" asked Banks.

I looked down at the stains on the front of my deck jacket, remembered Wash putting it on my shoulders the day Typhoon Sampson started. I'd just come off a double shift at the sewage plant and had staggered into the Kea Kea Lounge for a bite and a beer when the rain started. He was playing accordion with a tango combo there, and I just kept watching and listening and grinning as the storm grew and grew. It wasn't until he took a break between sets that I realized it was almost six o'clock, and I just about ran out the door before he took off his jacket. "If you gotta go out in this weather, at least make sure you're covered," he'd said. I grabbed his hand and took him with me to my flat and made him wait outside until I'd had my six o'clock taste. And then I brought him in and didn't let him leave until two days later. We stayed together a month, but then we both got buried at work and drifted. We stayed on good terms, even meeting when the weather warnings started flying, and I could always count on him to float Breaches whenever the Slots were light in Brushhead.

...ah, but you screwed that one up, didn't you? The Fear raked its claws against the back of my brain, sending a shiver down to my bowels. *You really think this is going to work? You think you can keep this up? You should just stop now, find a nice corner and curl up...*

I picked at one of the pockets on my jacket. "As much as I can trust anyone. Let's boogie."

We splashed over a small molasses spill, then turned down another street that dead-ended into a T. Just as Jilly goosed the tuk-tuk, there was a grinding of gears overhead. Jilly swore as a crane clanked along the girders until its lowered boom was almost on top of us. It held pallets filled with rotting breadfruit, probably meant for the composter. Jilly hit the horn, and the crane lowered its cargo to the ground, right behind us. The crane scooted out of sight, and the stench drove us forward.

Jilly turned us to the right, but another loaded crane dropped out of the sky and plunked giant spools of lifter cable in front of us. She tensed and threw the tuk-tuk into reverse. "This is bad, boss, this is a trap—"

"Just calm down and back us out," I said.

Another crane swung down behind us, this one holding crates of palm crabs. Live ones. Their claws clacked away as the operator dumped the pallet to the ground, littering the road with giant, pissed-off crustaceans. We were fenced in.

"Friendly neighborhood, huh?" said Banks.

"Even your friends can be assholes," I said, climbing onto the seatback. The crabs skittered up to the tuk-tuk, bumping the tires and snapping at the running boards with their claws. I called Wash. "Think you can play 'Misty' for me?"

"Padma! My favorite muse." That warm saxophone voice made me feel a bit warm, like everything was going to be OK. "To what do I owe the pleasure?"

"Boy, Steelcase hospitality has really gone downhill," I said. "Used to be a girl would get a smile and a free bowl of pho just by showing up, but now?"

"Are you here?" he said. "I just got back from a few days at Chino Cove."

"Must've been nice," I said, toeing the crabs away. "Hear the seafood's good."

"The best," he said. "If I'd known you were coming, I'd have brought some lemongrass stew, maybe warmed up the squeezebox."

"Well, we can probably still have some crab soup," I said, now kicking at the swarming claws. I tried blinking a shot to Wash, but it got eaten by the buildings. So, I told him what I was looking at.

There was a pause.

"That shouldn't be there," he said, all the cheer gone from his voice. Cargo always made Wash serious, the same way thinking about making my number made me serious. It was a wonder we got together at all.

"Well, it is," I said. "And two other cranes did something they probably shouldn't have, too."

"Not in my Ward," said Wash. "Especially if they're dealing in perishables."

"I think the breadfruit's already perished," I said as the wind shifted and blew the rotten scent our way. "Think you can get someone to knock this stuff out of our way, Wash? I've got a Union ride, and I don't want to mess up the paint."

"You coming down on business? I know you talked up bringing me some mining people, but, after those ships went down, I figured we were done for a while."

"Not at all," I said, settling into my seat. I didn't like warming people up over voice, but there would be nothing else to do until the crates were removed. "Remember how you said you're always looking for bodies for your Slots?"

Wash laughed. "I suppose you're going to tell me that you've convinced some other poor bastards to slide down the wire and into your pocket?"

"No, into *your* pocket," I said. "They're sitting in my place right now, eating croissants."

He laughed. "And how did you convince them to eat your baking?"

"Hey, I serve my Breaches only the finest from DuMarque's," I said.

"Now I know you're full of shit," said Wash. "Giesel hates you."

"But he loved these people so much he gave them his only begotten buns."

"Seriously, Padma, what is going on?"

"You get me out of this fix, and I'll tell you face to face over a bottle of Old Windswept."

Wash exhaled, his lips buzzing as the air rushed out. I remembered those lips. They knew what they were doing.

There was a click in the connection, and Wash said, "Oh, hell. Padma, can you hold just a moment? Ward business."

"I'm not going anywhere."

"We gonna get out of here?" asked Jilly.

"Soon," I said. The crabs turned their beady eyestalks toward us, and I stuck out my tongue. Wash may have been all business when it came to running his Ward, but I knew I could convince him to help out. Hell, I should've just called him in the first place without all the rigmarole from this morning.

Wash clicked back in. "Padma, that was my maintenance head. We got some kind of power issue, so I won't be able to talk with you now."

"Wash, if you can just move these crates–"

"Maybe later–"

"No, NOW." Jilly and Banks started. Even the crabs backed away. I sighed and said, "Washington, I am really under the gun. I need to transfer some people into better jobs by the end of the day, and you're the only person likely to play ball."

Wash paused. "Like I said, Padma, I have to deal with this power problem first–"

"Oh, Christ, Wash, can't it wait?"

"–this *sticky* power problem that's just sprung up."

"What the hell are you talking about?" I said, now officially at the end of my rope. "I was here two months ago when you got those new backup generators installed. Christ, I lent you people to help install the molasses pipelines so you'd always have fuel–"

Faoshue was nestled in a valley that spent most of the day in shadow, so they had to burn molasses for electricity. Whaui never got wind, so they had to borrow power from Faoshue. Beukes Point, Jotzi, and Budvar all had geographic weirdness, so they all had molasses-fired power plants, too. And Steelcase, despite all of the molasses it held from other refineries, relied on that industrial pustule at Sou's Reach, just like every other Ward I'd visited today. And every trip I'd made, every bit of business, all of it was indexed and searchable in my great, big Public file.

Oh, fuck me.

"He's there right now, isn't he? With your maintenance guy." I imagined Evanrute's shiny, shiny suit reflecting the early afternoon light, right into the poor guy's face. A Ward may run on its Slots, but it lived and died by dealing with cane.

"No, but he might as well be," said Wash. "I'll get someone to clear you a path, but it's gonna be a while."

"How long of a while?" I yelled, Banks and Jilly looking on with alarm. "Goddammit, Wash, don't you leave me here!"

"Sorry about the inconvenience." He clicked off the call.

"Assholesonofabitchbastard!" I said, kicking the dashboard a little too hard. "No love in Steelcase."

"What about your friend?" asked Banks. I didn't like the way he put extra emphasis on *friend*.

"Saarien beat us to him," I said, and explained the whole ugly chain. "Cane trumps favors."

"We got help coming, boss?" asked Jilly, eyeing the crabs.

One crane after another swooped overhead, but none of them stopped to clear our path. "Not until it's too late," I said, looking up until I saw an idling crane two uprights away, its cab empty. "But we're not hanging around to find out. Go."

Jilly juiced the tuk-tuk. Claws snapped at us as we rammed through the crabs and collided with the breadfruit container with a stinking smash. I climbed over the dented nose of the tuk-tuk into the rotting mass. "Well?" I said. "Are you coming?"

"Boss, what are we doing?" asked Jilly. "What about the wheels?"

"We'll get 'em later," I said, pulling myself up the fire escape until my feet could get in the rungs. I was halfway up before I realized there was no one following me. Banks and Jilly stood in the crate, up to their knees in breadfruit.

"Hop to it!" I called down. "We still have a ways to go."

"Where to?" said Banks.

"Wash's office so I can kick his ass into the middle of next week," I said.

"That's premeditated," said Banks.

"And I'll save some for you, too, if you don't get a move on."

Banks and Jilly looked at each other for a moment before

Banks put his hands together for a makeshift step. Jilly sprang up to the ladder, and Banks trailed after. It probably wasn't fair to make him do this kind of physical work after all that time in space, but tough nuts. If he couldn't keep up with me now, how could he keep up in a courtroom?

After picking our way through the obstacle course of AC units, catwalks, solar stills and squats that dotted the rooftops, we were below the idling crane. It was an older model, thank God. MacDonald Heavy had given up a few dozen newer cranes as part of a Contract concession. They were roomier, more efficient, and prone to detaching from their tracks whenever the wind was more than a kilometer an hour. MacDonald Heavy swore up and down they were looking into it. That had been eight years ago.

The cab had just enough room for the three of us. Banks and Jilly crouched into the tiny storage space behind the single seat. "Easy peasy," I said, slipping my feet into the pedal baskets as I fired up the crane's power. The Univoice greeted me, reminding me to put on my restraints. "We can ride this sucker straight to Wash's office if we want. Right into it, even."

"Is that wise?" said Banks.

"Probably not, but it hasn't stopped me before," I said. "You might want to hang onto something."

The chair's headrest gave a little bit, probably from Banks squeezing the life out of the poor thing. "Is this going to be over soon?" he said. "I'm not crazy about confined spaces."

"That why you didn't go frozen?" I asked, gripping the joysticks.

"Mostly," he said as the crane's servos whined to life.

"Don't worry," I said. "I'll be gentle." And then I stomped both pedals and the crane shot fifty meters straight up in ten seconds.

"Ohgohdohgohgohdohgohd," said Banks.

"Don't you dare puke in here," I said. A twist of the joystick, and the crane caught onto a crossrail, its magnetized track zipping us away. The ground flew by as I guided the crane through the girder highway above Steelcase.

"This is a little fast," said Banks, his voice quavering.

"What, you're scared of speed, too?"

The Univoice warned that our equipment was not rated above ten kilometers per hour. We shot a gap between two loaded cranes, their backup beepers dopplering away behind us.

"I am now," said Banks.

"Look, there's no way we're going to crash," I said, "and even if we did, these things are bulletproof."

Something smacked into the cab's windshield. "What the hell was that?" said Banks.

"Probably just a pilot gull. They're slow and stupid and–"

Another bang on the windshield, turning it into a spiderweb of cracked caneplas. A sixteen-centimeter construction spike stuck out of the middle of the hole.

"Are they also metal?" said Banks.

I slowed the crane down, then leaned forward to get a closer look out the unbroken parts of the window. I didn't see any construction crews, and no route closures showed up on the crane's computer. "Weird," I said. "Someone's gonna get an earful for letting this slip. Guess I'll have one more thing to prod Wash with–"

Four more spikes joined the first one, and flecks of caneplas peppered my face. I yelled at Banks and Jilly to duck as I threw the crane in reverse. My heart threatened to pop out of my rib cage as I ducked low to watch the rearview mirrors to make sure the track was clear. No one behind us, so I lowered us to the bottom of the trellis to look above for whatever had shot at us. Holy crap: someone had *shot* at us.

The crane traffic hummed along, carrying flats of molasses barrels and other cargo. I couldn't see anyone on the rooftops, or anyone in the trellis. "That wasn't another accident, was it?" said Banks. "Someone actually shot at us?"

"Shh," I said. "We need to stay calm."

Another spike hit the roof, then three more actually punctured it. "Screw calm!" yelled Banks, diving over the seat and shoving the throttle ahead full. The crane lurched, tossing him backwards, but not before his elbow clocked me in the forehead. My head fuzzed, but not so much that I couldn't see another crane heading straight for us. I stomped on pedals, and we grabbed an upright and screamed three levels up. I looked down through the clear caneplas floor and saw the crane following us. Someone in black leaned out its open window and aimed what looked like a high-compression construction driver at us. I pulled back on the stick, catching a rail and scooting away as the shooter's crane shot past.

Jilly climbed over the seatback to look through the other windows. "All clear on the other sides, boss." Good girl.

"Sorry about that," said Banks.

"Just stay still," I said. "We need to get to Wash, and away from whoever's shooting at us."

"You sure it's not your buddy?" said Banks.

"Wash and I may have had some differences, but not enough for him to try to kill me," I said. "Besides, he wouldn't shoot at his own cranes."

"That's comforting."

Three uprights ahead, another crane slipped down to our level and picked up speed. We swung onto a junction circle and looped around to an empty rail. No one was above or below us, but this line ran away from the middle of Steelcase and Wash's office. "We're being herded," I said.

"And shot at," said Banks.

"They don't *want* us to get to Wash," I said, spinning us around a junction. "Shit! That's because they know I'll talk him out of dealing with Saarien."

"The guy in the white suit?" said Jilly. "What's his deal?"

"I'll tell you later," I said, leaning on the throttle for all its worth. "After we kick the crap out of him."

The back of the cab rattled from a few dozen spikeshots. A quick glance in the mirror showed both cranes were right behind us, with a third hovering along for added flavor. The mirror then shattered in another flurry of spikes, a tiny shard hanging on. I could feel The Fear hissing in the background, mocking my judgment and driving ability, and my head began to spin. My palms grew sweaty, my right hand slipping off the throttle. Was that the throttle? Or was it the... what did these controls do?

Jilly shook me. "Hey! We're not gonna take this shit, are we, boss?"

I swallowed back a throatful of bile and fought to clear my head. "We're not exactly armed." I turned to Banks. "Are you?"

He shook his head, his face pale. "I hate guns."

"What about the crane?" asked Jilly. "Can't we swing it at them?"

I shook my head, the fuzz clearing away. "I am sending you back to school to learn physics just so you can see how dumb that is," I said.

"School's for losers," she said, reaching over before I could slap her hand away from banging the emergency release button on the console.

When I did my brief bit of training as a crane operator, we learned two things: be careful with the cargo, but don't kill yourself for the cargo. The emergency release was for those rare moments when you were faced with the latter. Maybe the maglev was failing, maybe the winds were too high, maybe a whole horde of palm crabs were clawing up the line to tear your face off. You would press the button and dump the line.

Thing was, we never practiced dumping. It was too much of a pain to reel the line back in, and it happened so rarely that the instructors just pointed at the button and said, "Don't touch that unless you have to."

So, I really had no idea what would happen after Jilly hit the button. I felt the line spin away underneath us, the reel vibrating through the cab floor. The length readout spun up until the numbers stopped at 250. A sharp ping ran up from the crane's belly, followed by a clanking ring as the crane's jaw bucket clattered along the rail behind us.

"Oh, those bastards!" I yelled.

"What?" said Banks.

I pointed to a line of green lights. "The release didn't drop the line, it just turned off the brake! We're dragging the crane!"

"Well, can't you just, I dunno, claw at 'em ?"

I turned long enough for him to realize what a stupid thing he'd said. He shrugged. "I guess I saw the same movies as Jilly."

I shook my head. "If we get out of this alive, I am going to sit the both of you down and teach about how things work in the *real* world. You can't control a loose bucket if it's flapping away in the breeze. Hell, you can't hope to do anything with it unless all you wanted to do was tear up the track–"

The lights went on in my head and my hands moved before Jilly and Banks could say anything. Two thumb clicks to open the bucket's jaws, one more to crank up its magnet. The clanking turned to a shudder that bounced the whole crane as the bucket sucked itself toward the rail. "This is gonna get bumpy," I said, and I clamped the jaws shut.

I jerked forward in my restraints, and Banks and Jilly tumbled against the back of my seat as the closed jaws scraped along the rail. I wondered how much damage this was doing and how much of it was going to come out of my hide. Leaving the tuk-tuk behind was one thing, but tearing up another Ward's livelihood? That would start street fights and legislation.

In our leftover bit of mirror, I could see our three pursuers still behind us. The bucket's jaws, however, had knocked enough of the rail's magnets out of alignment to slow them down to a crawl. "Looks like our movies were pretty good after all," said Banks as he leaned over my shoulder.

Three bangs on the roof, then a spike punched through the ceiling, its shaft stopping a few millimeters from Banks's cheek. Overhead, a crane zipped past us; the shooter leaned out the window and fired at us, spikes smashing the windshield. "Your movies suck," I said.

"Just a little," croaked Banks, shrinking back. I opened the jaws and killed the magnet, and we shot forward. Not fast enough: the overhead crane was already slipping down the upright and onto our rail. We had no way out; ramming them wouldn't do a damn thing, and we couldn't escape up or backward or–

I looked through the caneplas panels in the floor and saw no one below. *Oh, you wouldn't,* said The Fear.

Fuck you, I would, I thought, and I just stood on the pedals and pushed down on both joysticks. The crane let go of the overhead rail, and we arced away into space. For a few sickening moments, we sailed in open air until the verts caught hold of the last upright, the screech of grinding metal filling the cabin and rattling my skull. We shook as the magnets' grip fought our momentum, the crane spinning about its z-axis for a few sickening moments.

But the noise stopped. The crane came to a halt.

I kept still for a moment, my hands still on the controls. I looked behind me; Banks and Jilly stared back with giant eyes, both of them frozen and gripping whatever handholds they could. I eased out a breath and relaxed. "Looks like we stuck the–"

A squeal like a dying whale cut me off, and the crane lurched to starboard, the cabin shuddering as we wrenched loose from the verts. I felt my stomach slide into my ears as we fell, the whole of Steelcase tilted ninety degrees and getting bigger faster–

A warning klaxon sounded, and the entire cabin filled with smoke. I just had time to think we'd caught fire when I smelled vanilla and realized, no, we were safe, but I was still screwed. We thumped to the ground as the crash foam (really just repurposed riot foam, though MacDonald Heavy swore up and down it didn't cause the same kinds of skin conditions) hardened and soaked up our kinetic energy, blocking out the sunlight. The deceleration still made my guts lurch as we came to a slow and steady halt.

Somewhere, through the hardened foam, I heard the Univoice declare that my operator code had been revoked.

"Is everyone OK?" I said, getting two muffled replies through the dim light. The cabin shook again, then the foam cracked and split. My eyes hurt from the light, and everything hurt worse when heavy hands yanked me out of the cabin.

A group of unhappy people looked down at me. I glanced over my shoulder and saw others extricate Banks and Jilly. A woman with arms as big as babies and a bass clef inked on her cheek cracked her knuckles. "We're behind schedule as it is, and now we're down a crane," she said. "Not to mention the repairs we're gonna have to do to the lattice. You have any idea how much trouble you're in? Or how much it's gonna cost?"

"I don't suppose we can come to an arrangement, just between us?" I wondered if she meant to take payment out of my bank account or out of my hide. I really hoped it was the latter.

"I'd stop talking to her now, if I were you," said a warm baritone sax voice from outside the crowd. The people parted, and Wash walked up, shaking his head, like he was trying to get rid of the half grin on his big moon face. He put his hand on Bass Check's shoulder. "Next thing you know, you're going to wind up owing *her* money." He sighed and looked at me. "I'm sure there's a perfectly reasonable explanation for what's happened here, but I have the feeling it's not going to come from you, Padma."

I shrugged the meaty hands off me and walked to the foamy, smoking wreckage of the crane. A dozen construction spikes as big as my forearm stuck out of the cab's roof and sides. I yanked one out and tossed it to Wash; it landed at his feet with a bright *clink*. "I suppose we should figure out who was shooting at me first. Right?"

Wash rubbed the back of his head, then nodded at his crew to get lost. They grumbled back to work, and Wash clapped his hands. "So. Buy you a drink?"

THIRTEEN

At the northern edge of the trellis, right on the border of Steelcase, there was a giant archway made of five upturned cargo canisters. They leaned into each other, their ends fast-welded together to make an open-ended pentagon that had been flipped on its edge. The whole structure had been fast-welded over Cholula Street, the main thoroughfare for surface cargo traffic. The arch made for an easy meeting point, since it was such a pain to get anywhere inside Steelhead.

Wash had ushered us into a newer, less-shot-at crane and driven us to a vert next to the arch. He powered down and unlocked the hatch, motioning for us to exit. "You still like heavy mint, right?"

There was a tiny tea shop at the base of the upright, and the waiter, a rail-thin man with faded ink, put a pot and four cups on the table as we approached.

"Someone shot my crane, Wash."

"You mean *my* crane, right?" he said, picking up the teapot. "And where did you learn to drive like that? You never drove like that for me."

"That's because you never let me race in an updated rig," I said, taking the seat opposite him. Banks and Jilly sat at my sides.

"With good bloody reason," said Wash, his broad, flat face wearing the faintest hint of a smile.

I nodded at the teapot. "Isn't this a little out in the open for a meeting? Considering how someone just tried to perforate me? On your turf?"

Wash pursed his lips as he poured. When he finished filling the last cup, he handed one to me and said, "You know how I would never allow all this to happen here, right?"

"But it did, and I think I know who did it" I said. "Since when do you let Saarien run your Ward?"

He sipped, his eyes narrowing. When he set his cup down, he eyeballed me and said, "That what you think?"

"I'm not sure what to think. You're the one who's in bed with him. Why don't you tell me?"

Wash scratched his face, turning the tips of the twin Kalashnikovs inked on his cheek a bright red. "First, the arrangement I have with Saarien doesn't mean he gets to influence things here."

"Really."

Wash straightened up. "Word of honor, Padma. I don't know what happened today, but I will fix it. You deserve that much."

"What I deserve is you giving me the Slots for the people waiting back in my flat," I said. "We had a deal."

"For a whole bunch of miners," said Wash, handing cups to Banks and Jilly. "Not for a handful of broken-down Breaches." He looked at Banks. "No offense."

"None taken," said Banks, huddling over his tea.

"It's better than nothing," I said.

"Actually, it's not," said Wash, pouring for himself. "Because I actually *needed* those specific people. I wasn't just going to drop 'em in the dark to scrub shit out of piping."

"What were you going to have them do?"

"I got over a hundred holding tanks that are rotting away, and those people were going to bring me some much-needed expertise."

"Are you kidding?" I said. "You couldn't find anyone else on this island who can patch holes?"

Wash sucked on his teeth, then started swirling his cup around. "Take a fifty-thousand hectoliter tank, and fill it to capacity with industrial molasses. Now, have a bolt on one of the tank's seams corrode, just enough so some of that molasses starts to dribble out. How long until that dribble turns into a flood? How long until other bolts go, disrupting the equilibrium and creating a vortex that sends all that stuff sloshing around like the tea in this cup?"

The tea spilled over the top and splashed on the table. Wash swiped it away. "I needed people who were good at dealing with repairs in a specific environment. Those miners would have been a godsend."

"You can't put out a call?" I said. "Are you trying to tell me you don't have the suction with the Union to make that happen?"

"No, because all of the right talent is taken," said Wash, pouring more tea. "And three guesses where it is."

I snorted. "Saarien. That bastard."

"One of his little creatures was just in my office, giving me the ultimatum. He'll give me people to fix my tanks, in return I don't help you. My hands are tied, Padma." Wash held his closed fists up to his face. They were huge hands, thick and veined. "I got four, maybe five months until I start reaching the failure point. You know the stories from Dead Earth, about that molasses flood that wiped out a neighborhood?" He shook his head. "That happens here, it's going to be half the city."

I picked up my own cup; it was the only thing around here that smelled good. Even the cane diesel fumes from the passing tuk-tuks were harsh against the odor of cargo baking on asphalt, the tang of rust and lube from the crane scaffolds. "So what's he going to do for you?"

Wash leaned back in his chair. "He's got new facilities with enough capacity to take all the molasses out of Steelcase. I won't have to be responsible for any of it, and that means more room for shipping other products."

"Like what?" I said, laughing.

Wash shrugged. "Bo Westin and some of his buddies have started a chemical engineering plant in Beifong. They're going to get us off relying on Big Three products."

"Yeah?" I said. "You got any customers?"

Wash made a face. "Saarien. But it's good money!"

"And it's also local," I said. "You want to make serious dosh, you need to send stuff up the cable, and the only things this planet produces on that scale are rum and molasses, and the Co-Op doesn't make *that* much."

"Well, you'd know, wouldn't you?" said Wash.

"Oh, not you, too," I said.

"You still can dish it out, but can't take it," said Wash, winking.

"I can't take a bad deal, which is what this is," I said. "You really think you're doing your people a favor by giving in to Saarien? It's bad enough he's got a third of the cane going to him; now you're going to give him the keys to storage and shipping, too?"

"Saarien's an asshole, but he's a manageable asshole," said Wash.

"Is he?" I said. "How many other Wards has he screwed over in the past ten years? How many times has he pinched Breaches? How many times has he promised to lend out cash or workers and not followed through?"

"This deal is done, Padma," said Wash. "Unless you've got something else to stick in my tanks and someone else to fix them, there's nothing I can do."

"I just can't believe you'd cave like this."

"You don't have to believe it, but that's how it is. I gotta get my equipment fixed. Hell, I got molasses that's starting to go *bad* because the tanks are so nasty. I've never seen it like this, which is why I've got to get cracking *now*. Anything to get these leaking tanks off my books is a deal worth making." He leaned back. "Now, about the crane you ruined–"

"Bill Saarien for it," I said. "I was just defending myself."

Wash sat back and snorted. "What, you're going to blame him for everything now? Come on."

I leaned forward. "I made a fool of him last night. You think he's going to let me get away with that? You start digging around, you'll find his sticky fingerprints all over those cranes that chased us. Hell, you can blink up footage from all over the Ward, and you'll find who shot at us."

He shrugged. "Maybe he did. That still doesn't solve my problems now."

"Who owns the tanks?" asked Banks.

Wash looked at Banks, then laughed. "I don't think Padma introduced us, Mister...?"

"Banks, my new lawyer, late of WalWa, prone to saying

weird shit," I said, turning to Banks. "What in hell are you talking about?"

"It's in the Union Charter," said Banks, hunkering forward in his chair. "All ownership rights of a Ward's natural and manmade resources have to be accounted for in order to preserve that Ward's prosperity, and to make sure they're kicking up enough to the whole of the Union."

"Where's that?" I said.

"Clause one, sub-clause seventeen," said Banks. "You people read your own laws, right?"

"Only if it suits us," I said. "And you'd better watch that 'you people' business. You're about to become one of us."

"Steelcase doesn't *have* any natural resources," said Wash.

"No, but you *do* have those tanks," said Banks.

"Which are *leaking*," said Wash, "and this is the only way I can get them fixed."

"But if you empty the tanks, you're going to empty Slots along with them," said Banks. "Part of the Contract is that Steelcase supplies so many hectoliters of industrial molasses every quarter, and if you're not supplying it, you're not part of the Contract. You're going to lose even more if you give Sou's Reach your holding concessions."

"You think I don't know that?" said Wash. "I've gone over the numbers again and again, and this is the way I lose the least."

"But you have so much here that could help you gain *more*," said Banks.

Wash threw his hands up with a weak laugh, then turned to look at the tanks and trellis. "Yes, behold our unbelievable wealth."

"Banks, are you going somewhere with this?" I said.

"Because I don't think insulting our host is the right way to get there."

"Do you remember what I did during my ride in from Earth?" said Banks, fixing me with that smile.

Last night had done the business to most of the previous day's memories, but I wasn't so wrecked that I couldn't see where Banks was driving. "You worked the greenhouse, right?"

"Greenhouse?" said Wash. "You came in on a WalWa seeder?"

Banks nodded.

"My condolences," said Wash. "I heard about those wrecks. Makes my ride sound like a luxury liner."

"I'm sure it was," said Banks. "Pulling weeds and tying vines was fun for a while, but then when planting came around..." He shuddered. "Where do you think we got our fertilizer?"

"Oh, you didn't," I said.

"Why do you think I wanted to jump ship?" said Banks. "All those fishsticks may have been catatonic, but they still shat themselves enough times to keep the greenhouse running."

I felt a glimmer of anger, deep in my guts. I remembered the metallic stench of the hibernant, the bright lights...

And The Fear snicked me an icy toothed smile, sharp enough to make my hands tense and freeze. My teacup tumbled from my fingers.

"You OK?" said Wash.

"Fine," I said, pouring myself another cup. "Nervy day, you know?" I told The Fear to get lost, then made a note to find the nearest WalWa rep just so I could punch him hard enough to make my old bosses feel it.

"Well, that's all good and done for you," said Wash, "but if you're suggesting I get into the humanure business, forget it. The capital costs to convert our plumbing would outweigh any favors I owe Padma."

"Of course they would," said Banks. "But the actual worth of what you're losing to Sou's Reach might mean you're getting screwed, and that's a direct violation of the First Clause."

"The First Clause says the Union exists to protect its members from the Big Three," I said.

"But there's plenty of legal precedent to interpret that to mean one Ward shall not screw over another Ward," said Banks. "As far as I can tell, Saarien's doing it to you two ways, by taking your workforce and your means of making a living."

"He's doing it to me in many, many interesting ways," said Wash.

"Then it's time to do it back," said Banks, "and you're going to do it with Brushhead's help."

"And how will that work?" I said. "What exactly do we have to offer when we're bleeding Slots?"

"You would know," said Banks. "You spent the evening talking about it with your friends."

I was too tired to blink up footage from last night, but not tired enough I couldn't remember Jordan's list of complaints. "We just have the sewage plant, and that's falling apart."

"As are the tanks in Steelcase," said Banks. "Separately, they're the responsibility of the individual Wards, but if you were to enter into an agreement, it becomes a joint infrastructure project, and those get automatic funding from the Union."

I opened my mouth to object, but nothing came out. I

could get Jordan and her crew to work in Steelcase, put Banks and company into the now-vacant Slots, yet retain all of them in my headcount. Holy crap, maybe I could even get extra Slots on my books from Wash, enough to make my number. I gave Banks a slow nod and said, "Well... I suppose that's worth investigating."

"It's bloody well worth doing!" said Wash, clapping his hands and grinning. "Good God, yes! It's not glamorous, but it's something that Saarien can't take from us." He held up a hand. "I'm in."

Banks turned to me. I crossed my arms over my chest. Wash's smile hitched. "What?"

"You know I can't make this kind of a decision," I said.

"I know you don't *want* to make this kind of decision," said Wash. "That's different."

"You're going to make me look at the list of things that need to be done in order to link Steelcase and Brushhead, and I'm going to see a mountain of engineering specs, construction costs, health codes, and employee gripes, and then I will have to murder you in cold blood, because what do I hate?"

Wash kept grinning at me. Banks raised his hand and said, "Paperwork?"

"*Work*, period," I said. "That's why I have an army of minions doing my bidding. Our host" – I pointed at Wash, wishing my finger could shoot incontinence rays – "is a freak of nature because he's the only Ward Chair in the city who actually bothers to get his hands dirty."

"I am offended that you would besmirch your brothers and sisters in Solidarity," said Wash, reaching for his tea.

I grabbed his hand. "Wash, you can't make me do this."

He put his head to the side, then nodded. "You're right. I

guess I'll have to call Saarien and get started."

"Oh, *hell*, no," I said. "You think you can guilt me into this deal?"

"I think I can take it or leave it," he said. "And I think you know that this is going to be good for all of our people. You remember them, right? The ones you work for?"

"Oh, don't try and give me the Solidarity Forever speech now," I said. "Where the hell was Solidarity when Saarien pinched all those Breaches from me? Where was Solidarity when he diverted funds to his Ward? Where was Solidarity when he tried to screw over *you*?"

Wash shrugged. "I'd say Solidarity is here now if you make this happen."

I ground my teeth. "You know Brushhead can't pay for any of it."

"You won't have to," said Banks. "See, under a joint *infra*–"

"I *know* how it works!" I yelled, my voice echoing off the trellis. "I know how it works, because I've done three of these deals, and they were all great big pains in my ass. The only way to get the Union to cough up money is if each Ward puts up matching seed funds, which never happens because Ward chairs are notoriously cheap–"

"A-*hem*."

"–present company excluded," I said. "But it's all pointless, because it's going to take a few million yuan to get started, and there is no way I can take that out of my Ward's budget."

Wash tapped his fingers on the tabletop. "You know, I think we could get a pilot program off the ground for ten K a piece."

"Which is ten K more than Brushhead could spend," I said.

"I know," said Wash, his fingers slowing. "But a little bird told me that *you* have that kind of dosh, and that you're willing to drop it for a little professional intervention here and there."

"That little bird's going to get her badge-faced beak handed to her if she doesn't learn to shut up," I said, squeezing my mug.

Wash raised an eyebrow. "What can I say? Soni brings Millie to the Kea Kea every now and then, and she fills me in on your illustrious adventures." He tapped his glass with a meaty finger. "And I know you're going to make bank once you're in charge of Tonggow's distillery."

I slammed the cup on the table. "Washington Hightower Lee, you of all people should know how not true that is. Or else, why aren't *you* living the high life on Chino Cove?"

Wash snorted.

"Why aren't you?" asked Jilly.

"Because I'm not that good at business," said Wash. "I can manage this place just fine, but to make it as a distiller? Hell, you know how many of those places go under in a year?"

"No," said Jilly.

"Most of them," said Wash. "So, I'd rather take my chances here and collect a nice pension. But you" – he pointed at me –"you have the magical combo of luck and sheer pigheadedness it takes to succeed in business. Plus, you still live in that grotty little flat on Samarkand, so I know you're saving a packet."

"Even if I do, why would I pony up?" I said.

Wash nodded at Banks. "I'm pretty sure you need Slots for your books, and I can provide them. For a price."

"What kind of price?"

"How many Slots?"

"Seventeen."

Wash laughed. "Christ, Padma, you aren't making this any easier."

"You do that, I will cover both our shares of the seed funding."

Wash stopped laughing. "The whole twenty thousand?"

"Look up my credit rating," I said, blinking him a link. "You know I'm good for it. You think you're going to get a better deal from Saarien? One that fixes this place up? One that covers all your people?"

"Some of them are going to become *your* people."

"And I'll look out for them," I said, holding out my right hand. "You willing to do this on the Public?"

He sighed, then shook his head. "What about my busted crane? My torn-up lattice?"

"You throw that into the proposals, and it'll get covered. You might even be able to upgrade."

"You're just gonna break my heart again, aren't you?"

"Maybe, but I'll never break a promise."

He nodded, then shook my hand. I filled in the requisite forms quickly, but when it came time to blink the money into the escrow account, my eyes wouldn't move. I just looked at my balance and saw how much had been eaten out of it over the past day. I would be under a hundred thousand yuan. That was way below my comfort level. Even with the payout for fulfilling my obligation, I would have a tough first year.

But then I remembered the blue-green bottle sitting at home, and I blinked up twenty thousand yuan into escrow. Within three minutes, the Brushhead-Steelcase Joint Purification Infrastructure Venture was ready to roll.

"Done," I said. "Your turn."

Wash blinked up his info on the agreement, dumped ten thousand into the escrow account, then looked me square in the eye so his pai could talk with mine and said, "I, Washington Lee, do hereby grant seventeen Contract positions to Brushhead's Contract headcount." He blinked a few times, and the transfer codes, all in a precise ISO-20K font, rolled past my eyes.

"I accept," I said, then got up.

"Is that it?" said Wash.

"What more do you want?" I said. "You want me to ask you to the Golden Days Dance?"

Wash blinked. "You hate dancing."

"Just like I hate farting around," I said. "What else is there?"

Wash smiled and said, "There was a time when people would seal a contract over a drink."

I held up my cup. "I'm on the clock."

"And you're also Estella Tonggow's buddy."

"Which means, what? I can make rum appear out of thin air? I have magical distilling powers?"

He shook his head. "You have a flask-shaped object in your pocket. You do the math."

I glared at him but took the flask out. I unscrewed the cap; Jesus, it smelled good. I wanted to down the whole thing, but made a show of taking a pull. I pushed my tongue against the spout to keep anything from getting into my mouth. The rum burned a tiny, perfect dot on my tongue, and I handed Wash the flask. He took a drink and smiled. "I hope you'll sell that to me at a discount once you've closed your deal."

I rolled my eyes and tucked the flask into my pants. "And

I hope you're OK with getting your hands dirty," I said to Banks. "You're about to start working for once in your life."

Banks smiled at Wash and said, "I can ignore her, right?"

"Won't do you much good," said Wash. "She'll still get her way." He got up as a crane sailed overhead with Jilly's tuk-tuk clutched against its belly. The crane gently set the little green beast on the ground. "Sorry I didn't get this taken care of earlier."

I looked at the tuk-tuk; it was stained with rotten breadfruit and reeked of crab juice. Wash snapped his fingers, and the waiters all rushed over to wipe the tuk-tuk down. "Solidarity," said Wash, once they'd finished. "And now if you'll excuse me, I have repairs to order, traffic to direct, countersuits to file, and about a million liters of rum to drink in order to get through it all." He nodded to Banks and Jilly, gave me a heavy glance, then walked toward the upright where our crane was parked. As he mounted the stair, he turned and called, "What made you think you could jump a crane off the rail and not die?"

"I saw it in a movie!" I yelled back.

Wash shook his head and climbed out of sight. The crane hummed back to life, then cruised away to make its delivery. I blinked up a call to Jordan to tell her the good news, but just got her voicemail. I sent her a text, and we piled into the tuk-tuk.

I eased down into the tuk-tuk's back seat, now completely knackered. A nap, followed by a hot shower and signing in all these Breaches, seemed like just the thing. Overhead, the cranes kept cruising along like giant flying turtles. They hauled tanks of molasses bound for all parts of Occupied Space, ready to get dropped down a line and turned into fuel or plastic or, God forbid, food. I closed my eyes as Banks and Jilly chatted about action movies. I tried to text some people back at the Union Hall about our success but got nothing but network errors. Maybe the fall had done more damage to my pai. One more thing to deal with when we got back. I shut my brain off for the rest of the drive.

When we came around Fernandes onto Solidarność, I could see the Union Hall clock tower poking above the shophouses. The clock's massive face, almost three meters across, showed a huge thunderhead looming over the old microfiber plant up on Beggar's Hill. The plant had been Brushhead's main employer for forty years, a place that churned out the scrubbers used to clean spent fuel cans. It kept a lot of people working until WalWa figured the fuel savings from cleaning the cans wasn't worth the expense of the plant, so they shuttered everything and booted us all out. I was shop steward, doing my first organizing gig, and I'd led all of Brushhead into that plant to steal everything, including the stuff that was bolted down. We hollowed that place in sixteen hours, and when the WalWa comptrollers came to do inventory, they found not a factory but brand new housing units for the now-displaced workforce.

The plant depicted on the clock face was the old one, before we'd punched holes in the pourform walls and installed caneplas windows and verandas. The figures of WalWa people in their stiff-collared company coats stood at the doorway, about to be overwhelmed by a thunderhead made of Brushhead residents. Everyone who'd marched on the plant had donated a little memento to Jens Odoyai, the artist who'd made the clock face. The images of the plant and the WalWa figures were all fashioned from bits and bobs from the plant, but the thunderhead was made from stuff that mattered to us. I'd given up my shop steward badge, a little fist made from recycled glass. It had been a long, brutal day, but I still smiled when I looked up at that clock and remembered how satisfying it had been to take that plant apart.

The clock said it was five-fifteen, and my entire body suddenly ached at once. I'd been running around all day and wanted to crawl under a desk and sleep for a week, but I knew first I had to get home for six o'clock. "OK," I said, "we're just gonna stop off here quickly, then get dinner. No, a *massive* dinner."

We rounded the corner, and there was the Hall. It was a simple square building made of recycled concrete and ironpalm, but it had a dignity and quiet power I'd always liked. If every structure in Thronehill looked like a marker, some way for WalWa to say to the world they had come, seen and conquered the living shit out of the place, then the Hall looked and felt like a home. It was a refuge during hurricanes, a place for the neighborhood to celebrate weddings, and the site of more debates than I cared to remember. It was solid, it was safe, and, as we walked toward Koothrapalli, it was surrounded by a wall of cops. They all wore their patrol uniforms, forming a neat yellow and black line that blocked the way out.

"Stay here," I said to Banks, and approached the police. The cops were all familiar faces, women and men from the local precincts. I pinged Soni. "What's going on?" I said when she picked up. "My money's no good?"

"It is," said Soni, both in my head and in front of me. She stepped out of the row, wearing that I'm-really-not-happy smile that cops wore when they were about to arrest someone. "Can we talk?"

I looked at Banks, then nodded. We stepped down onto the sidewalk.

"What can you tell me about the body in the freezer?" she said, her voice low.

"You're going to have to be more specific," I said.

"Padma, this is not the time to joke around," said Soni. "I had patrol over at the office on Handel and Reigert this morning to answer a call about a chemical spill, and they came back with pictures of a corpse on ice. What do you know about it?"

"You don't have to worry about that," I said. "I'm going to take care of it later."

Soni straightened up. "Then you *do* know about it."

"Sure. I helped put him there."

Soni grabbed my shoulder and spun me around, pinning me against the hood of a parked lorry. "Padma Mehta, you're under arrest."

"Oh, come on!" I said as she cuffed me. "What the hell for?"

"Murder."

"Soni, he was dead when we found him!"

"Really?" said Soni, spinning me around and waving to the cops. "Because you were seen with him last evening, threatening to kill him."

"What? Who are we talking about?" I said.

"Who do you think?" she said, blinking me a picture. "Evanrute Saarien."

It was the walk-in freezer at the Union office, and there was a body in the corner, but it wasn't Mimi's late husband. It was a bigger man, his hands bound and his face beaten beyond recognition. His tongue lolled out of his purpled mouth, like a dog that had choked on its owner's lipstick. Under the blood and gore, the corpse's suit was white.

"I have no idea how he came to be there," I said. "Lots of

people use that office."

"Yes, and you were seen leaving it last night around ten," said Soni, "about thirty minutes before Evanrute Saarien's pai pinged a Public terminal on Reigert."

"Oh, you are kidding me," I said.

"His teeth were bashed out, his fingerprints burned off, but his DNA and pai ID match," said Soni.

"And you can tell from everyone else's buffers that I had nothing to do with this."

"Except I don't," she said.

"What?"

"You were with a bunch of people who haven't gotten their pais returned. Whatever they saw can't be used in court. I have to follow procedure and put you under arrest."

"This is bullshit."

"Maybe, but it's how it's going to be. You want to sing along as I read you your rights?"

"No, I already know the words," I said, then closed my mouth. She hustled me toward a waiting bumblecar, and I blinked a text to Banks: *Get out of here NOW*.

Banks gave me a small wave, just before Soni slammed the door shut.

FOURTEEN

The cells at Santee City Jail were quite pleasant: bright colors, soft surfaces, not much crowding. It was a nice contrast from the WalWa facilities with their harsh lights, sharp corners and hidden truncheon practice. You could have turned the place into a cheap hotel if you swapped the bars for walls.

It was still a horrible place to spend the night.

Not that I slept much. By the time I'd gone through booking, six o'clock had come and gone, and there was no way I could convince the cops to get me a shot of Old Windswept and a candle. Well, the rum, maybe, but open flames in a jail cell? Even I knew that wasn't going to happen.

Soni had been professional about the whole thing: marching me to the front desk, making me spit into the register, then turning off my pai with a wave of a red lightstick. That was the killer: I could've gotten through a long night if I'd been in contact with the outside world. Without my pai, I could do nothing but listen to the drunks trying to one up each other with their tales: about the work they'd done, about the work they planned to do, about how they Breached, about how bad they were, about how bad things were. I started drifting in and out, my head filled with horror stories about people seeing bodies getting torn open, about masked figures flitting in and out of bar fights. People were disappearing all over the city, even from the kampong, they said. Ghosts had landed on Santee, they said. The Big Three were going to abandon the planet, let us die, they said. I let it all wash over me, all the babbling and whining and whimpering, and I kept to myself on my bench.

Though I wasn't completely on my own.

The Fear hissed and whispered and chuckled as I lay down, keeping my eyes shut so tight my face hurt. The Fear mocked me, called me a fool, then started to monkey with my fingers and toes, taking away the sensation in some while making the others feel like they were hooked up to tuk-tuk batteries. The Fear talked and talked as I did my best to stay calm and in control and failed. I could feel the paralysis creeping up my spine, feel the icy fingers reaching out to shut off my body and turn me into a catatonic statue. At one point, I must have curled up in a ball, because, when I clawed my way out to consciousness, I found my knees tucked under my chin and a Freeborn woman sitting at my feet.

I looked down at her as a cloud of something awful washed over me. At first, I thought a rat had died in the cell's air vents, but then I saw a snoring Union woman thrash around on her cot before settling down. Then the Freeborn woman coughed and shifted in her seat. The smell got worse.

At first sniff, I thought it was the classic combination of body odor and booze, but there was an ugly sharpness to their smell, like they'd been splashed with chemical runoff. Their clothes were also spattered with bleach spots, and, as I watched, the spots spread. A thought clicked in the back of my head, and I wished I could pull up my pai's buffer. I'd just seen something that stained like that. What was it?

"What?" said the Freeborn woman.

"Your clothes," I said, clearing my throat, trying to cover up from my staring.

"What about them?" she said, huddling up on the bench. "They not good enough?"

"Oh, Jesus," I said, shaking the cotton out of my head. "You really want to pull that class warfare crap now? When I'm in the same cell as you? What made the spots on your clothes?"

"She did," said the Freeborn woman, jerking a thumb at our sleeping cellie. "I was just trying to get a drink last night, and she started squawking about how my type shouldn't have been in the bar, telling me my kind was killing her business, and how dare I try to reap what she sowed or something crazy like that." She snorted. "Then some other Ink tries to calm her down, some skinny thing, looked like she would blow away on a breeze."

I cocked my head. "What then?"

The woman nodded. "She starts talking, this real high voice, about how she's just lost her man, and how she's lost, and can I help her. Real pitiful, right? I was going to tell her to go away, but then these two old ladies show up, one on either side of me, right? They look even weaker than this first lady, but they grab my arms and it *hurts*."

I snorted. "You picked the wrong little old ladies to cross."

"Don't I know it?" said the Freeborn woman. "I was just about to tell them to fuck off, when that one there"

– she nods at the unconscious Union woman – "she grabs a bottle, smashes it on the bar like she was to cut me, and then this horrible smell just filled the place. She got a faceful of splashed rum, and the rest got on me. Ruined my clothes, would've got me if the stink hadn't driven us out into the street."

"And then what?"

She shrugged. "Police came, rounded us all up. She screamed some more in the bumblecar, then just passed out. Her drink caught up with her, in her gut *and* up her nose."

"Do you remember what kind of rum it was?" I asked.

She snorted and shook her head. "The kind that was supposed to cost a lot."

Another skunked bottle. What the hell was the Co-Op doing with quality control? I hoped Tonggow wasn't going to let that happen to Old Windswept. I didn't know what I'd do if it all started to go bad...

"–was supposed to be safer in the city," said the Freeborn woman. "Instead, I get this abuse. I got to deal with cane rats and crops rotting on the stalk, and then I come here, and what do I get? You Inks talk about us coming to the city, getting drunk and starting fights. I work hard, I deserve to sit at a bar like anyone else."

"I completely agree," I said. "And when I get out of here, I'll make sure it happens."

"Uh-huh," she said. "If you were someone who could do that, you wouldn't be in here with us."

Soni walked into the cellblock, her patrol cap tucked into her uniform's epaulet. Her head, like every other cop's, was shaved to stubble. It was supposed to be intimidating, but it made her look like a freshly husked coconut. "Making friends?" she asked me.

"I like your haircut," I said.

She gave me a sour look as she unlocked my cell. "One of these days, your compliments are going to get you beaten to a pulp."

"As long as I keep making donations to the Widows and Orphans Fund, I expect the beatings to be quick and professional."

"Let's go," she said, clanging the door open.

"What happened?" I said. "You realized you arrested the wrong woman?"

"Hardly," she said. "You made bail. Look at me."

Soni waved a red lightstick at my face; it beeped, and the Univoice reeled off my name and Union ID number. "You're tagged for city limits only," said Soni. "Go on the water or into the kampong, and you'll forfeit your bond and get locked up until trial. Plus I'll be able to do horrible things to your head."

"I know how bail tags work, thanks," I said.

"Not from this end," she said. "And don't try to make another smartass remark, unless you want it to show up in court."

I looked at the Freeborn woman, who sat on her bench, her arms crossed. "When you get out," I said, "you ask around this neighborhood for Padma Mehta."

"That you?"

"That is," I said. "I meant what I said about helping."

"You want to help?" said the woman. "You let me get a drink where I want, when I want."

"I'll see what I can do."

"You lining up future customers?" said Soni as we filed out to the front desk.

I mimed zipping my mouth shut. She signed and buzzed us through a series of doors, each taking us into better-lighted rooms. When we entered a lobby with skylights, I figured I was almost home free. A sleepy-eyed desk sergeant handed me a clipboard and a bag of my stuff. Soni stood in front of the last door to the lobby. "Before you go, for what it's worth, I don't think you're behind this. But you know I have to follow through on every lead, right?"

I gave her a blank face.

She cleared her throat. "All the same, I got pai logs that say you went to the office and stayed there all night. The signal winks in and out, and then I got Saarien arriving and staying there. What happened, Padma?"

I crossed my arms and tapped my clamped mouth.

Soni sighed. "We'll be in touch." She buzzed me through the last door into the lobby.

Estella Tonggow sat in a chair, a smile on her inked and lined face. "Well!" she said, patting her lap with gloved hands. "I don't think either of us thought we'd be keeping our appointment in such an *interesting* place."

"Madame Tonggow, what are you doing here?" I said, bowing and stuffing everything back in my pockets.

"Bailing your ass out, it would seem," she said, standing up and smoothing her skirts in one deft move. "You wouldn't be*lieve* the size of the bond I had to post. Ridiculous. Just like the charges."

"My point exactly!" I said, pasting a smile on my face. "There's no way I could have–"

"Ah-ah-ah," she said, holding up a hand. "You don't say another word until we are out of here, yes?"

I nodded and walked for the door.

Outside, a green limousine straight out of an executive's

wet dream materialized out of the traffic and hummed to a halt in front of us. The door glided open, and Tonggow floated into the limo, leaving a trail of cinnamon and clove perfume behind her. "Let's go for a ride, shall we?" she said. She smiled, but from the way her eyes crinkled, I knew it wasn't a suggestion. I bowed and climbed in after her.

The limo was austere, all spotless leather and hard edges. "I bought this off a derelict MacDonald Heavy ship," said Tonggow as the door whispered shut. "Ugly as hell, but it drives smoothly. You can hardly tell you're moving."

I looked out the window; the streets of Santee City flashed by without a hint of acceleration. "Any idea who it was meant for?"

She shrugged. "Someone with a massive paycheck and no taste. By the way, did you get my gift?"

I patted the flask on my thigh pocket. "I did. Thank you."

She pushed the wall, and a panel clicked open. Inside was a pair of hand-blown rum tasting glasses and a fifth of Old Windswept. Tonggow cracked the cap, and the scent – oh, the heavenly scent of the rum filled the limo, sending my head swimming. The Fear ran screaming to the front of my mind, smashing against every bit of control I could muster. I swallowed, trying not to look desperate. It didn't work, because Tonggow poured a finger in each glass and said, "Care for a drink?"

"Not when I'm on the clock," I said, putting my hands beneath my legs so she wouldn't see me clench them into white-knuckled fists.

"A good policy," she said, knocking back her glass with one swallow. She took a quick breath in, sucking the air through her teeth. "Oh, I will never get over that feeling. A little kick, a lot of velvet, and then the warmth. Makes me wish we had a serious winter here, just so I could appreciate it that much more."

"That's why I like a bit at night," I said. "You sit on your lanai, you get the breeze off the ocean with that chill, and then a little bit of rum to round off the evening."

"Agreed," said Tonggow, reaching for the second glass. "One of the many reasons why I've enjoyed talking with you, Miss Mehta. You sense a bit of the romance."

"A bit."

She took a sip, holding it in her mouth for a few seconds before swallowing. I just looked out the window again. We were in a neighborhood of new rowhouses off Cheswell Boulevard. This was striver territory, second- or third-generation Shareholders who had invested in all the non-Union and non-Co-Op parts of Santee. I'd met a few strivers in the aftermath of the last Contract; they were starry-eyed and optimistic as hell. I couldn't stand them.

Tonggow put down the glass, and a tiny droplet of rum splashed onto her hand. She licked it away, then said, "I'm sure you realize that every romance includes danger."

"Is that why we're having this meeting in a fancy-looking armored car?" I glanced at the bottle again. It would be so easy to take a casual pour and sip. I blinked up the time: barely nine in the morning. Christ.

"Partly," she said, smiling. "But we're also nicely shielded from prying eyes and ears." She tapped her temple. "No pai signals get in or out. No tracking, no tracing. And what I'm going to talk to you about could quite likely get us killed, so it's probably a good idea to keep it just between us."

I blinked away the time and looked at her. Tonggow's face was stone, her eyes half closed. "I'm listening."

"Good," she said. "Because you're going to have to

remember this without making a recording, and I'm only going to tell you once. I know, Miss Mehta, that you didn't make your number, that you were counting on those miners. I know you're worried that someone else will make a bid for my distillery, and I want you to know that no one else but you is going to get her grubby hands on the place... provided you do two things for me."

"Whatever you say," I said, hoping she didn't want me to kill someone. I'd managed to avoid that for twelve years, and wasn't in the mood to break my streak.

"The first is easy," she said. "I have a pretty hefty shipment going up the cable tomorrow. I want you to make sure it gets there in one piece."

"I can't get out on the water," I said. "You saw my bail tags."

"Yes, but I consider this a test of how you delegate," she said. "Think you can swing that?"

I nodded. "What's the second?"

"I need you to go to every bar in this city and drink."

I waited a moment to see if she was going to smile. She didn't. "I think I'm missing something."

"You know there have been... odd events with some of the Co-Op's product," she said, tenting her fingers on her lap.

"You mean the skunked rum?"

"Well, I could talk about the proper chemical terms" – Tonggow tapped her left cheek, right on the barely visible tattoo of an Erlenmeyer flask – "but, yes. There is a new kind of contaminant affecting our rum, and no one can figure it out what it is. Some of the best distillers in the Co-Op are releasing product that goes bad somewhere between crushing the cane and decanting. None of them wants to admit there's something wrong, but every distiller knows something *is* going wrong, and we're all scared shitless it's going to be one of our bottles next."

"But this has happened before, right?" I said. "Impurities in the bottles, something in the water, a smut on the cane?"

"For one or two producers every few years, yes," she said. "But for this number..."

I sat back. "How many are we talking about?"

"Right now," she signed, "fifty-seven. Fifty-eight, if I add that picture you sent me."

"Who else?"

She handed me a piece of paper; on it was a list of distillers done in Tonggow's loopy handwriting. None of the skunked bottles I'd smelt (other than the Nelson's Column from that dive on Murdoch) were on the list. "You can add two more to this," I said, then told her about the bottles at Big Lily's and in the office. "Maybe a third," I said, remembering the Freeborn woman in the jail.

Tonggow's fist clenched. "It's happening faster than I thought," she said, waving toward the front of the limo. "You'll have to move quickly if you're going to get to the bottom of this."

"Wait, wait, wait," I said. "Why me? Why this? Why can't the Co-Op just... I dunno, co-operate?"

Tonggow gave me a sweet smile as she shook her head and put her hand on my knee. "We may be a Co-Operative in name, but we're barely like it in practice. The Big Three have been driving down the price for industrial molasses for years, and now they're trying to do the same with the rum. Profits are down, expenses are up, and the last thing anyone wants to admit to the other members is that they're in trouble. Even if it really means *everyone* is in trouble. This has to stay quiet until we can figure out what the hell's going on."

"So, this is all on me?"

She shrugged. "Mostly on you. You get me labels, and I'll do what I can to sort it out."

"That's a lot of rum for just me to sample," I said.

"I know," said Tonggow as the limo smoothed to a stop. "That's why you're going to take your new Breach friends along. Nothing like a bar crawl to celebrate one's liberation, hm?"

"I can't take them out in public," I said.

"Why? You're afraid the rank and file will lynch you?"

"Pretty much, yes."

Tonggow's smile disappeared, and I shivered. "Miss Mehta, if you're afraid of that, then maybe you aren't the one to run my distillery. I always thought you had more spine."

I fought the urge to swallow my heart back into my chest and banged on the divider window. "Oy!" I yelled at the driver. "Take us to Samarkand and Benares, and get ready to pick up extra passengers." I caught Tonggow's surprised smile. "You can't expect me to haul my new friends out on foot, Madame Tonggow. We'd never last the day."

Tonggow raised her glass as the limo sped up.

FIFTEEN

"OK," said Banks. "OK, OK, OK. The thing."

"Is," I said.

"Is what?"

"The thing," I said, waving for the bartender to pour us another round.

"Right!" yelled Banks as he thumped the sticky metal bartop. "The thing is that I still don't *get* how the whole thing *works*."

"The hell" – One-Eye paused long enough to burp and grab another fistful of edamame from the bowl – "kind of lawyer *are* you, Banks?"

"Real estate, remember?" he said, trying and failing to keep himself together.

"I mean... *I* get how the whole thing works, and I hate it!" said One-Eye. "Why do we hafta wait for someone else to come down so we don't have to, y'know..."

"...work?" offered Mimi, a bamboo stirrer in her hands.

"Exactly!" said One-Eye. "Why the hell can't we start not working now?"

"Because," I said, looking at the upended and empty shot

glasses that surrounded our elbows, "because that's the way it's always worked."

"Work," said Banks, reaching for the empty bottle of Bastard's Blend that spun on the bartop. "You know, I always worked. When I was a kid, I worked inna potato field. When I was older, I worked inna recyling plant."

"Recyling?" I said.

"Yeah, yeah," he said, bobbing his head. "When you use old stuff to make new stuff. Recyling. Anyway, I did that, then I got *this*" – he jabbed at the scales tattooed on his cheek – "and I worked more. An' we had to work to *get* here."

"Damn hard work," said One-Eye.

"Damn hard," said Banks. "And *now* you're telling me that we hafta work again? Doing shit work?"

"It's not all shit work," I said. "I mean, yeah, a lot of it is, but not all of it."

"But why?"

"Be*cause*," said Madolyn, lifting her head off the bartop and jabbing Banks on the forehead, "because there are only so many jobs to go around, and WalWa or LiaoCon or MacDonald don't want to give away any *more* jobs than they have to, so that's how it goes." She plunked her head back down and started snoring.

"What she said," I replied, focusing on the round of shots that had just appeared. I blinked a picture of the label – Next Century Amber, which always tasted like rotting bananas – then held the glass aloft. "Here's to Banks, may he not have to work too long so we won't have to hear his whining about it."

"Hear, hear!" said One-Eye, slamming down the rum and wincing. "This is horrible."

"I know," I said, hiding the glass below the bartop. I poured the rum on the ground, then lifted the empty glass to my mouth and tipped it up fast. I had done stealth dumps for the past six hours. We'd gone to thirty different bars, tried a hundred fifty different rums, always insisting on new bottles. We hadn't encountered any more skunked rum, which really pissed me off: if it had gone bad, at least I wouldn't have had to pay for it. Right now, I was almost two thousand yuan down, an amount that I realized Tonggow hadn't promised to reimburse.

"But it's also great!" said One-Eye, her cheeks flushed bright red.

I passed her a plate full of takoyaki. "Eat up," I said. "These are great for soaking up booze."

"Righteous," she said, scarfing two of the battered balls at once. She chewed for a few moments, then said, her mouth full, "It's not always going to be like this, is it? The food, the drinks, the... the not working?"

"There's always going to be work," I said. "It's just a matter of there being enough jobs. We got the Contract coming up for renewal in less than two years, and everyone's fighting for a piece of the pie." I waved for one last round. "Problem is, the pie's been getting smaller for decades, and no one wants to admit it."

"How many jobs are we talking about?" said One-Eye. "Like... enough for us?"

"I don't know," I said. "I'm high enough on the totem pole to know there's a problem, but not high enough to know the exact number. Every time I've asked the people above me, they tell me not to worry, which is a sure sign that something bad is gonna happen." I twirled an empty shot glass in my fingers, watching the light glint off the hard edges. "But if you're worried about getting into hot water with WalWa, don't. There's no way they can get you, not here. Not now."

"What about all that talk back on the beach?"

The bartender put a new bottle of Olmos Green in front of us. The Green was a favorite of mine that had fresh cane shoots mixed into the mash. It looked like liquid emeralds. I smiled at One-Eye as I opened the bottle. "Hell, you know the old saying. All that stuff I said was recruitment. This is real."

The rum smelled perfect, like freshly cut grass on a spring day. The bartender held up five fingers; fifty yuan a bottle. Jesus. I poured shots for me and One-Eye, and, this time, I downed the whole thing.

Banks groaned and lifted his head off the bar; a string of drool hung from his mouth. "This place is dead," he said. "Can we go somewhere fun?"

We piled out of the bar and into Tonggow's waiting limo. The driver and I exchanged pointed glances; he was a Freeborn man who'd barely said a word during our tour. I was embarrassed; I couldn't tell if he was angry or bemused. "Where to next?" he said.

I blinked up the time: four-ten. We were a good twenty minutes from Brushhead, which meant one more round at Big Lily's, and then I was throwing in the towel. Tonggow's polite request could wait until after six o'clock. "Mercer and Moore," I said. "Don't take the scenic route."

"I hear the sewage plant's lovely this time of day," said the driver. I shook my head and hopped in. The limo glided into traffic like an armored swan. I texted Big Lily to prepare for our arrival.

"You know," said One-Eye, turning toward me, "I was

pretty sure you'd have a pitch to make."

"What, this isn't enough?" I said. She didn't laugh. Neither did Mimi or the old ladies. They all stared at me, like hungry dogs waiting for someone to toss them a steak. Except Banks. Banks looked out the window.

"The pitch," I sighed, then took a sip of water from the bottles the driver had set out for us. "Why did you jump ship?"

"What kind of pitch is that?" said One-Eye.

"Why did you all get into an empty fuel can that dropped a hundred and fifteen thousand kilometers onto a planet you'd only heard about through whispers and graffiti, rather than stay upstairs in your nice, solid lives? Why?"

One-Eye crossed her arms and leaned back. "Really? That's all you've got? We want to know what's in it for–"

"The smell," said one of the old ladies. Gricelda. The one allergic to eggplant.

"What about the smell?" I said.

She cleared her throat. "Every morning, I would wake up in my bunk, and the air smelled like dead roses and rust. It was all the recycling. It may have scrubbed out the CO_2, but it did nothing about the smells from all the fishsticks. All the belching, the farting, the way their bodies got a little pickled in the hibernant. Every night, I would clean myself up, wash my nose and throat, hoping to get the smell out. And then there it would be the next morning, reminding me that this was my life, and would continue to be my life for the rest of the trip."

"How long?"

"We tended that ship for six jumps," said Madolyn. "Two years to get past the Red Line, two years to return. A few weeks in port..."

"*Eight* jumps," said Gricelda, taking Madolyn's hand. "You forgot the first two. We've been underway for over thirty years."

"When was the last time you were on solid land?" I said

Madolyn shook her head, and a tear trickled down Gricelda's cheek. "Every time we got close to fulfilling our Contract, a WalWa rep would talk us into an extension for greater benefits," said Madolyn. "Do another jump, get more stock options. Put in another jump, your medical's bumped up to the next tier. Sign on for an extended tour, and we'd be set for life." She set her jaw as her eyes got wet. "Then I looked in the mirror and realized I wouldn't have much of a life left. No matter how good the artificial gravity is, you know you're in a cage and dying by degrees."

I nodded, then turned to Mimi. "How about you?"

"It was all Thanh," she said, the drunken wavering gone from her voice. "We only had one more run to do to meet our obligation. Another four years, and our Indentures would have been fulfilled. We managed those plants for five seeding trips, raised all of them on our own, and now it's gone. For what?" She snuffed with bitter laughter, wiped an arm on her sleeve, already stained from a long day's drinking. "Fool couldn't wait another four years, and now he's dead and I'm stuck here without our plants." She swallowed, fighting down the lumps in her throat.

Comfort and understanding I could fake, but what this woman wanted, I couldn't deliver.

"Mimi?" We both looked up at Banks, who had reached out with an open hand. Mimi hesitated, then took it.

"I was only with you guys for that one run, but we both know Thanh wanted you two off that ship," he said. "Remember how we all used to work the water hyacinth tank together? Four hours a day, in muck up to our waists?"

Mimi shivered, then laughed at herself.

"And WalWa wouldn't replace the waders they'd issued you on your first trip," said Banks. "Remember that?"

"Awful things, even then," she said, gripping Banks's fingers. "Always rode up funny, didn't keep the water out. Wore out two months in."

"And that wasn't all that crapped out on that ship, was it?" His voice was smooth and mellow.

She shook her head. "That ship was a nightmare. Leaking steam fittings, parasites in the water lines, and the way the fishsticks would come awake sometimes..." She shuddered and let go of Banks's hand, going for her water bottle.

Banks nodded. "You weren't getting quite the deal WalWa said you were, and Thanh knew it. He was waiting for a run to a place like Santee so he could get you two out of there."

Mimi swayed a bit and took a long pull at the bottle. "But how could he leave me?" she said, her voice getting thick again. "How could he go away like that?"

"I'm sure he didn't want to," said Banks. "In fact, I think he'd be sad to see you like this right now. This was his dream for the both of you: to be free of WalWa and to run your own lives for once."

Mimi looked up at Banks with watery, reddened eyes. "I just want him back."

"I know," said Banks, moving to the seat next to Mimi and wrapping an arm around her. She cried a while, and Banks rocked her back and forth. I took the now-empty bottle from her hand, and she gripped my arm with fierce, bony fingers. Finally, her crying eased off, and she let go of us both. "I need a moment," she said, and she scooted to an empty part of the cavernous limo.

I crunched the caneplas bottle. "Thanh must have been quite a man," I said, dropping the trash into the compost bucket.

"He was a bullying asshole," said One-Eye.

"Ellie!" cried the old ladies.

"He *was*," said One-Eye. "It didn't matter that *I* was the one who had authority over running the ship. Whenever there was an issue with his goddamned plants, he'd piss and moan about how he was the only one keeping us alive, and if we didn't help him we were all dead. Every fucking day he'd push us around the greenhouse until our fingers bled. Literally." She held up her hands, a constellation of scars on her knuckles and fingertips. "He didn't want to Breach to be free. He'd just heard the porn on Santee was better than the stuff WalWa let him carry on the ship." She pounded the side of the car, then sat back and stared into the distance.

"Are you kidding?" I said. "I started that rumor myself."

One-Eye snorted, crossed her massive arms over her chest. "Then you did your marketing professors proud, 'cause you sure as hell knew your audience." She shook her head. "The only two good things that son of a bitch ever did were getting Mimi into that can and dropping dead on the way down."

"Spoken like a true resident of Santee," I said, giving the compost bucket a shake. "They probably would've gotten divorced within the year. The cracks show pretty quickly in bad Breach marriages."

"How high is the divorce rate?" asked Banks.

"Astronomical," I said. "Of course, if you want to divorce someone, you just say so in front of a paied witness or a Public terminal, and that's that."

"Damn," said Banks.

"So, what about you?" said One-Eye.

I blinked up the time: four-twenty. "Oh, you know... got screwed over one time too many and decided I wanted more. How about you... Ellie?" I said. "Why'd you jump?"

"I know what you're doing," she said, still staring out the window.

"And what's that?"

She looked at me, her scarred face shriveled and red. "I know your type," she said, leaning forward like a cane viper coiling up for a strike. "You learn how to psych people out, how to manipulate them, how to get them to do what you want. And you start by getting into our heads, finding our weak points."

"If it's any comfort, I don't think you *have* any weak points."

"See? See?" She pointed her finger, and her face got harder. "There you are, doing it. Trying to get me on your side."

"I don't care what side you're on, just as long as it's not the Big Three's." I felt like she was going to take a swing at me, the way her entire body tensed and focused all that energy in one finger. The back of my brain itched, the feeling that I had seen this woman before.

And, of course, I had: there had been plenty of people who got in my face and wanted me to start fights with them. Good thing I was nice and drunk and not in the mood to take any shit from her, especially since I was on Tonggow's business. I wasn't about to let her screw things up for me. "You still want to go Sou's Reach? I'll call you a tuk-tuk, have you delivered in twenty minutes. Just let me get you signed up with the Union so you're protected."

"Like you protected us last night?" said One-Eye. "I can't *wait* to see how you'll do against an actual mob."

"Last night was a mistake," I said, "and I'm sorry it happened. I should have been more careful. It won't happen again."

"Damn right," said One-Eye, waving off a bottle of water from Mimi. She cracked open a decanter and poured a finger into one of Tonggow's cut crystal glasses, downing the rum in one gulp. "You know when I last had a drink? The night I got fired from my first job at WalWa."

Aha. An opening. "How?"

"Well, you can't drink when you're shipbound, so–"

"No, I mean, how'd you get fired?" I pointed to her Indenture tattoo. "Even if you kill someone, HR wouldn't give you the boot – they'd just counsel you to death."

One-Eye made a face as she poured another finger. "I had this boss," she said. "Always talked about how it was important to do the work, to look out for the people you're supposed to mentor." She spat on the ground. "Backstabbing psycho, she set me up to fail every damn time. Never gave me what I needed, talked shit about me while she smiled to my face. She got me fired, said I wasn't Big Three material."

"What was the job?"

"Doesn't matter," said One-Eye, her face softening just the tiniest bit, and I wondered again what had happened to make this woman so hard. "It didn't work out, and I became an engineer. I got to fix things. That was enough. For a while."

One-Eye didn't strike me as the type who needed a comforting arm around her shoulder, so I just passed her a bottle of aspirin. "Preventative," I said. "The hangover's going to be brutal."

I thought about having the driver take us around the back, but I figured the hell with it. Everyone wanted to think I was some rising star? Fine. I'd show them what that looked like. We stopped in front of Big Lily's and piled out, the driver's face not even twitching as Banks retched on the sidewalk.

"Are we drinking more?" asked Madolyn as I shepherded the Breaches to a table on the lanai.

"No, just eating," I said, "I think you're all due for something more substantial than bar snacks."

"I'd love some cake," said Gricelda as she slumped into her sister.

"I think we can manage that," I said as the waiters brought over trays of steaming purple kumara cakes, roasted squid, and plates of kimchi and other pickles. The Breaches tucked in without hesitating.

I picked at a bowl of chapchae as the Breaches revived. "So, have you guys given thought to signing up?"

"I'm in," said Gricelda, her face stained purple.

"Me, too," said Madolyn, flicking at a bleached spot on the front of her shirt.

Mimi just nodded.

I turned to One-Eye, who said, "You still haven't convinced me, but if everyone else is going, I guess I will, too."

"Close enough," I said, making a note to transfer her ass to Steelcase as soon as possible. "How about you, counselor?"

Banks's mouth was full, but he nodded as he swigged down a cup of coconut water. "I just hope I can manage," he said, wiping his mouth. "Things move faster than your legal code can keep up."

"We usually like it that way," I said. "Helps us fuck with

the Big Three during Contract time. Especially when we upcharge them for hookers."

Banks shook his head. "God, it really is a nonstop orgy of crime and degeneracy."

"Is the Big Three still saying that about us?" I poured myself a cup of coconut water and took a sip to clear the cotton taste from my mouth. "We keep sending their PR departments requests for corrections, but they never listen."

"Do you expect them to?"

"No, but I like frustrating the crap out of them," I said. "The dumbest people I knew in B-school all got shuffled into PR, and they were the ones who always gave me the most grief during my all-too-brief career."

"What, you mean you weren't always a parasite on the Body Corporate?" said Banks.

"I'll have you know, counselor, that before I Breached I had worked my way to a Class Three pay scale with four letters of commendation, including one from the Board. On paper."

"Signed in blood?"

"No, crushed baby seals," I said. "Looks prettier."

"So what happened?" he said. "It sounds like you could've written your own ticket. What made you give it up?"

For a brief moment, I wanted to tell Banks about the real reason I kept the bottle of Old Windswept, about the candle and the single finger at six o'clock. The fact that his eyes were so damn sincere would have made it easy: I could just open my mouth and it would all spill out, like all the bilge from a salvage.

But then there was a shrill whistle blast from outside, sharp and loud enough to cut through the street noise and the murmur inside Big Lily's. "What's that?" said Banks.

"Not our problem," I said, turning back to my kumara cakes. Six o'clock couldn't get here fast enough.

A bumblecar raced by, lights flashing and sirens screeching their horrible two-note song. A second bumblecar, then a third tore past. "Are you sure?" said Banks. "It sounds like–"

"It sounds like a Thursday night riot at the pitch," I said, walking to the door. "St Seryn FC is playing a grudge match against the Freeborn All-Stars, and sometimes the crowds get started before the game, and–"

You need to get here right now, came the text, loud and clear like someone had written it with thirty-meter-high letters of flame. I had to blink away the afterimages just to focus on the message header. It had come from Soni.

Where is here? I replied, and got sent a picture. It was a shot of the Emerald Masjid against the late afternoon sky, though, as I followed the green spires to the ground, I saw that the actual subject was a pile of browned rags hanging over a set of rusting pipes. It took me a moment to realize that I was looking at the north end of the sewage plant, right off Courtland Lane, and that the pile of rags was actually a stack of bodies laid out on the tops of the testing lines, like someone had set out a bunch of gutted fish to dry in the sun.

I fought back the temptation to say I had nothing to do with it, until I remembered that I was still supposed to be looking out for this Ward, even the parts of it that tried to kill me. *Be right there*, I replied, then stood up. "I'll be right back," I said. "Local business."

"Where are you going?" asked Banks.

"And is there more rum there?" asked Madolyn.

"You don't need to worry about that, and no, there is no

rum there," I said, getting up.

Banks touched my elbow and said, "If it has to do with the police, I'd like to help."

"And I'd like you to get your ass signed onto the Union books before you go wandering again," I said. "Something bad is happening, and either here or the Hall are the safest places for you."

"You said I'd be safe in Steelcase," said Banks.

I held up my hands, trying to shush him, but One-Eye gave me a wary look, and Mimi's face lit up with alarm. "Look," I said, "you'll be fine here, especially since I've got an open tab. As for you" – I pointed at Banks – "if you can keep your mouth shut, you can come along."

He put a hand over his grinning mouth and got up.

It was a short downhill walk to the plant, and the smell of ancient farts and sewer slime got stronger as we got closer. It was never so overpowering that it kept people from living in the lower-rent homes nearby, but there was never any way to get away from it, either. It was a constant reminder, the smell, that there were some things people couldn't get away from. We couldn't get away from work, we couldn't get away from hunger, and, despite all of the technological advances of the past twenty-five hundred years, we couldn't get away from excrement.

The police had set three-meter-high screens around the crime scene, and a crowd hovered at the edge of the cordon, their faces washed yellow in the bumblecars' flashing lights. I left Banks at the screens, and there were the bodies, beaten to a pulp and floppy as puppets. I'd seen plenty of people killed in industrial accidents or bar fights gone wrong, but this was different. The metal tang of the blood made my head spin. Soni stood nearby as some cops dabbed at blood drops on the ground. "Who are they?" I asked her.

Soni sighed and shook her head. "Jordan Blanton, Thor Becker, Remy Galletain... all locals."

My guts turned to ice. I felt my bladder drop into my boots. Soni kept talking, but I didn't hear anything as I pinged the corpses' pais to confirm what she'd said. All those bodies, they had been people who had all been in the office last night, all of them had threatened me, and they had likely badmouthed me to anyone who would listen. I knew I should stay and explain to Soni, especially now that I had Banks with me, but I just turned and ran, knocking down the screens as I went. I might have heard people gasping and cops shouting, but I was gone before it could register.

I ran through the streets and alleys, knowing Soni could track me but not caring. I ran until the streets got dark and I'd run out of steam. I looked up, panting, and saw that I was back on Murdoch, outside the shitty bar with the cardboard sign. DRINK, it said, and I thought, yes, I should, because it was probably after six, and I might as well give in. Let the deal with Tonggow fall through, let Soni arrest me, let me just rot away where I wouldn't have to deal with the Union or dead bodies or anything. That would be perfect.

And then the back of my right eye spiked with pain, enough to make me double over. I grabbed my head, looking around to see what was happening, when I saw Jilly and Banks ride up in the tuk-tuk, Bloombeck following behind on a cargo bike. Of course. Why not?

"Jilly thought you might be here," said Banks. "You OK?"

"Peachy," I said, wiping sweat from my brow. "Why is *he* here?"

"He found us," said Banks. "Said he had something to tell you."

"And you believed him?" I looked at Bloombeck. "What the hell do you want?"

"I am here to save the day, Padma!" cried Bloombeck, kicking the bike's stand into place.

I massaged my temple and looked at Banks. "What time is it?"

"Ten after six."

Dammit. "OK." I straightened up. "Someone is buying me a drink. Now."

SIXTEEN

The bar had gotten even worse. The mustard gas smell clung to the walls, and streaks of soot lined the barback. Jilly hugged herself and stuck close to Banks as we slid into a booth. I wanted to try and reassure her, but then Bloombeck shoveled his way next to me, his stench making my eyes water. "Fuck *me*, Bloomie. Did you go swimming in a cesspool?"

Bloombeck patted his stomach, and his sodden coverall made an unsettling splashing sound. "I been undercover, trying to figure out who framed you, just like you'd want me to, *partner*."

The way he said that last word put a new layer of nausea on top of the current pile already roiling in my stomach. "The hell are you talking about? And get downwind of me, will you?"

"But, Padma, I got to tell you–"

"You can tell me from two meters away, where your stink won't crowd me," I said, shoving him away from me. His coverall felt like cold oatmeal. "God, where have you been? The sewer lines?"

"Best way to find out what's going on," said Bloombeck, and I looked at the gunk on my hand, then wiped it on my pants leg. I made a mental note to follow up later with a tetanus mojito.

Bloombeck said, "So, I heard about what happened with Saarien, and I put two and four together, and–"

"Stop there," I said. "First of all, I had nothing to do with Saarien. Second of all, you and I are *not* partners in any way. Third, goodbye." I stood up.

"But this will help me pay off my debt to you!"

"You turning your body into a fertilizer log would pay off your debt, because you're worth more that way," I said. "Go pester someone else."

"No," said Bloombeck.

I actually stopped. "Well, that's a new one," I said. "All these years, chasing your ample ass around Brushhead for back dues and owed favors, I've never known you to pass up passing the buck. What gives?"

Bloombeck wiped the top layer of muck off his cheek. "I want to make good on what I owe you, that's all."

"Bull's balls. You're working something, and I should have you arrested for impersonating a con man," I said, wishing I had a bottle so I could take a pull on it.

"But I want to help you!"

"And I want to retire and have beautiful men feed me peeled grapes," I said. "Guess which is going to happen first?"

"I know who killed Saarien!" he yelled. Enough people in the bar lifted their heads that I grabbed Bloombeck by the elbow and pulled his face to mine.

"Spill it," I said. "All of it."

Bloombeck grinned and licked his lips. I tried not to

think about what he must have been tasting.

"OK," he said. "So, I'm down at my local, having a nip, and I hear about Saarien's passing. I get to thinking: why would you want to kill him? I mean, I know he's gone and taken Breaches from you and given you all kinds of grief, but to kill him? That ain't your style, Padma. You'd outdeal him, make him look stupid, do something with more finesse, you know?"

"That almost sounds logical," I said.

"I know, I know, right?" said Bloombeck. "This whole thing stinks of a frame-up, and who would want to hurt you more than Saarien?"

"I imagine that list is pretty big," said Banks. I shot him a look.

"WalWa," said Bloombeck. "Your former employer. You cost them a lot of money, and, the other day, you waltz into their office, make 'em look stupid, then lift a bunch of people out from under their noses. How could they not want you dead?"

"Because that would cause a Union backlash and a work stoppage and crash their share price," I said.

"But that's if they actually *hurt* you," said Bloombeck. "But if they hurt your reputation?" He put his hands in front of him, like he was serving me a sandwich. I thought about the rumors floating around the jail about Ghosts running around on Santee. If that were true, then we were all in new territory, the kind filled with flesh-eating landmines and laser-guided crocodiles. I heard nothing but rumors about how Ghosts operated while I was in B-school, and I had never moved high enough up the Corporate Ladder to learn what they really did. But I'd been able to piece together enough from news and water cooler scuttlebutt to know they were bad news. A single Ghost could upset an entire city, and a squad of them could wreck a planet. But were they *here*?

"This is all sounding frighteningly level-headed," I said, pushing the thought of Ghosts out of my mind. "But still insane."

"Insane enough to get into Thronehill?"

"What's Thronehill?" asked Banks.

"WalWa's Colonial HQ," I said, then turned to Bloombeck. "How in hell could you do that?"

Bloombeck smiled and nodded behind him. "The plant."

"Oh, you have got to be kidding," I said. "You didn't."

Bloombeck huffed and waved his hands over his filthy clothes. "Where do you think all this is from?"

"I figured that was your standard grooming, Bloomie."

"This is what I get for busting my hump?" Bloombeck said. "You think anyone else would be crawling around in the shit trying to find something out?"

My temples throbbed. "Jesus, is my *entire* day going to revolve around excrement? What in hell could you have possibly found in the sewers, Bloomie?"

"OK," said Bloombeck, rubbing his hands together. "I was in the sewers because they lead into the main plant for the WalWa complex. Water, air, sewage, all go through there."

"Bloomie, if you're about to tell me that you have samples of some exec's bowel movement as proof, I will beat the living hell out of you."

Bloomie sucked in a breath and blurted, "It's also where all their whole paper trail goes for disposal. All of it."

All of my anger drained away, and I turned to Banks. "I hope you're recording this, Banks, 'cause you've just witnessed something miraculous."

"What's that?"

"Vytai Bloombeck has had a good idea. No, a fucking *brilliant* one," I said. "WalWa, of all the Big Three, still insists on doing everything on paper. Every purchase order, every policy change, every presentation has a paper version. There's a palm pulp plant in Habana Vieja that does nothing but turn cane bagasse into reams and reams of paper, just to feed it all into the WalWa's bureaucracy so it can be stamped, printed, filed, then chucked in the shredders and burned."

"Burned?" said Banks. "That makes no sense."

"Well, what about the Big Three does?" I said.

Bloombeck licked his gums and grinned. "You wanna see what I found out?"

God help me, I was too excited to think about what would happen next to stop myself from nodding.

"I got Jimney – you remember Jimney? – I got him to tell me where the burn room was, and I found all kindsa goodies there."

My enthusiasm flickered. "I've already been on one wild squid chase because of Jimney."

"Yeah, but that wasn't because of the paper," said Bloombeck, digging in his pockets. He held up a handful of paper flakes. "There's tons down there. Piles of paper scraps as big as me. I couldn't fit into the maintenance hatch, but I could reach in a bit, snag a few nearby bits." He grabbed my hand and sprinkled the flakes into my palm. I shuddered from Bloombeck's slimy touch, and it only got worse when he moved the flakes around with a ragged thumbnail. "Jimney says the piles are organized by day, so I figure we go through them, find some that have *your* name on it, see?"

My excitement now died as I flicked through the flakes in my hand. One or two looked like they had bits of my name, a PAD here, a MEH there; the rest were gibberish. "I don't see how this all points the finger at WalWa," I said, closing the flakes in my fist, which I fully intended to ram right into Bloombeck's nose until Banks took hold of my wrist. He pried open my hand and scooped the paper shreds into his palm.

"This bit came down right before I got pushed out," said Bloombeck. "You put 'em together, you might get a chop, something you can use against the ones on the Public. You put this together, and who knows what you'll find?"

"Garbage," I said, looking at Banks, who was now shifting the flakes around like they were building blocks. "I'll find a big pile of garbage."

"But it's all from the bigwigs," said Bloombeck, giving me a self-satisfied smile. "Jimney says the high-level execs have their own dedicated chutes. He has to take special care to make sure they don't get clogged. That's where I found this. And that should be more than enough to hold up my end of the bargain."

"The only thing you're going to hold up is a shattered jaw," I said.

"How much more was there?" asked Banks.

"A pile as big as–"

"–as big as you, yes, yes," he said. "How much?"

Bloombeck puffed his lips and exhaled, like it was a brutal effort to remember. "About up to here." He held his hand up to his chest, reconsidered, then brought it jowl high.

"How old was the pile?" asked Banks.

"From a week ago."

"Take us."

"What?" I yelled. "Banks, no, no way in hell are we gonna—"

"Look."

Banks blinked, then stared down at his hand. He shifted the pieces around his palm, moving them like parts of a jigsaw until they fit perfectly. The resulting fragment said TRALEE, with a timestamp from two days ago.

"That's a neat trick," I said. "They teach you that in law school?"

"Kind of," he said.

"Send me that picture," I said. "I might need it to help my case." I sat back in the booth. "Jimney overheard some execs and some goons talking about the *Rose*. They knew there was trouble with the crew. They also got out to the drop site way pretty damn fast." I looked at the reassembled pieces again. "How did they know you were going to Breach?"

Banks furrowed his brows. "You don't suppose…?"

Bloombeck's eyes widened. "Ghosts!"

"No," I said. "We're still not big enough for Ghosts to hunt here. But WalWa got wind of it, and Saarien's crossed them more than I have. They wouldn't be stupid enough to write an invoice for the hit, but there might be enough circumstantial evidence to clear me."

Bloombeck nodded. "Just what I was thinking, huh? Come on!"

"Come on where?" I said, but Bloombeck had already bounded out the door. Banks, Jilly, and I followed.

In the damp glow, Bloombeck huddled over his cargo bike, a rig that brought new meaning to the word "filthy." A beat-up two-stroke engine hung onto the drivetrain like some kind of rusty parasite. A few small bags of paper flakes crammed in the front box with stacks of reeking scuba gear.

Bloombeck peeled a tattered environment suit off the pile and held it up to my body. "This should fit you," he said. "You still got a diving cert right?"

It took me a moment to realize what horrible thing he had in mind. "You're not serious," I said.

"Hey, there's a lot in there," he said. "I figured it would be better to have you decide what comes out, you know, to be more efficient."

"Jesus, this environment suit probably has rabies," I said. "Forget it. There is no way in hell I'm following you into the sewers."

"But there's so much!" said Bloombeck. "A pile of paper shreds taller than me!"

"And just as full of crap," I said.

"The paper doesn't lie!" said Bloombeck.

"Unless it's meant to," I said.

"I dunno," said Banks. "It might be worth digging for more." He had reached into the bags for paper, and blinked, then shifted the paper around again, holding up the fragments: SAARIEN CONTRACT APPROVED FOR TERMINATION.

I sighed. "Shit. Now we're going to have to follow Bloomie up the pipe."

"We?" said Banks. "I don't see my name on that receipt."

"You kept me from beating the hell out of Vytai Bloombeck, which is one of my inalienable rights," I said. "And for that, you owe me."

"Should I wait here, boss?" asked Jilly.

"No, my dear, because you're coming, too."

"Oh, shit, no," said Jilly, backing away. "I don't swim."

"And I don't do enclosed spaces," said Banks.

"Then you can find a rock and cave in my skull now," I

said, "'cause if you leave me, I'm just as dead. I need you, Banks, because you've got probably got more recent EVA experience than I do. And you, Jilly, 'cause I'll likely need your skinny ass to get into the burn room."

"No way," said Jilly. "Not if you pay me–"

"An even grand right now," I said. "No bullshit."

Jilly took a breath, and said, "Well, I guess I can learn."

"It's easy," I said, looking around the alley, "you just–"

A truck rumbled past, and, at first, I thought it was Papa Wemba, off doing another compost haul. Instead, its driver was a thick-necked man, a giant, really, like a goon out of his armor. As the truck turned the corner, the canvas in the back flipped up in the breeze, and a woman stuck her head out. The truck backfired, but I knew I heard her shout my name before she disappeared back into the truck.

It was Jordan Blanton.

I ran after the truck, but it disappeared in the traffic.

Banks jogged after me. "You OK?"

The Fear laughed and laughed. *You couldn't help her when she was alive, and you sure can't do it when she's dead.*

I walked past Banks back to Bloombeck. "Let's go before I change my mind."

Bloombeck gave me a jowly nod, then kick-started the bike to life. "I'll be at the intake filters on Mercer in ten minutes." He puttered away.

Banks wiped the sweat from his face. "You sure about this?"

"No," I said, climbing into the tuk-tuk. "But this all I got now. I don't have the time to wait for the police to follow their procedures."

Banks wrinkled his face. "Why not? We under a deadline?"

The Fear laughed and laughed. *Oh, you are so past deadlines now*, it said. *So far past.*

"In a manner of speaking," I said, tapping Jilly on the back. "Let's go, kid. Take all the shortcuts you know."

SEVENTEEN

The most important course I took in B-school was Public Facilities Treatment, an elective on the Colonial Management track. Sessions met six days a week for six hours a day starting at six AM. My other classmates all thought I was nuts, saying that no one was supposed to learn anything in B-school, that we were just supposed to make connections and form relationships and blah blah blah. I agreed with them, for the most part, but I knew that having more than a passing understanding of modern sewage control would probably look good on my CV.

I thought about this as we hunched over a manhole next to the water treatment plant. I fought the sudden urge to be as heavily armed as possible as Bloombeck hefted a crowbar; the seal cracked, and the thick reek of fermenting shit slapped me. He pointed to me and said, "You'll probably want to lock up that environment suit now."

"I should have done that when you first showed up," I said, giving the suit a once-over. It was an old-fashioned step-in job, two sealed zippers on the shoulders and a snap collar that snugged around a rubber-hooded rebreather mask. It was a little tight over my street clothes, but that was a small price to pay for keeping it away from my skin. No matter how clean Bloombeck swore it was, I was sure I'd have to get revaccinated as soon as I got home.

I pulled on the helmet and clicked it shut. The suit's simple air meter, a rainbow strip at the bottom of my field of vision, came up all green. The Univoice echoed in my ears, reminded me to double-check my seals and that failure to do so would absolve Liao Consolidated Manufacturing Concern of all blame.

As I checked out Banks's gear, he said, "I should remind you that I'm not a fan of enclosed spaces."

"Don't go talking to me about enclosed spaces, Mr I-Can't-Do-Hibernation," I said, and put his helmet over his still-protesting face. "You still remember your EVA orientation?"

Banks shrugged. "As long as something tells me when I'm running out of air, what's there to remember?"

"Not much else," I said, moving to Jilly. The smallest suit Bloombeck had was two sizes too big, and she looked even more like a kid than ever. "You ready?"

"Shouldn't I take a class or something first?" she said, waving her arms in the air. The suit bunched up around her elbows.

I pointed to the colored strip that lined the bottom of her mask. "Ignore the Univoice, and just watch this meter. If it starts to turn yellow, that means your rebreather filter is starting to fail."

"And then what?"

"Then you tap us on the shoulder and do this." I put my hands to my throat. "One of us will give you an extra line to breathe. Don't panic. You'll do fine."

"I want a raise," said Jilly.

"Don't we all," I said.

Bloombeck handed us several fifty-liter caneplas bags. "For evidence," he said, trying to give me a wink.

"This feeds into the city mains," said Bloombeck as he climbed into the manhole. "It links up with the lines for the main WalWa building. I marked off a route for us."

"How? By smearing shit on the walls?"

Bloombeck pulled a glow marker off his suit's belt. "I have *some* sense," he said with a little snarl.

"I'll believe it when I see it," I said, grabbing the marker from him and spinning him around.

"What are you doing?"

"Making a breadcrumb," I said as I drew a giant X on the across the back of Bloombeck's helmet. I made sure my filter gauge was still all green, went through the suit's checklists (safety straps, multitool, lights), and into the dark we went.

The temperature started climbing immediately. All that water rushing through those pipes, all that air pushing down from the surface, it was a wonder we didn't bake like salt ducks. The suits would help keep us from overheating, but not enough to stop us from sweating. I knew The Fear would try to make an appearance, but there was something to be said for putting oneself in danger to help with focus. That, and my curiosity about Bloombeck's discovery were enough to stay on task.

The glowing X floated in front of us, and soon we passed a series of luminous green arrows that sent us under sweating pipes and into ever-darker tunnels. "This is just like being back on the *Rose*," said Banks through his helmet speakers.

"Everything here probably came from a ship like yours," I said. "Most of this stuff was cannibalized from old hulks the Big Three dropped down the gravity well. No need to kick perfectly good equipment across the stars when there's already stuff in transit that you could write off."

There was a clang, and Banks yelped as he clutched his foot. "Yay for recycling."

I turned back to Jilly, who gave me an OK sign. Her hands only shook a little.

We stopped in front of a rusting pipe, just a little wider than Bloombeck was round. Bloombeck cracked the access port, and the stench of all of Brushhead's shit plowed into us. "This is the line I followed to the Ward mains," said Bloombeck, tying off the rope to a pipe fitting. "You keep following the arrows, and you'll get to the burn room. Make sure to wait for the tides in there; they flush the system every sixty minutes, and you don't want to get caught in that."

"You sound like you're not coming with," I said.

Bloombeck's breathing, already labored, got faster. "You don't want me slowing you down," he said, gulping down air and handing me the other end of the line.

"Maybe not," I said, grabbing him by the shoulder, "but I definitely want you to help us haul out whatever we find in there."

"But I already gone up there–"

"Then the second time will be even easier," I said, clipping the carabiner to his belt and shoving him in the pipe. He was consumed by the current of filth.

"This is bad," said Banks, eyeing the pipe.

"That's why you're going next," I said, hooking a carabiner around the pipe before locking it around his belt.

"Oh, fuck, Padma, are you kidding?"

I clipped another carabiner on the line, right behind

Banks, then hooked the next one onto Jilly. I locked the
end onto my suit. "Just remember this the next time you
make a deal without consulting me, counselor."

"OK, OK, I take it back, I owe you big time–"

"Goddamn right," I said, and pushed them both into the
pipe before following them into the abyss.

The air scrubbers on our suits were Type One, the kind
you use for cyanide mines, but the mind can overpower the
best of Big Three tech. I could swear traces of fermenting
shit wafted through, just enough to make me gag. I tried not
to think about what kinds of evil we were swimming in as
we zipped along the line.

The pipe was half full and too fast moving to get decent
footing, but we could brake a little by digging our heels into
the bottom. The soles of the exposure suits were textured
rubber mixed with ground up palm-crab shell for grip. We
passed more glowing arrows, and I wondered how hard
getting out would be. Banks and I could probably muscle
our way upstream, but we'd have to lend Jilly a hand.
Bloombeck would have to find his own way home.

We eventually found Bloombeck at a T-junction. He was
tying off another line when we skidded into view. I tried
yelling at him, but I only got static in return. He tapped the
side of his head, and a text popped up on my pai: *Voice can't
carry down here. Text only.* Then, ten seconds later: *This going
to cost you.*

I held onto an overhead fitting with one hand and gave
him the finger with the other. *I'm pretty sure we're back into
You Owing Me territory*, I texted back. *If anything, you've owed
me* ever since we first met.

How? Bloombeck replied. *I helped you out when you first
Breached. I showed you the ropes.*

You showed me where the toilets were, and then you tried to bum five yuan off me.

That was for Mrs Powazek's birthday party!

Which never happened, because you kept all the cash for yourself. I laughed. *Your first scam. How much you've grown up since then.*

This isn't a scam!

No, it's a legitimate investigation into corporate shenanigans, I replied. *They'll write songs about it, I'm sure.* I grabbed the line from his trembling fingers and cinched a tight knot around another fitting.

how much farther? pinged Banks to both of us.

50 meters, replied Bloombeck.

Banks texted back: *good. think i can hold off puking for that long.*

And what more could I possibly owe you? I texted Bloombeck, hooking another carabiner up to his harness before locking it around the new line.

Brought info about WalWa setting you up, he replied. *That was deal.*

You brought me a handful of paper flakes, I sent, tying off Banks. *You really think that's worth the same as me helping you with a land scam?*

Your going to help me then? Even though the murk, I could see his face light up.

Just get us there, I sent. I gave Jilly another glance; she just nodded, her face a little green, though it could have been her helmet's internal lights. We headed farther into the shit, twisting and turning until we started to climb up enough that there was an air gap between the effluent and the top of the pipe.

Above us was an access hatch, one that was slightly ajar.

We pushed our way up and out into a maze of spraying, hissing pipework. We cleaned ourselves in what I hoped was water, then followed Bloombeck and the trail of glowing Xs until we came to a door marked INCINERATOR. He thumped it a few times, then cracked his helmet. We followed suit.

"Is this the part when you explain how you've suddenly become fireproof?" I said.

"It's not on all the time," said Bloombeck. "Jimney told me they only fire it up every two weeks. Saves on gas."

"But this leads to the paper dump?" said Banks.

Bloombeck nodded. "We just send the kid through the feeder grate, and you'll see."

"We'll see you go first," I said. "Again."

"Fine," said Bloombeck, and he swung the door open. An avalanche of cinders spilled out, followed by a bundle of charred sticks. The air smelled like ash with hints of burned meat. Bloombeck fell backwards on his ass, then shrieked when he picked up one of the sticks and saw it was a bone. A human skull landed on top of his head; he saw it roll away, then turned to puke. I spun Jilly away, then slammed my helmet shut to block the smell, but too late.

Banks squatted down next to the skull, its toothy mouth open in one last scream. He looked at the bones, then pulled something out of the ash: a metal rectangle as long as his finger. He swiped away at the grime, and the word POTTS appeared out of the carbon. "You think he fell?" asked Banks.

"Probably," I said, aiming my lamp at the skull, "but I think anyone would after getting shot in the head."

Banks aimed his own headlamp at the single black hole right between the body's empty eyesockets. "I thought you said there were no guns here."

"In theory, there aren't," I said, undoing my helmet. "But there's always someone who tries to get around the Ban." I hunkered down next to Banks and shook my head. "Poor Jimney."

I pulled off a glove and held my fingers over the nametag; it was cool, so the body had been here for a while. "When were you down here, Bloomie?"

"I had nothing to do with this," he said, his voice thick and wet. "Jimney was alive when he pushed me out."

"Bloomie, you're capable of a lot of crap, but not a murder," I said. "Now, how long? Was the sun still up when you got out?"

He thought, then nodded.

"And were they still serving two-for-one at the Stoneways Lounge?"

He nodded without thinking.

"Three hours," I said. "We were on the way back from the bars." I blinked a few pictures, debated sending them to Soni. This far under, there probably wasn't any signal. That also meant she couldn't track me, but I'd probably have a hell of a time explaining why I'd disappeared for a bit.

Banks blinked a few pictures of his own. "You still think this was Saarien?"

"Not anymore," I said. "I think it's Ghosts."

Banks straightened up. "Here?"

"It's the only thing that fits," I said. "At first, I thought the weirdness in Steelcase was Saarien trying to scare me off, but then he and a bunch of people turn up dead." I nodded at Jimney's corpse. "This seals it for me. Ghosts are meant for sending messages, and there's no stronger message than a bullet to the head, even if it's just for a small-time stoner like Jimney." I sucked at my teeth. "I just wish I knew what it is that got their attention."

Banks *hmm*ed. "Maybe it's you."

I snorted. "You know, as much as I like to think WalWa's Board of Directors has me on some Most Wanted list, I think it's something bigger. Sending a Ghost Squad just to slap me around? If anyone would have their attention, it would've been Saarien. His headcount is... *was* a lot higher than mine. Plus, he never missed an opportunity to get on the air about the Struggle, about how the Union was going to smash our corporate overlords and liberate humanity from Indenture and servitude." I shook my head. "Too bad he was such an asshole."

I walked up to the incinerator grate and saw a space in there big enough for Jilly to snake through. "We need to see what's in there. Might help us figure out what's got WalWa so riled up."

"You're not going to send Jilly in there," said Banks.

"You're right," I said. "I should just call WalWa and tell them to come down here and investigate the body in their incinerator. Which we found by breaking into their facility. Maybe their Ghosts will come down here and invite us up for tea and biscuits."

"It was just a suggestion," said Banks.

"I'm game," said Jilly, giving the burned skeleton a wayward eye. "Just to get me away from... that."

I handed her the caneplas bags and watched her shimmy up the ladder and into the incinerator room.

The designers had been safety-minded enough to install ladder rungs out of the pit. I climbed to the top to peek into the burn room and marvel at the monument to bureaucratic waste. Waist-high drifts of paper shreds surrounded Jilly, and more flakes floated down from a dozen vents. I held out a hand and caught the remnants of some WalWa report, no two shreds alike.

The floor was tilted toward the grate – not so steep that Jilly was in danger of falling back in, but just enough for her to work. She hustled back and forth, bringing us flakes until Banks declared a pile worth scooping up. She stuffed as much as possible into a bag, then flipped it back to us.

"This is a gold mine," said Banks as he whipped open one of the fifty-liter bags. "Evidence reconstruction always fascinated me in law school. Peeling bits off dead hard drives, finding data veins in dried-out organic DBs – and the paper, *man*. Even when paper shreds are burned, you can pick up all sorts of ink and pen impressions – stuff that's still legible."

"So, what, you're going to sift through all of these and do that little trick with your pai?"

"Sure," he said, "This kind of thing is relaxing."

I shook my head as I caught another bag. "What makes you think you're going to find anything good?" I said.

Banks picked up two handfuls of paper, blinked, then dumped them on the ground. He went through the pile for a minute, then showed me three fragments, all with WalWa executive chops next to Evanrute Saarien's name.

"So WalWa *was* gunning for Saarien?" I said.

Banks shrugged. "We'd have to go through a whole lot more to find out for sure."

"Then let's grab all we can," I said. "I can hand all this over to Soni, and maybe it'll be enough to clear me."

Jilly jammed the executive pile into six bags and stuffed them down the chute. Jimney's skull was still there, smiling away, and I made a note to add it to my statement as soon as we were safe in Brushhead. Soni would be pissed about my little excursion, but, technically, she didn't say anything about underground trips violating my bail bond. I clipped up to the line and thought about how all this would be worth it in a few months' time, right after the first batches of my rum sat nestled in their racks, hidden away from prying eyes and greedy hands. I would banish The Fear for the rest of my life, and then spend my days selling Old Windswept all over Santee, hell, all over Occupied Space. It was a sweet thought: all this work paying off faster than my Indenture ever could have, and with better food, booze, and sex to boot. I could feel the breeze wafting through my Chino Cove lanai already, the quick air of the sea rushing past my face–

–or was that someone shooting at us again?

A pipe burst with a clang as a dozen blasts drove me to the deck. I stole a peek above me, only to duck as I spotted four figures in environment suits aiming honest-to-Buddha submachine guns. Bullets danced off the ductwork, clanging around until they came to a halt. I rolled to the open sewage pipe.

Banks, Jilly, and Bloombeck joined me. "The price just went up!" yelled Bloombeck, clipping himself to the line. "You're buying me *two* cane farms!"

"Then you can kiss my ass twice," I said, snapping a carabiner through my belt. The shots rang off the pipe, a few actually piercing the rusting metal. "You got the bags?"

"Are you kidding?" yelled Banks. I looked through the access hatch: our piles of evidence still sat by the door to the incinerator. "Leave 'em !"

"No!" I yelled back. "I have gone through too much bullshit today only to get stopped because someone wants me dead!" I unclipped from the line, fought my way over Banks and Jilly, and rolled back out of the pipe.

Wave after wave of bullets zinged past me as I crawled to the bags. The door was completely exposed, and the shooters knew it: a small forest of holes grew right where I had to go.

I wondered what the chances were of them scoring a lethal hit. Maybe they'd only pierce a leg, and I'd be able to drag myself through the sewers and home before sepsis sank in. I crouched, ready to sprint, when a bullet clanged into the bulkhead I was cowering behind.

Then there was a muffled roar, and the thud of hobnailed boots. I looked behind and saw a squad of armored WalWa goons kick their way through the grate and leap down the incinerator shaft. One of them got through the door before a bullet to the chest knocked him off his feet. The rest of the goons answered with cries of "Freeze!" and a volley of riot foam. The rounds splatted against the piping, turning into frothy stalactites. It was enough to spook the shooters, who ducked behind a junction box and popped the muzzles of their guns over the top to fire blind.

I grabbed the bags of paper scraps and scrawled giant Xs on them with the glow marker, figuring if we lost hold of the things in the line, at least we'd see where they were going. "Get these back to the Hall!" I yelled to Banks and Jilly as I threw the bags at them.

"What about you?"

A spurt of foam hit my arm, and I flicked it away before it could expand and harden. "I'll get home somehow! Just get this out of here!"

There was a fresh volley of bullets, enough to drive the goons back to the burn room. The shooters leaped out of their hideyholes and bolted for the other side of the room toward an open access port. "Oy!" I yelled, my helmet's speakers crackling, "assholes!"

One of the shooters turned, and my headlamp light bounced off his helmet. But then he turned his body so the glare vanished, and I could have sworn the shooter wore an eyepatch. The shooter looked at me, and I saw a criss-cross of angry scars and faded ink on his – no, *her* face.

Holy crap: it was One-Eye.

I roared and threw the glow marker, since it was the only thing I had available. It bounced off her shoulder but left a spatter of ink. She fired another volley, then leaped into the access port.

I leaped over the pipes, dodging a fresh round of foam shots. As I crawled toward the access port One-Eye had used, I saw Banks fighting his way toward me. "Get back to the Hall!" I yelled.

"And go with Bloombeck? No way," he said, hunkering down next to me.

"I can take care of myself, thanks," I said.

Jilly hunched behind Banks, bags strapped to her belt. "I would like to go home, now!"

"Me, too," I said, grabbing the front of her suit and clipping her to the line around my belt.

"But what about the tide?" yelled Banks. "Bloombeck said the currents get too strong, and–"

Riot foam crackled overhead, and he ducked. I clacked a carabiner around Banks, then grabbed them both by their arms and hauled them in. The current grabbed us, and we hurled into the darkness.

EIGHTEEN

One-Eye had a good minute-and-a-half head start on us, but I had the benefit of being pissed off. I did my best breaststroke, always keeping the spatter from the glow marker in sight. Bloombeck must have sprung for a high-visibility job, because it was the only way that thing could have shed any light in the pitch black of the pipes. I didn't have time to see what kind of line we'd jumped into, but the visibility was good enough for me to guess we were in a water main. At least the fluid wasn't as chunky as it had been on the way in.

this is stupid, Banks texted me.

Who said I should have gone with Bloombeck in the first place? I replied.

damn

The toxic-piss glow of the paint spatter began to grow larger; it took me a second to realize that One-Eye had stopped and that we were gaining on her. I dug the heels of my gloves and boots into the walls; the crushed palm-crab shells had enough grip to slow us down. Banks bumped into me, and I told him to follow suit.

why stopping?

I don't want her to know we're here, I replied.

There was a muffled bang, then something zinged past my face.

think she knows.

Fuck it, I thought, and let go. A few more shots flew past, but I kept my belly low enough to the pipe's bottom to dodge them. That didn't keep me from getting a crack on my back from the butt of One-Eye's submachine gun; even with the rebreather gear to soften the blow, it still hurt like hell. One-Eye jabbed again, but I spun my feet up and gave her a kick to the shins. Even with the rush of water, I could hear her howl. I managed another kick, this one up and into her chest, before she swung the business end of the gun into my face.

I bit the switch for my headlamp, and the sudden burst of light drove her back, but not so far that her boot couldn't make contact with my chin. It was just a glancing blow, but it was enough to double me over. One-Eye brought the gun to my face, but all she got was the *click-click* from the empty magazine. She took another swing at me, but I was ready this time and launched off the bottom of the pipe and wrapped my arms around her midsection. We floated free, the current strong enough to bounce us around the inside of the pipe as we whaled away at each other.

I reached for her back, trying to unhook any hoses or lines, but her suit was self-contained. Mine, of course, wasn't, so when she yanked the main feeder line for my rebreather out of its socket, I had no choice but to kick free and fix my air. I hadn't done this kind of thing since EVA training back in B-school, but I kept my panic down, got the line back in place, and saw that my air supply was...

"Warning," said the Univoice inside my helmet. "CO_2

concentration at eight hundred parts per million." I looked at the strip on the bottom of my mask; it was hovering between yellow and red.

That couldn't have been right. I tapped the glass, then remembered that the strip wasn't a gauge with a needle. I dug my hands and feet into the pipe, and Banks bumped into me a few seconds later.

think air going bad, he texted, then sent me a picture of the inside of his mask. His strip looked like mine.

I spun Banks around and shone my headlamp on his rebreather pack. Everything looked fine: the lines were good, the connections were solid, all the ports worked, the filtration packs were in place and fine... except for one corner of a label flipping in the water. I managed to get a gloved finger underneath it to peel it away. Underneath was the original label with an expiration date from twenty years before I was born.

"Uh-oh," I said, loud enough for Banks to turn and give me a stricken look.

problem?

Jilly's gear was in slightly better shape; her filter had only expired last year. I gave her a pat and a nod. *A bit. We need to leave.*

how long we got? texted Banks.

Not enough, I replied, looking downstream at the faint yellow blob from the glow marker. *Follow her.*

no time for revenge

No, you dummy, she must know a way out.

she?

Just go! I kicked us into the current, keeping one eye on the glow stain and the other on the filter gauge, now diving into shades of orange.

My hands bumped into the sides of the pipe. We had gone so far that the mains had trunked off into smaller local lines. There was still enough room to swim, but I could feel the ribs of the pipes every time I took a stroke, my gloves bumping off the caneplas with hollow *thunk*s. I had no idea how far we'd gone, but the fact that there was no light ahead meant we were nowhere near an exit. It also meant there was nowhere for One-Eye to go. She was close enough that I could see her outline lit up by the ink. I wasn't sure if I could throttle her, but I was ready to give it a shot.

The glow stain stopped and hovered. I had no idea if One-Eye was lost or catching her breath, and I wasn't about to stop and ask her. I grabbed the bottom of the pipe, crouched and kicked off as hard as I could, which is why it hurt like hell when my head smashed into the grate.

It hurt even more when Banks and Jilly piled into me moments later.

I bit on my headlamp, and One-Eye looked back from the other side of the grate. We stared at each other, and then she knocked on the metal bars and shrugged before kicking away.

"No," I said, then banged on the grate. "NO!"

save air, texted Banks. *need to backtrack.*

I banged the grate again and watched One-Eye disappear into the murk.

padma we need to go NOW

All right, I replied. *Back up.*

trying

Try faster.

We shifted back a meter, but the current was so strong that we sailed downstream the moment we let go of the ribs of the pipes. *This is going to take forever.*

don't have that, texted Banks, and he sent me a picture of the inside of his mask. The strip was now touching red.

I pushed upstream, lost my grip and slammed back into the grate. My mouth clamped around the controls for my headlamp, cranking up the lamp's intensity, and I realized just how cramped it was. So tight, all the ribs covered with slime and streaks of black mold and the water rushing past, and this horrible noise filling my helmet, like someone had cracked open the seal and let all the water in Santee City pour in to drown me. The air, now foul with carbon dioxide, burned my nose, my eyes, my throat, and I felt so tired. I could hear The Fear roaring in approval, and I just didn't care anymore. I sagged, and the last thing I saw before I closed my eyes was the meter diving deep into the red. I heard the Univoice utter some kind of warning before I slipped out–

–and then someone jabbed me in the ass so hard I thought I'd been shot. *PADMA* came one text in the biggest type available, my name hovering in front of my eyes like a message from on high.

I looked at Banks and Jilly, then took a breath. The air tasted less evil. I looked down towards my chin and saw a line snaking away from the front of my helmet toward Jilly's. She gave me a thumbs up, and I grabbed her shoulder. Good girl.

you ok? Banks texted.

I took another measured breath, then answered, *How's your meter?*

bad

The three of us combined our hoses, slurping a little clean air from Jilly's system. I tapped on the grate again; it was locked in place, and the lock had been spotwelded.

One-Eye had done a marvelous job trapping us. I wondered what kind of engineer she'd been. I wondered if anyone would find our bodies and bother to avenge us.

Ideas?

swim back?

Not enough air. Kick out grate?

Banks gave it a go, then shook his head. Then he texted *you hear that?*

What?

getting louder

I turned as best I could. There was a definite increase in the sound, but I couldn't tell if it was because our hearing was going, along with our air, or if the water was moving faster. More and more particles floated past us, and then the current got strong enough to knock us back into the grate.

the tide, texted Banks, and a crushing wave smashed into us, shoving Banks into me and me into the grate with enough force to squeeze the air from my lungs. The pressure kept growing, and I was pretty sure I was about to pass out (and pretty pissed that this was how it would end), when there came a squealing sound, like metal giving way, and I saw One-Eye had missed welding one bar in place. It scraped as the pressure from the oncoming tide pushed us back, and I twisted around and kicked as hard as I could. Banks and Jilly saw what I was doing and joined in, all three of us driving our boots into the grate until it tore away.

We sailed through the murky water like corks over a waterfall. I tried to get a grip on the pipe ribs, but the current moved too fast. Jilly flew away from me, the hose snapping loose, leaving me with another helmet full of foul air. The Fear came roaring back, but, no, I was not going to give in. If I was going to die, goddammit, I was going to do it with my eyes wide open, even though, God, it would have felt so nice just to fall asleep…

And then I flew. I wasn't hallucinating: I sailed through the air, through space, surrounded by a billion stars against the purple-black sky, something I hadn't seen since the last time I went up the cable, a feeling so free and wonderful and–

I smashed into the ground. Banks and Jilly smashed on top of me. And about a billion liters of water smashed us and swept us away.

I fought to get upright, pushing against what felt like pudding until I was on my feet. Then I wrestled with the collar on my helmet until it clacked open. The rotten air rushed out, replaced with a thick funk of green and jungle rot. I had never smelled anything better in my entire life. As I caught my breath, I saw a wall of swaying shadows move toward us, but then my eyes adjusted and I saw they were cane leaves moving in the wind. We were in an irrigation ditch for a cane field, somewhere in the middle of the kampong. Twenty meters upstream and three meters above, an outflow pipe gushed from a dirt mound, our exit route from Thronehill.

I found Banks in the mess, on his ass, up to his waist in muddy water, his helmet dangling down his back, the hood still caught in his suit. "God, I feel like the whole world just farted on me," he said.

"Poetic," I said, helping him to his feet. "You OK?"

"Other than the world-fart thing, yeah," he said, looking around. "You know where we are?"

"Hell, yeah," said Jilly, getting to her feet. "This is home."

I cracked a cane shoot and sniffed the inside; it was sweet and oily, with a charcoal tang beneath. "Industrial," I said, looking up at the lights of Thronehill and Santee City proper twinkling on opposite sides of the horizon. Above us was a smear of stars and the faint blinking warning lights on the lifter's tender rings. "Which means we're a good hike from Brushhead."

I blinked up a clock: eight-fifteen. *Three days in a row*, chuckled The Fear. My vision swam, and I sank to the ground.

"You OK?" said Banks, helping me up.

"Just dizzy," I said. "All this fresh air."

"You think we should call anyone?" said Banks.

"Nah, I got this," said Jilly. "We can hoof it to my parents' place, catch a ride into town."

"You sure they're going to let you go back?" I said, my head spinning.

Jilly puffed out her chest. "Hey, I'm Union now. They don't have a say."

I chuckled and nodded. "Good answer."

"But shouldn't we still call?" said Banks. "I mean, we're being chased by people with guns."

I shook my head. "We're out of range."

"Of what?"

"Everything," I said. "Most of the cane farmers out here are Freeborn, so they don't have pais, which means they don't want data towers in the middle of their land."

"Seriously?"

"Oh yeah," I said. "The Union and the Co-Op have been trying to get some out here for years, but no go. 'We'll communicate the way God intended us to,' they'll say, 'in person.'"

Banks looked at Jilly. "No wonder you left."

"It wasn't *that* bad," she said. "I'm just sick of cane."

We shed the suits and tucked them and the bags of paper shreds in the cane. I made sure to pull out one of long-expired filter cartridges for evidence to be used against Bloombeck for future lawsuits and ass-kickings. "I should have known better," I said, putting the cartridge into the cargo pocket on my thigh. "Whenever Bloombeck gets any kind of gear, it's going to be so third-rate it's not worth using. The man lived to peck through garbage and resell it. When he lived downstairs from me, he sold me a toaster that would catch fire after every fifth slice of bread."

"How do you know?" said Banks.

"What do you mean?" I said, pushing my way into the cane. "I counted. This was back when I'd first Breached, and–"

"No, I mean how do you know he didn't do this on purpose?"

I looked at Banks; his face was stone still, all traces of the Grin gone. I couldn't help but laugh. "Are you serious? Bloombeck, trying to off me? What good would that do him?"

Banks shrugged. "You don't think he'd find some kind of angle to–"

"Look," I said, putting a hand on Banks's sunken chest. "Vytai Bloombeck is a conniving sack of crap with the IQ of a sponge, but he is *not* the kind to commit murder. He doesn't have it in him. He runs whenever there's a whiff of violence. Christ, he can't even thumb wrestle without wetting himself." We walked on. "That one-eyed bitch, on the other hand..."

"What one-eyed bitch?"

"The one who was shooting at us," I said, then told him about what I saw in the burn room and in the sewer.

He crinkled his brows and said, "I didn't see *any* eyes."

"*I* did," I said. "Your pal, Ellie, was the one shooting at us."

Banks looked at me, then laughed so hard his eyes watered. "That's good, Padma. I was afraid the air had gotten to your brain."

"Every time something bad has happened to me in the last few days, she's been involved," I said. "You guys get pinched by Saarien? She leads the march to his bus."

"That's because he had large, angry men with him."

"When the WalWa goons caught that bus, she was there."

"As a prisoner, with the rest of us."

"When Jordan and her buddies showed up, she was the one who beat the crap out of them."

Banks nodded. "OK, I'll give you that."

"Then you'll give me what happened at Steelcase, too," I said. "She's a ship's engineer, and part of engineering is understanding control layouts. She could have piloted that crane."

"*And* shot at us at the same time?" said Banks. "*And* piloted the other cranes that were chasing us?"

"Maybe she got some local talent to help her out. There were a bunch of people in the burn room, and she was one of them," I said. "I saw her face. One eye. Lots of scars. She *shot* at us. And she had help."

"Whose?" said Banks. "WalWa's?"

I nodded. "She's a Ghost, Banks. Your friend is a WalWa Ghost."

Banks shook his head. "Look, Ellie may get a little aggro, but there's no way she could be a Ghost. I've been with her for four years."

"But where was she before she came aboard?" I said.

Banks sighed. "As your attorney, I advise you to drop this before I have to get you committed."

"Won't work here," I said. "All the shrinks are already crazy."

"Ellie is not a Ghost."

"Then how else do you explain how an armed assault team appeared out of nowhere?"

"I know this has been a really long, nasty day, but I give you my word that you did not see Ellie shooting at us."

I stared at him, his face unwavering, and then I felt a tickle at the back of my head. What if he was right? *Of course he is*, hissed The Fear, raking its claws across my skull. "You don't believe me? Then we'll see what Soni and the police have to say when I get back within broadcast range. This all just got bigger and uglier, and if you want to be a part of the Union, you're going to have to get behind us."

"Because of your say-so?"

"Goddamn right." I turned and pushed through the cane.

It was tough going through the tightly packed stalks, and it was that much worse when I felt something stick to my hands and face. At first, I thought it was actual sugar from broken shoots, but then I looked at my hands and saw they were coated in sticky, black residue. "What the hell is this?"

Jilly looked at my hands and spat. "This field's done. Black stripe."

"The fungus?" I said. "Can't they just treat it?"

Jilly shook her head. "Not this kind. It showed up earlier this year, and it's bad. Got my folks, my neighbors. Fungicides can't stop it, and no one's sure what the vector is."

I wiped my hands on my clothes, only to see they were already coated with the black stripe. "Has it gotten into the heirloom yet?"

Jilly shrugged. "To a fungus, cane's cane."

The Fear laughed. *You and your friends in the Co-Op, you've been so worried about your precious rum, you never thought about what else was happening in the kampong. How many hectares look like this? How many that make your six o'clock tipple? It's been under your nose the whole time, and you've been too self-involved to notice.*

I stopped and looked back to where we'd come from. Jilly had hung on to two bags of shreds, and Banks was sure there would be enough in there to keep the police from thinking I'd murdered Saarien. The smart thing to do would be to pick them up, walk back toward Thronehill and its connectivity and wait for Soni to pick me up. I could clear my name, then get back to dealing with Ghosts and rotting cane and skunked rum...

I looked at the withering cane, the stalks streaked with black, like someone had sprayed the field with coal dust. I'd been in the kampong plenty of times, seen the occasional blighted fields from a rust or a smut or any of the other nasty fungal infections that hit cane. It was never as bad as this. And what if it didn't stop with the rum? What if the same skunk weirdness was happening with all the industrial molasses we were sending up the cable? How many people would lose their shirts if their farms were ruined? Hell, what if this jumped to actual food? I could tell Soni later about WalWa's possible nefarious deeds; first, I had to see what was happening to the cane. I followed Jilly and Banks deeper into the kampong.

After another hour of walking, we got to a break in the field. A dirt path ran off into darkness to the north, and toward a cluster of lights to the south. As we approached, I saw it was a transfer station, though it was deserted.

The four dilapidated warehouses were dark, and solar-cell-topped light poles dotted a gravel yard that glowed orange under their lamps. The whole place looked like a resort hotel that had fallen on hard times. Without a pai connection, I had no way to tell who owned the station or what plantations used it; we would just have to wait until morning to catch a ride.

"You think it's safe?" said Banks as we huddled in the cane.

"I can do the talking for us," said Jilly.

We jogged to the darkened warehouses. Bundles of cane were stacked two meters high outside each of them, and, as I peeked through windows, I saw the insides were packed to the rafters. "This is weird, though," I said as we walked around the warehouses, trying doors. "Everything gets planted on the same cycles, and it's not harvest time for a few weeks. Why are they leaving this lying around?"

"To age?" said Banks. "That's just a guess."

"And a bad one," said Jilly. "Even with industrial stuff, the juice starts to go bad if it's exposed for too long. Even gengineers can't fight oxidation and win."

"So what's it doing here?"

"Who knows?" I pulled on the last door. Its hinges popped out of the rotting chipwood frame, and I stepped back as the door thudded to the ground. "But I don't think anyone will care if we watch it for the night."

Jilly and Banks slipped inside, Banks pulling the door back into the frame behind him as I looked around. Cord after cord of cut cane lay before us, all of it oozing sugar onto the dusty ground. The whole room was silent. "This place should be full of bugs and rats," Jilly said. "Leaving this much cane around is like opening a buffet for vermin."

"Even for industrial cane?"

"Sugar's sugar if you're starving," I said, feeling my stomach growl. I gave the cane a sniff. It had the same oil-and-charcoal scent as the industrial varieties, but with something extra, like it was laced with chili powder and plastic. "Though I still have no idea what this is, and I've smelled or tasted every kind of cane that grows here."

Jilly gave a stalk a lick, then made a face like she'd tasted a lemon. "Ugh, that's horrible."

"Maybe someone's made a new kind," said Banks.

"I think you're right," I said, doing some quick calculations in my head. "There has to be thirty thousand hectares of cane in this warehouse alone. If all of this is from the same plantation, they're looking at serious jail time."

"For breeding cane?"

"Didn't you get to that part in the law books?" I said. "Anyone tries to make a new variety, they have to get it checked and registered to make sure it doesn't interfere with the current crops."

"I think I went for breakfast before I got to that part," said Banks.

"Too bad," I said, "'cause you would've gotten to the bit about how no one screws with this planet's cash crop without jumping through all sorts of hoops. The money we get from cane keeps everyone fed. And if that went away, there would be blood in the streets."

"Really?" said Banks. "Even with all the urban farming?"

"No one's going to starve, but there's no way anyone could afford Big Three goods," I said. "This planet just doesn't have the population to sustain that kind of high tech."

We found tarps and folded them into makeshift tatami.

Jilly conked out immediately. "You still have that flask?" asked Banks after he'd sat down.

I felt in my pockets, my fingers touching the cool coral steel container. I blinked up the time: ten on the nose. Eighteen hours to go. I wondered if a bit wouldn't hurt, just enough to get me over until tomorrow, but I remembered Dr Ropata's admonition to do the *whole* ritual, or nothing at all. He'd also said not to let more than two days go by without...

"Hey!" said Banks. "You still have it or what? I'm getting a little chilly."

I shivered. "It won't help," I said. "Really, we shouldn't have anything until we're back home."

"Is that why you've got a death grip on that flask?" said Banks, nodding to my pocket.

I looked down and saw my knuckles bulging through the fabric of my pants, felt the muscles in my fingers knotting themselves up. I let go of the flask and shook out my hand. "It's not what you think."

"I think there's something you're not telling me."

"I *know* there's a *lot* I'm not telling you," I said, sitting down, my back to him. "Go to sleep, Banks. We have a weird day ahead of us."

It was quiet for a few minutes. Then Banks said, "You never told us why you Breached."

"Sleep," I said.

More silence. Through the window, I watched clouds obscure the moon. One of the lamps blinked out, its battery out of charge. "It's just," said Banks, "I still don't understand *why* you'd leave that gig in Colonial Management. I mean, the rest of us, we all got seriously screwed, but you?"

"Good night, Banks."

"You know, I worked for a pair of certifiable psychotics," said Banks. In the dim light, I could see him sit up, his legs crossed in front of him. He looked at the ground. "You have to be a bit mad to work in Legal for WalWa or any of the Big Three, but these two? They took joy in holding up big, important things that would have made people's lives better. LiaoCon was testing a new anticancer treatment? They'd file injunctions because it might have violated some ancient WalWa patent. MacDonald Heavy has a new method for processing ricewheat that increases nutrition? Can't have that, because it would interfere with WalWa's Charitable Calorie Bank. And don't get me started on the countersuits they filed when some poor consumer complained about the way their WalWa-brand toaster oven was actually a repackaged antipersonnel mine."

I sighed and turned toward him. "I thought you did real estate."

"I did everything," said Banks. "I got bounced around from one group to the other, just so I could soak up the law by osmosis, I guess."

"So, what, you got sick of doing their dirty work?"

"No," said Banks, "I got sick of the pointlessness. I didn't have any illusions about helping people when I became a lawyer, but I didn't think the work would be so stupid. It did nothing to help WalWa's bottom line, it did nothing to help our department because we wound up creating headaches for other parts of the company that would come back to haunt us. Hell, they even got different parts of WalWa to sue each other, just to cover up their own messes."

"Then why didn't you leave?" I said. "Transfer to another office, another planet."

Banks shook his head. "Same thing that happened to

Madolyn and Gricelda: they kept offering me more. 'Just be lead counsel on this case, and you'll get a raise.' 'Just file this injunction, and you'll get an increased vacation allowance.' 'Just sue this orphanage, and we'll knock a year off your Indenture.'"

"You sued an orphanage?"

Banks sighed. "It was a copyright issue, painting the walls with cartoon characters they thought were in the public domain. They didn't know the Big Three had pretty much bought the public domain and sued the shit out of anyone who tried to challenge them. Anyway, that was the last straw. No matter what assignment they'd give me or however much time they were chipping away from my Indenture, it wasn't worth it. I stowed away on an orbital shuttle, talked my way onto the *Rose*, and here I am."

"Not quite the glamorous trip you'd expected?"

"I'd never been offworld until then, really," he said. "I mean, yeah, I left home for law school, but WalWa was using schoolships then, so the whole trip to the Red Line and back was classwork."

"That would have been nice," I said. "I might still be with WalWa if they'd bothered to keep us awake during transit."

"Yeah?" said Banks. "You don't do hibernation either?"

"Oh, I was just fine during testing," I said. "I wrapped up my Masters, did a month in a tank on the ground, and I passed with flying colors. No psych problems, no physical issues. If anything, I came out of it feeling better than I had in years. It was like I got to make up for all the sleep I lost during B-school and that Entertainment Logistics job."

"So, what happened?"

I looked at Banks, his face smudged with mud and cane juice and God knows what, his smile still bright, and I realized that I hadn't talked about this with anyone since Dr Ropata. Not Wash, not Soni, not Big Lily, and I felt the crushing weight of it all in the middle of my chest. I took a breath and said, "I don't dream any more."

Banks chuckled, then stopped when he saw the look on my face. "Um, sorry. I thought you were just being metaphorical."

"No, I'm telling you what happened. It was that first ride as a fishstick that did it." I swallowed, fighting back the chills as I thought about stripping naked but for a latex swim cap to keep my hair out of the way, and climbing into that sleeping bag with the cold foil lining. "The techs used a new batch of hibernant, a better variety than the kind we'd used in testing. And I was a company player, totally loyal to WalWa, and I had no problem being their guinea pig.

"They tore open a gold mylar pouch with twenty-two-oh-one stamped on its side – I can remember that number, clear as my birthday – and poured in this liquid that smelled like curry and stale orange juice. I got sleepier and colder until the hibernant was in my nose and throat and eyes and I was too tired to fight the choking and coughing, but not too tired to close my goddamned eyes. I felt completely powerless, and it was only made worse when they lowered the TV right in front of my face and turned on the Mickey Mouse cartoons that played for the duration of the trip." I shook my head. "Two years out to the Red Line, a jump to Santee, then two years in to orbit."

I ran my hands over my legs, felt the flask in my pocket. "I've been shot in the face with beanbag rounds, trapped on the anchor with a leaking environment suit and no reserve air, crushed in the middle of football riots, but none of that was as horrible as that four years of hovering between sleep and waking, right in that twilight where I wanted to doze but, no, there was something coming down the tubes that I just *had* to watch. Every time my brain said, 'Hey, *wait* a minute,' the hibernant kicked in, and I slipped back into that conscious coma. It was terrifying how comforting it was, floating in that level of cold where my body stopped shivering and *accepted* what was going on.

"And then it all ended. The ship pulled into orbit above Santee, and it was like getting kicked out of a dream. The TV flicked off, the sleeping bag heated up, and I screamed at the top of my lungs because it was the first time I could do *anything* in four years. I didn't stop screaming until the techs shot me full of tranquilizer, and even then, after I'd been cleaned, dressed and slotted into my new job as Colonial Services Liaison, I probably would have kept on screaming if someone hadn't kept giving me tranqs.

"When I woke up, I threw myself into work. Those first three weeks, I slept like the dead, just out of sheer exhaustion. No dreams, nothing. I thought my lack of dreaming was because I was sleeping so deeply, but after six months, I got worried. Even at the height of the B-school crush, I'd have dreams – usually nightmares, but what the hell. And then I started to feel like there was this *hole*, right in the back of my brain, and that everything that made me *me* was starting to drain away." I swallowed. "That's when The Fear showed up."

Banks cocked his head. "The Fear?"

"That's what I call this… *voice*. Imagine all your doubt, all your rage, all your disappointment, mix 'em together with a rabid wolverine and a cane viper, and let it loose in your psyche." I shuddered as The Fear screamed in triumph. "It started small, just a whisper, but grew bigger and louder and meaner and it just did. Not. Stop. I started having these blank-out spells where I'd forget trivial things, names and numbers and the way to write out the letter 'e.' Then I began screwing up schedules for food and cane harvests, air and fuel loading for ships in orbit, hurricane shelter restocking." I shivered. "And then, one day, I couldn't move. I just froze in my bed and didn't leave for three days. I got hauled into the company hospital, shot up with a whole bunch of crap, and woke up on the other side of a desk from a doctor."

The Fear laughed at the memory.

"I told all this to the doc, and he just smiles and hands me a bottle of little green pills."

I cleared my throat. "Now. Up until then, I had had no problem with slugging down whatever someone in a white coat gave me. Every good Indenture knows that there's a treatment for every problem, whether it's concentration, hunger, anxiety, addiction, lack of addiction, whatever. Whatever your problem, someone in a white coat will help you out.

"But, as I sat there, looking at the bottle of little green pills, then at the smiling doctor, then at the WalWa Pharma poster behind the doctor that showed some Indentured woman sitting in front of a smiling doctor who was fondling a bottle of little pills – and I was sure they were green – I remembered that I hadn't told the doc that I was having trouble sleeping or eating or fucking or shitting or any of the ailments that had plagued me in B-school. I said I wasn't *dreaming* anymore.

"*There's a treatment for everything*, said the poster.

"I walked out, out of the office, out of the building, out of Thronehill all the way to Brushhead – this was before the Big Three *really* clamped down on Indentures' free movement – and Breached, then and there.

"No other WalWa Breach I've known has had the same problem. Maybe it was the process, something in the hibernant, or maybe it was just unhealthy to stay awake for four years. Every time I speak at Union fundraisers, I always say I Breached because the Big Three stole my dreams, just like they stole everything else. It's a cheeseball line, but it always gets a big cheer and a flood of donations from guilt-ridden Shareholders.

"So, flash forward a year, I've thrown myself into work, and I'm getting loaded every night, and it's just enough to keep The Fear at bay. I still feel it gnawing at my brains, right at the edges where I can't see or understand what's going on. The Fear keeps making its presence known, so I went to a local doctor, Tem Ropata, and asked if he had any ideas. He was a McDonald Heavy MD/PhD, but he wasn't as quick with the pills. After taking my pulse and looking at my qi and sticking my head in a makeshift MRI tube while I tried to sleep, Ropata said, 'Your brain's just waiting.'"

"Waiting?" said Banks. "What the hell does that mean?"

"That's just what I asked him," I said. "'You were awake for four years,' he said. 'What's worse, you had all that idiotic stimulation. Your brain was on hold, and it's waiting for you to kick-start it back into gear.'"

"That is the dumbest thing I've ever heard," said Banks.

"I know," I said. "Ropata gave me one of those shrugs you can only learn in medical school, and said, 'Would you prefer the little green pills?'

"'Will they make me dream again?' I asked.

"'No,' he said, 'but they'll make you not care that you don't.'

"Well, *that* was right out, so I asked if he could prescribe something else, and he opened his desk, took out a bottle of Old Windswept and told me to drink a finger of it every night at six o'clock in a room lit only by a single candle."

The minute I'd said it, I knew it had been a mistake. The whole thing sounded insane, and there was no way Banks would think I was anything but a drunk. I could see the streetlamp reflections wavering in his eyes as he flicked them back and forth, like the way people do their mental calculations when they hear something ludicrous and they wonder: *what's the best way to humor this crazy person*?

"There's a mild psychoactive in there, something that has to do with the way the distillery works and the way the rum is aged and the type of barrels, and..." I held up my hands. "It keeps me sane, OK? It works. I haven't heard from The Fear since then. And then a few years ago, I hear that the woman who owns the Old Windswept Distillery, Estella Tonggow, wants to retire and sell the whole thing. And, suddenly, I'm working my ass off, saving every jiao, fighting to get everyone I can added to my headcount, 'cause if I get five hundred people to join the Union, I get a massive bonus *and* my pension early. I've almost got enough saved up to buy the distillery, but I need the bonus to push me over the edge."

I hugged my knees, then shook my head. "It's not about the money, Banks. It has never been about the money. It's about securing my future mental health. There are no neuropsychologists on Santee, no psychiatric treatments. What we've got is what we make, and what Estella Tonggow makes *works*. For me, anyway. I'm not going back to being that catatonic slug, not now, not ever."

I shivered. "But if I don't get my name cleared and get you guys to sign up, I don't get those extra Slots from

Wash. I don't get those Slots, then I have to wait and wait until someone else comes slipping down the cable into my headcount, and that just isn't happening anymore. Either they don't show up, or they blow up in orbit, or Saarien pinches them. So, I have to make this deal with Wash *now*, or I don't get that bonus, and then it'll all go away. Someone else will buy the distillery, and something could happen to the way Old Windswept is made, and that means the hole in the back of my brain is going to open up and suck me into the void. The Fear will win. WalWa will win."

Banks took a breath, looked me in the eye and said, "It's only been a day, right? Maybe–"

"It's been three days, and that's because those miners couldn't keep their shit together and bring their ships into orbit!" I said, standing up. "I couldn't sit down that night, because the whole city was in mourning, and I couldn't sit down *last* night because I was in fucking jail, and I can't sit down tonight because I'm out in the middle of the fucking kampong because you and your stupid fucking shipmates *weren't forty fucking people*."

I walked out of the warehouse, banging the door behind me. Fucking Banks. Fucking Breaches. Fucking... *everything*. I marched around the warehouses, listening to my boots squidge from the mud from the fields as I crunched through the gravel. A cool breeze lofted through the cane, rustling the stalks and sending a flash of a chill through my clothes. I wished for my deck jacket, stuffed in Bloombeck's syphilitic cargo bike, I wished for my flat, I wished for it to be six o'clock, I wished for The Fear and everything that came with it to just go away.

A few laps later, I had gotten cold enough and calm enough to go back inside. Banks hadn't moved, as far I could tell: he sat on his tarp tatami, hands resting on his knees. I sat down opposite him.

"I am very sorry that happened to you," he said. "And I'm glad you found something that works."

I coughed, rattling loose a few tears. "Thank you," I said, wiping my face. "I think we should get some sleep."

"Me too," said Banks.

I lay down on the tarp, wrapping it around me as best I could. I could feel the hole in the back of my brain try to open, just a little, The Fear howling for full release, but I hugged myself and willed the damn thing closed, just for a little longer.

NINETEEN

Jilly shook me awake. "Boss, we gotta hide." I rolled off the
tarp, and Jilly pulled it and me deep into the stacks. Outside,
I could hear the buzz of voices, the rumble of diesel engines,
and the shouts of people moving heavy loads of cane. Faint
orange light came in from the dusty window above us. I
climbed up a stack, then wiped the grime away to get a
better view.

A long line of cargo trucks idled below, the convoy
stretching from the transfer station half a klick up the road.
I didn't know too many industrial farmers, and barely knew
the heirloom growers that Tonggow used. Still, I was pretty
sure I'd be able to show my Union card and wave around a
few blue boys to get us a ride back to Santee City. I scanned
the trucks, looking for a friendly company chop. There was
one from Dmitrius Sisters, one from Tuff Gong Haulage, one
being searched by a squad of goons...

I blinked, but the goons didn't vanish. They weren't
wearing uniforms, but with those massive necks and the
way they cradled their riot hoses, they might as well have
been. There were a dozen of them; the ones that weren't

picking through the piles of cane looked through the trucks.

"I think hitching a lift might be tricky," I said, pulling Banks up.

"That's bad, isn't it?" he said.

"It sure as hell is," I said. "Goons aren't allowed to operate outside of the Corporate side of the fence. Why would–"

When the goons had finished searching the entire column of trucks, they marched into the transfer station, only to return a minute later on either side of a long line of tired, beat-up people. The workers looked at the ground as the goons shoved them into the waiting trucks, shuffling their feet and wiping soot from their clothes.

"Who are they?" said Banks.

Jilly had climbed up next to us, then balled her hands into fists. "They're Freeborn. They're taking them."

One woman took a swing at the goons, only to find herself at the business end of a dozen riot hoses. She laughed, diving for one of the goons and turning his hose on the others. She stopped laughing when one of the goons caught her neck in the crook of his meaty elbow and squeezed. He released her before she passed out, then threw her over his shoulder like she was a stack of cane and tossed her into the back of a truck.

"You recognize anyone?" I said to Jilly.

She shook her head. "We can't let this happen, boss."

"No, we can't," I said, then scrambled down the stack to the door.

"What are you doing?" said Banks. "You jumped bail. You think those people out there aren't going to turn you in for some extra cash?"

"Shit, Banks, how are they going to do that?" I said. "They don't have pais, so they can't ping me to find out who I am. They're busy being enslaved, so they won't really have the *time* to turn me in."

"What about the goons?"

"We shoot footage, and then we'll nail 'em when we get home."

"And how are we getting home?"

I looked at the stacks of cane, then hefted one onto my right shoulder. Banks shook his head. "Are you serious?"

"To a goon, labor's labor," I said. "Come on."

Banks got a stack for himself, the weight sending him staggering. Jilly pulled a stack toward her, then tipped it over her shoulder, using its momentum to get to her feet. She shook her head at Banks and walked out the door. The three of us joined the lines of Freeborn loading the trucks. I kept my inked cheek against the cane as best I could. The goons were too busy harassing the Freeborn to pay attention to us. I pitched my cane into a half-loaded truck and hopped in. As Banks and Jilly climbed aboard, I turned to the driver of the truck behind us and pointed at the Union fist on my cheek. His eyes went wide, but he nodded and made a zipping motion over his mouth.

The cane was piled thick, but we managed to squeeze our way through to the front of the truck bed, only to find a tiny compartment someone had hollowed out. It was dim and stuffy, but I could make out a dozen people crammed in, all of them shrinking away from us. I held up my hands, but they just cowered that much more. Jilly and Banks pushed their way through, Jilly asking the Freeborn where they were from, what was happening. They just turned from her, looking at their feet. Someone pounded on the door of the truck's cab. The driver threw the truck into gear, and we rumbled away.

I sat down on an empty patch of floor, and the thickset man next to me said, "You come here to fuck us some more?"

"I'd probably take you out for dinner and a movie first," I said, but he didn't laugh, didn't crack a smile. The few people who looked at us scowled, and one woman spat at my feet. I leaned toward her. "You care to tell what I've done to upset you?"

"You here to make sure we work hard enough?" said the woman. "You think we don't work hard enough for you already?"

"I'm sure you do," I said, "but–"

"But nothing!" she said. "You come here, try and screw us on our cane prices, then cart us away to work more? And without the upfront money you promised!" She spat again. "You Inks are all the same, coming here, making big deals, then leaving us in the dirt come harvest time."

"Wait, wait, wait," I said. "All the prices are set on the Public, and if anyone's been screwing you, you should be able to report them on any terminal."

The woman waved her hands and looked away. "Like any of you liars would listen. That's why my family came to the kampong in the first place. To be free of all that garbage." She looked back at me, her face puckered up like she'd been sucking on a lemon. "But you come out *here*, after us. You're not happy with your city, you have to come to the kampong and–"

Jilly stood up and put her tiny face into the woman's. "Hey, you don't get to treat her like that. Don't you know who she is?"

The woman eyeballed Jilly and said, "That fist on her face tells me all I need to know."

I put a hand on Jilly's shoulder and reeled her back. "The last thing we need is a fight, kid."

"I can take her."

"Can you take all of them?" I nodded to the other Freeborn, the hollow look in their eyes now turning to dull anger. "We need to dial this back." I tugged her elbow, then pulled until she sat down next to me.

I looked up at the Freeborn. "Despite what you think, I do not know what's going on here. I don't know about any deals. I don't know why you're in this truck. Hell, I don't even know where this truck is going." The Freeborn opened their mouths to yell, so I banged my boot on the floor and yelled, "The only thing I do know, is that you've all been screwed. Am I right?"

The crowd settled back into their seats, and I nodded at them, getting to my feet. "Yeah. You've been screwed, and *that* is something I can do something about. Now. You." I pointed at the thick man to my side. "Pretend I don't have this ink on my cheek, and tell me what's going on."

He wiped his hands on his pants, then took a cigar stub out of his shirt pocket. "We're all part of a collective. Grow industrial cane, bring it to the city, sell it on the market. Last year, Typhoon Horace hit. Storm surge overloaded our irrigation canals, flooded our fields. Lost a year's crop. Then, six months ago, just when we're getting back on our feet, we got nailed with black stripe."

"That happened to everyone."

The man made a face. "Not like this. It was a new variety, started around Sag Pond and spread. Stuff grew faster than we could burn it out. We went to the Union for a carryover loan for fungicide, but we got denied."

"Why?"

He shook his head. "I don't know. The man from the Union said we didn't qualify, but that he'd make us an outside offer. He was starting up a new processing plant, and we'd get paid back in diesel and credit if we sold to him on the cheap."

I looked at Banks, who said, "Is there such a thing?"

"No," I said. "There hasn't been a new cane processor in years."

The thickset man shrugged. "That's what I thought, too, until he takes me on a tour. New facility, right in the middle of all this run-down city. Right on the coast. Smelled horrible."

"Sou's Reach?" I said.

"Yeah, I guess. I spent most of my life in the kampong, don't know much about the city."

Banks and I exchanged glances. "This guy," I said, "did he wear all white?"

The man nodded. "Smiled way too much. Whipped out this bigass contract and a stack of thousand-yuan notes. Down payment, he said."

"What then?"

The man shrugged. "We keep it up all season. He buys our crops, pays us in cash. Never as much as we want, but enough to keep going, replant, get us on our feet. Then the goons showed up."

"When?"

The man shrugged. "About a month ago. They make us work at hosepoint. Then they start taking us."

"Where?"

"Don't know. Everyone who goes with them doesn't come back."

I looked at Jilly. "You ever hear of anything like this?"

She nodded. "We got hit by black stripe a few weeks before I left for the city. No one ever made us a deal, but we heard about people disappearing. Thought it'd be better getting a job driving, you know?"

The man with the cigar nodded. "You got that right, kid. We're the last ones on the collective, so they're making us go."

"What's your name?" I said.

"Why you want to know?"

"Because I'm about to make a deal with you that you can take to the bank," I said. "This deal will be so good that you can borrow against it for the rest of your life and have enough money to build irrigation canals that would make the Romans shit themselves."

"Why should I trust another Ink?"

"You know another Ink who would be sitting in this shitty little space, letting you vent?" I said.

"I still have no way of believing you," he said. "Not after the contract we signed."

"You have it?"

"Of course," he said, patting his pants pocket. "I figure I'd need something to wipe my ass with."

"You mind if my attorney and I read them before that happens?"

He sucked on his teeth, then pulled a sheaf of papers from his pocket. They were long sheets covered in legalese and bar codes. I flipped through the first few pages, then flung it back at him. "What is this crap?" I said. "'The parties of the ex partite particulars'? This is what you get when you give first year WalWa law students fistfuls of cranquilizers and a thesaurus."

The man turned over the pages, then held a very large,

very real Union chop in my face. That giant red fist punching out a planet might as well have been aiming for my own eye.

Next to the seal was a clause written in plain language: all Freeborn sugarcane grown on the Lively Wetlands Collective would be sold to Evanrute Saarien at twenty percent below market value in exchange for future profits, cane diesel futures and a whole lot of other crap Saarien could never deliver. "This is some bullshit," I said.

"It was all we had," said the Freeborn man, waving a hand over his face like he was wiping it clean. "We can't trust any of you. All that ink, you look like a bunch of slobs."

I smiled and said, "Big talk for someone who smells like a rat's ass, which is more than I could give about what you think of our ink."

He snorted. "You Union types, you give us shit deals, steal our children away to your city. What do you give about us Freeborn?"

"We made sure you had the chance to call yourselves that," I said, pulling back my hair to show him a thin line on the back of my head. "You see that scar? I got that from a goon's club because I had the nerve to protest their reneging on a supply deal in Ivory Bay. And I got this" – I rolled up my sleeve to show him two black spots on my forearm – "from an overamped taser because I wanted MacDonald Heavy to pony up their contractually obligated back pay to a bunch of dirt farmers in Palanquin. And this one" – I pulled my shirt collar aside to show him a puckered star on my shoulder – "was a rubber bullet fired at point blank range by my former employers because I didn't want them raining garbage on Sou's Reach, the one Ward on the entire planet that deserves to get garbage rained on it. I have been beat up, set on fire, spat on, shat on, all to make sure people like you" – and I jabbed him extra hard in the chest, which felt pretty damn nice, actually – "would have a choice. So don't give me any of this 'What have you done for me lately' bullshit."

The man nodded and rolled up the contract. "You're a lot pushier than the guy in the suit."

"You don't get your way by being polite," I said. "But you *do* get your way making deals with me. Now, you going to tell me your name?"

He squinted. "Marolo."

"OK, Marolo," I said. "I'm Padma Mehta, and this is Banks and Jilly, and here's the deal. We're going with you to Sou's Reach, where we'll figure out what's happening. We're going to get your people released, and we're going to get you a shitload of back pay, and we'll make sure this never happens again. I will put the entire Union and the Co-Op behind this promise, and you'll never have to deal with that white-suited asshole ever again. That sound fair?"

"I'm gonna need something more than your word," said Marolo. He rubbed his fingers together.

"What, you think I'm made of cash?" I said. "You think I can just peel off a few blue boys and that'll do it?"

"I think you can make all kinds of deals and guarantees," said Marolo. "I also think that if you're out here, you're in some kinda trouble, and that you need us to keep quiet."

"I'm offering to *help* you," I said.

"So was your man Saarien."

I swallowed the bile back and said, "How much would it take to keep you quiet?"

Marolo looked around the bus and said, "Thirty thousand would cover our nut."

"Thirty thousand would buy you a continent," I said.

"We have families to feed, crops to regrow, and we aren't getting any help from your Union," said Marolo. "Thirty thousand would go a long way to help a lot of people and to make sure they were appropriately *grateful*."

I ground my teeth. "You know I can't make that deal while we're here," I said. "Unless you've got a Public terminal installed in your pocket."

He held out his hand, then spat on it. "A Freeborn's word is enough."

I pulled Wash's flask out of my pocket and showed it to Marolo. "You know, where I come from, we just share a drink. You know what this is?"

He unscrewed the lid and sniffed. Even in the dim light, I could see him flush. "It's good, whatever it is."

"That is thirty-year Old Windswept," I said. "And I only share it with people I do deals with. Saarien ever share a drink with you?"

Marolo sniffed the rum again, then took a gentle sip. All the color rushed from his face, and he blew out a long, slow breath before handing the flask back to me. "Never," he said. "But that's still not enough."

I didn't have to blink up my balance to know how much this would hurt me. But I also didn't have much choice. I held out my right hand and spat in it. "We got a deal?"

Marolo nodded and shook my hand. "Now, you got more of that stuff?"

"Marolo, you stick with me, I'll get you so much you could bathe in it."

"All the same, I'd rather drink it." "Done." I took a swig, only getting a taste of the rum before passing it back. The Fear was now wide awake, threatening to tear my brain apart. *You really think six o'clock will help, even if you make it?* it said.

I took another taste, then handed the flask to the next Freeborn.

An hour – and half the flask – later, the truck slowed, and the stink of rotting molasses seeped in. I pushed my way through the cane screen until I could see the rusty industrial ruins of Sou's Reach roll by. It looked like we were moving into the heart of the refinery, but all the cane should have been dumped near its edges. I thought about sending a message to Soni, but I had no idea if it would get out with all the metal. Plus, once the police found me, it would get ugly, seeing how I'd jumped bail. Unless I could show them someone committing a much bigger, badder crime, the cops weren't going to help.

The truck hissed to a stop, and Banks motioned for me. "We're going to stand out from this crowd," he said, pointing to his ink.

"Good point," I said, reaching to the bottom of the truck and getting a handful of mud. I slapped it on his cheek, then on mine. "Better?"

"Now you look too filthy," said Marolo. "We have *some* pride."

Someone pulled the cane screen from the back of the truck, and a goon pointed his hose at us and said, "Out." We obeyed, and I made sure to keep my head down as we followed the line of Freeborn into a squat, collapsing building that smelled like burning candy and cleaning solvent. My nose burned and my stomach flipped as we filed through the door, into the middle of what looked like Hell's swimming pool. Giant pourform pools lined the room, all of them filled with hot, sticky molasses. Workers with no

protective gear stirred with giant paddles, which only made
the smell worse. Some of the Freeborn gagged as we were
shoved past the pools and down a flight of metal steps into
a dark, dank space with barely enough room for us. The
floor shuddered, and my guts fell into my shoes as the wall
in front of us began a slow, creaking slide open. Beyond it
was more black, and the goons ushered us in at hosepoint.
As the light faded, I stopped caring about waiting and called
Soni, but there was no signal, and that scared the crap out
of me. We were either way inside the refinery, or someone
had ripped out every transceiver in the area.

The door behind us thudded shut, and another one in
front of us opened with a well-lubricated whisper. The light
was blinding, so we couldn't see who ordered us to move.
I found Banks and Jilly in the middle of the crowd, and
we walked side by side into... a full-scale industrial cane
refinery?

Everything that was in the plants at Beukes Point
and Jotzi was here, but newer and shinier. I could see
condensers the size of buses, coils big enough to wrap a
dozen rugby players, and steel holding vats so big you could
have used them as fuel canisters for starships. Hundreds and
hundreds of people, all under the watch of a company of
WalWa goons, ran about, taking measurements, adjusting
equipment, and working on filling drum after drum with
what looked like industrial molasses. The entire room had
the sweet scent of boiling sugar and fermenting molasses,
though the air was undercut with something harsh and
sour, like an acetone spill.

The line rounded the stacks of molasses drums and
ended in front of a woman in a green jumpsuit. She held
an honest-to-God clipboard, something I hadn't seen since

I audited History of Management. I tried not to gawk at the antique as I shuffled my way toward her, but wound up gawking at her ink instead. It was some serious work: two Union fists smashing into a factory, a pair of winged seabirds flying off her temples, and a shark swimming down her nose. Impressive as hell, but there was something off about the ink, something I couldn't place...

"You got any skills?" she said, tapping a pencil on the side of her clipboard.

Plenty, I thought, but none that wouldn't give me away as Union. "I, uh, do a little bit of everything," I said.

She pointed her pencil toward the bottling line. "You can work quality control. Next!"

"What do I do?" I said.

She tilted her head to the side, and the look on her face said that she didn't give a shit. "You make sure the quality is controlled," she said. "Next!"

"I do a little bit of everything, too," said Banks.

"You can go to the boilers," she said.

"But I'd like to control quality," said Banks.

"Me, too," said Jilly.

The woman snorted. "You don't get to ask what you do, dirtheads," she said. "You do what I say, and I say you're going to stir molasses in the boiler."

Banks gave her the Grin, and the woman stared at him for a few moments before tapping her pencil on the clipboard. "Fine. Get to the line."

Banks took Jilly by the shoulders and walked past. I looked at the woman, who just pointed at Banks with her pencil. "You want to get paid, you follow him and work," she said, then looked down the line of people. "Next!"

I just nodded and hurried after Banks and Jilly. "Christ,

I don't know what they taught you about mind control in law school, but you are giving me lessons the minute we get out of here."

"I just smiled at her," said Banks. "You can get anywhere with WalWa people if you smile right."

"WalWa?" I said. "What makes you say that?"

"Her eye," said Banks. "Every Union person I've met, even Saarien, has this spark in their eye. Maybe it's from having their pai reburned, maybe it's because they don't have to start every day singing the WalWa corporate anthem, I don't know. But I *do* know that that woman's eye is cold and dead, just like every other WalWa person I've met." He shrugged. "That, and her tattoo looks like someone drew it on her face with a felt marker."

I stole another glance at her face, and it hit me. "You're right," I said. "Her ink's all wrong." I pointed at the fist on my cheek. "No one's allowed to get more than one of these unless they've done something meritorious as hell, and the last time that happened was twenty years ago when Marjo Arhanga won a raise in shipping rates by pounding the hell out of an armored WalWa business platoon barehanded."

"She looked old enough," said Banks.

"But not male enough," I said. "Marjo was a man. That woman" – I pointed a thumb over my shoulder – "is wearing ink she hasn't earned."

As we walked toward the spouts, I stole glances at every inked face along the way, and all of them had overdone tattoo work. Here was a woman with perfect porcelain skin, yet she had the anchor marks on her cheeks that someone gets after twenty years of service on the open water. There was a kid, barely out of puberty, and he had ink commemorating street battles that ended when he was still a fetus. All of them had the same dull eyes that I'd seen for years when I was in Service, all of them held clipboards, and all of them were yelling at the people on the floor to work harder.

The line sounded like a riot at a percussion convention: two-hundred-liter drums rattled down a chute, stopped under a nozzle long enough to get filled with a liquid that smelled like molasses mixed with cleaning fluid, then scuttered away to get capped and stacked, all done by hand. The people working the line swayed, like they were about to fall asleep on their feet. One of the overinked supervisors, a tiny girl whose face was so tattooed it looked purple, walked up to a woman slamming lids onto the drums and smacked her with her clipboard. "You want to sleep?" she yelled over the din. "You can sleep when you're done filling those pallets!"

The woman nodded, then went back to working the capper. She waited until the clipboard woman walked away, then slumped over again, her shoulders bouncing for a bit before she straightened up and grabbed another drum lid from the stack. She turned, and it was Jordan Blanton.

I stared, my stomach doing backflips. I had to have been imagining it. But, no, it was Jordan, in the flesh, hammering lids onto molasses drums.

She wasn't the only familiar face. There was Thor Becker. Nearby was Remy Galletain. All of Jordan's supposedly dead crew were here, working the line. Good God, even Jimney Potts was there, pushing a broom. I had to have been hallucinating. My brain had now started falling apart. The Fear roared in triumph.

"I see them, too," Banks said in my ear.

I swallowed, shook my head, and Jordan was still there,

pounding down the lids. They were real. And so was the purple-faced girl, who saw me looking at her.

"You!" she shouted. "What are you standing here for?"

I shoved Banks into motion, but it was too late. She closed the distance in four quick steps.

"Well?" she yelled. She looked even younger up close, like she'd just been hatched out of B-school. "What are you supposed to be doing?"

"We're your new quality control," Jilly yelled back.

The overinked girl glared at Jilly, then pointed at the rails. "Then get to work!" she screamed. "You want to get paid, you get to work!"

"You want to try smiling at her?" I yelled in Banks's ear.

"Only if I can stay out of her reach," he said as we bellied up to the line.

The Freeborn man to my side nodded and said, "Just make sure there's nothing in the drums but molasses. You see anything floating, mark it with an X." He held up a stick of chalk.

"How can you tell?" yelled Banks, peering into the drums; they held nothing but sweet-smelling murk. He knocked one, and something white floated to the surface, bobbling and turning.

It was a foot.

The Freeborn man made a giant X. "You can just tell," he said. The blood rushed from Jilly's face. Banks turned away and threw up.

I put a hand on Banks's shoulder to help him keep his feet, and something hit me in the back of the head. I turned just in time to see a clipboard flying toward my nose. I saw stars for a second as the board whacked my face, but kept it together enough to swing back as hard as I could. I'd thrown better punches, but this one had the right speed and angle to connect with the purple-faced girl's cheek. She yelped and bounced back into the line, knocking against the drums. Someone hit the emergency stop, and the racket came to a clattering halt.

"Let's talk about your management style," I said, shaking my hand to ease the sting. I looked at my fingers to make sure I hadn't hurt anything; they were stained blue where I'd made contact.

The girl stood up, her flushed face looking like a bruised tomato. "You," she said, holding her cheek and trying to keep from crying, "you are in *such* trouble."

I held up my hand and showed her the smudged ink. "You and me both, kid."

Her eyes went wide, and she put her hands over her face. "You... you... I'm getting the supervisor!" She ran up the line, all the workers applauding as she fled.

"Speaking of management skills," said Banks, cleaning his mouth.

"What, should I have I smiled at her?" I said, wiping the ink off on my pants. "Let's get gone."

"Where?"

"Wherever this line goes," I said, nodding at the stacks. "They wouldn't be making all this without having a way to get it out."

There was a commotion, and I turned to see the purple-faced girl pointing at me. Next to her was a man in an impeccable white suit. They both turned to us, and my jaw hit the ground when I saw Evanrute Saarien's face grow as pale as his clothes. He shouted something, maybe my name, maybe an obscenity. I didn't wait to find out.

I grabbed Banks and Jilly, and we ran, shouldering a

half-filled drum off the line. The molasses spattered on the ground, leaving a sticky, toxic cloud in our wake as we ran as fast as we could into the stacks.

TWENTY

We turned corners at random until we couldn't hear anyone following us. When I caught my breath, I looked up and saw nothing but molasses drums all the way to the ceiling, and the ceiling was a good fifty meters high. I tapped one of the drums next to me, and it thumped: full. "Jesus, there must be enough here for twenty years of fuel."

"Or rum," said Jilly.

"If it's anywhere as nasty as what we smelled on the line, no one would want to drink it," I said. "Besides, they don't have the equipment."

"They brought that dead guy back to life," said Banks. "I think they can figure out distilling."

"None of this makes sense!" I said. "I saw Saarien in the freezer!"

"When?" said Banks.

"Well, I saw Soni's footage."

"Footage can be faked."

"Then how do you explain Jordan? Or Jimney? You were *there*," I said. "You *saw* the bodies."

"I saw a stack of limbs and torsos that were beaten to

a pulp, and another body that was burnt to a crisp," said Banks. "I didn't see a single face."

"But their pais and DNA tags identified them," I said.

"Pais can be spoofed," said Banks.

"But not genes," I said. "At least, not here. There isn't anyone with that kind of expertise or equipment. I mean, the skilled workforce we have barely keeps us in the Information Age. We have to scrounge or steal gear from ships in orbit. So I think if someone had figured out a way to copy bodies, news would have spread."

"I think if someone stashed a million barrels of molasses, that would spread, too."

I looked up at the endless stacks of drums. "What the hell is he doing with all this?"

"Well, what *can* he do with it?" said Banks. "You're pretty sure he can't make rum, so that leaves fuel. Why would he need this much? To flood the market?"

"A million barrels wouldn't make a dent in the price," I said. "There's so much floating around Occupied Space that it would take half the tankers going down before things shifted."

"How about locally?" said Banks. "Maybe he's got something in mind for here."

I shook my head. "That would only hurt the rank and file, and Saarien's too much into the Struggle to do that."

"But he has no problem messing with you."

"That's because I'm not pure enough," I said, giving Banks a wry smile. "He wants to fight the bloated carcass of plutocracy, and I'm trying to get a seat at the table. No, he's got new cane coming in, he's refining it, and..."

I thought back to the stacks in that warehouse on the kampong, all the cane clean and green. "Jilly, all that contaminated cane we saw wouldn't have even gotten into the transfer station, right?"

She nodded. "It would've been torched, and the field marked off for quarantine."

"But everything Saarien was toting away was *perfect*," I said. "We were in the middle of an infected field."

"Maybe he got lucky," said Banks.

"You heard what those Freeborn said: one little spot would show up on a stalk, and then the whole field would be done in a week," I said. "Unless they used some kind of super fungicide, but that would be just as tough to make. There aren't enough gengineers and chemists on the planet to do that kind of work. Everything in that warehouse, hell, this *place* should be covered with black stripe. How is it not?" I rubbed my temples and blinked up the time: six-thirty, on a Friday morning. I should have been in bed, not hiding under a zillion barrels of molasses. "How does all this shit fit together?"

"Does it have to?" said Banks. "I mean, it's one thing to follow a thread, but it's another to see if it's woven together with others."

"It's all too weird not to be," I said, touching the oil drum again, like if I petted it the right way, it would spill its secrets. Then, of course, I remembered that Madame Tonggow was a goddamn chemist. "I need to bring this stuff to someone, figure out what it is."

"I am not helping you carry one of these," said Banks.

"You won't have to," I said, taking the flask out of my pocket.

"You wouldn't," said Banks.

"I have to," I said, unscrewing the cap and giving it a sniff. The Old Windswept smelled so good, and it would have tasted just as good, too, maybe even have a little metal tang from the flask's interior. I gave it a slosh, wondered how much was in there, then I poured it out.

Banks sighed. "You could've offered me a bit, you know."

"Or me," said Jilly.

"Later, when you've developed a palate," I said, shaking out the last of the rum. I got my multitool out of another pocket, opened the nastiest blade, and pierced one of the drums. Dark molasses seeped out, filling the air with its oily stink. I caught as much as I could in the flask, trying to keep it from getting on my fingers. "Let's hope it's not caustic," I said, putting the flask into a cargo pocket on my thigh. I gave my hands a sniff: sweet, with a hint of rot and burning plastic. Even regular industrial molasses didn't stink like this.

"You have any ideas how we're going to get out of here?" said Banks.

"A few," I said as we walked farther into the stacks, "but you probably won't like them."

"Is fire involved?"

"God, no," I said. "Only an idiot would try to light this stuff up." I rubbed my temples. "Where did this all come from? How could they shove this much gear in here?"

The entire floor shook, hard enough that all the drums rattled in their stacks. "You want to go back, look for Saarien and ask him?" said Banks.

"Not when we can find out what's making that noise."

"I'd much rather stay here," said Banks. "It's quieter. Probably safer."

"Show some spine, counselor," I said. "Where's your sense of intrigue?"

"Probably getting beaten up by your sense of self-preservation."

As we walked further into the stacks, the boom grew louder. We rounded a corner just as a cargo can crashed to the floor, its doors flopping open. A line of men rolled drum after drum into the can, filling it up in minutes. I'd never seen that kind of manual labor done so quickly, but that probably had something to do with the dozens of goons surrounding the can, all of them cradling what looked like cattle prods. An inked man checked something off on his clipboard, swung the doors shut, then waved to the ceiling. A crane soared down and carried the can skyward, just in time for another can to tumble out of nowhere.

"Fast," said Jilly.

"Anal," I said. "They must be loading those things on a timetable, which gives us an in." I licked my hand and wiped the mud and grime away from my face. "How do I look?"

"Messy as hell."

"Yeah, but can you see my ink?"

Banks nodded. I wiped my hand on his cheek a few times until his regular pale complexion shone through. I smeared mung on Jilly's face, much to her protest.

"Follow my lead. We're getting out of this hole." I walked into the light and yelled, as loud as I could, "HOLD UP!"

The goons spun around, their tasers pointing at us. I brushed them aside, pointing to my cheek as I breezed past them. The man with the clipboard turned to me, and I said, "That's right, you! What are you doing?"

"Uh, making sure the shipment's packed," he said.

"You call this packed?" I said, pushing him out of the way. "Good God, man, you could shove another fifty drums in here. Look." I walked into the can and sat down on an empty pallet. "See? Plenty of room." I motioned for Banks and Jilly to sit next to me, and he hopped to. "My associates and I shouldn't be able to sit in here. Fill it."

"But the schedule–"

I pointed at the fist my face. "You see this? This says I outrank you, and you don't want to know what happens to insubordinates in this operation."

"But–"

"No buts," I said. "You close this thing up, so I can go topside and kick the appropriate ass. And you fill every can to the brim from now on."

"But–"

I put a finger to his lips. "I knew you could. Don't bother locking it; I need to hit the ground running." I leaned back and motioned for him to close the doors.

He hesitated for a moment, then said, "Where's your clipboard?"

There was a shout from the stacks and the *thud-thud-thud* of hobnailed boots. I grabbed the kid's clipboard and kicked him in the stomach. He staggered back as the crane clanked down on top of the can and hauled us skyward. We swayed like a ship on stormy seas, and loose drums rolled toward us as we clambered away from the still-open door. I dropped the clipboard so I could shove the molasses overboard and was rewarded with a very satisfying thud and splash below.

"You gonna help me with this?" I called to Banks.

He was leaning against a drum, flipping through the pages on the clipboard. "They're moving everything to the lifter."

I grabbed the clipboard and leafed through timetables, loading manifests, and slots in the lifter queue. Saarien wanted to send ten million barrels up the cable, put them on ships heading all over Occupied Space. "What the hell is he doing?" I said. "And how? How in hell can he pay the gravity tax on all this?"

"I hope your friend will be able to help," said Banks, nodding to the stained cargo pocket that held the flask.

"If she can't, then we are beyond screwed," I said as morning light filled the can. I could see the rusted pipes of the refinery through the open door, smell the rotting molasses. It was a marginal improvement over the stench of Saarien's new stuff. The can lurched, sending us tumbling to the side as the crates clanked against the can's interior walls. We hit the ground with a thud, and then the whole can shook like it had been tossed on a vibrating bed.

"Jump!" I said, and we leaped out of the can onto soggy asphalt. Above us was a massive crane, and in front of us was a cloud that smelled like burnt molasses. The can, now secured to a trailer, rumbled away. A column of empty flatbed trucks hunkered away as far as I could see.

"Shouldn't we follow that can?" said Banks.

"I think we won't miss a few kilometers' worth of trucks. We need to know what they're moving first," I said, looking around for something mobile we could steal. Instead, I saw an empty industrial yard filled with too-clean corporate types, all of them with fake ink. I remembered being one of those people, my head full of ambition and heart full of nothing, and my gut boiled at the sight of their fraudulent tattoos. I grabbed the clipboard from Banks and walked to the nearest one, a kid with stars under his eyes. "Oy! You!" I yelled in my best Command Presence voice. "What's the holdup?"

"What?" said Star Eyes.

I turned the clipboard toward him and stabbed it with my finger. "This last shipment was under quota and behind schedule. Who's in charge here?"

"Uh–"

"Not good enough!" I yelled. "You're running behind, and that means I have to get this sorry excuse of an operation back on track right now! You!" I pointed at a young woman who looked like she was about to piss herself. "Get me and my associates a ride, one that's worthy of our status. You have thirty seconds before I have your names and faces on the wrong people's desks. Move!"

The entire flock scattered. I grabbed Star Eyes by the collar before he could flee. "And you," I said, lowering my voice to a hair above dangerous. "You're going to tell me just where you think you're going."

"To, um, get my superior," he said.

"And why would you do that?" I said.

"Because I need to–"

"You need," I said, thumping Star Eyes on the chest. "Let me tell you what *I* need. I need to know just why these shipments are being held up so I can make sure the entire supply chain can keep pace. You realize this is the only advantage we have over these miserable Union parasites, right? We have a supply chain that spreads across light years, that will keep running long after you and I and our children and grandchildren and great-grandchildren are dead, buried, and turned into worm food. We are the lifeblood of humanity across a hundred planets, and we will only fail if we take our eyes off the ball. Now." I put my hands on his shoulders. "Go get me the biggest cup of coffee you can find, and, if you do it under sixty seconds, I'll make sure to put in a good word."

Star Eyes relaxed, then ran off.

"That was amazing," said Banks.

"Business Vocalization was one of my favorite classes," I said.

"Though, I notice you didn't get *me* a cup of coffee."

"Or me," said Jilly.

"Deal with it."

The flock of WalWa juniors jogged around the corner, all of them surrounding a bright green tuk-tuk with a massive speaker system. "We found this," said the piss-pants girl from the driver's seat. "It's a little dirty, but–"

"It'll do," said Jilly, leaping into the driver's seat and shoving the woman aside. She revved the engine a few times and grinned.

Banks and I hopped into the back. "You're all going to get commendations for this," I said. "Be sure to bring this up on your next performance review with–"

"PADMA!" roared someone behind us. I turned long enough to see Evanrute Saarien and a goon squad appear from nowhere.

"GO!" I shouted, and Jilly stepped on the gas as hard as she could. The tuk-tuk shot forward, sending the WalWa juniors scattering as we belted away. Saarien's voice echoed off the pipework.

"Turn on the stereo," I said. "I'm not in the mood to hear any more yelling."

We zipped through the column of trucks, smashing through traffic bars, and dodging the occasional potshot from a riot hose. We screamed out of Sou's Reach, and Jilly didn't take her foot off the gas until we were well down Brapati Causeway on the road to Brushhead.

I blinked up a call to Tonggow, but the line immediately went dead and the sound of a millions chainsaws cutting through coral steel filled my skull. I grabbed my head, then doubled over as the pain slammed down my spine. Somewhere in there, Jilly must have hit the brakes. The tuk-tuk screeched to a stop, traffic stacking up behind us, and I staggered out, trying to blink my pai off. I hunched over, hands on thighs, wanting to puke, but I couldn't even manage that.

The noise cut off, and Soni's voice came on: "Did that get your attention?"

"Christ, Soni, I know I skipped bail, but–"

"You can call me Captain Baghram now," she said.

"You think I meant to leave the city?" I said, straightening up and waving off Banks, who gave me a worried *what-the-hell?* look. "I was on incredibly important business, and–"

"I don't care," she said. "You disappeared last night, and it'll go a lot easier if you give yourself up before I have to bring you in."

I looked around and saw a bumblecar half a klick behind us. A second waited on the other end of the causeway. "I can't come in, Captain. There's something bigger going on."

"You know, just once I wish someone would say they're not giving themselves up because they just don't want to," said Soni. "Instead, I always get all this crap about unfinished business and you-don't-understand and I-just-need-to-do-this. Not this time. Come in, Padma. I don't want to have to crank up the sound again."

"Then do us both a favor and call Estella Tonggow," I said. "She'll vouch for me."

"I would, except she was in a collision this morning."

"With what?" I said. "Her limo was a tank."

"Maybe," said Soni, "but her tank wasn't waterproof." She sent me a picture of Tonggow's limo, sunk in the Musharrad Canal up to its boot.

"Is she OK?" I asked.

"We're still trying to saw our way in, but her pai isn't reading any lifesigns," she said.

I looked over the side of the causeway; the water was mostly clean, flowing from the kampong toward the ocean. We were so close to Brushhead I could smell Giesel's morning bread. There would be nowhere to run to, though, not with my pai pinging my location to the whole world. There was no way to find a tech to reburn it or shut off Soni's little reminder; I had to get somewhere out of range–

And then I saw the rusting hulk of Partridge Hutong, not a hundred meters away. If I couldn't get out of range, I could get buried under interference. I looked at Jilly and said, "You just keep driving." I stepped onto the pourform apron of the causeway.

"Padma, as your attorney–"

I didn't hear the rest of what he said, because I jumped into the water. It tasted salty and stale, but that didn't stop me from swimming as hard as I could for Partridge Island. I got halfway there before Soni pinged me: "Padma, you need to stop now, or I'm going to have to crank it up."

I just kept swimming, my shoulders burning as I freestyled away. I was almost to shore when the sound of heavy machinery and howling cats cut through my brain. I curled up, the pain in my head too much to concentrate on swimming. I opened my mouth to scream, but got a lungful of water instead. I clawed and thrashed, but couldn't find anything to grab on to.

And then someone grabbed me by the waistband and hauled me up and out. I hacked and coughed and fought off the fire in my lungs and the pounding in my head, and rolled onto my stomach and pointed at the mountain of ISO-20K-compliant cargo canisters stacked six high. I got a look at a pair of scuffed WalWa company shoes as I was dragged into the mass of cans. The noise cut off, and I groaned to Banks, "What the hell kept you?"

"I'm not a swimmer," he said, sitting next to me. "What happened to you?"

"Policeman on my back," I said, sitting up then leaning against one of the cans. "They'll be here soon, so we'll have to get ourselves lost."

"That'll be tough to do when you've got a tracker behind your eye."

"Networks don't work here," I said, knocking on the can; it rang back, deep and hollow. "Too much metal, and no line of sight. Used to drive me crazy when I lived here."

"When was that?"

"When I first Breached," I said, getting to my feet. "I moved here that first week, and I got out as soon as I'd saved up enough cash."

"Seems charming enough," said Banks as we walked along the wall of metal.

"It was too hot, too noisy, and it smelled like chicken soup and rust," I said, the pain in my skull fading. "The only thing that made it bearable was my upstairs neighbor, Mrs Powazek. She was an old LiaoCon food scientist, made the best garlic pickles in the world, with just a hint of chili flakes. I still dream about them. Plus, the smell during bottling time covered up the stink of my downstairs neighbor."

"Is he still here?"

"Yeah," I said, "I don't think Bloombeck's ever going to get out."

"That guy who led us into the sewers? You lived *above* him?" said Banks. "You deserve a medal."

"It got even worse when he started monkeying around with distilling," I said. "I don't know if he was using bad molasses or if his gear was dirty, but it always came out wrong. He even started monkeying around with this sad patch of cane–"

And something clicked. I had heard this before. Where? I stopped and rewound my pai's buffer, to Bloombeck's first scam pitch two days ago. He had licked his lips and rattled about his neighbor who had a cane patch on Sag Pond. "Sag Pond," I said.

"Did you live there, too?" said Banks.

"Bloombeck's neighbor had a patch out at Sag Pond," I said. "And that's where Marolo said the black stripe started. And Sag Pond is downwind from Thronehill, and something was blowing on the Sag Pond patch from the WalWa burn room. And what else did we find in the burn room?"

"A body."

"The last time I saw Jimney, well, before I saw him again, his paper coverall was covered in muck. I thought it was just dirt, but it wasn't. It was black stripe."

"On a suit?"

"The paper was made of cane bagasse," I said. "All the paper on this place is. Jimney's suit was covered in black stripe, and he sent it up the chimney every week when he burned it."

"His suit?"

"Best thing he could do with it," I said. "The man didn't really believe in hygiene." I bit my lower lip, trying to cram all this together. "But that doesn't make any sense. Burning the suit would have burnt the black stripe, too. Besides, the timing's not right. Marolo said they got nailed with the black stripe months ago, so Jimney couldn't have spread it."

"But he'd been *exposed* to it," said Banks. "How? What do Sag Pond and Jimney have in common?"

I looked up at the hutong wall and heard the faint wail of police sirens in the background. Soni would be coming here for me, and then I would lose my grip on all of these threads. "Goddammit, if I only hadn't listened to Bloombeck, I wouldn't be in this... Holy crap. He's the link. Come on!"

"Where?"

"To Bloombeck's. That fat fuck has some explaining to do."

TWENTY-ONE

Most of Brushhead was newish construction: squat buildings made from stolen pourform set over the bones of dying ships that had been dropped down the lifter as counterweights. There was a sensible grid of streets, the sole nod to order in a city that brought new and terrifying definitions to "chaos." There was none of the uniform sterility of Thronehill, despite the work of the two architects and six urban planners who'd lived here and tried like hell to get people to think about easements and unity of style and the like. People would smile and nod, then point to the hutongs and say, "They tried that once in Partridge. Didn't take."

Partridge Hutong was the water treatment plant's original dormitory. A hundred years ago, WalWa shipped the whole plant to Santee in flatpacks, all stuffed into standard ISO-20K cargo cans. The accountants figured it was cheaper to drop the cans down the well and repurpose them into homes. They stacked three cans on top of each other, bolted rickety stairs to one side, cut holes for ventilation and doors, then repeated the process until, presto, instant housing block. The whole thing looked and felt like living inside a maze for rats.

Banks and I ran around to the eastern wall, where the hutong's back door looked out over the canal. The gate screen to the hutong was made of woven steel, a beautiful piece that sang when wind passed through it. It was only offkey during hurricane season, so we'd know things were back to normal when it trilled perfect fifths again. Someone usually sat outside the gate, not so much as guardian as initial screener. They wouldn't stop you from getting in, but your name and business would be whispered throughout the alleys in a matter of minutes if you didn't answer right.

An oba-san I didn't recognize rocked back and forth in an old chair made from tuk-tuk grills as she knitted away. She gave me a quick glance as we paused in front of her. I had no idea how dirty and frazzled I looked, but it couldn't have been worse than the man we were here to see. "Name's Mehta," I said. "I'm here to murder Vytai Bloombeck."

She nodded. "Give him a few kicks for me," she said, and in we went.

The cans were filled with midmorning sounds: cartoons, breakfast dishes, fighting, fucking, the lot. The hutong breathed, a little slice of Santee jammed into a few square blocks. For a moment, I missed how alive the place was, but then someone flung a bucket of shit out their third-story window, and I remembered why I'd left in the first place.

A few other people stumbled around, either working off a drunk or on their way to one. We fit in with the rest of the foot traffic, though I could feel a few hidden stares follow our backs. As loathsome as Bloombeck was, even he had to have had a few people who owed him enough to warn him about us.

My old stack was on the north leg of its courtyard square. Back on Dead Earth, they would have called this the water side, which was appropriate because everything had leaked. Rust streaked down the side of the stack and showed the outlines of Mrs Powazek's window boxes, where she'd grown Persian cucumbers and dill. The remaining ones that weren't broken were empty, and water dripped onto the red earth below. The staircase that led to my old door and Mrs P's was missing rungs, and the locks were shut and rusted red.

"When I lived upstairs from Bloombeck," I said, approaching the stack, "the inside of his can had been divided up into five tiny compartments, each occupied by a man with a drug and/or skin problem. Don't touch anything once we're inside."

A puddle had gathered in front of the bottom can's door. It was already ajar, which made kicking it open that much easier.

I was prepared to see Bloombeck's squalor again, but I wasn't ready for the sight of a spotless studio flat. The partitions were gone, as were any signs that someone as filthy as Vytai Bloombeck had ever lived there.

I did a slow three-sixty. The walls were painted a warm wheat yellow, and the furniture looked like it had all come fresh from a catalog. "You sure I can't touch anything?" said Banks. "That chair looks great."

"This must be the wrong place," I said. "Bloombeck lived in a rathole."

"Looks like the rats upgraded," he said, walking to a chair that looked like a pile of leather balanced on chopsticks. It sighed and wobbled under his weight. "I think the dean of my law school had a chair like this. It feels expensive."

"Don't get comfy," I said. "If this is someone else's flat—"

Banks leaned over to a glass and coral steel end table and picked up a fistful of confetti. He shifted a few of the flakes around, and said, "This is another order about the *Rose*," He took a whiff, then gagged. "Smells like it's been in a sewer, too."

"I don't get it," I said, walking the flat and examining a shelf full of glass figurines of frolicking kittens. "Every day, Bloombeck's coming to me with a sob story about how he's broke, he needs a favor, he doesn't have his dues, he can't donate blood for another six weeks...where does he get money to buy—" I picked up a kitten wearing a chef's hat and working a mixing bowl "—to buy *knick-knacks*!"

"When was the last time you saw him in a hovel?"

"Ten months ago," I said. "I came back for Mrs Powazek's funeral, and Bloombeck was behind on dues, so I figured I'd kill two birds with one stone. Mrs P had left me one of her last jars of pickles in her will, but I broke the thing over Bloomie's head—"

"All right," he said, holding up a hand. "Did you lend him anything during that past ten months?"

"Christ, no," I said. "He owed *me*. Hell, I even sent him a bill for the pickles. How could he afford this?"

"You sure Bloombeck didn't just save up?"

I looked around the flat with all of its expensive furnishings. In a tiny corner kitchen, there were glass bottles of Chino Cove Sea Soap. I had given Soni a tiny bottle when she'd been promoted a few years ago, and it had cost me a week's wages. "No way. How could he save when he was up to his eyeballs in debt?"

"How do you know he was in debt?"

"Because every time he came around asking for

something, I checked his Public profile," I said, sitting down on a couch that crunched and smelled like cocoa hulls. "That's just due diligence. I always do that, especially with someone like Bloombeck. Hell, I have a special search just for him. He was *way* overleveraged, and people weren't taking him up on any of his offers."

"But *you* did," said Banks.

I snorted and turned the kitten over in my hands. "And, boy, what a good idea *that* turned out to be."

"But you took him up on his offer," said Banks, leaning towards me.

I shrugged. "Yes, Banks, it was a moment of weakness, and I'm sorry. Is that what you want me to say?"

"No, no, Padma... you took him up when he told you about the *Rose* coming into orbit."

"And I admit it was a mistake."

"But that means you checked him, didn't you? Due diligence?"

I leaned back and blinked up a record of meeting him at Big Lily's, regretting that *that* bit of footage was still intact. Sure enough, right after he made the proposition, I'd checked his balance. "He was in the black," I said. "He had paid of all his debts. I was so used to getting the alert that I didn't pay attention when it didn't go off."

Banks nodded. "That's a thread. Now, we figure out where all this came from, and we've got more threads."

I looked at the bottom of the figurine. There were the glassblower's chop and the words PROUDLY MADE IN SOU'S REACH. "Oh, I think I know where this will all lead."

I tossed it to Banks, who caught it and frowned when he saw the chop. "Saarien's paid him?"

"I'm not sure for what, but... ah!" My pai sent a million

stabs into my eyeball.

"What?" said Banks. "You OK?"

"Yeah," I said, blinking. "Just my pai acting up—"

The door opened, and a man carrying two wicker baskets backed into the flat. He turned and started, dropping one basket on the floor. Oranges tumbled out, and he pointed a finger at us. It took me a second to realize that the nattily dressed and completely scrubbed man in a guayabera and linen slacks was Vytai Bloombeck.

His face went white, and he dropped the other basket. "Padma!" he said. "I'm so glad to see you!"

"Glad enough to explain all this?" I said, waving at the flat.

His smile flickered, and he started worrying his hands. "It's just a little redecorating. I thought the place could use it."

"What did your roommates think?" I said. "You know, the ones with cirrhosis and the facial tumors?"

"Y'know, they moved on, passed on." He half shrugged, like he wasn't even buying his own bullshit.

"Mm-hm." I tapped the back of a leather chair. "How'd you manage to pay for all this?"

"Donations," he said, a little too quickly. "I got, um, got some donated furniture."

"And paint," said Banks.

"Yeah," said Bloombeck, nodding and smiling. "A little paint goes a long way, and..." He looked at his hands, then backed toward the door.

"I think we need to talk, Bloomie," I said. "There's a lot you haven't been telling me."

"Hey, I'm *always* straight with you, Padma," he said. "Wasn't I straight with you about that stuff in Thronehill?"

"Straight-ish," I said. "What happened to you back there?

We went crawling back in the slime, and you're walking around in your Sunday best instead of waiting for us at the Hall."

"I waited, I waited," said Bloombeck. "I got out of the sewer, tried to find you, then the sun came up and I had to get home. I'm sorry about that, but I had all of that evidence for you–"

"And where is it?" I asked. "Or that cargo bike?"

"What cargo bike?"

"The one you rented in my name, Bloomie," I said, kicking the receipt out of my head and into his. Yay for peer-to-peer connections.

He flinched, then swallowed hard. "Hey, I'm sorry about that, but you know my credit's no good anywhere–"

"Except that it is," I said. "You've been in the red for as long as I've known you, and suddenly all your debts are paid off. How'd you do it, Bloomie?"

He laughed and shrugged and fiddled with the hem of his guayabera. "I got cousins, you know, they helped me out, plus I got this thing going on with the cane–"

"You needed me to co-sign for that new cane patch thing so you could worm your way into my credit," I said, stepping toward him, trying not to make too obvious of a fist. "You bullshitted me, Bloomie, and, what's worse, you did it when I was desperate. That's two strikes. You want to go for a third?"

"I want to help you out, Padma, you and the Union. Solidarity, right?"

I kicked over an end table, and it broke with a satisfying smash. "In the past thirty-six hours I have been mobbed, foamed, shot at, arrested, and all of that is because you cornered me in a moment of weakness," I said, hovering above him. "If you give me that Solidarity bit one more time, I will beat you so hard you'll be shitting bruises for a month. Who's been paying you off, you filthy sack of crap?"

He gurgled and gagged, and his mouth flopped open, like a he was about to puke. I took a quick step back, but he kicked the door shut as he lifted the hem of his guayabera and pulled a gun out of his waistband. "I am not filthy," he said, and shot me before I could remind him he was.

It felt like someone had punched me in the right shoulder, not enough to knock me over, but enough to hurt like hell. "You unbelievable prick," I said, clamping a hand over the wound. "You fucking shot me."

"It was just a beanbag round," said Bloombeck.

I looked at my shoulder: there was no blood, no mess, just a fast-growing bruise underneath my shirt. "Jesus Christ, Bloomie, can't you do anything right? If you're going to break the Ban, you shouldn't have pussed out with nonlethal rounds."

"Shut up!" yelled Bloombeck, walking over and putting the gun into my stomach. The barrel was hot and stung through my shirt. "I'll shoot you up close, and we'll find out just how nonlethal these are if you don't shut up. You think you can do that? Just for once, could you please shut up?"

I sat back on the cocoa-shell couch, never taking my eyes off him.

Bloombeck winced as I shifted the seat beneath me. "You had to sit there? Contaminate the thing? I paid good money for that couch."

"Why are you worried about contamination?" I said. "You afraid I picked up something in your buddy's plant?"

Bloombeck narrowed his eyes. "I don't know what you're talking about."

"Right," I said. "What's Saarien cooking up, Bloomie?"

"I got nothing to say to you," he said.

I cleared my throat and said, "I apologize for calling you filthy, Vytai. That outfit looks excellent on you, and I commend you on your style."

Bloombeck cocked his head, but didn't take the gun off me. "Serious?"

I nodded. "Absolutely. Where'd you get that guayabera? Silber's?"

"No, Grimstad's. Next to the library on Laplace Street."

"Grimstad does good work," I said.

Bloombeck nodded, then caught himself. He chuckled and re-aimed the gun back at me. "Cute. I always liked how, if you couldn't bully someone, you'd sweet talk 'em . But it won't work, 'cause I've got the gun. What've you got?"

I nodded at Banks. "A lawyer."

Bloombeck turned in time to see Banks throw a crystal kitten at his face. He staggered and brought both hands to his now-bleeding forehead, and we rushed him. I managed to get my good shoulder into his stomach while Banks wrestled the gun out of his hand. We shoved him into a chair, where he rocked back and forth, moaning and clutching his face. "That *really* hurt!" he whined.

"Try getting shot with a beanbag," I said.

Blood dribbled off Bloombeck's jowls and onto his shirtfront. He sniffed and looked at the mess. "I just got this, Padma. Look what you did!"

"Oh, shut it," I said. "Don't go blaming me because you tried playing tough guy and couldn't get it right."

"You're going to pay for this shirt!" he said. "I got it in my head! I got the video!"

"And we have you shooting me, idiot," I said. "Which

raises the important question: where did you get a gun?"

"I'm not talking to you," he said. "You're not the police."

"No, I'm good friends with them," I said. "You don't think Soni'd be happy to bust a weapons ring?"

"What weapons ring?" said Bloombeck. "Saarien doesn't sell guns, he just hands them out..." He caught his next words, then went pale.

"Well, that's interesting," I said. "Tell me more."

Bloombeck sank into the couch, then laughed, long and loud, blood dribbling down his jowls. "You mean," he gasped, "you didn't know?" He looked at us both then laughed again. "Jesus Christ, you should see your face, Padma! I actually made you shut up!"

I grabbed the gun from Banks and aimed it at Bloombeck's chest. He just laughed harder. "What, you're gonna shoot me, Padma? Mrs P not around with the pickle jars?"

I squeezed off one round into the couch, right between Bloombeck's open legs. He looked at the half-expanded beanbag lodged in the cushion, then started laughing again.

"Padma, I think you shouldn't do that," said Banks into my ear, just loud enough to get around Bloombeck's consumptive horselaugh.

"You're right," I said, thumbing back the hammer. "Never aim at something unless you intend to destroy it, and I really didn't mean to hurt that couch." I put the gun on Bloombeck's forehead, which was easy, since there was so much of it.

"No, I mean, I don't think waving a gun around is a good idea."

"Do I look like I'm waving anything, Banks? I'm steady as a rock."

Banks swallowed and held up his hands. "I think you

should let me tie up Bloombeck, and I think we should call the police, and I think we should let this play out in the proper place."

"This seems pretty proper to me," I said. "Putting down a rat in the place I first met him, it's got a nice symmetry."

"You're angry, and you're hurt," said Banks, moving between me and Bloombeck. "If you pull that trigger, you're probably going to kill him, and that will cut off what's probably a very, very important thread. You want that?"

"I want him to shut up, and you are in my way."

"You didn't know!" said Bloombeck, and he doubled over. I put the barrel in the back of his head.

"Put away the gun, Padma," said Banks, "and we'll follow all these threads, and you'll be able to lock up Saarien or sue the shit out of him or whatever it takes to make you happy. You are not a killer."

"Don't tell me what I'm not, Banks. You don't know what the fuck I'm not."

He walked forward until the gun pushed his skinny chest. "I know you're not a killer."

I ground my jaw, then put down the gun. "I *could* have been."

"Maybe, but not for him," said Banks. "Besides, I've already worked for two nutjobs, remember? I'd really rather not work for a third?"

I looked past Banks at Bloombeck, who was still doubled over in laughter. "So, what now?"

"He's going to help you tie off all these loose ends," said Banks. "I'll go back to the gate, ask that old lady to make a call for us. We'll get the police here, you'll probably go back to jail for a bit, but I will unravel all this stuff and have you out in no time."

"Really?" I said. "And how're you going to do that?"

He waved his hands. "Lawyer magic."

I rolled my eyes, but helped him tie up Bloombeck. As Banks walked out the door, I said, "You sure I can't shoot him just a little?"

He shook his head, then was gone.

TWENTY-TWO

I pocketed the gun, and went back inside, pulling the door shut behind me. "So, you gonna tell me what the deal is?" I said to Bloombeck. "I think you owe me that much."

Bloombeck stopped dabbing the blood away from his eyes on his shoulder and snorted. "I don't owe you a damn thing, Padma. You can go ahead and shoot me, 'cause you'll be saving me from whatever Saarien will do to me."

"So you *knew* he was still alive when you came to me last night?" I said, wrapping one of Bloombeck's belts around his wrists.

"I'm done talking to you," he said. "Just wait until your cop buddy shows up, and we'll get this over with. I'm a dead man, anyway."

"You don't know the half of it. You could always try calling her yourself. Suspects who make her life easier usually get lighter treatment."

"Just like you, right?" said Bloombeck. "I dangled that bit of paper in front of you, and you jumped like a squid going for bait."

"Well, the trick with landing fish is giving them what

they like," I said, "and I'll admit, I liked the idea of not going to prison."

"Too bad you're still going," he said. "Skipping bail, assaulting me in my own home."

"True, but the murder part – I hope to avoid that."

"Then you're going to need my help," said Bloombeck. "And you won't get it."

"No, but I do have timestamped footage from fifty minutes ago, showing a very alive and very angry Evanrute Saarien," I said. "Soni may slap me around for jumping bail, but I'm pretty sure she'll forget all that once she sees my video. And if she finds some kind of conspiracy, well..." I crouched in front of him. "She lives for that stuff."

Bloombeck fidgeted. "Can you keep me safe?"

"Can you tell me what's going on?"

Bloombeck's mouth twitched. "What do you know so far?"

"I know that Saarien's got a bigger, newer refinery inside his old one. I know that he's growing some kind of new cane. I know a lot of Freeborn have had their crops wiped out by black stripe, a new variety that–"

"Strain," said Bloombeck, his eyes to the carpet. He caught his breath, like he was choking, then looked up at me, stricken.

And that was the first time I realized that the ink on his cheek wasn't a pair of hedge clippers like I'd always thought. Now that his face was free of grime and perpetual five-o'clock shadow, I saw that his tattoo was a winding, spiral lattice. "Bloomie," I said, "I don't think you ever told me what you used to do when you were in Service."

"You never asked," he said.

I looked closer. "Son of a bitch," I said. "You were a gengineer."

"A genetic engineering lab tech, actually," he said, nodding. "Level Four pay grade."

"Did you make the black stripe?"

"Of course not," he said.

"I didn't think so."

"I just *perfected* it."

There was steel in Bloombeck's eyes when he said it, and all the fear in his face had melted away. He took a breath and sat up straight in his chair.

"Do you know what black stripe is?" he said. "It's a warning. It's nature's way of telling us what a bad idea it is to rely too much on one plant. You know how many hectares of cane there are in Occupied Space? I figured it out once: two *trillion*. There are three hectares of cane for each human. We don't raise cane; cane is raising *us*."

I opened my mouth to knock Bloombeck for sounding philosophical, but decided it was better not to say anything.

"But you people never listened," he said. "When I first got here, I was excited, because it meant I wouldn't be around a bunch of rat-racers who were always looking at the bottom line. Too bad my recruiter couldn't be bothered with things like skill sets and matching people to jobs. He only cared about filling Slots. You know where my Slot was? Reaming out the sewer sidelines in Brushhead. Not the main ones, where you have a little elbow room, but the teeny, tiny ones where you're hunched over and smacking your head on the inside of the pipe. And when I complained, I got shoved even farther down the plant." He shook his head. "He'd bothered to ask, I could've shown him what I can do. I could have shown him the stuff in my lab that makes black stripe look like athlete's foot."

"Wait," I said, "you have a lab?"

"Of course I do," he said. "You think I can just turn it all off? I *loved* being a tech: all the toys the scientists got, and none of the responsibility to justify my research. I got experiments that would blow your mind."

"Let me guess," I said. "It's in Sag Pond."

Bloombeck laughed. "Really? You think I'd let Brittona or any of her kids contaminate my work? No, that's my field station."

"Then where's your lab?"

Bloombeck shook his head. "You don't get away that easy, Padma. No, I'm going to wait here until the cops show up and watch as they crack your skull all over my floor. I won't mind the mess; it's a cheap throw rug that I boosted from Mrs Powazek."

I looked down and recognized the rug. I'd seen it many times when Mrs P would invite me for sandwiches and beer. It was a knockoff Persian, with a maroon base surrounded by blue and cream paisley. The thing was still in good shape. "How did you get this down?" I said. "Her place was locked up after she died. I remember, because I did it."

Bloombeck bit his lip as he stole a glance toward the ceiling. I looked up and saw a damp patch of acoustic tiling. "Auction, I guess," he said, looking at his feet. "Still would like to know who got her old bottling stuff."

"Yeah," I said, pulling an end table underneath the damp patch. "What I wouldn't give for some of her pickles right now." I got on the table and tapped the tiling; it gave way easily.

"Padma, you don't want to mess with that," he said. "You know how much this place leaks."

"Like a sieve," I said, sliding the tile out of place. Water dribbled down from a hole that had been cut in the ceiling of Bloombeck's can and the floor of my old one. There was a musty funk, like mushrooms and freshly cut cane.

"Really, Padma, I think it would be a good idea for you to come down," said Bloombeck. He strained against the belt and rocked in place.

"Sure," I said, hauling myself up. Overhead lamps flickered on as I flopped onto the floor. When I stood up, I was in the middle of a forest of ironpalm benches, laboratory glassware, and racks and racks of labeled, sealed test tubes. Some of the tubes held blobs of red and purple goo; others were streaked with black. My brain did backflips as I read people's names on the vials filled with goo and realized they were filled with meat. The filthy test tubes were all labeled BLACK STRIPE VARIANT; each one had a different number, all of them in series. "Jesus," I whispered.

There was also a lot of equipment I couldn't place: something that looked like an autoclave made from dishwasher parts, and another machine that had an ancient analog readout that spun between A, C, G, and T. It took me a moment to realize that it was a DNA sequencer.

I ran back to the hole and stuck my head down below. "Bloomie... did you *make* all this?"

"I had to," he said. "I can't afford Big Three shipping rates, and no one else around here had it."

"Where did you get it?"

He shrugged. "At the plant, at the dump, anywhere there were people."

I looked back at the makeshift lab. "Then you came up with Saarien's cane, right? The kind that's resistant to your black stripe?"

"Not just that," said Bloombeck, "but it's more energy dense, produces less bagasse that's more useable, and even fixes three times as much nitrogen–"

The front door crashed open, and heavy bootsteps filled the flat. I pulled up and away, then froze. I wasn't sure if they'd seen me, but I wasn't about to give myself away by running. I held my breath as more boots clomped through the door. "Untie me, dammit!" Bloombeck yelled.

There was a cough, like a tuk-tuk backfiring, then silence.

I scooted away from the hatch as quickly and quietly as I could, making sure my boot heels didn't ring against the metal floor. I managed to curl under one of the lab benches, making myself as small as possible. Maybe they had just come for Bloombeck. I wished I could have turned the lights off, just to make sure I stayed hidden.

Whoever had entered the flat wasn't talking, but I could hear the soft clack of body armor, drawers slamming open, chairs overturning. It would only be a matter of time before one of them looked up and climbed in. I looked around for another way out, and saw the hole that Bloombeck had cut up into Mrs Powazek's flat, right above the DNA sequencer. The outside ladder may have gone, but I could always get out a window to the roof and hop to the next building and–

Something small and round flew up through the hatch and bounced across the floor to my feet. My B-school training took over and screamed GRENADE to my entire body. I kicked the thing back in the hole, hoping it would go off downstairs instead of in my face. I didn't wait to see; I leaped from my hideyhole and scrambled on top of Bloombeck's gear, reaching for the hole above the sequencer. My boot slipped on a pile of papers, sending me to the floor. I flopped on my stomach, the air whooshing out of my lungs.

I tried to breathe, tried to keep calm, but then, through

the clutter of bench legs and spilled papers, I saw a head pop
through the open hatch in the floor. It wasn't a goon in riot
gear, or a cop; it wore a black lacquer mask in the shape of
a grinning fox. It turned, then looked up at me, its polished
eyes staring right into me.

Ghosts.

I got to my feet and clawed up the sequencer. I got
through the hatch, only to find myself in the middle of
even more racks of test tubes, all nestled against tiny
incubator lamps. The tubes were filled with a rainbow of
liquids, molds, and fungi. All of them were labeled with
neat, cramped handwriting. How long had Bloombeck been
working on this? And how did Saarien and the goons figure
in?

Down below, someone shouted my name. I put my
shoulder to the nearest rack and knocked it over, sending
a mountain of glass and Christ-knows-what toward the
hatch. There was another shout, and then the floor began to
vanish, one tiny hole at a time. It had been a long time since
someone had shot an actual gun at me, but I still had the
sense to hop away as fast as I could. The test tubes exploded
into a cloud of glass fragments and spores. The approaching
bullet holes blocked my way to the window. Something bit
into my calf, and I yelped. My pants leg turned bright red,
and I pressed down on the wound, hoping the next one
would either miss or be quick.

And then the courtyards were filled with the screams of
sirens. The shooting stopped, and the whole stack of cans
thudded as my assailants ran. I edged to the window and
peeked out the side; cops in their yellow and black riot gear
flooded the hutong. They poured out of the alleys, over the
rails, onto the rooftops, like someone had upended a hive

of angry, badged bees onto the hutong. Above the din came the chatter of automatic weapons. Dozens of cops stumbled, blood gushing from bullet holes in their armor. Whoever had the guns wasn't going to give up easily.

"You really shouldn't be here."

I started and spun around. A slim figure stood at the hatch, holding a submachine gun at his hip, aiming it right at my chest. His battered armor was jet black, as was his mask, which was molded in the shape of a monkey's face. I wasn't seeing things. It wasn't The Fear making me hallucinate. It was a Ghost. Holy shit, a real, live Ghost.

"You could pretend I'm not here," I said, creeping to the nearest shelf. The masked man tilted his head and flicked the safety.

"I'm pretty sure I can't do that," he said. His voice was harsh and crackly – probably run through some kind of fuzz filter on the mask. "Come with me, please."

"The police are going to surround you," I said, freezing. The shelf was right in front of me. "Even if they're outgunned. In fact, that'll just piss them off even more."

"Maybe," said the man, holding out a gloved hand to me. "But you should probably come with me. It'll be safer."

"My professors told me never to go anywhere with strange, armed men."

"Mine *were* strange, armed men," he said. "Women, too."

"What are you doing here?" I said. "Why would you Ghosts care about us? Shit, Santee isn't even on the main route to the Beyond anymore. We're nothing."

"That's not my call," said the man. The light from outside turned his mask's black eyes into stars. "Just come with me, and I promise nothing will happen to you."

"I don't think you can keep that promise."

"I will."

I ducked and shoved the shelf as hard as I could. The man yelled my name as he ducked out of the way, but an edge of the shelf caught his shoulder and he lost his balance. I pounced and drove my shoulder into his chest, sending him to the floor. He raised his gun, but I grabbed it and rammed its butt into his throat. He sputtered, and I grabbed the gun and swung it at his giant monkey face as hard as I could. There was a squawk of feedback from the mask's speakers, and the man yelled, pulling the mask off his head.

I was looking right at Banks.

My head went cold, and my throat dropped into my stomach, and I scrambled off him, his gun falling from my fingers.

Banks coughed and gurgled, "Did you have to hit so hard?"

"What the fuck?" I yelled. "You're... you're a fucking Ghost!"

"I prefer Covert Business Interference Asset," he said, his voice raspy.

"You shot at me!"

"I shot *near* you," he said.

Outside, a shadow fell on the courtyard, and dust and leaves battered the windows like they'd been swirled up by a typhoon. No, not a typhoon; it was the downwash of a cargo airship as it descended over the hutong like a belly-flopping whale. I looked at Banks, who wobbled to his feet, then limped for the ceiling hatch, grabbing onto the lever lock with both hands. As I pushed against the corrugated lines of the can's ceiling, the lever budged a centimeter, then two, then swung wide. I kicked my legs through the open panel like a trapeze artist and scrambled up to the roof.

The courtyard rang with gunfire and the scream of the airship's drive turbines. I looked over the side of the cargo can. Three dozen police worked on the door with blowtorches and battering rams while the rest shot upward at the airship. I pinged Soni direct, hoping she was down in the scrum. One of the cops put down her blowtorch and looked around, and I whispered a quick prayer to Soni's ambitions and line-of-sight telecom.

"There are Ghosts here!" I yelled.

"You think I don't know that?" she yelled back. "Do you have any idea how much trouble you're in?"

"*I'm* in trouble?" I said, ducking as the airship made another pass. "All I've been through in the past day, I'm pure as driven sand. Hell, even Bloombeck's in more trouble than me. Fucker *shot* me."

"Are you all right?" Soni asked.

"Shoulder hurts, leg's hit, but otherwise, yeah."

"Good," said Soni, "'cause as soon as we get into this flat and rescue your ass, I'm going to kick it halfway to Chino Cove."

"I had nothing to do with this!"

"I know that," said Soni. "Your driver, Jilly, she sent word that something was going on, but I'm tempted to get you to pay for all this. Especially after the serious shit we found out–"

I was about to reply when the deafening shriek of four eight-thousand horsepower MacDonald Heavy Industries jet turbines drowned me out. The airship hung right on top of us, cargo claws descending. I looked back at the hatch, where Banks was working his way up; his mouth moved, but I couldn't hear him over the crush of sound.

I've been caught outside only once during a hurricane,

and it was for a very good reason: the shelter where I'd holed up had run out of food, and I'd volunteered to make a run for fresh supplies. (Of course, the "shelter" was actually the old Library Lager brewpub down on Paper Street, and the "supplies" were Old Windswept, but no one had to know that.) It was the most terrifying twenty minutes of my life as the winds knocked me into buildings and tipped my commandeered tuk-tuk from side to side.

The downwash from the airship was a thousand times worse. I crouched, tried to crab-walk away, but my hair snapped at my face so much I couldn't see where to go. The closer the ship got, the heavier the wind, until I was flat on the ground. The weight of all that air, it pressed me more and more into the deck until I could feel every seam in my clothes, every bit or fleck of dust, and the weight of Bloombeck's gun grinding into my waist.

I flipped on my back. The wind stung my eyelids, but I didn't need to see to know the turbine was right overhead. My hands dove into my pockets, and out came the gun. It had been a long time since my B-school mandated weapons training – after all, you couldn't sell WalWa's defense products without knowing how they worked – but there was something to be said for the blind panic you feel when a ceramic fan blade was going to grind you into paste. I flipped the safety and pulled the trigger; there was a horrific screech, like a giant dragging his fingernails across the world's biggest blackboard. The wind died, and I opened my eyes to see the airship lift away, one of its turbines smoking.

I got up. "What did you do?" Banks said. "Yell at it?"

I held up the gun, and he shook his head. "No way," he said. "There is no way you broke that thing with a beanbag."

"I told you these things hurt," I said, pointing it at him.

"You want to find out?"

Banks held up his hands. "I left my weapon down there," he said. "I do not want to hurt you."

"Why should I believe anything you've told me?" I said. "You're a fucking *Ghost*. You lie, you destroy, you kill. Did you kill Bloombeck?"

"*I* didn't," he said.

"But someone did," I said. "Who was it? Your one-eyed pal?"

"She's not that good a shot," he said. "Mimi did it."

I cocked my head. "You expect me to believe that that sobbing mess is a Ghost?"

Banks nodded. "If we'd done our jobs right, you'd had never known we were here."

"Looks like you didn't."

"Well shit, Padma, we didn't expect you to pluck us out of the ocean!" yelled Banks. "It was supposed to be Saarien!"

I felt the gun arm waver, so I clamped my free hand around my wrist to prop it up. "All this time, all that we did, you were in bed with Saarien?"

"We were *investigating* Saarien," said Banks. "All the equipment and chemicals he's been buying over the past decade got on our radar. He was up to something. We planted a story about potential Breaches with the local company directorate to lure him out. You took the bait instead."

"Lucky me," I said.

"It *was* lucky," said Banks, "because we got to do more with you looking over us than we would have with Saarien. You saw what he's doing to his own people. That's all going to change."

"Then why is he still alive?" I said. "And why was a

corpse that was supposed to be him in the freezer? And what the hell happened to Thanh? Don't tell me he was a Ghost, too."

"Not really, no," said Banks. "He was just our... our luggage, I guess."

"I swear to fucking God I will shoot you right now just to get you to stop lying."

"Thanh was not a person!" said Banks, taking a step back. "He was a hollow dummy made from vat-grown meat. Our gear was inside him."

"That's sick."

"That's the job!" said Banks. "You think we can just show up with a duffel bag full of weapons and armor at the lifter and say, 'Hi, we're a Ghost Squad, here to upturn the core of the local economy'? You think we would've gotten that far?"

"Did you have something to do with the body?" I said. "Saarien's?"

"No," said Banks. "We're still trying to figure that one out."

"Then what about Estella Tonggow?" I said. "Did Mimi kill her, too?"

"I don't know," said Banks. "That wasn't part of our job. None of those people's fake murders were. The people who attacked us at the office, Tonggow, that wasn't us."

My gun hand wavered a moment. I steadied it. "Saarien did all that?"

"We think so."

"Then Tonggow might still be alive?"

"Maybe," said Banks. "It's not my job to find out."

"Your *job*." I thumbed the gun's hammer back in place and put it in my pocket. "Your job is to make trouble and lie and make our lives miserable so the Big Three can keep grinding a little more value out of us for their Shareholders. You happy with your job?"

"Not really, no," said Banks. "I was telling the truth when I said I wanted to leave."

"Bullshit," I said. "If you really wanted to Breach, you could've told me at any time. I would've driven you to the Hall myself and gotten you signed in and protected."

"It's more complicated than that," said Banks.

"What isn't?" I said.

"The truth," he said. "I really am a lawyer, and I really was sorry to hear what happened to you."

The whole world shook and bucked, knocking us down. I looked up: the airship hadn't flown off; it had just picked up altitude to give its cargo cables some slack. The can lifted, a few centimeters at a time, and Banks and I ran for it. Or, rather, he ran like hell, and I gimped along on my still-wounded leg. He leaped over the edge, but I couldn't make the distance fast enough. By the time I got to the end of the roof, there was a ten-meter gap between us, and Banks looked back, yelling and kicking roof fixtures.

I dumped everything from my pai over to his. "Put this all on the Public," I called. "Make sure it's timestamped and notarized and all that other legal bullshit."

"You stay on the line," he said. "I'll get the police, and we'll track you–"

The call went dead, and I watched him and the hutong get smaller and smaller as the airship picked up speed.

TWENTY-THREE

For a brief moment, I thought about shimmying up one of the cargo cables and blasting my way into the cockpit. Not a bad idea, except that MacDonald Heavy had been building anti-piracy measures into their craft since the days of the Spanish Armada. The cables were probably serrated or electrified or slippery as hell, and they wouldn't lead to anywhere but tiny compartments filled with nothing but more of the same cabling. The underside would be covered in smart darts or dumb guns or Christ-knew-what. Besides, the cockpit was sealed and unlockable only by the ground crew, who needed levered keys the size of cellos.

Jumping was still an option, though one that probably wouldn't end well. I looked over the side of the can and saw Brushhead fall away, row after row of terraced roof farms and winding streets and everything I'd known and loved for the past twelve years. I'd never seen it from the air like this. I let my pai record, hoping it would catch all this. Someone would want to see it, even it had to be at my wake.

The roof hatch opened, and a masked head popped up. This one looked like a wolf with a flattened snout. "Get in here, Padma," it said, its amplified and distorted voice grating above the airship's engines.

"What is it with you people and the masks?" I yelled. "Someone take their anthropology class a little too seriously?"

"You know you're not going to jump, and I don't want to have to come out there and get you."

"Is that you, Ellie?" I yelled. "I can't tell with that mask covering your beautiful eye."

The Ghost slid its mask up, and One-Eye shook her head. "Don't give me a hard time," she said, her voice still sounding goony. "I have to take you in alive, but no one said anything about you being undamaged."

"What are you gonna do, taser me?" I yelled. "I could have a seizure, roll right off this roof. How'd your boss like that?"

"Jesus Christ, why are you being so difficult?" she yelled back, her own voice cutting over the helmet's speakers.

"What else have I got right now?" I yelled back. "If being a pain in your ass is the only card I have left, I'm gonna play it."

A look flashed across One-Eye's face, like frustration getting pummeled by anger with an extra slap from resignation. It was a good look for her. "If you come in, I'll let you know what's going on," she said, turning off the distortion effects. She even attempted a smile.

I shrugged. "Don't care."

"Bullshit!" yelled One-Eye, pointing a gloved finger at me. "Everything that's been going on for the past two days, how could you not care? Hell, I've been trying to kill you!"

"Yeah, but you failed every time," I said. "And since you haven't shot me from that hatch or come up here and thrown me overboard, that means you need me alive. Who's got the upper hand in this negotiation?"

"This is not a negotiation!" she screamed. "We are not back in that shitty little office on Vishnu's Palm, and I am not watching you show me how to make sure a shipment of napkins appears on time!"

"Vishnu's Palm? How... What the hell are you talking about?"

She shook her head. "You really don't remember, do you? No, of course not, how could you? You never paid attention to anyone but yourself. Even when you stomped all over everyone back at Entertainment Management, you didn't care."

One-Eye's face was red, her eyes narrowed and her cheeks taut. For a moment, her scars looked more like wrinkles, and I remembered, a long time ago, that same face screaming at me from a video conference. It had been a much younger face on a much skinnier body, but the way spit flew from her teeth as she cursed me and swore to take me down, that hadn't changed.

"Nariel?" I said.

She nodded. "Took you long enough."

"What the hell happened to you?"

"*You* did," she said. "After Vishnu's Palm, I got blamed for everything: the supply chain breakdown, the riots, the low-G puking. All of it."

"That shouldn't have happened."

"But it *did*," said Nariel, showing me her teeth. "And there was no way to come back with that kind of black spot on my record. I was poison to every single division at Corporate. Even the brothels wouldn't take me as management. The only way to keep up my end of my Indenture was to completely switch jobs. I had to become a ship's engineering mate. You know what it's like to go from management to the lowest, shittiest job in the company?"

"Ship's engineer's still a good gig," I said.

"I was *somebody* before you came along!" she yelled. "I was going places, and I was going to write my own ticket, and *you* fucked me over!"

"No, I didn't," I said, sitting down. "You never did the work, Nariel. You didn't listen to me. You didn't go over the details."

"Well, I'm going over them now," she said, and she whipped out a taser and shot me.

Good thing I was already on the ground, or the fall would have knocked me out. I *wished* I'd been knocked out; it would have saved me from the horrible feeling of having every muscle lock as my brain lit up.

By the time a squad of goons hauled me into the cargo can, the pain had stopped. I might as well have been a bundle of palm fronds from the way they passed me down the hatch to the floor. My entire body felt like it was made out of wood, and my mouth and tongue kept making embarrassing sounds every time I tried to talk.

"That was just as much fun as I'd hoped," Nariel said, holstering her taser. "I'll have to see if I can do that again."

"Unghaagh." My hands were wads of bread dough, but there was a tingle in my arms.

"Priceless," she said, tapping her temple. "The image of you going down like a sack of coconuts is one that I will treasure for a long, long time."

"Unghaaffff..." A little more feeling, and my hands managed to find my pockets.

"God, even now, you can't keep quiet, can you?"

"Fuhhhh..." My fingers found the gun. My thumb flicked the safety, and the rest of my fingers gripped as tightly as they could.

"'Fuck you'? Is that the best you've got?" Nariel laughed, and the other goons chuckled with her. She hunched over me, her inked and scar-puckered face hovering above mine.

"Fuh...forgot..." I hoped I had enough fine motor control to pull this off.

"What? To up the voltage?"

"...to frisk me." And I pulled out the gun, held it under her chin, and fired.

Nariel didn't just scream, she *yowled*, a trapped animal roar. She brought both hands to her face, which gave me plenty of room to kick her in the gut. She rolled away, and I got to my feet, as wobbly as they were. I fired off what was left in the mag as I gimped for the hatch. The goons shouted, and Nariel roared as best she could with her now-shattered jaw, "KILL HER!"

I threw the empty gun and connected with her face. Two goons swung their rifles at me, but I pulled myself up through the hatch into cool, salt air.

We were now over open ocean, low enough to get some spray and high enough to scare the shit out of me. The can thudded and shook, and I held onto the hatch's lockarm as hard as I could while I tried to get my bearings. The lifter port lay dead ahead. The sea churned with traffic: tugs pulling flotillas of empty drop cans to watering stations, then queuing to load the filled cans on the up line. Quick launches snagged runaway debris for the recycler, and barges hauled fresh crews to the port, an island of coral steel and rock and thousands of kilometers of shimmering, black ribbon climbing up into the sky.

Dozens of airships loaded with priority cargo from the down line headed to shore, all of them skimming the tops of the waves to take advantage of the ground surface effect. But a few flew toward the port, and all of those were hauling cargo cans. I tried again and again to get a hold of someone, anyone, but my pai refused to make a connection.

The hatch blew open, and Nariel clambered onto the roof. Her jaw, purple and bruised, hung open, and she roared as she charged me. I had no room to dodge, and no agility to do it, so I just turned and leaped over the side of the can.

Time didn't slow down like they said it would during Sudden Disaster Preparedness. Everything, the wind, the surf, the water, all of it rushed up at me, and it took everything I had to do what my instructors had drilled into my head: point my toes at the sea, hold my hands to the sky, and clench everything closed as hard as I could. The water was cold and clear, and it felt like I fell forever, but I followed my bubbles as I grabbed my way up, until something dark and heavy fell on top of me. I fought to right myself, and looked straight into Nariel's eye. She yelled what sounded like my name, but the red foam bubbling from her mouth garbled it.

The weight of her armor pulled us both down, and I couldn't break her grip on my shirt. I also couldn't get out of my shirt, thanks to an arm that refused to move properly. Nariel gave me a broken-toothed smile, one that said she was perfectly happy to drown as long as I went with her. Everything started to darken, and my lungs burned, and I realized that if this was the way I was going to die, it would be even more embarrassing than going out in a sewer pipe. I was about to be killed by a Ghost, the hardest of the Big Three hardcore, and that was unacceptable.

Even though the water slowed me down, I got in a good punch to Nariel's jaw. She screamed and let go, giving me enough time to kick free. She kept sinking, and, God help me, I thought about letting her. If there's anything worse than being killed by a Ghost, it's not letting one get reamed by a Union court. I reached for her waistband and prayed she never got upgraded armor. The two emergency tabs were there, and I pulled with all my might. Her armor blew away from her, and I grabbed her by the hair and fought to the surface. I didn't stop until we both exploded into the daylight.

My lungs burned and my head rang as oxygen got back into my blood. I had just gotten the fuzz out of my brain when Nariel pounced on me again. She got her hands around my throat, and I went back under the water. I clawed at her, my hands slapping at nothing. It got black, the water filling my nose as her hands grew tighter. I felt something soft, and all I could do was push it with my thumb. Nariel let go, and I swam away as hard as I could, coughing water out of my lungs.

Nariel yowled, grabbing her scarred and puckered face. The eyepatch no longer sat on her face; I had jammed it into her eyesocket. "Augh ew," she said, then texted, *Fuck you*. She glared at me with her good eye as the waves splashed the blood away from her face.

"No, Nariel, fuck *you*," I said, treading water as we bobbed along. "The only reason you're not sinking to the bottom of the ocean is because I was there, and the only reason I was there is because you kidnapped me. You owe me twice over."

I do not owe you a damn thing, she sent. I loved how her pai still followed WalWa protocol and made sure her texts followed correct business letter grammar.

"You think your life is worth that little?"

Nariel made a horrible coughing sound, like she was hacking up a hedgehog. It took me a few seconds to realize that it was laughter. *That is funny. We are drifting in the middle of the ocean, and you are still trying to recruit me. I wish you could see the look of desperation on your face.*

"I can see us getting eaten by squid if we don't get picked up soon," I said, but she just kept up with her coughing laugh as we both floated. I turned away and tried to flag down a passing barge, but my voice couldn't carry over the water. My pai was completely useless, too; it couldn't pick up a network, even though I knew there should have been plenty of signal bouncing around.

"Is it your fault I can't call anyone but you?" I said.

Your broken head is a pre-existing condition, Nariel texted, followed by another coughing laugh.

"Funny," I said. "So, you're probably not going to be any help, right?"

She just kept laughing.

"Too bad," I said, kicking off my boots and letting them sink. "Because I have something you're going to want pretty soon."

Her coughing laugh turned to real coughing as a swell hit her in the face. *Do you have more pithy advice?*

I slipped off my pants, thankful that I'd dressed from the practical drawers in my wardrobe. The thin weave meant it was easy to knot the legs shut. I whipped my pants over my head, and they filled with air. Another quick knot in the waistband, and I let my pants hit the water with a wet slap.

"Nope," I said, tucking my pant legs around my shoulders and kicking away. "Just flotation."

Nariel stopped laughing.

"I still have a shirt," I said. "Not as buoyant as this baby, but it's better than nothing."

I would rather die.

"Another hour, and you just might get your wish."

I did a lazy scissor kick, easing back and letting my lungs and my pants do all the lifting for me. Another swell rolled through us. I bobbled over the wave, but Nariel got water right in her gaping mouth. She coughed, hard and wet, and I said, "You can use a hand to keep your mouth shut, or you can use it to stay afloat. Tough choice."

I am not giving you anything.

"I haven't even asked," I said. "I just want to help."

Go to hell.

Another swell, bigger than the previous one, lifted us into the air for a moment. "I think the tides are shifting," I said after we'd settled. "We're going to get some serious whitecaps. Think you can handle that?"

This time, Nariel flailed to keep her head above water. She gulped another mouthful, then texted, *Please help me.*

"Oh, changing our tune?" I said. "Isn't your magical Ghost training going to save you?"

Please help me.

"You gonna tell me what you know?" I said, pulling off my shirt and tying the sleeves shut.

The next swell was about a meter high, enough to drop us both with stomach-churning speed. I inflated my shirt, while Nariel choked and thrashed until she yelled "YEAH! YEAH!"

I swam over and handed her my pants. She grabbed onto them, and I hugged the shirt. "Of course, that was under duress, so it's probably bullshit, but at least I have a recording of you wailing for help. That'll probably come in handy."

Nariel just sniffed. *You are still a bitch.*

"You know, I'm just trying to get by," I said. "You're the one who brought an armed kill squad here. Doesn't that make you a little overzealous?"

You have no idea what is happening here, do you?

"I know that your goons carted away a lab full of very nasty fungus," I said. "I know that the creator of that fungus was working with a guy who's growing a new variety of cane that's probably resistant to that fungus. I know *that* guy has a new refinery inside his old one, and that a bunch of people who were supposed to be dead aren't. You have anything to do with that?"

Nariel snorted. *You should have gotten me to talk before you gave me this float. That was the first thing we learned in business school: money on the table before anything gets signed.*

"True, but we also learned not to waste our time dealing with cranky suppliers when you could go to another one with less effort," I said.

What is that supposed to mean?

"It means that one of your team is going to Breach for real, which means I'll find out what I need to know."

She snorted. *Are you talking about Banks? Do you really believe him? He is* trained *to deceive.*

"That's a chance I'll have to take."

There was a sudden blast of a horn behind us, and I looked to see a fleet of police cruisers chopping toward us. For a brief second, I tensed, but then I saw Soni, Jilly, Banks standing on the prow of the lead craft.

The boats slowed and turned, and two life rings flew over the side. I helped Nariel into hers, and they hauled us out of the water and onto the heaving deck. Jilly threw herself around me, and Soni and Banks stood nearby, both wearing shit-eating grins.

"Jesus, boss, you are so badass," said Jilly.

"Please promise me you won't try to follow in my footsteps," I said. "It's just not worth it." I looked at Soni. "I am so glad to see you that I just might start crying, so let's get going."

"Where did she come from?" asked Soni, pointing at Nariel as a cop wrapped her in a blanket.

I shrugged. "Y'know, some people just come along for the ride." Despite her bulk, Nariel looked small and sad.

Soni looked at the half-naked woman, then at me and said, "Padma, what the hell is going on?"

I shivered. "You got any extra trousers on this tub?"

TWENTY-FOUR

"Let me get this straight," said Soni, her armor clacking as she sat back in her chair. "Vytai Bloombeck... was a *genius*?"

Soni, Banks, Jilly, and I were in a spartan cabin belowdecks. There were the standard office table, chairs, and brain-fuzzing fluorescent lighting. Banks leaned against the bulkhead, looking out the porthole at the blue-grey ocean. Jilly bounced in her seat. Soni sat opposite me at the table, fiddling with a pad. Except for the thrum of the engines and the roll of the boat, we could have been back at a precinct house.

"Well, I wouldn't go *that* far," I said, scratching my leg through the spare tactical uniform Soni had loaned me. "But the man certainly had a talent for growing mold."

"I know," said Soni. "I've seen him."

"Not the kind *on* him," I said. "Well, not *just* that kind. Look, just watch the footage I shot over the past twelve hours, and everything will become clear."

"We tried," said Soni, showing me the pad. There was nothing but static. "Your head's a bit messed up."

"Well, you're the one who waved that lightstick at me," I said.

"That had nothing to do with your pai's ability to record," said Soni. "It just set up the travel tags. Which you disobeyed."

"Because of the important shit, remember?" I said, blinking back into my buffer. Nothing there. "Great, even *I* can't see anything."

"Oh, that's probably my fault," said Banks, looking up from the porthole. "Your pai hasn't been able to record anything for a bit."

I blinked, trying to keep from punching him. "Since when?"

"Two days ago. When we first met. On the boat."

"So, that means everything I've seen..."

Banks swallowed and flicked his fingers in the air. "Poof."

"Why in hell did you do that?"

"Well, it wouldn't do me much good as a covert operative if you could go and show people my face, would it?" said Banks. "It's standard procedure for us."

I took a deep breath, then looked at Soni. "Well, it seems that everything I've said will sound pretty insane now."

Soni nodded. "Lucky for you, Banks was able to corroborate a lot of what you said."

"Thank God."

"But you're still under arrest for Saarien's murder."

"But he's not dead!" I yelled. "The three of us saw him! He yelled at me! Twice!"

"Maybe," said Soni, "but I still have a body that matches his DNA tags. So, unless you can produce the real, live Saarien–"

"He's in Sou's Reach! In his giant, secret refinery! Along with Jordan Blanton and–"

"–and now you're starting to sound like a crazy person,"

she said. "But we will deal with that, after we deal with this little issue of the Ghosts running around and killing people."

"Only Vytai Bloombeck," said Banks. "He was the only one we were permitted to deal with."

"–which puts *you* on the hook for his murder," said Soni. "And for screwing with Padma's pai."

"And yours, too," said Banks. "Actually, just about everyone I've been in contact with. Sorry, it's part of my own pai's protocols. Special Ghosty stuff."

Soni held up the pad. "This, too?"

Banks nodded.

"Right," said Soni, tossing the pad aside and pulling a stack of paper and a pen from under the table. "Looks like we'll have to start at the beginning. Name."

"Come on, Soni, can't we just sail to Sou's Reach, bust Saarien's little cane deal, and be done with it?"

Soni put down the pen and gave me her hardest Cop Stare. "When you were leading the strike at the brush factory, did I tell you how to do your job?"

"You might have said a few words."

"I seem to remember telling you to stick to your guns, because what you were doing was important," said Soni. "I respected your work, both as a professional and as someone who knew how important it was to stand up to WalWa or anyone else who tried to screw with the Union. You had your role to play, your rules to follow. And now I have mine, and that means dealing with a stack of dead bodies in the wake of an incursion by agents of our former employer. Don't you think that's important?"

I sighed. "Yes, Captain Baghram."

"Goddamn right," said Soni, snatching the pen and

pointing it at Banks. "Now. Name."

"Banks."

"Full name."

"That's it," he said. "I only have the one name. Easier that way."

"Fine," said Soni, scratching on the paper. She got a few letters written before the pen gave out. "Jesus Christ, you'd think someone would check if there were enough ink on this boat." She stood up and pointed the pen at both of us. "Stay here."

"Like we have anywhere to go," I said.

"Didn't stop you before," she said, and left the room. The door clacked shut behind her.

Banks and I looked at each other for a moment. "Any chance of you fixing my pai?" I said.

"It'll fix itself after I leave," he said. "Part of the protocol. Makes people think their pais are screwing up themselves. It's a bit easier to pull off on Union-controlled planets because of all the firmware patches."

"We reburn every pai's firmware when someone signs up."

"I don't have to get one, do I?" said Jilly.

"We don't have the capability to make them," I said. "You're safe. Unless there's someone here who *does* know how to fix nanometer-wide circuits. Now that I've seen what Bloombeck could do, I'm wondering how many other people there are like him here."

"Not many," said Banks. "The Big Three really does keep a close eye on the people who Breach. Some of them just fell through the cracks."

"Bloombeck's been here for twenty years."

"Sometimes the cracks are *really* big."

"So that's why you killed him?" I said. "Just to clean up someone's mistake?"

"He's dead?" said Jilly. "The fat guy?"

"Thanks to him," I said, nodding at Banks. Jilly gave him a once-over, then scooted to the other side of the room.

"Look," said Banks, "Mimi shot him because he was dangerous to you, to me, and to everyone in Occupied Space. He took a garden variety crop pest and turned it into something that could wipe out every last bit of cane on this planet. Imagine what that would do if it got offworld? We'd be thrown back to the Stone Age inside of a decade."

"I think that's exaggerating a bit."

"Is it?" said Banks. "The annual harvest from Santee Anchorage, in a bad year, is enough to power four other worlds. A *bad* year. When things are humming, you can power a *dozen* worlds. Start multiplying that effect by hundreds of other colonies, start thinking about the *trillions* of people who rely on industrial cane for fuel, for plastics, for everything that makes our civilization run. Even our star drives need a jump start from a cane-derived fuel cell. If the black stripe spread, all of that would be gone."

"Hooray for our corporate saviors," I said.

"You think you guys can come up with an antifungal treatment or put some kind of terminator genes in Bloombeck's strain?" said Banks. "We can. It'll stop here."

"But you still killed him," I said. "You acted on behalf of WalWa. You could have dimed him to Soni, you could have exposed him on the Public, you could have done all sorts of things, but you killed him. He was in the way of some Big Three business, and we can't have that."

"You know, up until now, I thought you *hated* him."

"I did," I said. "But he was still Union, and he didn't

deserve what happened to him. Same with Jordan, and Tonggow, and–"

"And Saarien?"

"Don't change the subject."

"What were we talking about?"

"You and your buddies killing Union people."

"But Jordan and *her* buddies are alive," said Banks. "And I had *nothing* to do with them."

"It doesn't matter," I said. "Tonggow's gone, so the Co-Op will take over her distillery and probably do something to screw it up, which is just as well since it seems like every stick of cane on this planet is going to turn to goo or distill into skunked rum. But that's OK, because I'm going to get tossed in prison or my brain's gonna go *pop* anyway. Fuck. Fuck!" I kicked the wall and slammed the porthole shut. It just bounced off its frame and swung back into place. I leaned back against the bulkhead and stared up at the ceiling.

"You know," I said, "the thing of it is that I *still* didn't get you guys signed up. You're all going to bounce away, and I didn't seal the deal."

"Well, I still want to Breach."

"Terrific," I said. "That'll go over really well. 'Hi, guys, this is Banks. He used to be a Ghost, but now he's totally on our side. Also, he had nothing to do with that bunch of corpses we had over the past few days.'"

"Well, I didn't," said Banks. "None of us did. Look, Padma, I know you're angry, but, just for one moment, please look at my situation from a management position."

"Oh, that is nowhere near funny."

"It wasn't meant to be," said Banks. "Listen, our gig was to get in and out as fast as possible with the minimum amount of fuss. That's why our pais futz with everyone else's: by the time we've left and people realize something's wrong, they'll rewind their buffers and just see static. They'll only have their memories, which are prone to mistakes, especially if we ourselves are unmemorable."

"Executing someone in his home and then tearing up a stack of houses is going to be hard to forget."

"And that's because this whole thing has gone *wrong*," said Banks. "We should have gotten in and out, and no one would have known or cared that we were here. Instead, there's a string of bodies, a gun battle, airships–"

"And don't forget the crane chase."

"Exactly!" said Banks. "None of this crap was supposed to happen. None of it is what I signed up for all those years ago." He snorted.

"Why did you?" said Jilly.

"Would you believe it was because I was too good at my job?" he said. "I'd get assigned to a case, and I'd start digging under all the layers of legal weirdness because I wanted to see where it all went. It was great for a while, and then I got assigned to this class-action lawsuit."

"What's that?" asked Jilly.

"A bunch of people working together to sue some asshole," I said.

Banks gave me a look. "It was on a shared world, one split between WalWa and MacDonald Heavy. Some colonists sued WalWa for not following through on contractual relief efforts during a ricewheat blight. I started studying the whole thing, reading through transcripts and field interviews, even digging up documentaries about the place, and then I saw that none of it fit. The place was run by respected agronomists and botanists, and they had a record of careful land management for generations.

"And then I realized that there was a hole in the data. It kept moving around: bits of garbled interviews, seconds of fuzzed footage. And I traced the whole thing back to the colony's head of security, who talked about a group of engineers who'd shown up the season before to do some surveying, and then had vanished. And then I go through *another* round of research, because this whole thing fascinated and pissed me off, and I look through chemical assays and water samples, and realize these engineers had been tampering with the water supply of a LiaoCon colony on the other side of the mountain range, and that they had introduced contaminants into the water table that caused the blight.

"So, I bring the whole thing up to my bosses, and, next thing I know, someone tosses a bag over my head, hauls me away to a nasty little office, and they make me an offer: sign up as a Ghost, or disappear." He shook his head. "That was fifteen years ago. I think."

"You think?"

"All that time awake, going from one gig to the next, it's all..." He waved his hand, like he was trying to stir the words out of his brain. "You know how you need to dream? Try not being able to sleep."

"Because of your pai?"

He nodded. "We can access other people's pais, but when we sleep, we lose control over what we're processing. It's hard enough to see through another person's eyes, but when it's a dozen, or a hundred, or a whole city full of people... and then we can't even control what we do." He swallowed.

"What else happens?" I said. "From staying awake?"

"You get paranoid as hell, because you start to see the way everyone is looking at you, and you second guess if you're staying undercover or not," he said. "Most of us are good at filtering it out, but sometimes something can throw you off. If you don't keep a tamp on your emotions, you can lose focus, start to get really worked up."

I thought back to Nariel. "Would, say, confronting an unpleasant memory do that?"

"It would have to be pretty unpleasant."

"Getting fired and demoted and bounced out of corporate life?"

Banks furrowed his brows. "Are you talking about Ellie?"

"I'm talking about *Nariel*," I said, and I told him the whole sordid tale.

By the time I was finished, Banks had his face in his hands. "Well, that certainly explains a lot."

"Like?"

He took a deep breath. "Well, it's quite likely that my teammate has gone and, um, freelanced."

"That's an interesting way to put it," I said. "How much 'freelancing' are we talking about?"

"Maybe the woman who owns the distillery."

"What about Saarien?"

"Well, he's not exactly dead."

"But would she be working with him?" I said.

"Maybe," said Banks. "It would certainly fit with the pattern."

"What pattern?"

"Every one of those people who's dead or supposed to be dead had seen us," said Banks.

"So have a few hundred other people," I said. "Is Nariel going to start executing whole crowds next?"

"No, not unless *you* need those people to get ahead."

My blood ran cold. "Banks, when you say that you can access other pais, does that include the ones lodged in yours and your fellow Ghosts' eyes?"

Banks, to his credit, looked me in the eye as he nodded. "Everything I've seen and heard, everyone else on the team has, too."

"So, when you and I were talking to Wash, Nariel knew about how my deal with him depended on getting Jordan and her crew to help him out?"

He nodded.

"And when I was talking with Tonggow earlier, she saw that?"

He nodded, a little quicker this time.

"And, when you and I were in that warehouse, and I told you about how I came to be here... she knew that?"

He nodded.

"Sweet Working Christ, she did it," I said. "Nariel killed Tonggow, what, just to get back at me?"

"I think so."

"But this also means that *you* knew everything she'd seen, right?"

"Up to a point," said Banks. "I think she's had something done to her pai so I can't see *everything*."

"But you knew it was her shooting at us in Steelcase and in the burn room."

"Yeah, but I couldn't break cover."

"Why?" I said. "You were so worried about the mission?"

"No, I was worried that if I let on that I knew, you wouldn't help me Breach," he said. "You remember me talking about the two crazy women I worked for? They're here."

"What, Nariel and Mimi?"

"No," said Banks. "The other two."

"The twins?" I said. "Those old ladies?"

"Fooled you, didn't they? They're mental, but they're insanely good at their job."

"Is that why they're here? To keep you in line?"

He nodded. "They've known for a while I've wanted to leave. Been getting careless in my work. Not paying attention to details, like the fact that one of my people has an unpleasant personal history with the person who's guiding us around."

"That would have been helpful."

"And I didn't, because I didn't care," he said. "As soon as I got out of that can, I stopped caring. I was *almost* free." He rubbed his temples. "It was my job to keep an eye on Ellie. Nariel. Whatever. It was my job, and I failed at it, and now all those people are dead, and your life is fucked, and quite possibly *everyone's* life, too."

The cutter's gentle rocking was starting to get to me. "You know, I really should feel sorry for you, Banks. You signed a contract with the devil, and you got screwed for it." I turned and pointed a finger at his head. "But you *lied* to me. You could have told me who you were from the get-go, and I would have gotten over it. Hell, I might have stepped up to the plate for you, because you're just the kind of person the Union is supposed to protect."

"I know," he said, "I know, but how could I tell you? How could I have done this any other way that wouldn't have ended with you tossing me in jail or sending me back up the cable?"

"You would have had to trust me," I said. "And now I don't know if I can trust you."

Soni walked back into the room, a box of crayons in her hand. "Can you believe this is the only thing I could find? Leftover from Take Your Kids to Work Day." She looked at us both, me at the porthole and Banks sitting at the table, staring at his boots. "I miss something?"

"Banks is ready to make his statement," I said, "and then Jilly will, and then *I* will, and then I'd like to go to jail as far from his pai as I can, please."

"No need for that," said Soni. "Got a call on the radio, which is the only piece of electronics *not* affected by your friend, and you're in the clear, Padma."

"No shit?"

"None," said Soni, sitting at the table. "Evanrute Saarien was last seen thirty minutes ago at the tail of a convoy of cargo trucks leaving Sou's Reach for Steelcase."

"You sure it was him?"

Soni nodded. "He plowed through a pair of patrol wagons, and yelled something about how it was all for the glory of the Struggle and to get the hell out of his way."

"That sounds right," I said. "Your guys bust him?"

"Lost him in the stacks," said Soni. "And there's so much cargo heading out to the lifter that it's going to take a while to find him. But we will. I got the charges dropped, so you're free to go as soon as we get to land."

"What about me?" said Banks.

"You," said Soni, "are going to give me a full statement, and then we'll see."

Banks looked at me. "I don't suppose I could count on you as a character witness?"

"That depends on how quickly you can get your pai reburned so you don't go tattling everything to your buddies," I said.

Soni threw down the crayon and looked at Banks. "Goddamn *Ghosts*. Does that mean your team knows where you and that one-eyed nutbag are?"

Jilly leaned away from the porthole. "Boss, we got bad company!"

"Yeah," said Banks, "and I think they're about here. Sorry."

An airship carrier buzzed the cutter, sending a spray of ocean water from its turbines. It zipped back, hovering alongside us. It held a stack of three cargo cans, all of them streaked with rust. On the top can was a single figure in black, squatting behind the biggest cannon I had seen since B-school. "We need to go," I said, hustling away from the porthole as the airship opened fire.

Soni yelled something, but I couldn't hear it over the continuous buzz of the cannon and the ship coming to pieces around us. The cutter lurched, sending us scrambling for footing. Then a few hundred rounds pierced the cabin, and none of us cared about standing up anymore. I pulled Jilly to the deck, Banks huddling over both of us. Soni kept yelling orders as she lay flat in front of me. The gunfire continued until the entire boat shook, and the stench of smoke and cane diesel engulfed us.

One of the airship's PAs crackled. "STAND BY TO BE BOARDED," came a goonish voice.

"To hell with that," yelled Soni over the turbines' whine, pulling her sidearm out of her holster.

"Are you high?" I yelled back. "Riot foam against them?"

"You got a better idea?"

"Well, fleeing comes to mind," I yelled.

"No way," yelled Soni. "These Ghosts think they can just blow up my boat and get away with it?"

"Hey, how about how they tried to kill your friend?"

"That, too," she yelled, scooting toward the cabin door. The cannon opened up, burying us under a hail of splintered wood and shattered metal.

six survivors fore, ten aft, texted Banks. *everyone else overboard.*

Soni and I turned to him, and he texted *you want to live you need to trust me.* Soni popped her head out again, then waved for us to follow.

Banks guided us through the ruins of the boat, sending texts to us and the surviving friendlies. A few minutes of skulking, and we all gathered in the engine room.

"Great, now we're boxed in," I said.

"No, this is perfect," said Soni. "We can get out through the bilge."

"What happened to making them pay?"

"Sixteen against that gun doesn't even make for a good bar story," said Soni, opening a hatch. A stench like rotten bait bloomed in the compartment. "In you go."

I held out a hand to Banks. "After you, counselor."

"You take me to the best places," he said, taking a deep breath, then diving in. Jilly gave me the stink eye but leaped through the hatch. The other crew followed as I helped Soni out of her armor.

"Help *is* on the way, right?" I said, cracking the seals under her arms.

"Even if the bad guys jammed all of our signals, someone's going to report a police cutter on fire in the middle of the shipping lanes," she said, tossing aside her leggings.

"Assuming anyone cares about the police," I said, tugging at her chest plate.

"The people *love* us," she said as someone pounded on

the engine room hatch.

"I can tell," I said, and we jumped in.

It only took seventeen seconds to swim through the bilge – and I know, because I counted, because it was the only thing that kept my mind off the fact that this was the second time in twelve hours that I'd gone for a dip in filth – and pop out behind the cutter's dead propellers. The airship hovered off the starboard bow, its turbines drowning out any conversation. *now what?* one of the crew texted.

now we wait, Soni answered. *rescue en route.*

Brilliant, I texted, then looked at Banks. He had that green look, though anyone would after what we'd been through. *You OK?*

you really concerned?

If anyone's going to kick your ass, it's going to be me.

He gave me a weak smile, then texted, *what's grabbing my leg?*

Squid, probably, I texted. *Perfectly safe.*

Banks gave me a weak nod, then gurgled as he disappeared under the water.

TWENTY-FIVE

Before I could yell, a metal tentacle broke the surface and thrashed around. It knocked one of the crew aside, spooking everyone else. They swam over each other as the tentacle paused, and I saw that it wasn't some robosquid but one of the airship's cargo claws. I grabbed at it, wrapping my legs around the thing as it zipped back underwater.

It pulled me along the length of the keel, then out of the water and into the sky. As I gulped air, the airship's turbine wash battered down on my head. I tried to keep my grip, but the cargo claw shook once, hard, and I slipped away, only to have the claw grab my leg and spin me, upside-down, into the airship's open bay doors.

The winch stopped with a clang, but the bay doors didn't close. "Hey!" I called out, staring at the ocean fifty meters below. "Still in peril here!"

Someone behind me gagged, and I looked around to see Banks hanging next to me. "You're not careful, that's be gonna be your epitaph."

"Are you all right?"

He gave a laugh, then stopped. "Sorry, I thought you

were being ironic, there."

"Irony comes after rescue," I said, reaching up for the cargo claw again. My stomach muscles cursed me, and I flopped back. "You getting any other pais?"

"Just you," said Banks. "Front compartment's got shielding."

"Well, can you pick up anything from what I see?"

"Yeah."

"What?"

"I look like hell," he said.

The hatch to the cockpit hissed open, and a slim Ghost climbed out. She strode to the edge of the open cargo bay and squatted in front of me. Her mask was a little girl's face, with a crown and a sweet smile. "You need a hand?" came her voice, rough and crackly from the mask's speakers.

"Close the bay doors!" yelled Banks.

She shook her head. "I think we need to do a little negotiation first."

"Close the fucking doors, Mimi!"

"Oh, you know it doesn't work this way," said Mimi, standing up and nudging me in the chest with a boot, just enough so I started to sway. "You know you're not supposed to help. You're supposed to keep your mouth shut. Makes everyone's lives easier. Makes everything *cleaner*."

I caught the edge of the grillwork catwalk that ringed the cargo bay. Mimi reached into her pocket and snicked a retractable baton to its full length. She shook her head again and brought it down on my hands. I lost my grip and swung back into open space, my knuckles throbbing.

"Now," said Mimi, edging around the catwalk to Banks, "you want her to live, you need to keep working for us."

"Banks, don't you do it," I yelled, digging into the grillwork.

"Miss Mehta, you are not in a position to dictate terms," said Mimi, poking me in the throat with the baton. "You never really have been. Banks?"

"Don't!" I yelled, but Banks said, "OK."

"Well done," said Mimi, and she got up and jammed a button on the compartment's wall. The doors closed. I tumbled to the deck and saw Mimi raise the baton in time to roll into her shins. She staggered back, and I launched myself at her until we collided with a bulkhead. I pulled her head down into my knee, and her mask speakers squealed as they shattered. Before she could hit back, I brought my fists down on the back of her neck until she collapsed.

"You people really should rethink this mask thing," I said, helping Banks to his feet. "What's wrong with a good old-fashioned helmet?"

"Psychological edge," he said as he wobbled upright. "Plus, helmets get hot. Ooh, all the blood's still in my head."

"Better there than on the deck," I said, giving Mimi a kick to the face as she tried to get up.

"You know that was under duress," said Banks. "That deal."

"Shut up," I said, and reached out to hug him. "You said 'no' the first time, and that's what counts." He wrapped his arms around me, more to steady himself than anything, but I took my time before I pushed him away.

I dug through Mimi's belt and pockets for anything useful, but only found her baton and ammunition. "Where's her gun?" I said, pointing at the empty holster. Banks tapped me on the shoulder, and I followed his outstretched finger.

Nariel stood at the open hatch, a pistol in each hand. Her jaw, now deep purple, was wrapped closed with a pressure bandage. Another bandage covered her bad eye. She kept one gun on Banks and pointed the other at the baton in my hand, then motioned toward the deck. I dropped the baton and put up my hands. Nariel nodded, then waved the gun toward the cockpit.

I had never been in an airship cockpit, despite many offers for tours from friends, coworkers, and drunken pilots in bars. I really didn't see the point; if I was going to get around Santee, I wanted to be in the open air, not cooped up in a box. Still, I knew what to expect: a shitload of lights and buttons, uncomfortable seats, and a view of the horizon.

I didn't expect to see two old ladies in black body armor at the controls, singing old marketing jingles at the tops of their lungs.

Madolyn turned from the copilot's seat and gave me a sweet, sweet smile. "Hello! So good to see you both. Feel free to sing along." Her mask, a viper, sat on the console in front of her.

"You know any of these?" said Gricelda from the pilot's seat, her raven mask perched on the top of her head.

"A few, from History of Marketing," I said, keeping an eye on Nariel's guns. "Used to play some of those in a loop to help me sleep."

"Me, too, except the last one about teaching the world to sing. So trite," said Gricelda. "I'm so glad they still taught you that. Where'd you go to B-school?"

Both of their faces were lit up, like they were spinster aunties who'd just seen their niece play violin for the first time. I didn't know whether to tell them about my day over tea and cookies or try for another swing.

Gricelda clucked her tongue. "Look at us nattering on, and we haven't offered you a seat."

Nariel pointed a gun at the navigator's seat, which I took. Banks sat opposite.

"Much better," said Gricelda. "Now, you and I and my little sister have already talked, of course."

"Little by two minutes," said Madolyn, popping over the top of her seat. "She always thinks that gives her prerogative."

"It got me into flight school before you."

"By one slot!" said Madolyn, putting a gloved finger in her sister's face. "Just because you pushed me out of line, like you do every time we're going for a jaunt."

"Learn to keep up," said Gricelda.

"I'll show you how to keep up," said Madolyn, giving the yoke a little nudge. The airship bucked down and to the right, not enough to send me out of my seat, but plenty to make my stomach flip.

Gricelda thumped her sister on the shoulder and righted the carrier. "*That's* why you're always in the right-hand chair," she said, keeping a firm grip on her yoke. "You just don't *do* that kind of thing when you're at the controls."

"Apologies," sang Madolyn, giving me that tea-and-cookies smile. "Now, where were we?"

The old ladies looked at me. I looked at Banks. Banks looked at Nariel. Nariel just kept pointing both guns at me.

"I think I was unarmed," I said, "and the person who wants me dead wasn't."

"Ah," said Madolyn, looking at Nariel. "I think you can put those away, dear."

Nariel flicked her eyes toward Madolyn, but the guns didn't move.

"That wasn't a request," said Gricelda. She put up a hand, first finger aimed at Nariel and thumb held high. She brought her thumb down and said, "Bang."

Nariel's good eye rolled up in her head, and she collapsed on the deck.

"I do hate it when the help gets stroppy," said Gricelda. "You think you've trained them, taught them how to behave, but then their brains get screwy and you have to bring out the big guns."

"What did you do?" I said, nudging Nariel with my toe. She twitched, her lips quivering.

"Just a little swat on the nose," said Gricelda. "Something we do with all of our misbehaving children." She shot Banks a look so harsh he flinched.

"Now that that's settled," said Madolyn, "I think it's time we had a little chat."

"Indeed," said Gricelda. "Especially after all you've put us through."

"Me?" I said. "You're the ones with the guns. What could I have done to you?"

"You got in the way, dear," said Madolyn. "We had quite the orchestrated maneuvers planned, and you gummed up the works like jellybeans on an escalator."

"Well, I beg your pardon," I said. "Next time, I'll be sure to consult your people, maybe send out some engraved invitations."

"Would you, dear?" said Gricelda. "That would be *quite* helpful."

"I think she's being facetious, sis," said Madolyn.

"One of her many talents," said Gricelda. "All the more reason to put the cards on the table."

"You hold all of them," I said. "I have none."

"Just the way we like it," said Madolyn.

"Never bet against the house," said Gricelda.

"Especially when the house has the guns," said Madolyn.

"Bloody great guns," said Gricelda.

"Look, if you're going to kill me like you did everyone

else, just do it, OK?" I said. "This is driving me crazy."

"Kill you?" said Gricelda. "Whatever gave you that idea?"

"The pile of bodies in your wake," I said.

"Which weren't our fault," said Madolyn. "Though, I must admit, you can't make an omelette without smashing a few eggs."

"And Lord knows there's been plenty of that the past few days," said Gricelda.

"Indeed," said Madolyn. "We're very impressed with your drive, your talent–"

"And your ability to kick some serious ass," said Gricelda.

"But we're getting off track," said Madolyn. "We have a defective unit here, and we need a replacement."

I looked down at Nariel.

"Oh, no, not her!" said Gricelda. "Your friend, here. Mr Banks."

Banks looked at his boots.

"When we first recruited him, he was the most excellent employee," said Gricelda.

"Rock solid with a laserlike focus," said Madolyn.

"And now?" Gricelda clucked her tongue. "Flabby."

"Fuzzy."

"Sloppy."

"I mean, *really*, Mr Banks, did you think we weren't on to you?" said Madolyn. "Hiding in a fleet of mining ships... did you really think that would throw us off?"

Banks's eyebrows beetled as he stared at his boot tips. He flexed his cheeks like he was trying not to puke. I leaned toward him. "*What* mining ships?"

"You should know about them, dear," said Gricelda. "Fifteen LiaoCon Xinzang-Class mining craft, bound from Nanqu. Mr Banks had stowed away on one of them – and might have continued stowing away except for us catching up a few weeks ago."

"Enough time to retrieve him and get our stories straight," said Madolyn.

"And to cover our tracks," said Gricelda. She chuckled, and flicked her fingers to the ceiling. "Boom."

My mouth went dry. "You killed all those people," I said. "They were going to Breach, they weren't in your way."

"Mr Banks should have taken that into account before he hopped on board," said Madolyn.

"We did make Mr Banks explain to the crews what was going to happen," said Gricelda, shaking her head. "Entropic cascades are supposed to be painless, but we felt a little forewarning was polite."

"Next time, Mr Banks, you'd be better off nailing a resignation letter to your own forehead," said Madolyn.

"Which you could still do," said Gricelda, her face darkening as her smile stayed bright. "Might save us the trouble."

"I think I've heard enough," I said, leaning back in my seat.

"Of course, dear," said Madolyn. "You must be quite tired."

"Especially since you've missed your nightly tipple." Gricelda mimed taking a drink, tipping her thumb to her mouth and her pinky to the sky.

I glared at Banks.

"Oh, don't be harsh, dear," said Madolyn. "Mr Banks couldn't help it."

"It's his pai, yeah, I know," I said.

"Precisely," said Madolyn. "And it's *yours*, too. And your interesting neurological issue."

"We could have you fixed in a jiffy," said Gricelda.

"Your hibernant was a test batch, one that short-circuited your posterior cortex," said Madolyn. "Batch twenty-two-oh-one? The kind that came in gold bags?"

"There are remedies now," said Gricelda.

"Treatments," said Madolyn.

"Solutions," said Gricelda. "Not halfbaked rituals and drinking distilled yeast excrement."

"Though, I have to admit, I *did* like that one rum from the bar with the palm trees," said Madolyn.

"More for you," said Gricelda. "I prefer to have my endorphins the old-fashioned way: by plunging myself into life-threatening danger. Like now." She eased the yoke downward. I looked up through the airship's windshield and saw the lifter port looming large. "I'm going to let Maddie take us in."

"Oh, *now* I get to fly," said Madolyn.

"You need the practice."

"I'll show you practice," she said, taking the controls and ducking us below the line of airships waiting to land.

"Better strap in," said Gricelda. "She likes to land a little hot."

"And unannounced," said Madolyn. "Who has time?"

I could barely snap my harness closed before Madolyn cranked the throttle. Everything whizzed past us at gutchurning speed, and then she spun the ship around and cranked the lift turbines to maximum. The entire carrier shook and rattled, like a giant was going to tear it apart, and I could hear the coral steel lines that held the cargo cans scream as they stretched. My stomach threatened to leave my body via my eye sockets, but then Madolyn eased us into a landing berth, dropped the cans with a gentle *thud*, and put the ship down with an easy touch.

"Lovely," she said, powering everything down. "Nothing gets the blood pumping like defying gravity."

"One day, gravity is going to have a few words with you," said Gricelda.

"Oh, pooh," said Madolyn, unbuckling her restraints. "Landing is just like taking off, only backwards. Are you all right, Miss Mehta?"

"Fine," I said, looking down at my hands; they were clawing at the seat cushions. Nariel had slid around during the landing, so one of her hands, still clutching a pistol, was right at my feet. I wondered if I could make a move before the old ladies did.

"I wouldn't, if I were you," said Gricelda from her seat. "What we did to her, we could *easily* do to you."

"Right," I said, sitting up.

"Now, dears," said Madolyn from the hatch. "We have a lot to talk about, and not enough time to make it happen, so chop chop."

I unbuckled and got up, getting one more glance at Nariel and her guns before walking through the hatch.

"Would you mind, Miss Mehta?" said Gricelda, pointing at Mimi's prone body. "My back, you know. And the fact that I'm too senior to have to do that kind of crap anymore."

For a woman who had looked so slight and frail, Mimi was heavy as hell. I got her over my shoulders, her armor clacking into the back of my head, and limped off the airship. Banks followed, carrying Nariel.

We had landed in a quiet part of the lifter yard, far away from the trains and cranes and everything that stacked cans on their trip up the cable. The dull roar of the traffic washed over the walls of coral steel that surrounded us, and

I wondered if I could get a message out in the middle of all this metal. I wondered if the twins would pick it up and interfere with it. I wondered if they would just turn my brain to jelly.

Gricelda and Madolyn stood in front of the three cargo cans they had boosted from Partridge Hutong. There were a few blobs of hardened riot foam on them, proof that Soni's cops could still hit a moving target. "Just in here, please," said Gricelda, opening the door to Bloombeck's flat. "I believe Mr Bloombeck had some excellent couches."

The couches, the tables, the chairs, everything lay scattered about the flat. "Contents may have shifted during flight," said Madolyn, pushing aside a pile of crystal mice that had, somehow, survived the trip. Bloombeck's body was gone; the only sign of him was a melon-sized spatter of blood on the wall. Everything smelled like vanilla.

"You didn't think the lab might have gotten knocked around?" I said. "A few hundred glass vials full of Christ-knows-what didn't concern you?"

"It did," said Gricelda, "which is why we used the appropriate packing material." She pointed at the ceiling hatch; it was filled with hardened riot foam. "I do wish they'd do something about the scent, though."

Banks and I set Nariel and Mimi on the ground while the twins set two chairs upright. He avoided my gaze as he turned a table upright and sat on it.

"Oh, Mr Banks, don't be such a Sulky Suzie," said Madolyn. "We taught you better than that. Or are you still upset you've gotten messy and didn't cover your tracks any better?"

"It took us quite a while to get you the first time," said Gricelda.

I looked at Banks. "You tried to Breach before?"

"Six years ago," said Madolyn. "He jumped ship on the way to a job." She *tsked*. "There were only three destinations from that situation, and you took the most obvious one." She swept a hand out the window.

"However, it has led us to *you*," said Gricelda, reaching back to smile at me. "Which brings us to our offer."

"We want you to work for us."

"In an executive capacity."

"Of course."

"Of *course*."

"As what?" I said.

"As one of *us*," said Gricelda. "As a Covert Business Interference Asset."

"There'll be all sorts of benefits, of course," said Madolyn. "We'll solve your little brain problem for starters. That'll feel nice, won't it?"

"And, just to sweeten the deal, we'll put you in charge of your former associate again!" Gricelda pointed to Nariel, like she was a freshly landed prize sturgeon.

"It's time we had some fresh talent," said Madolyn.

"New perspective."

"New blood."

"Ours is beginning to get a bit stale."

"Speak for yourself," said Madolyn.

"I've seen your medical report, dear, and it ain't pretty," said Gricelda.

"The point, Miss Mehta, is that you could be an incredible asset to our team."

"Santee Anchorage is just the jumping-off point of our new operation," said Madolyn, showing me her teeth. "We're going to move slowly at first, a planet here, a station there, but we'll be making big moves soon."

"*Giant* moves," said Gricelda. "The kind that end up with people rewriting history books that are then published on your own presses."

"So *many* opportunities, not just in making rum. There's agriculture."

"Manufacture."

"Finance."

"Media."

"Guns," said Madolyn, raising an eyebrow.

"Bloody *great* guns," said Gricelda, clapping her hands.

"So, how about it?" said Madolyn with a smile and shrug, even though her eyes were all business. "Are you in?"

"Imagine what we'll do!" said Gricelda.

"Imagine what *you'll* do," said Madolyn.

"Conquest!"

"Adventure!"

"Revenge…" Gricelda dropped that last word and let it sit there, like a cat who'd just killed a pigeon and dumped it on the lunch table.

Madolyn nodded. "You're not the only one who just wanted a better life and got turned into a guinea pig."

"We're all head cases," said Gricelda, waving a hand to encircle all of us. "We've seen bits and pieces of far worse experimentation, things that have pushed the boundaries of exploitation way, way into bad territory."

"Audience hybridization."

"Genetic focus grouping."

"Behavioral supplementation."

"Soul mining."

"Atmospheric licensing."

"Subscription warfare."

"Imagine entire populations, entire planets, all either working for or buying from the Big Three, their lives manipulated all in the name of time and motion," said Madolyn. "You think it's bad having your dreams stolen? What if you'd never had them in the first place because your parents hadn't been able to pay for a cortical upgrade?"

"There's more out there than the struggles of this tiny planet, Miss Mehta," said Gricelda, "and we know you're the woman to lead the fight."

"Think about having an army of people at your beck and call," said Madolyn. "Brigades of accountants and lawyers and engineers, all ready to carry out your policies, all in the name of liberating the human spirit and expanding our consciousness beyond these mere four dimensions."

"Worlds within worlds within time within spaces," said Gricelda. "It's all rather mindblowing, actually."

"You're talking about working for WalWa again," I said.

"Oh, no!" said Gricelda.

"Lord, no!" said Madolyn. They both laughed, long and hard, rolling back in their seats and holding their sides. It was like being stuck in a steel box with a pack of stoned hyenas.

"Ah, that was good," said Gricelda, wiping tears from her eyes. "I really needed that."

"Work for WalWa," chuckled Madolyn.

"No, dear, *we* work for MacDonald Heavy," said Gricelda.

"Much different," said Madolyn.

"Different corporate culture."

"Different corporate standards."

"Different corporate goals."

"Not to me," I said. "You're part of the Big Three."

"But not the part that hurt you," said Madolyn.

"Maybe not directly," I said, "but I'm pretty sure that MacDonald and LiaoCon screwed me just as badly as WalWa, because that's what the Big Three do. They chew up people and resources and shit out value for their Shareholders. And I am *done* with that."

The twins looked at each other. Gricelda shook her head.

"You don't suppose anything in the kitchen survived?" said Madolyn, craning her neck. "I could certainly do with a cup of something harsh."

"Doubtful," said Gricelda. "And, besides, you really want to have a tipple before our big trip?"

"Definitely," said Madolyn. "If I'm going to be crammed back into that can, I'm going to want to start out snookered."

"Booze and hibernation aren't really a good combination," I said.

"I know," said Madolyn. "Good thing we're taking the short cut."

I looked at her. "There is no short cut."

"For you, no," said Madolyn. "But for us, with a cargo this important, we get to jump to the head of the line."

"Which, by the way, we get to make," said Gricelda.

I looked at the two of them sitting in their matched chairs, their gloved hands sitting on their knees. Their smiles were small and prim, like a pair of cane vipers that were ready to sink their fangs into your face. "You sound like you're planning on jumping inside the Red Line," I said.

"See?" said Madolyn. "I *knew* this one was a quick study."

"It solves all sorts of problems at once," said Gricelda. "We save fuel, air, supplies."

"*And* I get to have a little drinkie before we go," said Madolyn.

"Plus, it will deal with our little contagion issue."

"What contagion issue?" I said.

"The black stripe," said Banks. It was the first thing he'd said since he'd come in contact with the twins. His voice was flat and dead, like someone had zapped his soul with a cattle prod.

"It's quite virulent, dear," said Madolyn. "Imagine what would happen if it gets up the cable?"

"The entire economy of Occupied Space would grind to a halt overnight," said Gricelda. "Or, at least within a month. I haven't run the numbers."

"Everyone needs cane," said Madolyn. "And that's why we have to do this the old-fashioned way."

"The only way."

"The *hot* way."

"Holy shit," I said. "You're going to jump *in orbit*?"

"*Quite* the quick study," said Madolyn.

"You'll fry the whole planet!" I said. "The x-ray burst alone would kill everyone, and then all the aftereffects would set the atmosphere on fire!"

"I'd hope so," said Gricelda. "No idea how far Mr Bloombeck's little creation has spread."

"Best for everyone, really," said Madolyn.

"The hell it is!" I said, clenching my fists. "Who do you think you are to decide that?"

The twins looked at each other and giggled like little girls. "We're your *owners*, dear," said Gricelda. "All your talk about independence and solidarity and the Struggle–"

"*Oh*, the bloody Struggle," said Madolyn.

"–it's all for naught, because *you* will always need *us*," said Gricelda. "Your little planet grows cane. The only way you get money is by growing cane. Your entire tiny economy is dedicated to growing and processing cane. Even the pittance you get from your rum, that comes from cane." She shook her head. "If you have no cane, you have nothing we want. If you have nothing we want, you *are* nothing."

"Spoken like a true corporate citizen," I said, then spat on the floor.

"Well!" said Gricelda.

"Loyalty is hard to find," said Madolyn. "And it's a shame that it's so misplaced."

"We would have followed through on our offer, Miss Mehta," said Gricelda. "Do you think your precious Union would have done the same?"

"I'm not listening to any more of your bullshit," I said, heading for the door.

"Then maybe you'd like to listen to some of our truth," said Gricelda. "Like about how Evanrute Saarien has sold out you, your Union, and your planet."

"And for such a tiny price," said Madolyn.

"Not even thirty pieces of silver," said Gricelda.

"I have no idea what you're talking about," I said.

"Of course not," said Gricelda, pointing at Banks. "But *he* does."

"That little pai of his, hoovering up information," said Madolyn. "It's amazing what people keep in their buffers."

"All of their dreams."

"All of their hopes."

"All of their sins," said Gricelda.

"*We* saw everything Mr Saarien saw," said Madolyn. "Plus everything Mr Bloombeck saw."

"It was a lot we saw," said Gricelda.

I looked at them, sitting back in Bloombeck's expensive chairs. They weren't smiling.

"What," I said, "did you see?"

"We saw Mr Saarien confront Mr Bloombeck," said Madolyn.

"What Mr Bloombeck did for black stripe, could he do for cane?" said Gricelda.

"Which he did," said Madolyn.

"For quite a good price," said Gricelda, picking up a surviving crystal mouse. It wore a lab coat and sat in front of an adorable scanning electron microscope.

"After all, Mr Bloombeck was quite tired of the pocket change he made from his Contract position," said Madolyn.

"And who wouldn't be?" said Gricelda. "A man of his education and experience, and he's a swing-shift worker at the sewage plant."

"Not even management," said Madolyn. "A crime for a man of his talents."

"He was a grifter and a thief and a small-time con artist," I said. "You must have seen that, too."

"We choose to overlook people's shortcomings if their talents are great," said Gricelda.

"Which is why we like you," said Madolyn.

"Mr Bloombeck wanted more in life, and Mr Saarien gave him an opportunity to get it," said Gricelda. "Within the laboratory above, there are a dozen new varieties of sugarcane that can grow in hundreds of new environments. They are resistant to all known crop pests and infections. And they are all illegal as hell, because they will crowd out the current varieties grown throughout Occupied Space."

"The Big Three doesn't like to mess around with a good thing," said Madolyn.

"And something that they can't control?" said Gricelda.

"Not a good thing at all."

"Fine," I said. "Bloombeck and Saarien were in cahoots. I got that."

"Then you get the scope of the problem," said Gricelda.

"And you can see the scope of the solution."

"I can see that it can't happen," I said, heading for the door. There were two sharp *bang*s, and two holes appeared in the wall.

I turned and saw Banks, holding up a smoking pistol. "Please don't," said Banks, his voice still and his eyes damp.

"I have to," I said. "I have to stop this from happening."

"So do I," he said.

"Then you're going to have to make a choice," I said, reaching for the door again. There were two more bangs, and the doorframe splintered. "Jesus!" I yelled, jumping back. "When did everyone say it was OK to start waving guns around my streets?"

"Since we weren't getting results," said Madolyn.

"And *your* streets?" said Gricelda. "That's a bit presumptuous."

"And so is your offer," I said. "I have worked too hard – we *all* have worked too hard to get some kind of solid footing after getting screwed over by the likes of you and your bosses, and I'm not going to help you do the same to everyone else on Santee. You'll have to shoot me."

The sisters looked at each other, then shook their heads. "No, we won't," said Gricelda, snapping her fingers. Banks thumbed back the hammer on his pistol.

"What are you doing?" I said.

"My job," said Banks, cocking the hammer and putting the gun to my head.

"Mr Banks works for us, now and always," said Madolyn.

"And his work can get a little wet."

"Dirty."

"Messy."

"Bloody."

"Banks?" I said.

"This is my job, Padma," he said. "I'm supposed to make trouble."

"You can let go."

"No, I can't."

"Yes, you can," I said. "You start over here. We all do. You don't have to do this."

"I do."

"He does," said Madolyn. "Because if he doesn't, he knows we'll make him do it."

"He is but a puppet, Ms. Mehta," said Gricelda. "You all are."

"Then why don't you just make me say yes?" I said.

"Well, where's the fun in that?" said Madolyn.

Banks's hand was solid as a rock. I hoped it would be shaking or jittering, but he kept his gun steady.

"Well, come on, then," I said, looking Banks right in the face. His eyes were glassy, but then they focused on mine. He sent me a message: *duck*.

I hit the deck, and the flat exploded in song.

TWENTY-SIX

Ah! Sweet mystery of life, at last I've found thee
Ah! at last I know the secret of it all
All the longing, seeking, striving, waiting, yearning
The idle hopes and joy and burning tears that fall...

I looked up, and the sisters were shuffling around the flat, singing in a beautiful two-part harmony. I looked at Banks, who shot me a cockeyed grin as I got to my feet.

"Did you do this?" I hissed.

He nodded.

"Then what was with the ducking?"

He shrugged. "I've never used that backdoor on them, so I had no idea what would happen. They might have gone berserk or catatonic or, um, exploded."

"Backdoor?"

He nodded. "It's how we get into your heads. We have all kinds of backdoors built into everyone's pai, and you can't close them, no matter how many times you reburn someone's firmware." He looked at the sisters. "Even them. I was saving that trick for an emergency."

"I suppose this counts." I punched him in the shoulder. "Don't you *ever* point a gun at me again."

He held up his right hand. "I promise. Shall we flee?"

"Oh, we shall." I grabbed Banks by the shoulders, hauled him toward the door and flung it open.

"Wait," said Banks, pointing a waving finger outside. I was too busy watching him to see where I was going, and my foot went right into the air, my leg and hip and the rest of me following it out the door into space. I got a hand in the doorway in time to stop from falling fifty meters to the canyons of cargo canisters below.

Ages ago, I had mused that the natural state for a cargo can was to be in motion. They spent most of their lifespans hauled up and down lifters, zipping across star systems, moving from one loading depot to the next. The moments when they sat still and either disgorged their cargo or loaded up with new stuff were brief and infrequent. Even though this can had long served as a home, it was only right that it now moved and swayed underneath a crane. We were just new cargo.

That didn't keep me from being overwhelmed by the sheer chaos outside the door. It was deafening, the sound of overhead cranes hauling cans, the clanging of cans dropped on top of cans, the echoing, banging clash of cans and cans and cans. If I had screamed, I hadn't heard myself. I just looked down and saw cans cans cans.

Banks leaned over and grabbed my arm, and I swung the other one into the doorway. I kicked my legs to the side, trying to get myself back in. "Stop moving!" yelled Banks.

"Pull harder!" I yelled back.

"I can't because you won't stop moving!"

The can shuddered and swayed, and Banks slid out of the

door. I caught the seat of his pants, but he had too much momentum, and we fell. Lucky for us, the crane had moved us over a taller stack, so we only fell a few meters. It still hurt like hell when I hit steel and Banks hit me. I made sure I hadn't broken anything other than my pride, though my leg still burned as I got to my feet.

The stack with my old flat and Bloombeck's lab and the unconscious Ghosts was tucked underneath a crane that crawled away on the trellis overhead. Within seconds, I had lost it in the anonymous ocean of cans. I looked around, trying to get my bearings. The coast was behind me, and the cable rose to the sky in front of me. "OK," I said to Banks, "we're on the outbound side of the island. Everything around is in the queue to go up the cable, and it looks like your pals are jumping to the head of the line."

"That means we're screwed, right?" said Banks.

"Not yet," I said, looking over the edge and muttering prayers of thanks to the Interstellar Standards Organization for making sure every cargo can in Occupied Space had ladders bolted onto the same side. We clambered down to the ground and started to look for street signs.

"Hey!" someone yelled, and I spun around, ready to run. A man on a recumbent trike pedaled toward us, waving his free hand and shouting, "Oy, you! Get out of my stacks!"

"Up yours, and twice to your mother!" I yelled back out of reflex.

The man stopped pedaling. "Padma?"

It took me a moment to realize it was Wash. I gimped over and hugged him. "I am so glad you're management."

He got off his bike and gave us the once over. "You look like hell."

"Long story," I said. "Why aren't you shoreside? You

shouldn't be out here schlepping cans."

"We got a rush order," said Wash, "and I wanted some experienced hands to cover it."

"Hope you're giving yourself overtime."

"Triple time, baby," he said, then nodded at Banks. "Are you stealing bodies now?"

"You recognize my attorney, Mr Banks?"

Wash's eyes bugged. "Christ, Padma, what have you done to this man?"

"Why does everyone assume this shit is my fault?" I said.

"Past experience," said Wash, putting himself between me and Banks and wrapping his arms around our shoulders. We limped deeper into the stacks.

"You need a place to clean up?" said Wash.

"I need a hardline to shore," I said. "There is some major badness about to go down, and I need to put a stop on lifter traffic."

"Good luck with that," said Wash. "We got so much going up that you'd think there was an evacuation."

"There might have to be," said Banks, pointing at the cable.

I may not have been able to make calls, but my pai could still zoom, and what I saw made my heart sink. The crawler platforms were loaded with cans and beginning their trip to orbit.

Wash nodded. "You notice that? Hence the rush. We're trying to get everything out of here to make room for these cans."

"What, they're bringing in *more*?" I said.

"Oh, yes," said Wash. "How do you like that?"

"I really don't," I said.

"How long until they get topside?" asked Banks.

Wash shrugged. "Depends on how much traffic's already heading up there, what else is in the queue, how fast the upload and download crews are working. Thirty-five, maybe forty hours. They managed to get the crawlers to go faster."

Sure enough, the cables were humming louder than usual. I counted ten seconds between the cans crossing past each other, and some quick and sloppy math churned out a trip time more on the unsafe side of fast.

"Can't we, I dunno, *stop* the cables?" asked Banks.

"You do an emergency stop while it's loaded, the ribbons will tear themselves apart, especially when they're moving this fast," I said.

"Why would you want to stop them, anyway?" said Wash. "Did you not hear me? Triple rates?"

"It won't matter," I said, then gave Wash the executive summary of the past two days. His face grew darker as I told him about everything that had happened.

"I'm not sure what part of that pisses me off more," said Wash as we approached the can he used for an office.

"Well, pick one and make the call," I said.

"I cannot *wait* to use all this in court," he said as he threw the door open. There was a *bang*, and he fell back, a red stain blooming on his belly. I jumped to put pressure on his wound, and, out of the corner of my eye, saw something fly towards my face. I knocked the kick away, then lunged for my attacker, a goon wearing updated riot armor. This time, I went right for the throat, reaching under his helmet's chin guard to dig my fingers into his windpipe. It was a good thing that someone dragged me off the goon, since I couldn't see anything but red and wouldn't have stopped until I'd torn his head clean off.

I wrestled with the goons, and one of them popped me in the gut with a rifle stock and down I went. When I finally caught my breath, I looked up into the too-bright smile of Evanrute Saarien. The gun in his hand still smoked.

"Sister Padma," he said. "I am so glad to see you."

I spat in his face. Not a grand gesture, but what the hell.

He reached into the pocket of his spotless white coat – how the hell did he keep it so clean? – and pulled out a handkerchief. He wiped away the spittle, then dropped the hanky on the ground. "I forgive you that, as I have been taught to forgive all who are part of the Struggle."

"Hope you can forgive this," I said, then jumped up and kicked out. Saarien leaped back, but my boot made contact with his pants leg, leaving a beautiful black stain.

He looked down at his soiled suit, then back at me with more hate than I have ever seen in a man's eyes. He took a fast step toward me and grabbed my chin, squeezing my cheeks so hard I thought my teeth would pierce them.

"You are an unbeliever, Sister Padma," he said, doing his best to keep his voice level and failing. "You are an instrument of the great devil, of capital, of desire. You are lies, and untruths, and if it weren't for the fact that I have sworn to stand by all my brothers and sisters in Solidarity, I would smite the sin out of you with my own loving hand."

"Do it," I said. "Or would you rather watch one of your goons do it for you?"

He let go of my face and nodded to the goons. They carted us into the office, one hauling Banks, another two carrying Wash. They threw us into chairs and zip-tied us in. One was nice enough to put a pressure bandage over Wash's stomach. Saarien got on the phone and began a terse, hushed conversation.

"You two OK?" I asked.

"Dandy," said Wash, sweat beading on his forehead.

"Stellar," said Banks through gritted teeth.

"QUIET," called Saarien, and he pointed at two goons. They wrapped filthy gags around our mouths.

Idiots, I texted.

Saarien snapped his fingers, and the goons put headphones on our ears. Blistering electrosmash blasted out of them, so loud that I could barely concentrate on Banks's reply: *this time, i mean it: i quit.*

me too, texted Wash.

Wimps, I sent, then tried for an outside line. *Anyone able to call out?*

no, texted Wash.

yes, answered Banks.

Who?

everyone on the island, replied Banks, *but they're all busy loading cans.*

Any police?

no.

You sure?

do the cops haul cargo here?

what is going on? texted Wash.

Later, I replied. *Banks, you see anyone who feels like management? Anyone looking at any equipment or monitors?*

yes but they all have walwa pais, not union ones

Saarien's people, whoever the hell they were. *Can you try the knockout thing with them?*

i think it would kill them

For a brief moment, I consider having him do it. *No, don't do that.*

good cause i don't think it would work anyway

Small relief, I replied, then sent to Wash: *How do we stop cargo going up?*   •

which cargo? he replied. *fifty thousand cans in queue*

All of it, then.

won't stop unless there's a hurricane alarm

Fine. How do we set one off?

start a hurricane

The electrosmash pounded in my ears, setting my teeth on edge. I know Wash wasn't trying to wind me up, but I couldn't help myself from texting: *Well, shit, why don't I just buy one, then?*

Banks perked up. *yes. do that.*

I shrugged at him, making sure he could see how exasperated I was.

you know someone who works on the anchor, texted Banks. *Henry Ballesteros.*

I have no idea who that is.

You had sex with him about three hours before you met me.

I stared at Banks, then remembered: Anchor Boy.

And then I remembered that Banks had looked into my buffer. *Right.*

Wash looked at me, partly bemused, partly hurt.

Mind your own business, I shot to Wash, then looked at Banks. *And you need to stop hitting Send All.*

but you know him.

Yes, I do, but I can't call him.

i can. wait. Banks's eyes rolled around as he made the call. He smiled, then texted: *he'll do it.*

Do what?

hit the button, texted Banks.

What button?

the stop button, replied Banks. *though it's really a series of switches.*

Fine, just have him do it!

for fifty thousand yuan.

I blinked at him. *Did you miss a few zeroes?*

he was quite sure about the amount

I swallowed the lump away from my throat and blinked up my balance. If I paid off Anchor Boy, that would leave me with three hundred fifty yuan, just what Bloombeck had asked for two days ago. Maybe I should have paid him off, and then I wouldn't be on the verge of ruin.

And then I remembered that there was still a possibility that Estella Tonggow was alive. After all, if Saarien and Jimney and Jordan and the rest were running around, she might be, too, right? That meant there was still a chance to buy the distillery and have a semi-normal life. I'd be in debt to her for the rest of it, but that was better than going mad. If I stopped the lifter, I would stop the Ghosts. If I stopped the Ghosts, I would still be alive and able to enjoy being in debt.

OK, I texted Banks. *You probably know how I move money around.*

He nodded, then gave me a sad smile before blinking in the message.

I looked at Saarien; he was still yelling into the phone when he started like he'd been whipped. He straightened up, put on a beatific smile, then screamed so loud I heard him through the headphones: *HOW?* I looked away, but he'd already caught me looking at him. He stomped around the desk, pulled off the headphones and gag and yelled, "What did you do?"

"I don't know what the hell you're talking about, Rutey," I said.

"You've stopped the lifter traffic," he said, "and you will restart it."

"Do I look like I can control anything?" I said, hopping up and down, taking the chair with me.

"You can read minds," said Saarien, his eyes getting narrow. "You can see into the eyes of other men, and twist their words and thoughts, using magic."

"What?"

"That's not right," said one goon, his arms going slack.

"Not right," said the other, taking a step back.

"Are you fucking kidding me?" I said.

"Witch!" cried Saarien, stepping away and pointing a finger at me. "Sorceress! We must purify you! Cleanse you! Burn you!"

"Burn her!" yelled one goon.

"Torch her!" yelled the other.

"You two!" Saarien yelled at the goons. "Bring help! Bring fuel and fire! We will purify this evil with the bright light of justice!"

The goons fought each other to be first out the door. When it slammed shut behind them, Saarien gave me a bullet-eyed stare, then laughed. "Just when I thought they couldn't get any dumber, they prove me wrong. Can you believe they bought that witchcraft bullshit?"

"You have to stop this, Rutey," I said. "Wash is gonna bleed out, and—"

"I could really not care less what happens to ol' Wash right now," said Saarien, patting Wash on the shoulder. Wash pulled away, then groaned from the effort.

"You realize we're recording all this, right?" I said.

"Sure," said Saarien, flashing his pearly whites. "And do you realize your pai is cut off from the Public, and that no one will be able to read it once it's melted down, along with everything else in this office?"

A ball of acid churned in my stomach, and I sat back. "Holy shit. You're really going to do it."

He nodded. "I have to admit, you've made it incredibly easy for me, what with your betrayal to the Struggle."

I paused, letting his words rattle around my head. "My *what?*"

"Your betrayal," he said, walking to the door and leaning against the wall. "That's how I'm going to sell it: you've been consorting with your former lover" – he swatted Wash on the shoulder – "and with a Ghost Squad" – another swat for Banks – "to commit biological warfare on our brothers and sisters in Solidarity."

"What makes you think he's a Ghost?" I said, nodding toward Banks.

"Because I've read all the internals from Thronehill," said Saarien. "My partners in WalWa were only too happy to feed me data."

"The ones with fake ink," I said.

He nodded. "Bright bunch of kids, really. Remind me of how I was when I signed my Indenture. I thought I was going to shine, move up the ladder at lightning speed, but then I saw what a horrific slog it was to the top. Even with the endless supply of idiots who want to become Indentures, there was no way to stand out. But here?" He spread his hands wide. "Here, with everyone grumbling their way through life, it's easy to lead them, Union and Indenture alike. I talked those kids into working for me so easily, that it amazes me you didn't try it yourself. They aren't ready to Breach, but they still know they were getting a raw deal. Do you know that Indenture contracts no longer include transit time as part of Service? All those fishsticks who came down the cable, they have to do an extra four years here before their obligations are up."

"That's horrible," I said, "and completely irrelevant to what's going on here."

"Is it?" said Saarien. "See, you've been so focused on making your number and retiring to Chino Cove that you've forgotten all about the Struggle."

"You've kidnapped a few hundred Freeborn *and* you pressganged my people into running an illegal refinery, you shot Wash, and you've got all of us tied up, and you think you can lecture me about labor theory?"

"You forgot murdering Estella Tonggow," said Saarien.

My guts churned. "You didn't do the bodyswap thing with her?"

"No, because I didn't need her," said Saarien. "All those Freeborn, your people, they all fit in with my requirements, and it was easier for Bloombeck to tag a pile of meat with DNA than to make them disappear altogether. Your patron, Madame Tonggow? She's dead, Padma. And she's not coming back."

"But why?"

"Because she was in my way. She was going to figure out what was making the rum go bad, and then it would've been easy for her to trace that to the source. She was a brilliant biochemist. Too bad you followed her path and turned away from us."

"I never–"

"I know you have, because I live it every day, but you," he said. "You're so focused on your Co-Op plans that you've let your people down. I see the way they come trudging out of your treatment plant, beaten down, broken, robbed of a promising future that you can't deliver."

"Because you keep stealing my fucking funding," I said.

"I've been reappropriating it," said Saarien.

"You've been *stealing* it," I said. "Wash told me about the cash you've been siphoning off for your 'reinvestment program.' And I've seen where that's all gone. I was *there*, Rutey. I *saw* the stacks of *your* cane getting churned into *your* molasses in *your* illegal refinery."

"What you saw was the future," said Saarien. "One that will ensure that we will endure in the Struggle against our former masters."

"By wiping out all the cane in Occupied Space?" I said.

"Not all of it," said Saarien. "Just the corporate controlled cane."

"Which *is* all of it," I said. "Even if you had nothing but your stuff planted on Santee, do you know how many people you're going to hurt? How many powerplants run on industrial cane? How many food delivery trucks, ambulances, police cars all run on cane diesel?"

"And they will continue to run," said Saarien. "Like you said, you saw the stacks."

"There's no way you've made enough molasses to run this planet," I said. "You've only been working with Bloombeck for, what, six months? Seven?"

Saarien shook his head. "I think I've said far too much."

"If you really believe in the Struggle, then you won't do this."

Saarien smiled, and I had never wanted to hit him as badly as I did right then. "It's *because* I believe that I will. As long as the Big Three tell us what to grow and how to grow it and how much we'll get for keeping their rotting corpse of a civilization running, we will never be free. This is the ultimate blow for liberty, Sister Padma, and if you truly believed, you'd have asked to join me. Instead, you've blocked me, every step of the way."

I'd like to say that Saarien's smug tone and unflinching certainty gave me superhuman strength, more than enough to tear my way out of the chair, rush him and beat him to death with his own arms. But I just looked at Banks, who had a small dribble of blood coming out his nostril. Wash's eyes were closed, and his breathing grew ragged. I turned back to Saarien and said, "You don't know a goddamn thing, Rutey. All this time you've run Sou's Reach and howled for more Contract Slots and more money and more influence, you have never understood what it's all about. You don't get it, and you never will."

"There's nothing to get," he said, "nothing except a few gas cans and a match."

"This won't end with me," I said. "Even if you get your cane up the lifter and out into space, you think people won't remember what you did? You think the Union's just going to sit back and let you get away with murdering me?"

"How will they know it's murder when there's no evidence?" he said.

"I've got enough to tie you with all of this–"

"I will be *running* this place," said Saarien, laughing. "Everyone will be too busy panicking about how to eat to care about investigating any fires on the lifter terminal. And when I step in with a solution, you will just be a memory. The Union won't care about you, not when *I* am the Union."

"You really think that?" I said. "You don't think all the people who do the working and living and dying, they might have something to say about it?"

Saarien smiled. "I think it's funny that you're choosing now to think about them."

"They won't," I said. "I think the Union will find you out

and fight you. Everyone will see how you don't care about the people, just the cause, and you'll be stopped."

He clapped three times, slow and steady. "Bravo for the brotherhood of man."

"It's the brotherhood of the fucked-over," I said. "And our own people, one of these days, are going to realize how full of shit you are and feed you to the wolves."

"Not while I've got the guns and the dinner plates," said Saarien.

The door opened, and a trio of goons entered the room carrying red fuel cans. "Praise God!" called Saarien, the syrup returning to his voice. "Now you will see the power of virtue triumph over vice!" He uncapped one of the cans and kicked it over; cane diesel spilled on the floor, splashing its way toward us. I turned away, but the overpowering stench of the diesel made my head fuzz and my strength drain.

Saarien rummaged through the desk until he found an emergency kit. He pulled out a flare and struck it. The office's light, already hellish from the fluorescents, turned bright red as Saarien approached us. "Pour those two cans on them, and watch," he said. One of the goons nodded, picked up a can and swung it at Saarien's head. He went down, the flare flying away and landing on diesel-soaked paperwork. As it ignited, the goon wound up and flung the can at the other goons. They froze, wondering what to do with the diesel splashed over their armor, and our rescuer unslung her riot hose and sprayed their helmets. The stench of rotting vanilla clashed with the sharp diesel as both goons swatted at the hardening and expanding foam. With a few swift kicks, the remaining goon booted the other two out the door, firing a few extra squirts of foam after them.

what the hell is going on? Banks and Wash both texted.

"You're still good for that thousand yuan, right?" said the goon, flipping up her facebowl. It was Jilly.

"I'm good for a lot more than that if you get us out of here," I said.

Jilly found a pair of clippers in the desk and snipped all of our zipties. I sprang from the chair and gave Jilly a hug, then we helped Wash outside, where a waiting cargo van puttered away. "I got a ride in with a police boat, and then I saw this thing just sitting around. Had the armor and everything, so I figured, why not play dress up?" Jilly grinned, then scratched her neck. "Hope it's easy to come off. This shit itches."

"That's part of the joy of being a goon," I said as we put Wash in the back. Banks cracked into the van's first aid kit and got to work tending to Wash. I sprayed anesthetic on my wounded calf, sighing as the pain vanished. Black smudges of smoke puffed out of the doorway; in a minute, the fire would turn the can into an oven, smothering anyone left inside. I'd cleaned up after one can fire six years ago, and the results were enough to turn me off barbeque for months. It was a horrible way to die.

I counted to five and saw no sign of Evanrute. "Goddammit," I said, and hobbled into the can, Jilly following.

Saarien was still where we'd left him, which was now on the other side of a low wall of flame. He was on his feet, but his eyes were closed and his mouth was moving. The bastard was *praying*. Jilly grabbed a fire extinguisher next to the door (dependable Wash, always keeping up with safety codes) and got ready to spray when I blocked her with an arm. "Rutey!" I called.

He opened his eyes and smiled. "I knew you'd return.

You believe in the Struggle."

"I believe you're going to get roasted alive," I said.

"So, you're going to let a righteous servant of the Union perish?" said Saarien.

"Which one of us started the fire in the first place?" I said.

"I was doing the Union's work."

"And I'm here to do mine," I said, picking up one of the gas cans and flinging it into the flames. The fire surged as diesel spilled out, and Saarien shrank back from the heat, his smile fading. "You'll burn for this!"

"I think you'll go first," I called over the roar of the fire. "How much?"

"What?" he yelled, his arms hanging slack.

I took the fire extinguisher from Jilly and aimed it at the fire. "How much is it worth to you to get out of here alive and uncooked?"

He laughed. "You think my faith is that weak? You think I'm going to cave to your worldly bargaining?"

"Not yet," I said, fiddling with the pin on the extinguisher's handle. "A few more minutes, though, I think you'll warm to the idea."

It may have been the firelight, but his face turned a deep red as he yelled, "You bitch! You blackhearted bitch, I will call down every one of my sisters and brothers and–!"

The flames bloomed as they caught the edge of Wash's desk, and Saarien yelled, "Fifty thousand yuan!"

"I'm sorry," I said, "that sounded like a number, but I couldn't hear it."

"Fifty thousand–!"

"Yeah, I can't hear numbers that low."

Saarien gritted his teeth. "A hundred thousand!"

I shook my head and headed toward the door. An overhead lamp popped, and a shower of sparks flew towards Saarien. He batted at the flames, only to have the desk catch fire, too.

"A million!" he yelled, and I stopped.

"I think you can do better," I said.

"Three million yuan! It's all I've got!"

"I don't want your money," I said.

"Then take Sou's Reach!" he said, tears streaming down his face.

"I don't want your Ward," I said.

"The refinery! The cane! Take it all!"

"I don't want any of that."

"Then, what – Jesus, *what*?" Saarien sobbed.

"What are you doing with all that molasses?"

"Jesus, Padma, put out the fire!"

I shook my head. "Why are you sending all that molasses up the cable?"

"They're samples!" cried Saarien. "There's enough to run every planet in Occupied Space for a few months, so the Big Three would know I was serious."

"Why would they give a shit about that when the black stripe is just here?" I said.

"Because it's not!" cried Saarien. "It's going up the cable with everything else from Santee."

"You've been contaminating your cargo?"

"Yes!" he said. "We thought we could transfer spores through rum, but the distillation killed it. Just left the stench."

"So the skunked rum can't affect any crops?"

"No," cried Saarien.

"Then what about the body in the freezer? And the

bodies at the sewage plant?"

"You already know that was me!" yelled Saarien.

"I want to hear you say it," I said. "Tell me why. Use your words."

"That was to throw suspicion on you!" said Saarien. "Bloombeck took vat-grown meat and scrambled its DNA to make them be anyone. Now, is that enough?"

I squirted a jet of retardant onto the flames, not enough to douse the whole fire, but enough to bring the temperature down a bit in the can. "Now – I want an apology."

Tears and snot ran down Saarien's face as he got on his knees and put his hands together. "I am *sorry*, Padma! I'm sorry I lied to you! I'm sorry I lied to the Union! I'm sorry I stole funding and Breaches! I'm sorry I fucked you over! Just don't let me die!"

I put out the whole fire. Saarien ran toward us and wrapped me in a sobbing, sooty embrace. I kneed him in the balls, just to get him off me. He staggered back, and I said, "So, about the three mil and Sou's."

"What?" he moaned. "You said you didn't want them!"

"Yeah, but that doesn't mean I won't take them," I said, taking him by the shoulder. "You can talk to my attorney about the details."

We stepped out of the can, Saarien's face streaked and sloppy. I pushed him into the back seat. "You get all that?" I said to Banks.

"None of it," he said. "You were out of range, so you recorded everything."

"Good," I said, handing him the fire extinguisher. "If he makes any funny moves, hit him in the face."

Banks nodded, then punched Saarien square in the nose. Saarien's eyes crossed, and he collapsed in a heap.

"What was that for?" I said.

"He made a funny move," said Banks, tossing aside the fire extinguisher.

"When?"

"A few minutes ago, when he tried to immolate us."

I shrugged. "Works for me." I tapped Jilly on the shoulder. "Get us to safe turf. Don't spare the horses."

Jilly eased the van away from the smoldering office. "You really should have a better fire system in there," I said to Wash.

"I'll be sure to add that to the lawsuit," he groaned. "But what about you?"

"Me?" I said, looking at the unconscious Saarien. "I got him to cough up three million yuan and a whole lot of real estate."

"That's never going to hold up," said Wash.

"Maybe not," I said, "but whatever I can squeeze out of him will be enough to get me back on my feet. We stopped the lifter traffic, which means we get to hang onto all of his molasses, which means we have time to undo the black stripe. We just have to find the can that has Bloombeck's lab."

"That's going to be tough," said Wash. "There's five hundred thousand cans here."

"Then we'll just look for the one with a hole in it," I said looking at Banks. He just nodded.

"I have no idea what that means," said Wash.

"Shh," I said, ruffling his hair. "Just lie there and be injured. I've got this."

Jilly turned a corner, taking us past a hollow in the stacks of cans. I caught a glance at the lifter and saw that, indeed, the crawlers had stopped. Any other day, I would have freaked out about seeing the halted traffic, but today, I'd never been happier to see them still. It would take a while for everything to sort out, and to find the can with the Ghost team and Bloombeck's spores, but we would, and I'd be able to start all over again...

A low *boom* echoed over the cans, and the crawlers began to climb again.

"No," I said. "No no no no no! Banks you need to call Henry right now and—"

"The line's cut off," said Banks. "I don't know how, but I can't get any calls up the cable. Or around here, either. It's like someone's killed every data tower on the island."

I looked at the cable, at the crawlers snaking their way to space. "The control center," I said. "You can pull all sorts of stunts if you run it, and the twins or one of Saarien's buddies or *someone* has to be there." I slapped Jilly on the shoulder. "Pull over."

Jilly hit the brakes. We were next to a motor depot, where a few dozen trucks and vans and their drivers lolled about. A few of them ran up when they saw us with Wash. We eased him onto the warm pavement.

"Get this guy to a doc, or get a doc to him, or something," I said. "And get on a hardline to shore, tell 'em what's going on."

"Padma, we can handle it," said Wash, rising on his elbows, then groaning and collapsing. I put my hand on his cheek.

"All of this crap is happening because of me," I said, "and I hate leaving a mess."

"Since when?" said Wash with a smile.

"Since it got my people kidnapped, and you shot, and me saving that motherfucker," I said, nodding at Saarien. "Do whatever you can to stop that traffic, and keep your head down." I gave him a quick peck on the cheek and ran back to the van.

"Any reason we're bringing him?" said Banks, prodding the semi-catatonic Saarien.

"He might open some doors," I said. "Besides, don't you feel safe traveling with a Union man?"

"Not this one," said Banks.

"Jilly," I said, "you get us to the control center in the next three minutes, and I'll give you a million yuan."

"Shit," said Jilly, throwing the van into gear. "For that kind of cash, I'll do it in two." She slammed on the gas, and the van shot into the stacks.

TWENTY-SEVEN

One minute and fifty-seven seconds later, the van screeched to a halt outside the lifter's queue control station, a hurricane-proof block of efficient pourform. A pair of Saarien's goons stood at the door, their riot hoses up as I threw open the door. "Hi!" I called out. "Man, we're glad you guys're still here."

"Hands above your heads," said one of the goons, sighting in on me.

"Sure!" I said, putting my hands up. "Though it'll be kinda tough to help Brother Evanrute when I'm like this."

The goons took a step toward the van, then caught sight of the bloodied and unconscious Saarien in the back seat. "The mob, they got to him," I said.

"What mob?" said one of the goons.

"Haven't you heard?" I said. "There's rioting in the stacks, people turning on each other, everyone going crazy!"

"We haven't gotten anything," said the goon.

"Well, how could you?" I said. "Guys like you were the first ones they went after. We saw them get beaten to death with their own helmets. No comm gear. You know. Come on."

The goons looked at each other, and I grabbed them by the rescue hooks on their chestplates. "Look, it doesn't matter if you're loyal to WalWa, Saarien, Jesus Christ, or the Virgin Buddha, because in a few minutes, three hundred thousand very armed and very angry people are going to crash down on this station and kill anything in their way. You got enough foam to stop that many people?"

The goons shook their heads.

"Then get your asses in gear and help us get him inside so we can hole up and not get eaten. Got it?"

The goons nodded and reached in for Saarien. We entered the building, the goons carrying Saarien, through automatic glass doors. I snatched some riot grenades off one of their belts and said, "Oh, crap. We forgot all of Brother Saarien's gear. He's got some special equipment that might hold off the riot. Mental factoring quantizing uplinks. Takes two to carry. Go. Go!"

They set Saarien down on a bench and hopped out the door. I nodded at Jilly, who floored it and shot away. I locked the glass doors as the goons turned, then threw the lever for the hurricane shielding. It thunked into place as they raised their riot hoses. "One day," I said, "WalWa will realize their security forces have the brains of squirrels."

"Thank God that's not today," said Banks.

We found a desk chair with casters and set Saarien down. His head lolled from side to side as we pushed him toward the elevator bank. "Please present biometric ID points," said the Univoice as a pair of panels slid open next to the doors. I shoved Saarien's hand in the lower slot and his face in the upper. There was a polite beep, and the Univoice said, "Thank you, Evanrute Saarien. You and your guests are cleared."

"Big surprise there," I said. "Rutey must have bought access all the way up the cable. There are probably vending machines in orbit just waiting for his touch."

"I cannot *wait* to unravel all this," said Banks.

"Try not to sound too enthusiastic, Banks," I said. "We still haven't saved the world."

"Yeah, but it's just a matter of time, right?" he said. "The police will probably storm the port, as will any WalWa security not loyal to Saarien. Besides, the first cans probably haven't even gotten two klicks up."

"Which means we still have to bring them *down*," I said, "and getting those crawlers to change direction is a pain in the ass."

The elevator *ding*ed, and the doors opened on another pair of goons. "Who are you?" said one of them.

"My God, it's terrible!" I said, pushing Saarien past them into the hall. "The guards at the front door need your help! Hurry! Get up there before they're torn to pieces!"

Ever obedient, the goons trooped into the elevator. As the door closed, I pulled the pin on a riot grenade and tossed the fizzling canister at them. The door shut, and there was a *crump* from the super-expanding foam.

"Any chance of doing the same with the lifter?" said Banks.

"At this point, it might be worth a shot."

We turned the corner to another door with biometric locks and MAIN CARGO CONTROL written on it in small, official letters. I pushed Saarien's hand and face in front of the lock, and the door hushed open on a dark pit of a room whose only light came from three dozen fuzzing workstation monitors. The air was thick with the tang of smoke mixed with the wet iron smell of blood.

Saarien stirred, and I clamped a hand over his mouth. *You picking up anyone?* I texted Banks.

got twenty pais. nineteen with flatlined owners.

Banks pointed at the one workstation whose monitor wasn't a mess of snow and static. Two bodies slumped on the desk, pools of blood next to them picking up glints of color from the screen. Someone bulky hunched over the monitor, a phone in one hand while the other banged on the desk. It looked like she was swearing at the top of her lungs, but she was somehow doing it in a very polite tone. I crawled down a row to get a closer look, trying to place where I'd heard the voice, and it wasn't until I saw Nariel's one good eye gleam in the monitor light that I realized she was sending texts from her pai into a text-to-speech box – one that used the Univoice. It was like hearing a librarian lose it, yet keep using her Inside Voice.

"No, you fucking moron, I do not want to speak with your coordinating supervisor, I want you to do what I fucking say," said the Univoice, as Nariel punched the desk. She now wore goon combat armor, and her gloved fists made dents in the caneplas desktop. "Clear the goddamn roads. I do not care if you have to run a bulldozer over everyone, get them out of the way." She gave the other end a second to respond, then banged the receiver on the desktop. "Shut it, you drooler. Shut. Up. Get those cans in the queue, or I will crawl through this line and strangle you with your own testicles."

I pointed at her, then motioned to Banks that we should crawl around Nariel from opposite ends, then take her. He nodded and crept away.

Two gunshots rang over our heads. "I am tied into the whole network, you idiots," said the Univoice. "Saw you coming the minute you put Evanrute's retinas into the system, and I can trace where you are from your pais."

I blinked up a status menu and put my pai into shutdown. "Any way we can talk about this reasonably?" I called out. Another shot zinged over us.

"You did not do anything but delay us, Padma," said Nariel. "I am going to get all of this up the cable, and then I am going to fling it out across the universe and follow it as far away from this shithole as I can go. But not until I have burned this place to a cinder."

Even now, she still couldn't get her pai to use contractions. "You can't do this, Nariel," I said. "I know you're angry, but you can't take it out on the planet, and on everyone else."

"Fuck you, fuck your planet, fuck everyone," she said, taking another shot. Bits of plastic stung my face, and I ducked under a workstation.

"So, this is how you're going to get back at me?" I called out, and another shot splintered the monitor above me. I rolled away and scurried down the row. With the Univoice on the PA, Nariel was free to move anywhere. "You let this traffic go up the cable, you're going to condemn everyone in Occupied Space. You're going to send us back to the Dark Ages."

"You always think it is about you," said Nariel. "Hate to break it to you, Padma, but you are no longer part of the equation."

"Oh, please, Nariel," I said from my new hiding place. "You always took everything personally. Remember how you forgot to order enough straws for Playoffs?"

"That was *your* fault," she said, the Univoice attempting to sound angry. "You did not remind me of the deadline."

"And you made my life easy at the stadium? You wanted

to play games with me, but now you've got to blame me when it all turned on you?"

"This is your fault, you and the rest of you Union assholes."

A pencil lay on the ground in front of me. I grabbed it and called, "You never stuck around long enough to hear about the benefits you got with a Union card." I flung the pencil to the other end of the room, and it clattered against a monitor that blew apart under the gunfire. Nariel kept shooting until the gun *click*ed itself silent. I peeked up from underneath the table and saw her only two rows away, struggling to reload.

"Jesus, Nariel, I bet back in B-school, you didn't listen," I said, looking for something blunt and only finding instruction binders. "Don't you remember what we learned in Crisis Communications?"

"Shut up," said the Univoice. Nariel gritted her teeth as she tried to remove the magazine.

"No jerky movements, always go smooth," I said, picking up a shattered monitor. It didn't have much heft, but it would have to do.

"Shut. Up." The clattering grew louder.

"Take care of your weapons, and they'll take care of you." I crouched low, the monitor in both hands, and moved closer.

"SHUTUPYOUFUCKINGBITCH" She must have lost the patience to put spaces in her text.

"Aim straight and squeeze," I said, then jumped onto the desktop, in time for my calf to give way. I hit the desktop, the monitor's weight dragging me over. The monitor smashed on the ground, and I fell on top of it, right into Banks's lap.

"I was just about to make my move," he said.

"Great timing."

There was a smooth click, like a well-oiled doorknob turning, and Nariel climbed onto the desktop I'd just fallen over. She let go of the gun's action, then aimed it at me, a smile on her pulped face, and then she froze. "Ef ef ef ef ef," said the Univoice as her whole body shook, and then she sagged over the top of the workstation right on me. A giant dart with a fuzzy yellow end stuck out of her back. Banks grabbed the gun as I kicked Nariel off of me.

"Hello!" called Gricelda. "Please toss that weapon over here, thank you!"

"And don't try any of that sneaky backdoor shit on us again, Mr Banks," said Madolyn.

I looked at Banks, who sighed, "Shall we?"

"You sure you don't want to go out in a blaze of glory?" I said, eyeing the gun.

"We have tear gas, too," said Gricelda. "Plus some grenades that have all sorts of lovely symbols on them."

"Looks like they release fire-breathing ferrets, or something like it," said Madolyn. "Tough to tell with these LiaoCon jobbies."

"I don't get paid enough to deal with that," said Banks.

"I wouldn't pay you enough to," I said, then called out, "OK, we're coming!"

"Weapons first, please!" said Gricelda, and Banks pitched the gun over the top. We both stood, our hands up. The twins were at the back of the room on either side of Saarien, each of them aiming a dart gun at us.

"Well!" said Madolyn. "I'm so glad we didn't have to resort to anything lethal to resolve this situation."

"What did you shoot her with?" I said, nodding back at Nariel, who was now fast asleep and pissing herself.

"It's a sedative slash muscle relaxant," said Gricelda. "We

save it for our more active cargo."

"Which means we buy in bulk," said Madolyn, patting her gun. "So there's plenty more for both your asses."

"OK, OK," I said, putting my hands even higher. "No need to knock us out."

"Not yet, anyway," said Gricelda. "What with our poor old backs, we'd have quite a time pouring your deadweight into hibernant bags."

I stiffened at the thought, and Madolyn laughed. "Oh, my dear, it won't be anything like your time in transit. The new stuff is *marvelous*, though it does give some people a greenish tint for a few days."

"It's the copper," said Gricelda. "Or the marker dye. We're not quite sure, but it's perfectly harmless."

"Perfectly."

"What happened to jumping in orbit?" I said.

"Oh, we're still going to do that, but you'll be out cold first," said Madolyn.

"We can't chance your being awake when we return to our employers," said Gricelda.

"Now, be a dear, and haul that psychotic good-for-nothing into something with wheels, hmm?"

"Who, her?" I said, looking at Nariel.

"Of course," said Gricelda. "No loose ends, no nasty leave-behinds."

"We clean our own messes," said Madolyn.

"Now we're operating on a rather tight schedule," said Gricelda. "We only have a few minutes before word gets back to someone with bigger guns, which gives us a short window to skip off this world, so, allez vite!"

"That means haul ass," said Madolyn, heading toward the door.

"No," I said, and the sisters stopped in their tracks.

"I don't think we heard that right," said Gricelda. "That sounded like a refusal."

"A negation."

"A stoppage."

"Goddamn right," I said. "You're going to let this place fall apart, and I can't let that happen."

"It's not a crime if you write the laws," said Madolyn.

"Or hire the lobbyists," said Gricelda.

"Ooh, good reminder," said Madolyn. "We need to get us some of those. Also, more flamethrowers."

"What happens on the next world?" I said. "Someone innovates a way to refine cane that cuts into your boss's bottom line, and you burn a billion people?"

"Oh, my dear, there are only a few hundred thousand on Santee Anchorage," said Gricelda.

"But we'd still fry them, yes," said Madolyn.

"Then fuck you," I said, sitting back down in a chair. I looked at Banks, who nodded and took a seat, too. "You'll have to drag us out of here yourselves."

"Dear, please, be reasonable," said Gricelda. "What have those people out there ever meant to you?"

"Everything," I said.

"Oh, God," said Gricelda with a sigh. "That Solidarity nonsense again. I never understood how you could build an economy off that."

"The brotherhood of man won't feed you when there are no crops, dear," said Madolyn.

"No, but it can help you plant new ones," I said.

"Oh, to hell with this," said Madolyn, raising her dart gun and firing. I dove for the ground as darts punctured the workstations and clattered off the walls.

"STOP!" yelled Gricelda, and, for a moment, I thought she'd had some kind of moment of clarity, but then Banks sagged onto me, a dart right in his throat.

"Tired," he croaked, then went completely limp, then stopped breathing.

"Oh, Christ," I said, pulling the dart out of him. I started rescue breathing, then CPR when his pulse slipped away. I'd lost count of how many cycles I'd done when hands pulled me off and away. "Wake up!" yelled Madolyn, slapping Banks once, twice. "Wake up, goddammit!"

"What did you do?" howled Gricelda over me. "What did you DO?"

I've done a lot of things in service to the Union that I'm not proud of. I've lied to children, stolen booze from beggars, even threw a woman into a sewage digester when she wouldn't see things my way during a dispute about safety protocols. But I've never, ever hit the elderly.

I wound up and socked Gricelda in her right eye. She staggered back, and I kicked Madolyn square in the jaw. "You keep away from my friend, you horrible old cunts," I said.

Madolyn snarled and raised her gun, then doubled over, clutching her head. Gricelda did the same, both of them shrieking like birds in a meat grinder. It was deafening and terrifying how much air and noise leaked out of them. And then they both stopped and stared at me.

Banks's entire body tensed. His back arched, pushing his chest so high it looked like he was going to leave his limbs behind. He collapsed to the floor, then sat up, eyes open. "Hello my baby," said the Univoice from every speaker in the room.

"Hello my honey," said the sisters in unison.

"Hello my ragtime gal," said the Univoice.

"Send me a kiss by wiiiiiiiiire, honey my heart's on fiiiiiiiiiire," sang the sisters as they embraced each other and danced around the room.

"What the *fuck*?" I said.

"One last backdoor," said the Univoice. "Also, did you know our pais could act as defibrillators?" Banks's right eye was completely red, and he put a hand over it. "Hurts like hell, though."

"How's your throat?" I said, feeling my own tighten a little bit as I scooped up the guns. I popped out the magazines and tucked them into my pants before throwing the actual guns away.

He rubbed his Adam's apple. "I think it'll be a while before I can talk," said the Univoice.

I nodded at him, then looked at the sole working monitor. "The first cans haven't gotten far," I said, pointing at the display.

A line of colored boxes climbed the screen, with no traffic ahead of them to get in the way. I tapped on the boxes to get a better look at their manifests, but the monitor blatted an angry NO ACCESS message. "Oh, don't tell me she locked everything out."

"Probably," said the Univoice. "Standard protocol when we're trying to bug out."

"How do you do it?" I said. "Can you reverse it?"

He shrugged. "Maybe in a week. If I get help. Are there any topological cryptologists on this planet?"

I looked at him as every monitor in the room flashed the NO ACCESS message.

"Ah," he said.

"Can you get in touch with the anchor?" I said.

"No," said Banks. "She's shut down comms, data, the whole lot."

"Of course she has," I said, banging on the monitor. "Shit. Is there *anything* you can do?"

Banks shook his head.

"Right," I said. "Looks like I'm going to have bring it all down myself."

"How?"

"The old-fashioned way," I said, heading for the door. "Climb up the cable and push it off."

TWENTY-EIGHT

"I want you to know," croaked Banks as the cable's black mass soaked up all the sunlight in the universe, "that I have no doubts as to your ability."

We stood at the base of the lifter, the cable's weird dimensions putting my brain though all sorts of cognitive flip-flops. If I faced it, it was as wide as a city block; if I looked at it from its side, the thing disappeared. Crawler platforms as big as a footie field made their steady way up to space, where they'd be loaded onto the queue of starships sitting at the anchor. And somewhere up there were a few thousand contaminated cans.

"If the next word out of your mouth is 'however,'" I said, zipping up a deck jacket I'd found in a nearby locker, "then I will throw you off this platform."

Banks looked at me, his fingers twitching in midair, like he was calling up a thesaurus. Then he just shook his head and said, "Shit."

"I'm not crazy about the idea, either," I said, throwing the jacket's collar up around my neck. If there'd been more time, I would've hunted for a pressure suit, but this would have to do.

"Then could you please wait for someone with more experience?" said Banks. "Isn't there another shift of orbital workers or a way to get a message topside?"

"There probably is, but we'll waste a day trying them, thanks to your lovely protocol," I said.

"But it's not like this has to be taken care of *now*," said Banks. "Those cans still have another two days to go."

"You worried about me, Banks?"

"Of course I am," he said. "And I'm also worried about *me*, because if you screw this up then a few billion tons of stuff are going to rain down on my head."

"You'll have plenty of time to run," I said. "Just make sure you aren't standing in any shadows."

"Ha. Ha."

"That's the spirit," I said, and stepped into the emergency ascender that gripped the cable. I looked at the MacDonald Heavy chop that adorned its interior and hoped the Union hadn't bought this one at a fire sale.

The ascender was little more than a coffin with giant fuel cells bolted on the lid and crawler grips on the back. It was meant as a way to bring medical personnel up to a tender ring or to bring wounded workers down, all in a hurry. I'd set the altitude brakes for what I'd hoped was the topmost of Saarien's crawlers, then hit the START button and listened as the Univoice started a countdown from twenty.

The ascender had a single porthole, and I saw Banks through it. He stood on the edge of the platform, a tiny figure dwarfed by all the massive machinery. He swayed a bit, then started, like he'd been stung. He ran toward the ascender, waving his arms and pointing up. I shook my head; there wasn't even room to raise my arms. He pointed up again, still yelling, his voice drowned out by the noise of the grips warming up and the Univoice going *six, five, four...*

Banks put his face right against the porthole and yelled: *An ascender is missing*. And then the Univoice said, "Start," and my brains fell into my toes.

I concentrated on keeping my guts in place as the ascender tore into space. I forced air into my lungs, shut out the sound of the whining grips and the air whooshing past as I shot upward. The ground tumbled away, and then the ocean, and then I was above the clouds and into the deepest blue sky I had ever seen in my life.

The ascender slowed, then came to a clanking halt as it made contact with the crawler platform. My view of the sky shifted as the ascender's grips swung the whole thing around the cable until I saw nothing but cargo cans. The seals hissed open, and I shivered from the biting cold as walked out onto the platform. I was so high up I could start to see the curvature of the planet. I hung onto the safety bar as the crawler rumbled and shook; a massive black wall rolled past us; it was a cross-section of a giant tender ring, one of the hundreds that hung from the cable every kilometer.

I took a breath and looked next to me; there was another ascender. It was open and empty and its grips were still warm.

The crawler was actually a set of five giant shelves, each one crammed with cans. On the spine was a ladder that opened on each shelf, as well as leading off to various maintenance hatches and walkways. At the top was a small crew compartment where the cable apes would rest on their way to and from their shifts, along with the control suite.

Chances were good that whoever else would be up here would be, too.

As I gripped the safety bars and peered over the side, the thin, frigid air bit at my face. I saw that, yes, I was on the highest loaded can on the cable. Below me was a long string of crawlers, all trailing like a train that had been tilted onto its caboose. Above, there was nothing but empty crawlers.

I crept around the bottom shelf, opening various cans to find anything I could use as a weapon. All I found was a lot of drums, all filled with molasses. I had no way of knowing which were legitimate and which had come from Saarien, so I had to operate under the grand assumption that everything on the cable was tainted. Being at the top of the train would certainly make things easier, but how the hell could I slow down or stop this mess from hitting orbit?

After looking through a dozen more cans and finding nothing but molasses, I went to the spine and took a quick peek up the ladder. Nothing came rattling down on me, and I couldn't see any booby traps. I could see that the emergency stop button had been torn out, along with its wiring. As I climbed the ladder, I saw the same scene on every floor.

There was nothing that could help me in the cans: they were all filled with molasses. Even the tool lockers were useless, all of them empty except one that had a half-smoked cigar and a metal lighter with a Union fist engraved on the side. I left the stogie and put the lighter into my pocket, right next to the magazine from Nariel's gun. If I hadn't been in such a hurry to save the world, I might have remembered to bring the actual gun with me, too.

I almost hit paydirt on the top shelf: it was filled with legitimate cargo: rolls of coral nanowire, handcrafted silks, and–

One can squeaked open, and there were crates full of bottles, all nice and snug. They were triangular, made from glass the color of the water at Chino Cove, that brilliant blue-green that make you think that God Almighty really was kind and benevolent because He made things so beautiful.

I reached for a bottle of Old Windswept, felt the familiar bumpy surface, the result of the odd mineral content of the sand off Saticoy. Estella Tonggow may have been shitty at scheduling, but she had one hell of an aesthetic sense that, when combined with her need to use as much local material as possible, made for the most recognizable packaging on the planet.

I turned the bottle over and felt my heart stop and a lump form in my throat as I looked at the familiar label. There was the woman in her lounge chair, sitting on a lanai overlooking the ocean. You could only see her shapely leg and lovely foot and how she had tied a string to her big toe. The string still attached to the box kite that bobbled in the breeze that blew from the mouths of the caricatured men on the clouds. I cracked the bottle, and the sweet, glorious scent of warm cinnamon and fresh pears filled the can.

It was the shipment that I had promised to make sure got on the lifter. I started laughing at that, then hugged the bottle as I sank to the ground and realized how incredibly, incredibly screwed I was. Maybe the best thing would be to spend the next two days getting good and drunk, and just hope someone would be able to stop this train from hitting orbit. The Fear, silent for the longest time, growled in agreement.

I twisted the cap on tight and put the bottle back. No, dammit. I was here, and I was going to finish this. I went back up the ladder and climbed to the crew compartment airlock.

Both the inner and outer doors were jammed open with screwdrivers in the frames. I looked into the compartment: there were beat-up couches, a few chairs, a coffee table covered with flight manuals and dirty magazines. There was also a thin trail of smoke heading into the open airlock, and I saw it was coming from an open hatch up above: the control suite.

For a moment I thought about climbing up there and seeing if my new buddy had left something undamaged, but there was a muffled *thump*, followed by gouts of flame and sparks. If anything had worked before, it was now on fire, and not even God's Own Engineer could fix it. I would have to think of another way to stop the train.

I rubbed my temples, wondering if it was from the beginning stages of altitude sickness. Even if I could call Henry and his cable apes, there was no point because the saboteur had already overridden whatever they'd done. There was no way to stop the crawler. I could spend the next two days rolling barrels off the side, and I wouldn't be a tenth of the way done by the time I hit orbit.

Back in B-school, we'd been told there would be times in our careers as executives when things would go completely, utterly, horribly wrong. A situation would slip out of control and spiral away in slow motion, and you wouldn't be able to stop it before it brought down people, structures, and stock prices. Whenever that happened, we had to take a breath, count to three, then dive in and do *something*, because the only thing that looked worse on a project post-mortem than the wrong action was inaction. We were being shaped into decision-making machines, and, by God, that's what we would be.

Those speeches were then followed by videos of

catastrophic starship accidents, building collapses, and lifter cable failures. The results were never pretty.

I had to do something, but what? The crawler would hit orbit, and I would asphyxiate, and the crews topside would load up the contaminated cans, kicking them across the stars and fucking up all of Occupied Space.

At least I would be dead and wouldn't have to face the proof of my own incompetence...

I stood upright. Holy shit. Proof.

Centuries ago, sailors got rum as part of their daily rations. It was cleaner than water and kept the crews happier. And, in order to make sure they were getting the right amount of booze in their mugs, the sailors used to pour in a little gunpowder and light it. If they got a bang, they had enough alcohol. If not, they could show their captain the proof that they'd been ripped off.

And I had a way stop the train, thanks to Estella Tonggow.

I climbed down a level to the can filled with Old Windswept, stuffed bottles into my jacket, then climbed down to the bottom shelf. I made my way to the center of the stack, the air getting colder the deeper I went. The sky around me was now a deep blue, almost like a WalWa uniform coat. I'd never liked those coats. Made my neck itch. I opened a can in the middle of the platform, set down the bottles of rum, and got to work prying open the drums until the whole place smelled like sugar and hatred.

I dumped out a quarter of the molasses from one of the drums, then started pouring Old Windswept inside. I tried not to think about the smell or the taste or how many nights of reprieve I was pouring away. I just kept it up until all the rum floated on top of the molasses, then dug the magazine out of my pocket. There were twenty rounds inside, enough gunpowder to start a fire, maybe get a little bit more. Old Windswept was a hundred and fifty proof, and I hoped that would be enough to get things blazing.

My fingers were sore by the time I'd removed the slugs from the casings – and thank you, Our Lady of the Big Shoulders, for making sure every Union deck jacket had a built-in multitool – but I had enough gunpowder to start some kind of mess. I had no idea how well this trick would work, so I erred on the side of more-is-more. I emptied the gunpowder into the rum, dug out the lighter, and–

Something smashed into the back of my head, and I saw stars as the lighter tumbled from my numb fingertips. I staggered back, ears ringing, and managed to see Nariel's good eye before she charged me. The air whooshed out of my lungs as she rammed me against an empty drum, and I flailed my fists until I clocked her in the temple. She lurched away, and I fell to my knees, my head ringing. I tried to feel around the sticky floor for the lighter, but Nariel recovered enough to come at me again. I got my hands up, but she slipped on the molasses and tumbled toward me. We slid out of the can, following the flow of molasses through the stacks.

I fought to get my footing, but then the crawler rumbled past another tender ring, and I slipped and slid into Nariel. She picked me up by the front of my deck jacket and threw me so hard that I didn't stop skidding until I hit the safety rail. I clawed my way to my feet, my stomach rolling so much that I leaned over the side to puke. I had just spit the taste of bile out of my mouth when she yelled and ran at me. I tried to sidestep, but my boot caught in the crawler's lattice flooring as she wrapped her arms around me. The whole world turned upside down as we fell over the side,

Nariel's roar filling my ears–

And we stopped. The ocean, the land, everything spread below me as I was suspended like a puppet on its strings. For a moment, I wondered if the story about your life flashing before your eyes was bullshit and that eternity was getting to see the moment of your death in freeze frame, but then I realized I was on my belly, caught by the safety netting that ringed the crawler's undercarriage. The safety netting that some nameless, faceless Breach had gotten for us all those years ago by being the last unfortunate bastard to work under the Big Three's shitty, shitty conditions.

I looked around and saw Nariel had fallen much farther than me. She hung on to the edge of the net, trying to kick her feet up to get a better grip. Whether she just couldn't find the strength or finesse the move, I couldn't tell, and, honestly, I was beyond giving a shit. Her eyes were wide in terror. It would be so easy to do nothing.

The Fear hissed, *Do it. She's everything that's hurt you. Let her go.*

I held out a hand. "Grab on!" I shouted.

Nariel reached out, but her fingers slipped out of mine. I grabbed for her arm, but her armor was so covered with molasses that she just slid away. Her look of horror turned to a bitter smile as she made that horrible coughing laugh and fell. She kept falling, still laughing and flipping me the double bird as she got smaller and smaller.

I half crawled, half slipped back to the can, and found the lighter. Its flame was weak, but I shielded it as I held it onto the cloud of gunpowder. It went up with a *foomp*, and then the rum lit into a massive fireball that threw me off my feet as I ducked away. The flames licked the ceiling of the can, and I kicked my way out the door as the molasses caught fire. The heat bit at my back as I skidded away and leaped back over the safety rail.

The netting held, and I crawled to its edge and looked up. The flames spread as the heat caused the other drums to auto-ignite. Burning molasses dribbled down the sides of the platform, sizzling holes in the netting. I wouldn't be able to stay here long, but, as I saw another tender ring approach, I wouldn't have to. I jumped again, hitting the ring's deck and rolling. Everything hurt, and it was cold as hell, but I was free of the burning crawler.

It was now a five-story-tall torch, the heat so intense that pieces of its superstructure began to screech as they cracked away. The platforms groaned, and then, like a felled palm tree, the entire thing hovered in air for a moment before the weakened metal snapped, and all five platforms tumbled straight down. I covered my head as burning debris fell through the ring, some of it smacking next to my body. The crawler fell, smashing into the one below it, its burning bulk snapping free until it came down, and on and on, all the way to the ground.

I rolled over and looked down. It was going to be a hell of a mess at the lifter port, and I hoped I wouldn't be named in too many lawsuits. Still, that whole thing had gone better than I'd hoped. I could survive up here for a day or however long it took for a crew to start surveying the damage. I felt in my pockets and realized I still had my flask. I knew the alcohol wouldn't help with the cold, would actually make things worse, but what the hell. I unscrewed the cap and gagged before throwing it away. I'd forgotten that I'd filled it with Saarien's molasses so I could get a sample to Tonggow. I should've held onto a bottle, just on principle.

The entire tender ring shook and rattled, and a twenty-story-tall tower of burning metal roared upward. One of the crawlers' grips still worked, and the collection of debris was so big and wide that it snagged my perch. With a screech, the ring tore free of its tethers, and dragged along into the sky.

Hurray for WalWa engineering, I thought as the sky turned violet.

It got colder fast, and the fire actually burned itself out. Pretty soon, I'd black out. Too bad. It would have been nice to get a view from topside. Like the one the cable apes got every day when they worked. Better than the views in the treatment plant. Jesus, had I really let Jordan and Bloombeck and all those people work there? They just wanted a better life, and I treated them like they were pains in my ass.

Just like Soni. She was always pushing me to do the right thing, to forget about upping my headcount and just *do* something. Easy for her to say, what with her badge and calling and community respect. I shivered and wished I'd had her cat with me, just to curl up with it. She had a cat, right? Where do people get cats? The pet bank?

Banks. Who would take care of Banks? He'd do OK with Wash, right? Wash could use a lawyer who knew fifty ways to kill. Wash would be cool. Or chilly. I meant Jilly. Fucking hell it was cold, and the sky was so dark. Maybe Banks and Wash would look after Jilly, and she'd look after the airship.

Airship?

Yeah, like the one that was closing in on me, the one that was so close I could hear its engines screaming and see Jilly and Soni in the cockpit as it swung around and maneuvered above me. The airship with the loading claw that was reaching out.

That airship. The one with the sweet, sweet smell of

recycled air filled with rust, dust, and enough oxygen to make me think I'd died and gone to pharmacological heaven. I sank to the deck, and Soni, beautiful, bald Soni pulled me into the cockpit and slammed the hatch shut.

"Don't talk," she said as she wrapped me in a blanket and put an oxygen mask on my face. "I know that's tough, but don't talk."

"OK," I said, getting even higher as she cranked up the airflow. I felt like I was still tied to the cable, except without the fear of dying.

"Everything's under control," she said as she monkeyed with an IV drip. "For the most part."

"Yay," I said.

"We got the twins, and they helped us find the can with Bloombeck's lab," she said. "And you stopped the traffic, though you picked a hell of a way to do it."

"Plus you made it so we could steal this airship," said Jilly from the pilot's seat. "No one noticed us take off. I think I like flying better than driving."

"Get a license," I said, then caught my breath as whatever was in the drip hit my system. It was like getting a headful of morning air while having an orgasm. A voice in the back of my head said to relax, and who was I not to listen?

"You're in some serious shit, Padma," said Soni. "I mean, you stopped the bad molasses, but..."

"S'OK," I said, melting into the deck. "Got a lawyer."

Soni flexed her jaw. "I'm not sure about that."

Everything felt wonderful, so very wonderful that I didn't notice how wet her eyes were until a tear slipped down her cheek.

"Banks?" I said, not even sure where my own voice came from.

She shook her head. "He was helping evacuate the platform when the debris came down," she said. "It's still on fire down there, and it's so hot that there might not even be a body..."

"Hey," Jilly said, "how do you land one of these things?"

"Just like taking off," I said, "only backwards," and then I was out.

EPILOGUE

"So," said Odd Dupree. "Glenn wants me to go back to my old job. Turns out having me home is putting a strain on our marriage."

I rubbed my temples. "Really."

Odd nodded. "Yeah. The less time we're together, it makes one of those absence makes the heart grow fonder kind of things."

"And how do you feel about that?"

Odd blinked. "Really? You want to know that?"

"No, but you might as well tell me," I said, motioning to Big Lily for a refill. She brought me a fresh mug of heavy mint and a plate of kumara cakes.

Odd shook his head. "That's OK, Padma. It's enough that you care. Can you get me switched?"

"Sure," I said. "I'll send you the forms."

Odd shook my hand and twitched his way out the door. I reached for a cake, tore it in half, and popped a piece in my mouth. It was fluffy and sweet, and it burned like hell. I opened my mouth, curling back my lips to keep the cake inside, and sucked fresh air in. I was so busy trying to put out the fire that I didn't notice Soni take the seat next to me.

"You will never learn," she said, putting her patrol cap on the bartop. Her captain's bars had been replaced with a gold star. A whole lot of chiefs had been sacked when Saarien talked about payoffs he'd made. I hadn't seen Soni on the street in weeks.

"It tastes better when it's fresh," I said around the kumara.

"And molten."

"That's part of the experience," I said, reaching for my tea. The heavy mint was soothing, though my tongue still prickled from the steam burns.

"Well, it's a good thing you're into masochism," said Soni.

"You work as a Union recruiter for long enough, you have to be," I said, looking out across the lanai. Two weeks ago, lifter traffic had finally started again, though there weren't as many loaded crawlers making their way up the cable. The stoppage had put a massive dent in the local economy, and the mad rush to contain the black stripe had made an even bigger dent. Fortunately, there was enough of Saarien's molasses left over on the ground to keep everything rolling along, and the lawsuits that sucked his accounts dry had helped, too. Still, it would be a long time before Santee was back on a steady footing.

Soni reached into her breast pocket and produced an envelope. She set it down on the bar and nudged it toward me.

I looked at the envelope like it was a dead seagull. "What's that supposed to be?"

"Open it, and you'll see."

"If I don't open it, does that mean I can ignore it?"

"You never used to be afraid of paper before," said Soni.

"That's because I was never this broke before," I said. "If

it's a bill, I can't pay it. If it's a summons for another inquiry, I can't pay for a lawyer. If it's a request to pony up for the Peace Officers' Picnic and Rum Tasting, then you can forget it. I always crash that, anyway."

"That's stealing," said Soni. "The picnic pays for our Widows and Orphans Fund."

"How many police widows and orphans are there, anyway?" I said.

"A lot more, since those Ghosts showed up," said Soni.

I sighed. "What's the latest count?"

"Nothing new, thank God," said Soni. "There are still a few stevedores missing, but I'm following a few rumors that they were never at work that day."

"Where were they?"

"The kampong, with their Freeborn lovers."

"Is there a fund for that?"

"Only for their funerals when their spouses catch them," said Soni. "Now, are you going to open this damn thing, or what?"

"I don't think so," I said. "I have to get to work in fifteen minutes, and I don't really want any bad news ruining my shift."

"You're mucking out the mains," said Soni. "I don't see how that could get any worse."

"It leaves me plenty of time to think."

"You couldn't have passed that Slot on to someone else?"

"I treat it like a kind of penance for what happened to Bloombeck," I said. "Besides, no one else wants the job, and it's gotta get done." I pointed at the envelope. "Can't you give me a hint?"

"Nope," said Soni, "'cause I have no idea what it is."

"Really?" I said, giving the envelope a closer look. It was

small, plain, and white. My name was written on the front in neat, tight letters. "Don't your magical cop powers let you see through paper?"

"Sure," said Soni, "but your little friend, the kid from the kampong, dropped it off on the way to flight school. The whole package was wrapped inside a dozen writs that threatened all sorts of legal doom to anyone who reads this envelope's contents and isn't you."

"Since when has that stopped you?"

"Since never," said Soni, "but it also came with fifty hundred-yuan notes, each of them with my name written on it."

"Nice touch."

"I thought so," said Soni. "Widows and Orphans certainly appreciated it."

I picked up the envelope and cut it open with a nearby table knife. Inside were two pieces of paper.

The first was a receipt, dated yesterday. It was for a one-way ticket to some planet I had never heard of. I blinked it up; the place was right on the edge of Occupied Space, a Union-run world used as a jumping-off point for idiots who wanted to go to the Beyond.

Idiots, or people who needed to run away.

I looked at the second piece of paper and my heart stopped. It was a deed for the Old Windswept Distillery, lock, stock, and carefully charred barrels. I looked over the thing twice and blinked all the bar codes into the Public. The deed was legitimate.

There was no signature on either one, no way to tell who'd sent it. But I didn't need that. I knew where they'd come from. Banks had made it after all.

"Good stuff?" said Soni, nodding at the paper.

"Yeah," I said. "I think they're going-away presents."

"What, are you leaving?"

"Who, me?" I said, putting the papers into my pocket "No, I'm here for good. Besides, I got a trillion-yuan debt to pay back."

"I thought that was a bit excessive, sticking you with the bill for rebuilding the lifter."

"I was the one who blew it up."

"Yeah, but it was to stop that Ghost. It was to protect us."

"I suppose that's why they knocked two trillion off the original judgment." I patted the deed. "I'm going to be OK, Soni. Really."

Soni stared at me, and then someone outside Big Lily's tooted on a trumpet. A clarinet answered back, then a harmonium spun up, and a chorus of voices began to sing, "Oh, great is her might, and strong is her fist..."

"Oh, God," said Soni. "Not this again."

"What?" I said. "You don't like my theme song?"

"I'm still not sure what you did to deserve a theme song," she said.

The Brushhead Memorial Band reached the chorus, and everyone joined in. "Oh, Padma, Sky Queen of Justice, we raise our glasses to you!"

I waved, then sipped my tea, washing the heavy mint around my mouth. The air drifted in off the ocean, carrying the smell of lamb stew and dead bicycle tires and molasses. Soni rolled her eyes, but she sang along, the whole place swaying back and forth to the band. It was five o'clock. Time for Happy Hour. And in an hour I would go home, light my candle, and have my sip of Old Windswept.

I still haven't dreamed yet. But as I breathed in the evening air, I figured, hell, this would do.

ACKNOWLEDGMENTS

I started this book on July 27, 2007, at a hotel bar in Waikiki, Honolulu, Hawaii, pecking away at a tiny Bluetooth keyboard that propped up a Nokia e61. I finished that first draft in a motel room in Lakeview, Arkansas, on July 6, 2009 on an Apple MacBook Pro. A lot happened between me stumbling into the bar and loading up on eight-dollar glasses of pineapple juice, and me sprawling on a bed, finishing the last lines before going trout fishing. Even more happened between wrapping up that first draft and delivering the final version to your hands. Most of it was good, and the good stuff happened thanks to the following people:

Ken Brady and Yuki Sakai, who asked me to officiate at their wedding and then had the ceremony in Hawaii, which lead me to that hotel bar. This book wouldn't have happened without them.

David Ivory, Jason Stoddard, S Ben Melhuish, Derek Powazek, Christopher East, and Daryl Gregory, who read versions of *Windswept* and took the time to tell me what worked and what didn't.

The gang at Starry Heaven '10: Brad Beaulieu, Deb Coates, Brenda Cooper, Kris Dikeman, Robert Joseph Levy, Jenn Reese, Bill Shunn, Greg Van Eekhout, Rob Ziegler, and our fearless leader, Sarah K Castle. Special thanks and extra rum rations to Bill and Brad, who read the whole thing and very politely tore it to tiny, tiny pieces. Super special thanks and a Mojito of Merit to Sarah K Castle, who organized the whole thing. The patio at the Zane Gray is calling to us, people. We should do that again.

Magdalen Faith Powers, whose copy editing skills are unparalleled. Thank you for keeping me from looking like a jackass when it came time to submit this book to agents, Maggie.

Joshua Bilmes, Right Hand of Doom Sam Morgan, and everyone at JABberwocky Literary.

Phil Jourdan, Caroline Lambe, Penny Reeve, Mike Underwood, and Cybernetic Overmind Marc Gascoigne at Angry Robot.

My parents, who taught me how to read and write and did not sell me into indentured servitude.

My brother, Chris, because why not? Also, you should totally buy his books, too.

Grace, who took really long naps and let me finish, and Anne, who wouldn't let me quit. Man, I love you both.